THE SHADOWS OF DARK ROOT

DAUGHTERS OF DARK ROOT: BOOK FIVE

APRIL AASHEIM

For My Readers
Who have made Dark Root real
Thank you

FOREWORD

I never planned to write a series. Originally, the Dark Root story was going to be only one big book. But as I started to develop Maggie and her family, I realized her tale was MUCH larger than I first envisioned. This wasn't just a story - this was a saga.

I hope you enjoy reading The Shadows of Dark Root as much as I enjoyed writing it. I leave a piece of myself every time I visit Dark Root, and I know you do, too.

Cheers and happy reading!

April Aasheim

THE FORMATION OF SHADOW

(FROM THE WANDERING WITCH, CIRCA 1892)

*In the beginning, there was only darkness. And then the
Goddess, in her infinite wisdom, gave us light.*
*But in those moments when she separated the light from the
darkness, she created shadow.*
Formed by her divine hands, the shadow grew and grew.
Larger than our own world and without the limitations.
*Though mortal eyes cannot see the shadow realm, it coexists
alongside our own.*
*It is the realm of dreams and fantasy, faeries and imps,
demons and angels, nightmares and madness.*
It is the bridge between the past, the present, and the future.
It is the divide between the living and the dead.
*It is the Netherworld. One gate opens to another. And then
another.*
Beware of the false lure of this shadow world.
*For most who wander in - even witches - are never heard from
again.*

PROLOGUE

*L*arinda swaddled the gangly child in his downy blanket, clutching
him to her chest as she flew toward Eagle Mountain. The launch
was bumpy - as passing between worlds usually was - but soon the
broom between her slim legs sailed effortlessly across the midnight sky,
casting her silhouette against the full yellow moon.

She stifled a laugh as she picked up speed, her spirit buoyed by a giddiness
she hadn't felt in years. She had done it! The baby was really hers! She
chanced a peek inside the bundle to ensure he was still in her arms. The child
slept peacefully, her enchantment spell locking him into his dreams. She
smiled, then bent forward, clutching the broom handle tight with her free
hand and picking up speed.

"Screw you, Armand!"

She cursed her former lover as she veered hard right. She alone had done
what the all-mighty Armand could not - take his first male heir. Granted, it
had taken time and preparation, but fate had also been on her side: Had
Shane Doler not returned when he had, Maggie never would have let the
child out of her sight, let alone allow him to leave Dark Root. But once
Michael took the child out from under the protective dome, all she needed was
a series of lesser cantrips - rolling fog, twinkling lights, a minor confusion
spell. Abracadabra! Just like that! The baby was hers!

At last, her castle perched atop the gray peak of Eagle Mountain loomed before her. Larinda maneuvered along the contours of the steep slope in her hurry to reach the safety of the castle door. As she landed, she snapped her fingers. The broom disappeared and the enormous vaulted door swung open, as if expecting her.

Click. Click. Click.

Larinda's wooden shoes echoed across the marble floors and throughout the vast hall. She went straight to the main chamber, now carrying the baby carelessly beneath her arm like a football.

"Leah? Leah! Show yourself!" she called for her daughter. "I know you're here. I can smell your apathy a mile away."

Larinda fell back into her tall throne atop a raised platform and waited for her daughter to appear. Once settled, she pulled the blanket away from the boy's face and smiled. He was cute, she had to admit. In fact, he looked rather like Armand. Even the way he smiled sideways when she stroked his cheek. She was seized by heartbreaking nostalgia as she remembered her time with the warlock. She quickly covered the boy's face again, lest her emotions get in the way of her judgement.

Leah appeared in one of the many corridors leading into the throne room, wearing baggy jeans and an old sweater. Larinda's lip curled as she took in her daughter's slovenly appearance. She let it go, for now. Perhaps over dinner they'd talk of the proper way to dress in castles.

"What is it, Mother?" Leah asked, her words as pinched as her thin face.

Larinda snapped her fingers and another chair appeared beside her own - not a throne, but not a chair for a commoner either. She patted it, motioning for her daughter to join her. "I want you to meet your new brother, Leah. Isn't he a lovely little imp?"

Leah ignored the chair and stood over her mother, surveying the bundle. "My new brother?" She pushed back the blanket, revealing the boy's bright auburn hair. When she saw him, she smiled. "This is Maggie's baby! Mother! You did it! Daddy will be pleased."

"Oh, he will, won't he?" Larinda said, standing. She handed over her new charge to Leah, then smoothed the wrinkles from her long black gown. "I was thinking, perhaps we should wait on telling Armand. You know how he's always wanted a boy? I'm afraid that if he sees this child, he may not want to spend time with you."

"He doesn't spend time with me now," Leah said. "I don't even think he knows my name."

"That's nonsense," Larinda said, though she knew it was a lie. Aside from a pitying glance now and again, Armand never noticed Leah at all. "Your father loves you, he just has many burdens."

"Bringing about the end of the world will do that," Leah said, nuzzling the child.

"But every end brings a new beginning!" Larinda reminded her. "And if all goes well, this end will be a new beginning for us. We won't be trapped here, Leah! Just think of it!"

"I'm not trapped here now."

Larinda fought to keep her composure. She hated being reminded that her daughter was free to roam both worlds, while she was mostly confined to the Netherworld. She also hated defending Armand, even though she felt compelled to do so. But this wasn't the time for squabbling. "We will keep the baby with us a while, just until we figure out the best course of action. You've always wanted a sibling."

"But Maggie will be coming for him!"

Larinda pursed her lips in disapproval. How she had managed to raise a witch with so little magick and backbone was beyond her. She opened her palm and the image of a large hourglass appeared before them, spinning in the air.

"Don't worry, my darling. We have all the time in the world," Larinda said. "Now go and find the child a room. Summon him toys. Just amuse yourself while Mommy comes up with a plan."

Leah nodded uncertainly. She took the baby and left through the lone corridor, which was guarded by a row of stone gargoyles. Leah's 'pets.' The girl had strange tastes, but as long as she was obedient, Larinda was willing to tolerate her odd daughter.

Once alone, Larinda stroked her chin thoughtfully. Gleefully. My, how times had changed. For once, she had leverage - real leverage- against Armand. She had wanted marriage from him before, but now she could demand anything. Money. Power. Even immortality, once Armand's deal went through. The Netherworld, the Upper World – all Worlds! - were her oysters now. Armand would do anything she asked in return his male heir.

Still...

Could she trust him to keep his end of the bargain?

He had, after all, imprisoned her here. He had used her heart, her body, and her magick to help travel through the Netherworld. And then he had left her here to rot. And here he kept her, trapped like a genie in a bottle, always promising to release her – someday.

Larinda's eyes narrowed as her fingers drummed the arms of her throne. "How dare Armand? How dare he steal everything from me?" She seethed as she thought further of her current situation. How had she allowed herself to be taken advantage of, and by a man, no less? Her own mother had warned her of the fickle hearts of warlocks, but she hadn't listened. Why?

Love, her heart answered quietly. Love was to blame. But whatever love her soul had once possessed had long ago been eaten away by Armand, and this entrapment.

No matter. The day of reckoning had come!

Armand had his share of enemies. Hers wasn't the only bridge he had burned. Perhaps it was time she made deals of her own.

The raven-haired witch reached into a bag at the foot of the throne, producing a glass mason jar. A cross on a chain dangled from its lid. The jar was cool to the touch, though it vibrated in her fingers, as if something large and horrible was seeking to escape.

"Hello, Gahabrien," she cooed as she tossed the cross onto the floor and unscrewed the lid. "We met years ago in Dark Root. Do you remember me?"

She set the jar on the floor and an inky cloud rose up out of it. Soon, the entire room was filled with mist and shadow. The dark form collected itself into a tight column at her feet, ready to receive its orders. It smelt of sulfur and rage.

"I'm sorry that Maggie did this to you," Larinda said, sympathetically. "A powerful demon like yourself shouldn't be caged." She stood and greeted her new guest properly. "I am Larinda, your queen and protector. You are home again, where your powers cannot be contained within a simple jar. You are strong again, Gahabrien. Avenge your enemies with me, and I'll even give you one of their own as payment."

She conjured an image of a sleeping baby with red hair. Gahabrien slithered around the picture, seeming to taste it with his numerous inky tendrils. His eyes glowed red, and Larinda thought she glimpsed a smile somewhere in the darkness of his face.

"Are we in agreement?" she asked. "Destroy Maggie and I'll turn over the child to you. In doing this, you'll also get revenge on Armand. All of this is yours, so long as you serve me."

It was a risky barter, as demons weren't known for keeping their word - but neither were warlocks. If she pulled this off, three generations of trouble would fall with a single blow.

The shadow pulsated, and Larinda was certain of its answer.

"Yessssssss, myyyyyyy queeeeen."

THE FOOL

$\mathcal{T}$he earth surrounding the once-majestic Harvest Home was a dry, arid brown, parched and cracked like the binding of an old book found at the bottom of an attic trunk. Sickly gray vines crept out from an otherwise empty garden, seeking out moisture like a pack of snakes seeking their first meal after a long hibernation. The flowers in their beds had also shriveled, their stems so delicate that a stiff breeze might disintegrate them to salt. And though it was high summer, the trees had all dropped their leaves and needles; their boughs were at half-mast, as if paying homage to my despair.

I sniffed the air. It was still charged with the scent of heavy rain from the night before. But that rain had been born of magick - my magick - and these days magick dried up quickly in Dark Root, no matter how powerful the witch.

An assembly of fat crows and steely-eyed ravens gathered on the front yard, raising billows of dust as they scratched at the dirt and flapped their metallic black wings. They had swarmed overnight. I had watched their sharp-beaked silhouettes cut through the heavy rain from my porch. When the sun finally rose above the trees - illuminating the peak of Eagle Mountain, where Larinda had undoubtedly taken my son - their ranks swelled further. They squawked out warnings in raspy caws and piercing screeches, steadily encroaching upon the house as their reinforcements joined in.

I stood up, a blanket wrapped around my shoulders and a cup of tea in my hands. The cup hadn't been warm for several hours. If the birds were trying to scare me, they clearly had no idea what kind of a mood I was in. I caught the eyes of one of the larger birds, who was hopping towards the porch. Just yards from the steps, he stopped and puffed out his chest.

"Caw!" he challenged, locking eyes with me.

His squawk hurt my ears, but it was the gleam in his eyes that got me. There was a human quality to his expression, as if he knew, and enjoyed, my grief.

"You have no power here," I said, shedding the blanket and dropping the cup as I descended the steps. The cup shattered, fragments bouncing from the ledge.

The fat leader-bird blinked, exchanging glances with the others, as if considering their collective next move. I waded into the flock, scattering them. They cried out, hopping away, but all the while readying themselves. There were hundreds of birds, and I knew they could easily rip me to shreds if they chose.

But they didn't attack. Were they waiting? Or only watching?

"Leave," I ordered, raising both arms high into the air and stretching out my fingers. I couldn't pull from the earth any more, as all its local magick had been tapped by my mother, Jillian, and my Aunt Dora. But I didn't need to.

The air was mine to control.

I felt the familiar tingle in my fingers as I drew in energy, letting the charge trickle all the way into my toes. The birds watched, curiously. Once full, I snapped my fingers as I had seen my warlock father, Armand, do in my snow-globe visions.

"I SAID LEAVE!"

The ground trembled, from the Victorian house all the way out to the edge of the surrounding woods that marked Harvest Home's property line. The birds looked around, hopping, squawking, and confused.

I pointed to a nearby cluster of dried leaves, then spun my finger in the air three times. The leaves rose up and formed a whirlwind, gathering twigs and stones and even a few birds as it slowly twisted across the yard. With every pass, the funnel grew larger, sucking in new fodder along the way. The birds cried out, scurrying to avoid the flying debris. A few less-disciplined crows even flew away.

I thrust my hands forward, as if closing a double door, and there was a perceptible roll to the air, a wave. Vines, twigs, rocks and birds were swept into the surrounding forest. Not a creature remained.

"This is my house! Mine!" I called into the woods. "Tell Larinda I'm coming for her!"

"Impressive, Maggie," said a voice behind me.

"How long have you been watching?" I asked, turning to face Jillian, trailing down the steps in her robe and slippers. She handed me a fresh cup of tea, which I took absently.

"All night." She smiled wearily and I felt a wave of love for her, knowing she hadn't slept at all.

"My patience ran out."

She lifted a strand of my curly red hair, staring, as if it brought a memory. "I knew you were powerful, but that was the work of more than a mere witch." She dropped my hair and sighed, filling up her lungs. "Dora and I have been magickally neutered, so to speak, but you remain strong. Even as the magick of Dark Root wanes."

"I'm not even sure how I did it," I admitted, still feeling the charge inside me.

"*So mote it be*," she said, her jade eyes twinkling. "You are a wilder, but you are learning to gain control. It's almost like breathing to you now, Maggie. You're creating reality with every thought and every word."

The notion did nothing to encourage me. "I wasn't able to create a reality strong enough to save my son." I rolled a pebble into a crevice in the ground with my toe. The crevice then sealed itself shut, as if it had reached its occupancy. "Jillian, I'm so scared. I've never been so scared in my life. What if... oh, God...Jillian...what if..."

My earlier bravado disappeared and I was overcome with fear. How could I find Montana in the Netherworld? What kind of fool believes in the impossible?

Jillian clapped her hands before my face, bringing me back. "Maggie, darklings and demons can smell fear. And who knows what else lurks in the Netherworld? You must control your thoughts! You cannot let yourself imagine the possibilities, because they are infinite. If you want to make it out of there, you'll need discipline of both temper and mind. You can't be reckless in the Netherworld. It's too dangerous."

"I don't care about danger or making it out," I said. "I just need to find my son."

I know, darling, but please hear me out. Magick is more than just words and intent. It's about how you feel and think, too. The more powerful you are, the more you need control. You are going to the world where magick runs even deeper than in our world. Do you understand?"

"Yes. No." I massaged my temples. I was a wilder. Reckless was my natural default. "I'll try," I said.

"You'll need to do more than try." Jillian passed the back of her hand across her brow then stared at me, matter-of-factly. "You are taking your sisters with you. And Shane, Michael, and Paul."

"Yes, I know."

"They are depending on you, Maggie. Not on Shane. Not on Ruth Anne. On *you*. *Trying* will get you all lost. Or worse. And what good will that do Montana?"

I swallowed, nodding. It was time to step up. This was my son and my quest. "I understand," I said.

"Good." Jillian's eyes softened, the deep jade shifting to a rich emerald hue. She took my hand and I felt her 'reading' me. "Stop blaming yourself. There's nothing you could have done to stop this, Maggie. We tried to disrupt destiny, but the wheel of fate won't stop turning for a few old witches. You and your sisters are the new order now, stronger and more cohesive than any Council before it. You are bound by love. If Sasha did nothing else right, she gave you each other. Stay strong. For now, at least, your son is fine."

"Why did you say 'for now'? And how do you know he's fine?"

"I pulled The Star card from the Tarot this morning. It is a card of hope."

"A Tarot card is what you're going on? Hope isn't the same as reality. Hope is just a feeling."

"Hope is one of the most powerful feelings in all the universe. Hope is the essence of miracles."

I rubbed an eyebrow, absorbing her words. If I ever needed a miracle, I needed one now.

"Maggie," she continued. "I'm linked to him too, remember? He is my grandson, and DNA is a powerful thing. I know he's fine because I can feel his presence. You can too, if you listen. Try."

I held still, *listening*. At first, I heard only the wind and the distant, squawking birds. I extended my reach, listening with every part of my body. As I concentrated, I noticed that *silent* things made noise, too. Trees rustled. The gray vines cracked. The rocks hummed. Even the dead earth vibrated, creating an inner noise I could sense rather than hear. It was a subtle purr, but it grew in strength the longer I focused. Even the rising sun and the waning moon had a pulse. Everything had a vibration, like musical notes all playing together. The world was alive, playing a symphony I could hardly fathom yet knew completely, like a lullaby sung to you as an infant and recalled years later.

In happier days, this realization might have made me smile. But not today. I opened my eyes. "Jillian, I still don't feel Montana."

"Did you *feel* his absence? Not only his physical absence, but the absence of his light?"

"How would I know that?"

"You're a mother, Maggie. You'll know."

"No. Actually, I felt strangely at peace. That means he's okay, right? For now?"

Jillian brushed my shoulder. "Yes... for now."

I understood what she meant about hope being a powerful magick.

I had been offered just a drop of water, and yet, it filled my entire canteen. "Thank you."

I looked towards the rising sun, feeling its warmth while I *listened* to it hum. My amber bracelet sparked and the golden ankh around my neck – the one I had discovered in Shane's attic crawl space - flashed brightly. I lifted the glowing ankh and stared at it until it faded back to normal. "What does it mean?" I asked.

"It means Montana's calling to you," Jillian said. She tapped the ankh . "You'll always be able to reach him, if you are able to tune in. He'll show you were to go. Don't doubt yourself, or that ankh."

"How long do we have to reach him?"

Jillian shrugged. "I'm not sure. Time doesn't work the same way in the Netherworld as it does here."

"What does that mean?"

"It means you're about to enter a dimension where time does not exist."

"That's impossible."

"Everything's possible in the Netherworld. Never forget that."

I sat on the porch step, holding the mug between my palms as the sun continued its ascent. "I wish time didn't exist here. I need a lot of it to figure this out. Theoretically," I added, using one of Ruth Anne's words, "theoretically, we can leave at any time then? I mean, if time exists on our plane, but not in the Netherworld..."

Jillian smiled with one side of her mouth, and a new dimple appeared. "Theoretically, yes," she agreed, sitting beside me. "But Montana and Larinda are born of this world. Their rules are different. Montana will continue to age and grow there. And his abilities will be a product of his time there. That's if – IF - Armand lets him grow up."

"That doesn't make me feel any better," I said, finishing off my tea.

"I'm sorry, Maggie. I'm new at this parenting thing. One thing I do know is that it's important to prepare in this world, to be ready for the next one. Once there, everything shifts and changes. I've only read about it, and seen glimpses in my visions, but I understand it's a messy place. The clearer you are, and the more prepared, the easier it will be to traverse." She stood and stretched her arms. "As above, so below.

Everything you do here alters your reality in the Netherworld, and vice versa."

"Sounds so ominous," I said, rising to join her.

"I'm not going to lie, Maggie. It is. Time may not work the same there, but it is said that living souls have roughly three 'Upper World Days' before they are assimilated into the Netherworld."

"Assimilated?"

"Become a part of that world. That is what partly what happened to Larinda. Armand left her there, and her window for permanently returning to The Upper World closed. She expends a great deal of magick just to visit periodically, but she is always pulled back."

I clutched my constricting chest, finding it suddenly hard to breathe. "I only have three days to reach him? Why didn't you let me go last night, then?"

"Maggie, do you trust me?"

I looked into her eyes. Though I had just discovered she was my birth mother, there had always been a bond between us that I couldn't explain. I pressed my lips together and nodded. "Yes. I trust you."

"Then you can't go charging into the Netherworld without a plan. We will wait until this evening. There will be a full moon, which assists in veil crossings, and I will infuse you with whatever magick I can muster. We will use today to prepare. It is our best chance of saving Montana."

I shuddered, but nodded, hoping she was right. I liked that she said 'our' best chance - it made me feel less alone

Jillian took my hand and we went into Harvest Home together. Although it wasn't quite seven, almost everyone was awake. Eve and Paul were huddled up in a far corner of the living room, talking intently to one another. Eve's smeared mascara drew dark streaks across her alabaster complexion. Her normally sleek hair was a frazzled mess. She sniffled and nodded as Paul did his best to reassure her.

Near the stairs, Merry was arguing on her phone with her ex-husband Frank, who lived in Florida and currently had their six-year-old daughter, June Bug. "Just let me talk to her, please," Merry begged. Fear rattled her voice, then anger. "Fine! I hope you go to where I'm about to go! And that you never find your way out!" She cursed him, before tossing the phone back into her purse.

Merry caught me looking. "I'm sorry. That wasn't very nice. But he wouldn't even let me hear her voice, and this might be my last chance." She found a tissue and blew her nose and plodded off to the restroom, most likely to cry in private.

I wanted to console each of my sisters, but I couldn't. I was the reason for their grief. They were coming with me to the Netherworld, leaving behind all that they loved, uncertain if they'd ever return. Only my eldest sister, Ruth Anne, had managed to sleep. She was nestled in Aunt Dora's recliner, her head resting on her shoulder. Every now and then she'd snort herself awake, look around, then nod off again. I couldn't imagine how she was able to sleep - I'd give anything for that kind of magick.

"Come with me, Maggie," Jillian said, gently pulling me into the kitchen.

Aunt Dora sat at the breakfast table with my son's father, Michael. This room usually felt charming and warm, but in this moment it felt tired and sterile. Glass 'witch balls,' expertly crafted by my aunt's own hands to ward against evil, hung in the windows, motionless as witches hanging from the gallows. The copper teapot sat on the gas stove, for once not steaming. Even the blue checkered pattern on the starched curtains had faded to winter gray.

"Good morning," I said, hugging my aunt's shoulders while purposely ignoring Michael.

"Ain't nothin' good about it," Aunt Dora said, hugging me back from her chair. The lines circling her eyes were an endless well of troubles. I had never seen her expression so stark.

"We're all here," I said. "That's something. Right?"

"We're not all here." Dora opened her hand, revealing a blue baby

14

bootie. Montana's sock. "I found this in the pantry. Don' know how it got there." She choked, curling her fist around the bootie.

I had cried all night and thought I'd run out of tears, but the sight of Montana's sock in my aunt's hand turned me into a whimpering child. Aunt Dora knocked over her teacup in her hurry to stand and comfort me. Jillian's arms were around me, too. We cried together while Michael stared into his lap. He didn't dare offer any condolences. I hadn't spoken to him in hours, and I wasn't about to start now. I needed someone to blame for this, and he had been the last person to have my son. I would lift Michael's sanctions only when my baby was back home.

Aunt Dora's spilt tea rolled towards a card in the center of the table, and I scooped it up before it could get wet. A Tarot card: The Star. A woman sat at a well, her eyes lifted towards the heavens. The well was empty but she was full of hope as she gazed at the bright star above her. I slid the card into the pocket of the long skirt I'd been wearing since yesterday. Hope was something I could probably use in the Netherworld.

"I'd go with ya if I could," Aunt Dora said, wiping her nose with a paper napkin. She blew twice, folded it once, and tossed it into the trashcan.

"I know you would," I said.

"I would too, Maggie," Jillian said. "But I think I'll be more useful here, watching."

"Watching?"

"Yes. It is one of the reasons I asked you to wait until tonight to go."

With that, Michael went into the living room, returning with an old-fashioned hat box. Eve, Paul and Merry straggled in behind him. He set the box on the table and looked at me, expectantly.

"What's this?" I asked.

"Open it," my aunt instructed.

I placed my hands on either side of the lid, feeling the rich magick radiating from within the container. I reached inside and removed a beautiful crystal globe from its prison.

"It's so light," I said, lifting out an orb the size of a bowling ball, with just the tips of my fingers. It was delicate as a bubble, and I balanced it on my palm for fear of crushing it.

"It needs to be activated," Aunt Dora said. "Where's the charger?"

Michael left again and returned with a small gold pedestal in the shape of a lion's paw. I placed the globe upon the open paw, and stepped back, waiting. But the globe didn't react. I tapped on it lightly, twice. "I don't think it's working," I said, blowing on the smooth glass.

"It's not like the memory globes," Jillian said. "There's nothing inside this one. It's a blank slate, created for scrying." Her eyes fell on the ankh around my neck. "Maggie, we need to attune your energy to it. This is how I can keep an eye on you, and intervene if necessary."

"How will you intervene without magick?" I asked, glancing at the witch balls hanging in the windows.

"Leave that to me. Now, place both hands on the crystal ball and stare into its very center. Relax your eyes, but don't blink or look away until you feel me pinch you, okay?"

"Are you sure it's safe?" Merry asked, looking from me to Jillian. "I trust you and Aunt Dora, but things are so topsy-turvy right now. What if it backfires? Or she gets sucked in and can't get out?" Merry shifted her weight from one foot to the other, her voice escalating as she spoke.

"Merry, it will be okay," I reassured her.

She twisted the rings on her fingers, nodding too quickly. "I know. But what if it isn't okay? We have no way of knowing anything right now."

"Don't be frightened," Jillian said, patting Merry's shoulder. "The Netherworld, like our own world, is unpredictable and endless. You'll never be able to prepare yourself for every scenario, so you'll need to rely on your intuition. And if you find yourself lost, you have each other."

Merry looked from Jillian, to me, and then to the globe. She exhaled audibly. "Okay, let's do this."

Jillian nodded. "Maggie, are you ready to start the process?"

I chanced a quick look around to see if Shane had slipped in unnoticed. He'd been gone since before sunrise, leaving almost immediately after Michael performed our wedding ceremony. There was a faraway look in his eyes as he kissed me goodbye, one that rattled my nerves. I told myself that Shane would come back in time, but my unease deepened with each passing hour.

"I'm ready," I said.

Michael closed the curtains, shutting out the morning light. Eve lit three candles, setting them around the room. Merry drew a circle in the air with her wand, invoking a blessing of protection. All this done, Aunt Dora tapped a silver bell with a small fork, vibrating the room with sound.

"Clear your mind and focus on the crystal ball," Jillian instructed.

I took a seat, clasping both hands around the cool sphere, staring into its core. At first, the crystal stared back, giving nothing away. But as I continued, feeling the weight of my eyelids surrender to the globe's magick, colors emerged within. A rainbow prism sprouted from the center of the sphere, expanding until it filled the entire globe.

I was no longer in Aunt Dora's kitchen.

I was somewhere else - inside the glass ball, bathed in white light, standing in a rainbow. I lifted my hands, watching the many colors surge through me. I felt a sense of joy, of utter wonder. But it didn't last.

On the curved walls, shadow creatures of all shapes and proportions shuffled along. Some had long rubbery arms dragging behind them, others had broad, hulking chests and misshapen heads. Some were almost sprite-like in their delicate appearance, as they flitted about on the glass screen. Their silhouettes marched in circles around me, carrying their burdens like pack mules. I shivered. These were the beasts of the Netherworld. And I knew, instinctively, that their only joy was in trapping other souls inside that miserable realm with them.

"I can't do this," I thought, as one of the creatures licked its lips. "I'm not strong enough."

In the far distance, I heard a baby cry. *My son!*

"Montana!" I called. His cries echoed around me. I grasped at the air, no longer concerned about the shadows at all. "I'm coming!" I called, running towards the glass wall that separated us.

A sharp pinch on my wrist brought me back to the kitchen. I was sitting at the table again, shaking, my hands glued to the globe. The others were staring at me.

"What the hell happened, Maggie?" Eve demanded. "You were tripping out. Screaming about shadows."

"I was?" I stood and wiped my wet palms across my skirt, brushing The Star card in my pocket along the way. "I heard Montana. He was in there." I pointed to the globe. "I need to go back!"

"You heard our son?" Michael crouched down, looking me in the eyes. He wore his reading glasses and his dark hair had a sizable streak of gray that hadn't been there before. I nodded slowly, reticent to share the shadow creatures with the others, hoping it had been my imagination and not truly the world I'd be taking them to.

Jillian tapped the globe with her knuckles and it went dark. "You were safe the whole time. There is nothing actually inside of the ball - it's just a window."

"Aye," Aunt Dora agreed. "I commissioned it long ago, from a witch in Denmark. It was made ta watch yer father in the tunnels, but he left Dark Root before we could attune him to it."

Jillian narrowed her eyes. "Maggie activated it, so as long as you all stay together, Dora and I can watch over you. And intervene if absolutely necessary."

I glanced towards the back door, and then into the living room where Ruth Anne still snored on the couch.

"Don't worry," Jillian said. "Ruth Anne and Shane will be under our watch, as well."

Paul raised his hand. "Um, I don't really have any abilities. Are you sure I should go? I don't want to muck things up."

"E'eryone has a lil' magick in them," Aunt Dora said. "It's yer birthright. Some forms are just more obvious than others."

"All of your talents will be necessary in the Netherworld, magick or otherwise," Jillian said. "Don't sell yourselves short."

Aunt Dora chimed her fork once more, signaling the ritual had ended. I looked at the clock over the stove. Nearly an hour had passed! Time might not have meaning there, but with each passing moment here, my anxiety grew.

"Maggie, you're glowing!" Merry said, her blue eyes widening as she pointed at my ankh.

Sure enough, it *blazed* around my neck. I touched it carefully, though it was as cool as the crystal ball on the table.

"Hey, look!" Paul pointed to the globe.

In its center, an ankh appeared, identical to the one I wore. It spun slowly in space.

"Excellent work, Dora," Jillian said, clapping her hands together. "Now that the crystal is charged, we'll be with you the entire time, in spirit at least. We won't be able to hear you, but if you break the chain on your ankh, we'll know it's time to take action and pull you home. But please only do it when you're absolutely ready to come back."

Aunt Dora nodded in agreement, but there was a subtle doubt in her eyes that I hoped no one else noticed.

"I won't come back without my son," I said, regarding the globe as both friend and enemy.

"I know." Jillian met each of our gazes individually, as if to offer a quiet moment of comfort. "We will use the portal in the Sister House nursery at dusk. Spend your day in preparation."

"You just said there are endless possibilities in the Netherworld," Eve said. "How can we prepare for that?"

"Listen to your inner voice. You won't need food or water, though it may feel like you do at times. Eating is more pleasurable than necessary in the Netherworld. And you won't need a change of clothing, either. If you get cold or hot, remind yourself it's illusory. Bring only what calls to you, no matter how silly or strange it seems now."

Jillian placed the tip of her index finger on the bridge of her nose, squeezing her eyes shut. "Remember, your thoughts, hopes, and fears will be used against you. Don't give the Netherworld any extra leverage. Understand?"

We all nodded like obedient children.

"Let go of the past, because there is no past in the Netherworld.

And most importantly, remember who you are and your love for one another. Through all the trials that await you, your love will be what guides you back home." Jillian opened her eyes and shrugged.

"So... do we pack tents?" Paul asked. "I'm guessing there aren't any hotels in the Netherworld."

"There is everything in the Netherworld," Jillian said. "And there is nothing. It is a collection of all planes, dimensions, times, memories, and dreams. From what I understand, each person's experience is individual, and we have no idea where you'll end up. That is why attuning is so important, as is staying close together. Some areas of the labyrinth already exist, and some will be created as you go."

My head pounded from trying to absorb all this information. "A labyrinth? How are we ever going to find Montana? I'm not sure we can do this, Jillian."

"I am."

We all turned towards the back door.

Shane Doler stood in the entry, wiping the mud from the bottom of his boots. His face and hands were dirty, as if he'd been digging. His faded cowboy hat was drawn low, revealing soft gray eyes, red-rimmed with exhaustion.

I caught my breath, my heart beating unexpectedly fast at seeing my new husband. I found it strange that I could be filled with such love while still grieving for my missing son.

"You have a dreamwalker and tracker with you," Shane said, stepping into the kitchen. He put his hat on the counter and washed his hands. "I've traveled these landscapes while sleeping. I'll figure them out when I'm awake."

"Well, aren't you the hero?" Michael said.

Shane released me, staring Michael square in the eye. "Someone has to be."

2

THE MAGICIAN

"I'm not sure how to repay you, to repay any of you, for coming with me," I said, taking Shane's hand. Though he had washed his hands in Aunt Dora's sink, there was still a layer of grime on them. He offered no explanation, and I didn't press. He was here now and that was all that mattered.

My husband leapt onto an ancient tree trunk that had fallen across a brisk stream. He reached out his hand, pulling me up to join him. From this vantage point, we could see much of the forest; it was thinner in this region, opening up into many glades. To the east, the ruins of Jillian's old studio called to me.

I laid my head on Shane's shoulder, squeezing him tight. The sun cut through the gathering clouds overhead, illuminating us like actors on a stage. For a moment, I was a princess and he was my grimy-handed prince. I had never been a fan of fairy tales, but now I realized the allure of everlasting love.

He kissed the top of my head and ran his hands along my back. "I love you, Maggie Mae."

"I love you, too Dork," I teased, relishing even the smallest movements of his hands as they ran over me.

Shane looked into my eyes, one hand now stroking my cheek, the other brushing my hair. He smelled like wet leaves and earth. He was only slightly taller than me but seemed much larger now. My body reacted. I closed my eyes and our lips met.

His kiss was gentle at first, but grew more insistent and demanding. Our bodies were pressed tight and I felt his desire build beneath his jeans. I bit his earlobe as his warm breath tickled my neck. Our hands roamed wildly. Finally, I moaned and pulled away. I didn't want our first time as a married couple to be under such circumstances.

My child is missing. I looked at my husband apologetically.

He held up a hand. "You don't have to say a word. We both deserve better than this. But the second we get back from the Netherworld, I'm taking you on a honeymoon you may never recover from."

I laughed. "Is that a promise?"

"More like a threat."

He pulled me into his side, and I felt a surge of pure happiness. "I feel so guilty, Shane. I shouldn't feel happiness right now." I looked down at the ground, ashamed. "Right?"

He pointed towards the sky. "Maggie, take any happiness you can find in this world. Happiness is like that sun - we need it to sustain us. Without it, there's really no point."

I pressed my lips together, sifting through the guilt. What Shane said made sense. Moments like these were what kept me charged. And if there ever comes a time I can't remember what the sun feels like, I'll probably surrender to the shadows.

"Thank you," I swallowed, my words drying up as I held back more tears.

"Deep breaths," he said, as I fanned myself.

Jillian had told me to keep a rein on my emotions. So far, I wasn't doing well. I inhaled and let it go. "Okay. All better."

He looked dubious but gave an affirmative nod. "We will find Montana, okay? You have to trust me on this. And stop acting like I'm doing you a favor. I blame myself for this entire thing."

"How can you blame yourself? You weren't with Montana when he disappeared. Michael was."

"Yes, but if I hadn't been… occupying your time, Michael wouldn't have taken him out of town."

"Stop it." I cut him off. "It's all my fault, although I'll never admit that to Michael. I knew Larinda was out there. I should never have let Montana out of my sight." My body trembled and my breath quickened. *Control, Maggie.* If I couldn't maintain myself here, how would I possibly deal with my emotions in the Netherworld?

"I suppose we both need to quit feeling guilty," he said. "The wheels were set in motion long ago, and not even the Council could stop it. Sometimes fate is too strong."

"Yes," I agreed, remembering Jillian saying something similar. "Larinda was just waiting for her opportunity. I couldn't have watched Montana every moment of his life."

Shane removed his hat and ran his hands through his shaggy brown hair. He looked ruggedly handsome with the new growth on his chin, though he was still thinner than I was used to. "Are you ready to let Michael off the hook, then?" he asked. "He did marry us, after all."

"I find it amusing that you're concerned about Michael," I admitted.

"I'm not his biggest fan. But I do feel a little sorry for the dope. He lost you and his kid… Oh, God, I'm sorry… Maggie. That was completely insensitive." He looked at me with pleading eyes. "Forgive that comment, please."

"You're right." I slid down from the trunk. The hem of my skirt caught on the bark and ripped, but I didn't care.

Shane hopped off in one nimble leap.

"I *want* to forgive Michael, but I can't," I said. "Even though it's illogical, part of me will never forgive him until I have Montana in my arms again."

"Larinda may have her limitations, but she's an adept witch," Shane said, leading me down the narrow path towards the abandoned studio. "There was a reason Sasha kept her around, and it wasn't because of family loyalty. Uncle Joe and Sasha worried what Larinda would do if she were ever snubbed. They kept a close watch on her. If they were that worried about her, there's not much Michael could have done."

"I suppose," I said, my feet as heavy as my heart. Twenty-four hours ago, life was perfect. Today, there was an emptiness I couldn't even fathom. When you bring a child into the world, your world becomes your child.

We trekked through the woods, taking turns leading the way. The tree shadows followed, their arms stretched out like the gangly creatures in the crystal ball. The path opened up and we were greeted by a small meadow filled with summer wildflowers. The grass was lush, dotted with jeweled flowers in shades of lavender, topaz, and amethyst. I wrinkled my brow. They hadn't been here yesterday. But that was how Dark Root worked.

"It seems like the world should stop when you're grieving," I said, picking a flower and twirling it in my fingers. "How can everything just go on?"

"When your heart's broken, it seems a mockery that cows still give milk."

I laughed so hard I nearly choked. "Thank you," I said, wiping my eyes. "Your cowboy poetry is just what I needed to cheer me up."

"You like that? I got a slew more pearls of wisdom tucked away in a journal somewhere."

"No, thank you. I can only digest so much wisdom at once." I pointed my chin at the ruins that sat in the center of the clearing. The day was passing too fast. I buried my nose in Shane's neck, inhaling his familiar scent. We trod through the dense meadow towards the studio. It was strange to see this area so abundant with life and magick, while only a few miles away at Harvest Home the world was depleted.

"I can see why you come here," Shane said, smiling pleasantly. "It's very peaceful." He removed his hat and held it to his chest in reverence. The sun caught the highlights in his hair, and he looked like a grubby angel standing beside a place of pilgrimage.

"Look!" I pointed towards a small tree behind the building. "That wasn't here yesterday!"

"Are you sure?" he asked.

It was a squat tree, only as tall as I was, with a sturdy trunk and thick branches that swooped gracefully upwards. It was in full leaf, perfect and dewy and green. It seemed to glow, as if kissed by a fairy. We circled the tree, neither of us touching it.

"Is it me, or is it growing even as we stand here?" I asked. I stood perfectly still, watching. Yes. It was taller than me now, by a smidgeon.

"This is either the result of a miracle, or a shit ton of magick," Shane said.

"I'm beginning to think those two things aren't entirely unrelated." I continued my inspection, gazing at it as a child would a Christmas tree, freshly doused in lights and tinsel. It was so beautiful, and so out of place. "I feel very connected to this tree for some reason."

"This ground is very fertile," Shane said, digging the toe of his boot into a patch of moist earth. "Do you feel that? Its concentrated. I don't think this is all Jillian's residual energy, or yours either." He poked one of the branches with the tips of his fingers and quickly pulled back. "Wow. That must be what it's like to shake hands with an electric eel."

I scratched my head, wondering how it had gotten here. Merry had some life-enhancing abilities, but nothing on this scale. Jillian and Dora were essentially out of magick, and hadn't left Harvest Home in days. Larinda was ruled out as well - green magick is not a dark witch's forte.

"Hey, Mags. There's a dark spot near the bottom. It looks charred."

Sure enough, there was a mark on the trunk, as though it had been singed. I didn't dare touch it, for fear of damaging the tree further. Just above the burn mark, there was something tucked into the crook of a branch. It was sky blue, and at first I thought it was a small roosting bird. I carefully plucked it from the tree, and rolled it in my hands, hardly able to believe my eyes.

"Mags? Is that the cap Aunt Dora knitted for Montana?" Shane asked.

"Yes!" I nodded tearfully. He was wearing it the day he disappeared. But how did it get here? I held it to my nose and breathed in the scent of my infant son. It suddenly occurred to me he might be nearby, and I immediately raced into Jillian's studio, half expecting to see him lying on our picnic blanket, just as he had so many times before.

"Montana! Where are you!?" I called out. "Mommy's here!"

I raced out into the meadow, and then back again, and then circled the building frantically. Eventually, Shane stepped in front of me.

"He's not here, Maggie. I've tried tracking him. He's not on this plane."

"But the tree! And the hat! He's sending me signs, Shane. I know it!"

I returned to the tree, focusing so intently I feared I'd set it on fire. I felt its power, stemming from deep within the earth. I placed both hands on its trunk and braced for the shock. Though the magick was strong, it didn't repel me as it had Shane. In fact, it felt reassuring.

"I'm Maggie," I said, feeling a proper introduction was important. The tree's lower branches rustled gently. I pressed my ear to its trunk and listened. The tree had a heartbeat!

I looked up at Shane with wide eyes, my ear still pressed to the smooth trunk. The steady beat of a small heart echoed from within. I knew that beat. I had listened to that beat many times while Montana slept on my chest.

"He's in there!" I said, tapping the trunk. "Montana's in there!"

"Maggie, are you sure?"

"He's inside the tree!" I said. "I know it's crazy, but..."

Shane squatted down and put his own ear to the trunk. We stared at each other, listening to the beat together. Our smiles mirrored one another, growing with every passing thump. "He's in there," I whispered, giddy.

Then, abruptly, the beating stopped.

Oh, God. I felt panic rise from the pit of my stomach.

Shane grabbed my wrist, trying to steady me. "It's a sign, that's all," he said. "A sign that your son is okay. Hold on to that."

"But what if something happened to him?"

"I got a read when I heard him. He's not in there, exactly. But I think this was his way of letting you know that he's alive and well, for now."

For now. There's that line again. Two of the most beautiful - and dreaded - words ever spoken. I prayed Shane was right.

We stepped away from the tree and I cradled the hat in my hands.

"Hang in there, okay?" Shane said, lifting my chin.

"I just want my happily ever after."

"And you'll get it. But if you've read any of the stories, you'll remember there are no happily-ever-afters without a fight first. Now let's get ready for that fight."

"Take a picture first, please? I want to show Jillian the tree."

He took several photos from various angles while I massaged the hat, absorbing every bit of my son's energy. But the tree, or the Netherworld, had already taken its share. The hat was merely a shell now - but it was my shell.

I reluctantly followed Shane into the studio. It was a place where Jillian had painted long ago, and where I had later come to find my own inner peace. Some of my things were still there: a notebook, a pen, candles, flip-flops, and the small blanket I had used to lounge the afternoons away.

"Sit," Shane ordered, spreading the blanket. He sat down and crossed his legs, motioning for me to do the same, opposite him. As I did so, he held up his hands and told me to press mine into them.

"Slow, deep breaths," he said. "I can't lead you through the Netherworld when your emotions and mind are jumbled. If it's like the dream world, every thought creates or destroys... and can bring chaos or tranquility. Let's practice."

After several guided breaths, I felt my body and mind go soft. "Let go of your fears, Maggie. Can you do that for me?"

"How?"

"Fear is a trick of your mind. Ignore it. Montana is linked to you, and I won't be able to find him if your mind is disorderly. So just focus on the good stuff."

"But every good thought simply leads me back to fear. Fear of what's happening to my son. I can't go anywhere in my mind, Shane."

"Remember our shared dream world?" he asked, setting his hands on his knees.

I couldn't help but smile a little. Shane and I had carved out our own fantasy world in our collective dream, when we couldn't have one here. "I've never felt so safe or happy as when I was there."

"Go into those dreams, but this time, create them as you wish."

"I'll try," I agreed, closing my eyes.

Shane spoke, guiding me back to our private world. At first, it was his words.

"You are in a lush meadow, surrounded by trees. Everywhere you look there are beautiful flowers, in colors so bright they are only possible in a dream..."

Soon, my own imagination took over. I smelled the scent of grass and sunflowers. I felt the breeze tickle my cheeks. I heard birds dancing overhead. A white butterfly floated before me, then settled on a pink flower. We regarded one another with happy curiosity.

"It's all so real," I said. It seemed as real as anything I had ever experienced.

Unexpectedly, a wash of vibrant pastels splashed the clear blue sky, as if someone had taken a giant paintbrush and hastily added in... *A rainbow.*

"You couldn't stay away, for even a minute?" I asked, smiling as Shane appeared beneath the arch of colors.

He grinned as he sauntered towards me. He was no longer in his cowboy hat and grubby clothes, but in a faded pair of jeans and a clean t-shirt.

"Are you really here?" I asked, reaching for him. We had rendezvoused in his night dreams, but never while we were both *awake.*

"We are linked, Maggie. Your dream world is now mine, and the other way around." He lifted my hand to show me the ring on my finger. Our wedding ring.

"Is this your rainbow?" I asked.

"No. If this were my work, there'd be a campfire and a saloon. Maybe a few dancehall girls." I slugged him playfully in the arm and he pretended it hurt. "The rainbow is all you. You can do anything, Maggie Magick. In any world, dream or otherwise."

"It's so beautiful," I said, as the scene slowly dissolved and we found ourselves back in the studio. Once reoriented, we both grinned.

"I wish we could've stayed longer," I said.

"No, you don't. If you did, we would have."

"I really hate riddles." I laughed. "But I love you. Thanks for showing me."

"I love you, too, Maggie. Forever."

I crawled onto his lap, pushing him backwards. I straddled him, my red curls cascading down across his face. For a breath, I forgot everything. I took off his shirt, and then my own.

"Maggie..." he whispered.

"Shhh..." I pressed my bare chest flat against his, just as our palms had been pressed together earlier. I needed to feel every part of him, to confirm that he was real. There were so many things that weren't real in this world. "I need you, Shane."

"Here? Now?"

"You're my husband. This might be our only chance."

Without a word, Shane traded places with me, expertly rolling me onto my back. His hands ran over my body, from my face to my thighs. His warm lips found my neck, his tongue tracing circles around my ears as he repeatedly whispered, ."I love you, Maggie."

"I love you, too, Shane. Forever."

I sunk into his embrace, the rhythms of our bodies becoming perfectly harmonic, rising and falling together as we breathed. But when he lifted my skirt, I grabbed his wrist. There was something behind him. Or rather, someone. My body went cold and limp while my mouth went dry. And just as quickly, the vision was gone.

"What's wrong?" Shane asked, his eyes searching mine.

"I just can't yet," I said, pushing him back as I scrambled out from under him. "I'm sorry."

"Did I do something?"

"No, I just feel dizzy," I lied. "I haven't slept or eaten much. It must have caught up to me."

"Let's get you some food," he said, lifting me to my feet and handing me my shirt. He hadn't bought my fib, but he didn't press. *Had he seen the phantom, too?*

The phantom - my father, Armand - peering in through the window, an hourglass hovering above his open hand. "Tick tock," he mouthed to me, before snapping his fingers and disappearing altogether.

3

THE HIGH PRIESTESS

e left the ruins quickly. Shane offered me a granola bar from his pack, saying it would 'perk me right up,' and asked no more about my sudden change in mood. I would tell him eventually, but I needed time to think about it privately first.

The domes must be failing if my father found his way inside Dark Root so easily.

Unless it was all my imagination?

It didn't matter. Armand's appearance, whether real or imagined, woke me up.

Tick tock.

hane and I made our way to the downtown district of Dark Root. A year ago, the quaint town had been in decline, but we had revived it. Today it bustled with shoppers, children eating ice cream cones, and summer tourists. It was a relief to feel a sense of normalcy, even if only for an hour. I drank in the sunshine and pushed the image of my father from my mind. For now. All the while, I massaged the baby hat in my pocket, nestled near The Star card.

"Days like this make you believe in miracles," I said, wondering how anything could be wrong when the air was so crisp and the sun so bright. I clutched Shane's hand as we made our way up Main Street. "Do you think things will ever be truly good again? Tell me the truth. And please, don't answer with more cowboy poetry."

Shane smiled, pressing my hand to his lips. "I think as long as we act with love and conviction, things will always be okay."

"Still corny, but I like it."

"I do my best work on short notice."

A gray-haired woman grabbed my elbow as we passed her on the sidewalk. "Maggie, are you okay?" She asked.

"Yes, Fine, Mrs. Newsome," I said, pulling out of her grasp. "Why?"

"Well, that's a relief! You look like you've seen a ghost. Your mother isn't haunting you, is she?" Mrs. Newsome chuckled nervously, looking about as if Miss Sasha were watching us at that very moment. "And how's the new baby doing? A boy, is it? I just bet he's the reason you're looking so tired and green around the gills. It's tough being a new mother. I remember when my baby Frankie was born..."

"Sorry, Mrs. Newsome, I have to go," I said, waving a quick good-bye. I grabbed Shane's hand and steered him away before we were trapped in one of her famous 'Baby Frankie' stories. The man was now forty-eight-years old and coached high school football. But in Mrs. Newsome's heart, he was still her baby. Did that happen to all mothers? I hoped more than anything to get the chance to find out.

We proceeded down the street, but it was slow going. I was a semi-celebrity in Dark Root these days, for better or worse. I squared my shoulders and pasted a smile onto my face as we walked, nodding here and there. Shane, bless him, did the talking when we couldn't extricate ourselves from a particularly chatty local.

We made our way past the book store, the pie house, and two ice cream carts, the owners shooting accusing glares at one another from their competing spaces. At last, we reached the apex of downtown - Miss Sasha's Magick Shoppe, located directly across the street from Dip Stix Cafe.

"Eve has the keys," I said, leading Shane around to the rear entrance. The back door was unlocked. "Remind me to write myself up for that," I said, knowing neither Eve nor Merry would have left the shop unsecured.

We went into the stockroom, skirting the life-sized nude statue of Adam that Michael had ordered. The sculpture brought fresh anger. "Michael can order garbage like this but can't keep our son safe," I said. It was an unfair accusation and I knew it, but I didn't care.

"Ignore it," Shane said. "We have other priorities at the moment."

We made our way to the front of the store. As always, Eve's displays were perfect. There were at least a dozen bins of multi-colored candles, and twice as many boxes filled with dried herbs. We had shelves overflowing with oddities - shrunken heads, bat wings, and other novelties. There were clocks that ran backwards and love potions that only worked on werewolves.

Then there was the meat of the store - a massive collection of anything the modern witch needed to cast spells, read fortunes, or avenge wrongdoing. I strolled through the short aisles, brimming with mood rings, Tarot cards, dragon's ink, parchment paper, pendulums, and crystals. I stopped at the DIY voodoo doll kit, wondering if I needed an actual lock of Larinda's hair for it to work.

"It's a shame we don't have the store open right now," I said. "We could be making a ton of money today." I sighed heavily, looking around. "I don't even know what I'm here for," I admitted, throwing up my hands. "But Jillian said to trust our intuition, and my intuition led me here."

Shane pulled a wand from an umbrella stand near the door, one of several, each carved from different wood. "This one smells like cedar. Do you need a new one?" he asked.

"No. Mine's back at Harvest Home."

I sifted through a bucket of crystals, then poked at a dreamcatcher. Nothing called to me.

"We should go," I said. I took a step towards the door, then stopped abruptly as I caught a glimpse of something in my peripheral vision. It was tucked away on one of the lower shelves, partially hidden behind an old recipe book. If the sunlight hadn't hit it just so, I never would have seen it. It was an hourglass, no larger than the palm of my hand.

On first look, there was nothing particularly special about it. In fact, it looked cheaply made, like the kind you find in a child's board game. But when I picked it up, I felt its dense magick. It couldn't be just coincidence. I had just seen my father holding one.

I held the hourglass up to the light. There wasn't much sand inside, only a light dusting on the bottom. I turned it over and read the inscription: Plane-Traveling Timepiece. Don't Leave Hope Without It.

"Okay…" I said, uncertainly. I put it in my skirt pocket alongside the cap and Tarot card. I swore, when I got back from the Netherworld, I was going to invest in a real purse.

"I think I found what I came for," I said, looking out the front window. A gangly woman with short, choppy hair hurried by, muttering to herself. It was my sister, Ruth Anne.

"Hey!" I called, stepping outside and joining her on the sidewalk. "Find anything useful?" I asked, eyeing the khaki backpack dangling from her shoulder.

"Just got my ghost hunting gear and a few things from my preppers kit," she said. "Otherwise, I have no idea what to take. Maybe some snacks?" Her eyes trailed to the nearest ice cream cart. I suppressed a laugh. Only Ruth Anne would dare to sneak Ben and Jerry's into hell.

"There's probably nothing that can prepare us for what's to come," I said.

"Right!" She held up a finger. "I'm off to the bookstore to do some research." Ruth Anne flapped away like a riled-up chicken in combat boots. I felt a swell of love for her, for each of my sisters, who were about to risk everything for me and my child.

S hane herded me across the street to Dip Stix Cafe. Several people saw him opening the door and asked if he were back in business. "Still fire damage, but we'll be open soon," he assured them. "Most likely by fall." They nodded, but lingered a few minutes, anyway.

"This town is full of gossips," I said, too loudly, as we slipped inside. Once the door closed behind us, I asked, "What are you getting in here?"

"Mainly, one last look."

The once-pristine restaurant now reeked of soot and ash. There was a chill to the air, though the air conditioner wasn't on. I hugged my chest as we wandered through the dining room and into the kitchen.

"Shane, we're going to clean this up and get it open as soon as…"

"Yep," he agreed. "As soon as…"

I took his hand and kissed it. Since my return home nearly a year ago, I had gained so much but I – we, had lost so much, as well. The café had been in Shane's family for decades, passed on to him by his late Uncle Joe, a member of Mother's original council. Now, it lay in ash and ruin. While I spoke confidently of restoring it to its former glory, I wasn't sure we could restore anything anymore

Shane took out his phone and began snapping pictures, catching the room from various viewpoints. "Memories," he said, putting his phone away.

"Won't those make you sad?" I asked, looking around at the mess.

"They'll make me determined. This place isn't just for me anymore. It's for family. *Our* family."

Our family. He meant me and Montana, and his son, whom I still hadn't met.

My lip quivered. I needed to comfort him, and myself. When Mother got into one of her moods when I was a kid, Merry would take it upon herself to boost our morale. No matter what was thrown at us, she'd put her hands on her hips, her blue eyes twinkling with both kindness and determination. Invariably, she'd say something like,

Here's the plan. We just need to stay out of Mama's way for a few days. I'll take care of dinners. Maggie, you are in charge of laundry. Mama will calm down. You'll see. We got this.

Then, we'd all stick out our hands and Ruth Anne would blow on them like dandelions. We'd wriggle our fingers and stack our fists, one on top of the next. "We got this!" It was our rallying cry, our declaration to the world that the Maddock girls wouldn't be defeated. I looked at Shane, wanting to share that memory with him but also needing to keep it to myself.

"We got this," I said out loud, and that was enough.

"Yes. *We* do." He looked at me from beneath his hat. "We can get through anything together. Now, give me a moment. I'll be right back."

Shane went up the narrow wooden staircase that led to his attic bedroom. I wandered the dormant café, listening to the sounds of Shane above me. Doors and drawers opened and shut. Something large was drug across the floor. And I wasn't certain, but I thought I heard breaking glass. What was he looking for? A few minutes later he reappeared, carrying a small pack.

"Good to go?" I said, not asking what he carried inside the pack. We were married now, and I had to learn to trust.

We left the shop and continued our walk through town, my eyes wandering towards the gray mountain peak in the distance. Larinda's castle was there, at least in the Netherworld. The mountain didn't seem so far from here, but how far would it be once we crossed the boundary of the veil? Would it be there at all?

"Ruth Anne put me in the mood for ice cream," I said, stopping at the cart in front of the book store. I gave the vendor a five-dollar bill. "We might as well live it up now. I hear calories don't count in the afterlife."

"Too bad," Shane said, patting his trim middle. "I could actually use a few."

We ordered a double scoop of rocky road and shared it. I savored the taste of the chocolate melting on my tongue and the feel of the creme rolling down my throat. It was now quite warm and we had to quickly lick the sides of the cone before it dripped. A woman passed by with the same double scoop and we exchanged guilty smiles.

How had I taken ice cream for granted for so long? It was one of the many, many marvelous things in the world. There were so many things I hadn't properly given their due - so many small joys I had forgotten to notice as I got busy with my life. I vowed that when I returned, I would never take ice cream for granted again.

We strolled Main Street slowly, taking it all in. It was as if we were seeing each shop, bench, and streetlight for the first time - or perhaps the last. This was our collective history, the town we grew up in, the place many of our memories resided. Where did memories go when there was no one around to remember them?

We ended our walk at the bench in the town square. Shane accidentally dropped the last of our ice cream as he sat down.

"That's a shame," I teased. "Now, you'll have to do something to make it up to me." I scooted close, so that our legs were touching.

"Yeah?" he asked, twisting a lock of my long hair around his finger. "Like what?"

"Hmm...let me think about it."

He licked his lips. "I, uh, may have a few ideas."

"Just a few?"

"A handful? A couple handfuls? No more than a few dozen, tops."

"I'm glad to hear that I haven't scared you off, after my freakout at the ruins earlier."

"You'll never scare me off, Maggie."

"Then I do have an idea of my own," I said, fluttering my lashes.

"Yes?"

"Well, I suppose you could escort me into the Netherworld. That might just do it."

The side of Shane's mouth curled up. "Bah! That's no way to properly punish a man for dropping an ice cream cone."

"Get me out of the Netherworld, then I'll punish you properly."

"You got yourself a deal."

"Ouch!" I felt a sharp jab into my shoulder. I looked around to see

Eve standing behind us, her arms crossed and her lips puckered. Merry was beside her.

"Honestly," Eve said. "How you two can be making kissy faces right now is beyond me."

"What should I be doing?" I asked. "Jillian said to take the day to prepare. Do you have any idea how to prepare for this? Because I'm clueless."

Eve circled the bench, so that she stood directly in front of us. "All I know is that Merry and I are busting our asses trying to figure out what to do, and you guys are here playing newlyweds!"

"I am a newlywed," I reminded her.

"And I'm about to risk my biscuit for you. I would think you'd be doing something...something more useful."

"Eve, please calm down," I said, standing.

"Calm down! I just want to remind you that it's your kid we're looking for." She waved her hands in exasperation. "If you aren't taking this seriously, why should we?"

I reached for Eve's hand but she stepped back, her eyes clearly saying 'don't touch me.' I looked to Merry , but she only shrugged

"Are you okay, Evie?" I asked.

"Evie?" She raised an eyebrow and laughed, rightfully suspicious. We only called her Evie when we wanted her to be agreeable. "I don't know if I'm all right. Are you all right?"

She jiggled the Crown Royal pouch she wore over her shoulder. "We spent the entire day trying to prepare for the unpreparable. So far, I have something called *pixie dust* that I found in one of Mom's old shoe boxes, which I suspect is actually some 1970s ground-up amphetamine. And for whatever reason, I grabbed a few moon rocks from the store. My intuition is telling me nothing. That's how okay I am."

"Eve, tell me what's really going on. It has to be more than moon rocks and pixie dust."

"I...I don't want to go," she said, adamantly shaking her head. "I've dreamt of it, Maggie. It's dark..."

She sucked in a breath and fanned her eyes before continuing. "But we can't leave Montana in there. And I'm not letting you go without me. I'm just freaked out... freaked the fuck out. How are we going to face whatever is in there? That's the world where nightmares are born! And that's not even counting Larinda, who probably has Superman powers on that side of the veil."

My younger sister clenched her fists and squinted her eyes, as if she were four-years-old again and had missed her nap. I grabbed her shoulders and forced her to look at me. She fought against me but I held firm. Then her body shuddered, and finally slumped. I caught her.

"Eve, stay focused," I said, stroking her hair. "It's going to be all right. I promise you."

"Your demon-loving father is in there, right? I'm just afraid this whole thing is going to end badly."

I lifted her chin and stared into her dark pupils. She didn't often let people see her true depth, but it was there, just beneath the lipstick and henna tattoos.

"I'm afraid too, Evie," I admitted. "In fact, I'm freaked-the-fuck-out, too. But I have no choice. You do have a choice. I'll still love you, even if you don't go."

Eve sighed, letting it out slowly. "Well, I can't let you guys go and come out with all these awesome stories. Let's go be scared together."

I squeezed her hand. "Thank you."

"C'mon Evie," Merry said, "I'll buy you an ice cream. I hear calories don't count in the afterlife."

Eve nodded, looking visibly better.

As they walked away, Merry called back over her shoulder. "Jillian's looking for you, Maggie. She wants you back at Harvest Home, right away."

"**I**s everything okay?" I asked.

Shane and I stood before Jillian and Aunt Dora, who were seated at the garden table in the back yard. Only now, there was no garden, and the ornate marble table looked as out of place as the giant heads on barren Easter Island.

On the far side of the yard, Michael had set up a mat and was moving through a series of yoga poses. I eyed the corner of his mat, tugging at it in my mind. Michael tumbled out of warrior two, falling on his ass. I kept my face expressionless as he looked suspiciously our way.

"Thank god yer back, Maggie," Aunt Dora said. "Can ya talk ta that man? He's been doing them poses fer hours, an' chantin' the whole time. Are all men such fools when they're about ta turn forty?"

Shane flushed. "This sounds like a conversation I don't want to be involved in. I'm gonna go put on a clean shirt," he said, turning towards the house.

"You called me back to stop Michael from practicing yoga?" I asked, annoyed but also relieved.

"No. Was just goin' ta use the opportunity since yer here."

My eyes drifted towards Michael. He was a buffoon, but a harmless one. And Aunt Dora usually appreciated his company. He must have been particularly exasperating today.

"Now Dora," Jillian said, patting her hand. "Not all men have a midlife crisis. And for the ones who do, that doesn't mean they all end up like…"

"…My father," I finished for her. I took a seat at the table, resting my elbows on it. "You knew him better than anyone, Jillian. What do you think went so wrong for him?"

Jillian pulled at the shawl draping her shoulders. She looked frail in that moment, not at all the vibrant woman I'd come to know. "I believe those dark tendencies in your father were always there. I saw it within him in his younger days, but I kept telling myself he'd outgrow it, or that I could save him."

I understood. Though Michael wasn't dark, per say, I had seen facets of his personality I chose to ignore when we were together. "If I knew then what I know now, I doubt I would have run off with Michael. But I got Montana out of it, so it wasn't all a waste."

"And I got you," Jillian said warmly.

Aunt Dora opened her mouth, then snapped it shut. She had always been second-in-command of my life, after Sasha. But now that I knew Jillian was my biological mother, my aunt probably felt she'd lost her place in my familial hierarchy.

"Auntie, if Michael's bothering you, I'll put an end to it."

I started to get up, but Aunt Dora stopped me, her veined hand closing around my wrist. "No. I shouldn't be addin' ta yer worries. It's bad enough I may ne'er see any o' ya again after ya go into the Netherworld." She clamped her hand over her mouth and widened her eyes. "Oh, no! I cursed ya. Oh, Maggie, girl. What have I done?"

"It's not a curse," I said quickly, before she properly worked herself up. "You said *may. May.*"

"Words have power, and *may* just softens them a bit." My aunt blew her nose with a tissue from the pocket of her housedress. "'Tis not the time to send mixed messages to the Universe." She made the sign of the cross on her chest, as she had seen Michael do numerous times, and I hid my smile.

We drank silently, all the while wondering if this was our very last tea party. Michael continued his sun salutations and I envied the peaceful look on his face. If – when - my son returned, I hoped that Michael's patience rubbed off on him. If Montana were indeed a warlock, he'd need to learn to weather the storms of Dark Root, rather than create them.

Shane returned, clean-shaven, wearing fresh jeans and a blue t-shirt. Only his boots and cowboy hat showed signs of wear. He eyed Michael. "If that guy stops to do a downward dog in the Netherworld, we're not waiting for him."

"Agreed," I said.

"Maggie, Shane, can I speak to you two in private?" Jillian asked.

I glanced at Aunt Dora. She winked, letting me know she could handle Michael if needed.

We followed Jillian towards the west edge of the woods, through a narrow opening between two slender trees. I began to sense magick ripening around me. The further we got from Harvest Home, the richer it was. The plants and earth still seemed affected, though not as severely as they were near Harvest Home. I pulled a leaf from an overhanging bough. It crumbled in my hand, as if it were late autumn.

"Jillian, did you and Aunt Dora draw magick from out here, too?"

She stopped, turning to look at me with a grave expression. "I suppose you should know, but please don't tell the others yet. I don't want them to worry." She looked around, though there was only foliage as far as the eye could see. "Magick isn't just fading near Harvest Home, it fading all over Dark Root."

"All over?" I asked, as she began walking again, faster than before.

"Yes. It weakens by the day - even here where its more concentrated than in other parts of the forest. But I can't let Dora know. She's so old now, and has worked so hard for so long." Jillian wiped her face with her hand, drawing in a long breath. "What I'm about to show you has been kept secret for many years. Sasha showed me when I was an initiate, and now I'm showing you. Discretion is imperative."

My mother turned abruptly, and proceeded down a marshy path. The trees seemed to know her, spreading their boughs wide to let her pass. Eventually, she came to a halt, and pulled back a branch with wide, fan-shaped leaves. I realized we had looped all the way around and were on the back side of Sister House.

"Why are we here already?" I asked, looking through the woods to the white Victorian home. "I thought we didn't need to be here until the evening."

"We won't be going inside. I just wanted to show you where we were first." Jillian backtracked several steps, spun to the right, and then parted another thick clump of limbs. We emerged into a welcome patch of sunshine.

"Here," she motioned to a tree inside the clearing. It was tall and wide and majestic, with golden upturned boughs that saluted the heavens. The tree was just like the one we'd seen at Jillian's ruins, only much larger.

"We've seen that tree! Shane, show her the picture!"

Shane produced his phone, showing her the image.

"It's the same tree!" Jillian gasped.

"Just smaller," I agreed, studying them both. In every way except for size, the two were identical. Even the trunk was charred in the exact location of its smaller doppelgänger. "The miniature tree appeared today, behind your old studio," I said.

"How unusual," Jillian said, pressing her palms and ears to the trunk, listening for its pulse as Shane and I had earlier. Next, she dipped a finger into a nearby puddle of clear water, and *drew* sigils over the tree trunk I recognized as health and serenity. She then gave the tree a silent blessing, and wiped her hands clean.

"I am the caretaker of this tree, and someday, someone else will inherit the task. Until recently, it's always been healthy. I can't tell you how much this troubles me."

Jillian stepped away, seating herself on a fallen log. She cradled her face in her hands, deepening the worry lines in her forehead. When she looked at me again, her normally vibrant green eyes had muddied. "I suppose I should have expected this sort of synchronicity."

"What do you mean?" Shane asked. "What synchronicity?"

"Come sit," my mother said, motioning to the log on either side of her. We flanked her and she took each of our hands. I could feel a hint of her old magick returning, either from tending to the tree or from venturing away from Harvest Home. It was muffled, but there. "There is a saying: As above, so below. That means, what happens in the Netherworld also happens here. The reverse is true as well. We are all connected. One world mirrors the other, to a degree."

"If the worlds are mirrors, why does Larinda have a castle in the Netherworld, but not here?" I asked.

Jillian sighed deeply and drew her hands back onto her lap, tapping her fingers along her knees. "Magick is much more concentrated in that realm. In fact, you can say that it is one of the sources of our magick here, in this realm. And Larinda's fortress was built on deception. She never wanted to share it with anyone but Armand, and so when she created it, she set that intention. Now, it's become her prison, as a house constructed of greed usually does.

"The tree I showed you is no ordinary tree. It is the Tree of Life. Or, more accurately, one of seven earthly representations scattered across our plane of existence. The original resides in the Netherworld. It is very old, born at the creation of this current Age, and will live until the end of this Age. Each of the seven earthly trees is assigned a female guardian, who cares for it until her seventh decade, or until another guardian is found."

"You're the guardian for the Tree of Life?" I asked, overcome with wonder. There was far more to Jillian than her appearance let on. In fact, her layers seemed endless.

"Just one of seven guardians. That was why Sasha recruited me. She had inherited the duty from her own mother, but Sasha admittedly wasn't suited for the task." Jillian laughed hoarsely as she called up the memory. "Sasha was a powerful woman, but she was no Green Witch."

"Is the burn new?" I asked.

"Yes. And this is what has me deeply troubled. The tree shouldn't sicken until the final days of this Age, which should last several more centuries, at least. I fear time is speeding up, and if that happens... well, that is what the Dark Root Council has been preparing for all along. The end of times. The domes. The white magick. All the protection rituals. Essentially, the Council exists to protect this tree."

She removed her shawl and folded it neatly onto her lap. "The original Tree of Life is hidden somewhere in the Netherworld. If it dies, so do we. The seven trees protect the one, and the one protects the seven. As above, so below."

Shane and I exchanged worried glances . "Die?" I asked. "As in everyone, everywhere?"

She swallowed, looking much older than her years, and nodded slowly. Her normally neatly-coiffed hair had fallen from its pins during our hike, framing her worried face with gray-streaked tendrils.

"Why weren't we told?" I asked. "This seems rather important."

"The end will come, whether we want it to or not. We hoped to delay it with enough light, care, and magick." She glanced at the burn mark on the tree. "I believe this is the work of your father, who is seeking to push through his deal for power and immortality. He is trying to hasten it, before there is a turn around. Going into the Netherworld is not only about saving Montana now, it's about saving everyone. Armand cannot be allowed to trade his first-born male heir, your son."

I stood, wiping off my skirt. "I can't save everyone! It's too much! I just want Montana back."

"I remember Uncle Joe talking about the Tree of Life," Shane said, rising to his feet. "Uncle Joe said that when the final tree succumbs to the darkness, our world will come to an end. I thought it was just a myth. Or alcohol."

"I'm afraid not," Jillian said. "I'm not sure what condition the other trees are in, as they are all kept separately hidden by their guardians. But if the magick is dwindling from Dark Root, it's fading all around the world. It will do you no good to find Montana, only to bring him back to a world of darkness."

"Our entire civilization hinges on trees?" I asked, in disbelief.

"It always has," Jillian said simply. She stood and wrapped the shawl around her thin shoulders again. "There is still hope, though." She reached into her hip pouch and produced a white acorn.

Shane and I inspected it, looking upon the acorn as if it were a holy relic. Perhaps it was. There was so much magick in it that I couldn't bring myself to touch it, feeling somehow unworthy.

Jillian proffered the acorn. "Take it, Maggie. If you find the original Tree of Life and it's in decay as I suspect, then you must plant another. But it can't take root in the same location, as that soil will be tainted. You will know where to plant it, when the time comes."

"Where did you get this seed?" Shane asked.

"Armand gave it to me as a gift, when he was courting me. I didn't know until later that he brought it from the Netherworld. It is from the original Tree of Life. He claimed he won it in a game of dice. Years later, your father demanded it back, once his greed had fully taken hold and he discovered what it was truly worth. He wanted to destroy it, claiming there was more to be gained by the destruction of the world than a new beginning."

"How did you keep it from him?"

"I took it with me when I left Dark Root the first time, and hid it under so many layers of magick that I almost forgot about it myself. Until today." She looked at her tree again, sadly. "I'm sorry," she said. And that was all.

I let my hand rest on the acorn a moment, drawing in its powerful otherworldly magick, before placing it in my skirt pocket. I felt the baby hat, and showed it to Jillian. "We found this in the tree," I said. "Montana was wearing it the day he disappeared. And I swore I heard his heartbeat from within the trunk."

"I think your son is sending you messages from the Netherworld! If this cap was with him on the other side, I might be able to tune in." Jillian clenched the hat, fingering it as she closed her eyes. She mumbled in a language I couldn't understand, invoking ancestors I'd never met.

"He's okay," she said, after a long and frightening pause. "I saw him in a woman's arms. He was physically fine, but I sensed his fear. I could feel him calling out for you."

My hand went to my heart. My child was afraid and needed me. "How much time do we have?"

"All the time in the world," Jillian said. "And none."

~

"As above, so below," I said, plopping down beside Jillian on the porch swing at Sister House. Our legs were drawn into our laps, and the swing moved of its own accord.

Jillian smiled at me. "You shouldn't waste your gifts on swings. Magick is a resource that grows scarcer by the moment, these days."

"I don't care. What good is being a *wilder* if I can't use it from time to time. Besides, it reminds me of Montana. Remember how he'd make his baby swing go, all by himself!" I smiled at the memory, holding it close to my heart. "Oh, Jillian. Montana was the best part of me. How can I go on if I don't find him?"

"You will find him. But I will give you the same advice Sasha gave me, when I lost my brother in the Vietnam War."

"You had a brother? I had an uncle?"

"Yes. I admired him so much. He was handsome and kind and good. He died saving a friend. But anyway..." she looked past me, at a ghost only she could see.

"When Sasha found me, I was a shell of my former self," Jillian continued. "I remember her telling me, 'Jillian, when the best of us are taken, the rest of us must step up.' It was simple and direct, but her words got through to me. My brother was gone, but I was not. The best way to honor his legacy was to be a light in the world, just as he was."

"That breaks my heart, Jillian. In so many ways."

"Mine too, but it also sustains me."

"Is there anything else I need to know?" I asked, looking out at the waning sun.

"Darling, there is so much to tell you, and not enough earthly minutes to tell them in." She spread her hand across her lap, and thought. "From what I understand, Magick is immediate in the Netherworld. On this plane, you need candles, stones, rituals and time to cast spells. But there, a mere thought can alter reality immediately. And focus items intensify the effects.

"It is a volatile world, and the rules will change as soon as you master them. Plus, there are many 'existences' in the Netherworld, and each operates independent of the others. There is no guide or roadmap. If your mind gets messy, you risk getting lost permanently."

"Shane's teaching me to summon rainbows," I blurted, wanting to impress her. "That should help keep my mind uncluttered."

"He's a good match for you, and his skills will be invaluable on the other side of the veil. But this is your journey, Maggie. This is about you and your son. Only you can plant the acorn, and only you can find Montana."

Shane returned, carrying a bouquet of wildflowers in his arms. I reached out to take them, but he handed them to Jillian instead.

"What's the occasion?" she asked, smiling as she inhaled their fragrance.

"Life."

"Maggie, take a bit of this lavender. It's cleansing." Jillian handed me a sprig, and I added it to the other things in my pocket. I could get a bag, but I wanted to touch them at a moment's notice.

～

At dusk, our tribe gathered in the Sister House nursery. Most of us wore our earlier clothes, though Eve had changed, wearing fitted pants and heeled boots, looking as if she were going for a night on the town, rather than a journey to the Netherworld.

We stood in the center of the room, looking warily towards the closet door. Decades ago, my father had opened a portal into the Netherworld inside this room. Now, I was literally going to follow in his footsteps. I prayed our fates wouldn't be the same.

Jillian read from a spell book, offering invocations of protection. When finished, she closed the book and spoke. "I have prepared the portal. You will enter here, though you likely won't return through this same passage. That will depend on many things, including timelines."

"Timelines?" Merry asked.

"This house might not exist in certain timelines. The same goes for dimensions."

"Roger that," Merry said, bouncing on her heels. "But then how will we get out?"

Jillian and Dora exchanged glances. "Break the chain of the ankh and have faith," Aunt Dora answered. "Ya'll know when."

Faith? I swallowed. With Dark Root's ailing magick, was faith enough to pull us back? And what if I accidentally broke the chain too soon? And if the house didn't exist at all, did that mean Aunt Dora and Jillian would still be on this plane? The worries piled up and I tried not to think of them. First, I'd go into the Netherworld and get my son. Then, we'd sort through the rest of the logistics.

At exactly 7:30, Aunt Dora lifted up a small wicker basket from beside her feet. She ambled about the room, using her cane to keep steady. She drew strange symbols on our foreheads with ash from the basket, muttering each time, "So mote it be."

At last, my aunt stood before me. I bent forward so that she could mark my own forehead and offer her blessing. Once done, she grabbed both my hands, squeezing them tighter than seemed possible for her age. "Ya'll find the boy, and ya'll both return ta fulfill yer destinies. Got it?"

"Yes?" I answered hesitantly. The only destiny I could envision for myself was in being a mother, a wife, a daughter, a sister, and a friend. But maybe that was enough. Who knows how long a shadow our lives cast upon others?

"Keep the light," Aunt Dora said, hugging me.

"Always." I returned her hug. Though she had lost weight, her body was like a comfortable old pillow that never lost its shape.

"I'll be watchin' ya," she said, disentangling herself and poking me in the chest. "I'll come pull ya out myself, if I have ta."

"And I'd pity anything in the Netherworld that got in your way." I kissed her cheek. Her skin tasted like rose petals and salt. I made note of that, in case the Netherworld tried to make me forget.

"We should go now," I announced, just as the final sunbeam disappeared and the full moon appeared in the lone window.

"Shane, will you open the closet door?" Jillian asked.

He squared his lean shoulders and turned the knob. A chill fell over the room as the door squeaked open. Everyone moved in a step.

"There are many worlds within the Netherworld, and you will meet many beings," Jillian said as we stared into the closet's black maw. "Some will be helpful, others will not, and you may not know which will be which."

"I have no intention of interacting with any *beings*," Eve said. "We're just going to go in, get the kid, and get out. The rest of the Netherworld can implode, for all I care."

"Unfortunately, you may not always have a choice," Jillian said.

I made my way to my mother, collapsing against her chest. She smoothed my hair, holding me. "I love you," I said, wiping my eyes. How unfair to be leaving her, I thought, when I needed her the most.

"I love you too, my daughter. Stay safe and bring back my grandson."

I saluted, then took a sidestep towards Shane and the closet. I had touched the portal before, when I thought Montana had disappeared inside. I remembered how dark, cold and vast it felt. And how lonely.

I couldn't dwell on that now. I looked around at everyone in the room and made a promise to myself. If we came back, I'd wring every ounce of joy out of every day - never taking anything or anyone for granted again.

If we came back.

"Stay together," Jillian warned everyone. "The Netherworld will do its best to pull you apart. Dora and I can only watch Maggie. If you wander too far from her when we pull you back, you may not be able to return."

"Let's do this," I said, stepping into the doorframe. Shane took my hand, and looped his other through Merry's arm. We formed a chain of seven, our hands linked like a mountaineer's rope.

"Maggie," Jillian stopped me, just as I lifted my foot.

"Yes?"

"Remember the laws of karma are stronger there. Harm no one... but take no shit."

"I'll remember," I said, feeling Montana's hat between my fingers before stepping in.

4

THE EMPRESS

"*Remember when we watched* Titanic *last Christmas?" I asked Merry. "And the people all fell into the water?"*

But it wasn't Merry I was talking to. It was a wisp of Merry. A fragment. A mere shadow.

We were kids, digging in the garden. I was confused because we hadn't watched Titanic *yet, not until we were grownups.*

Merry looked up from the ladybug in her hands and nodded, not confused at all. "The portal was as cold as that water in that movie, wasn't it?" she asked.

"Much colder."

I had been born again, into a new world. A world that was strangely like my own.

The chilling emptiness evaporated before I could remember how terrible it was. When I emerged from the blackness, I was back in the nursery. The room was stark and I was all alone.

I fumbled for the light switch, nearly tripping over a sleeping bag on the floor. The overhead light went on, buzzing loudly before shutting off again. The moon was still shining through the window, but it was only a crescent now.

"Shane!" I called out nervously, tiptoeing around the room. "Merry?"

I stood beside the closet, unsure how long I should wait. Jillian had said our emotions could fashion the landscape, and I wondered if that small shadow creeping along the baseboard was an invention of mine or a denizen of the Netherworld. Was I even in the Netherworld?

I lifted the ankh, flicking it with my finger. "Glow. Please… please…please." I shook it, hoping to awaken it.

There was a hint of cigarette smoke in the air. My eyes adjusted and I was able to look carefully at my surroundings. The wallpaper, the curtains, the ashtray on the windowsill - I knew this timeline. I had seen it in the snow globes.

This was my father's world.

I crept towards the window and looked out, my breath steaming up the glass. A half-smoked Marlboro sat in the tray and I nudged it away with my elbow. I remembered seeing Armand stand in this very spot, watching Jillian in the garden, or speaking of his deals with the Dark One to Larinda. His essence was dense. Not only could I smell his cigarettes; I could almost taste their ashes.

I jumped at a shuffling noise in the far corner. Sets of tiny red eyes blinked at me from the hidden nooks of the room, so quick to open and shut I wondered if they were really there. Instinct told me to run out the door, out of the house. But would I be any safer out there? Did 'out there' even exist?

"Jillian? Aunt Dora?" I whimpered, hoping the shadows wouldn't hear me.

There was a noise inside the closet. I heard Shane's voice call for me. "Maggie!" He appeared in the closet doorway, red-eyed and relieved. He pulled me to my toes and kissed me. "Damn, I was worried."

"Where are the others?" I asked, craning my neck to look past him.

"Coming. I think. We couldn't stay linked, but the portal can only lead here. I hope."

"Let's pray," I said, nervously watching for more red, blinking eyes.

Time, if it existed here, taunted us as we waited. The room stayed dark, frozen, and the moon didn't change its size or position. Even the sounds outside - owls, ravens, wolves – all repeated like a soundtrack played on a loop. I was thankful Shane found me, though my fear for the others grew with each passing breath. *Are they lost? Trapped? Separated from one another?* I shut down the thought, damned if I'd give this place any further fuel.

At last, Michael emerged, shaking his head, woozy. I hugged him fiercely. He looked surprised but hugged me back. The others emerged in quick succession, all equally dazed. We exchanged looks of bewilderment, then burst into giddy laughter as if drunk on too much champagne.

"We landed back in the nursery?" Eve asked, looking around. She tried flipping the light switch too, with no luck.

"Yes. The nursery as it was when Armand lived here," I said, motioning to the sleeping bag and the ashtray.

Shane and Paul conducted a more thorough assessment of the room. They checked walls and knocked on doors. "It feels solid," Shane said. "More solid than in my dreams. But so do I," he added, pinching his wrist.

"There's nothing more here," I said, looking nervously at the door leading to the hallway. The entire bedroom seemed to tilt, just slightly.

Shane put his hand on the doorknob. "Wait," I stopped him, turning towards Merry. "Can you check this?"

She chewed on her lip, worried. As an empath, Merry could be easily overwhelmed with emotions. Negative ones, especially, weakened her.

"I'll be right beside you," I assured her.

We held our breaths while Merry held her hand in front of the door, tracing small circles in the air around the knob. Then she took a tissue out of her purse and wiped her hands. "I don't feel anything unusual out there," she said. "Unless you count Mama."

"Sasha's out there?" Ruth Anne said, taking a step away from the door. "I don't think I want to leave this room anymore."

I understood her fear. Shadows were one thing; running into our dead mother in a feather boa and high-heels was quite another.

"I don't know if she is actually out there," Merry amended. "But her energy certainly is. This was her house for over a century, after all."

Ruth Anne rummaged through her pack and produced a flashlight. She grinned, as if seeing light for the first time. "Yay! The batteries work!"

"Let's go, already," Eve said, pulling open the door. We all shouted her name, and she snorted when a perfectly ordinary hallway was revealed, with a few buzzing lightbulbs dangling from cords above.

Eve bravely stepped over the threshold and into the hallway. We had no choice but to follow. We slunk into the corridor, looking both ways as if crossing a major road. Upon closer inspection, the hallway wasn't as ordinary as it first appeared. For one thing, the portraits on the wall were mostly of people I had never seen. They ranged wildly in age and fashion, from women in high-collared dresses to women in miniskirts and tube tops. Mother and Aunt Dora were in a few of them, but there was no trace of any of us.

And there were too many doors. It was like staring down a motel passageway, where each door was spaced only a few feet from the next. They seemed to go on indefinitely.

"What the..." I sidestepped to the right. The hall seemed to tilt in response.

"Maybe we could split up? Half of us go left, the other right?" Ruth Anne suggested. "We'd cover more ground."

"Hold on there, Scooby," Eve said. "We're not supposed to split up at all, according to Jillian and Aunt Dora. I'm not about to be lost in the Netherworld. Wherever that ankh goes, I follow."

"We don't need to split up," Shane said. "I've established a link with Montana. It's weak, but it's there. That tells me he isn't in this house, but we still need to find our way out. We can try some of these doors as we search for the stairs leading down."

"You've established a link? Oh, thank god!" I said. "Where is he?"

Shane tightened his jaw. "I can't say for certain. I see him in a cool dark room, surrounded by... giant stone... toys?" He raised an eyebrow and scratched the back of his neck. "It's a fuzzy image, but it's there. I'm sure I'll know more if we can get outdoors."

Michael pushed his way to the front, holding the crucifix around his neck up like a shield. "I'll open the doors. This ain't no dream world, cowboy. Things could get dangerous here. Don't pretend you have all the answers just because you've stomped around a few dreams."

"I'd stop dreaming altogether if you showed up in one of mine," Shane said.

"Trust me. I want no part of your dreams."

"Let's go right," I said, pushing between them. "There's enough doors for all of us to have a turn. Ruth Anne, stay close with that flashlight."

I opened the first door slowly. There was nothing inside but an old phonograph, a tall rocking chair and an old-fashioned baby cradle. We recognized none of them. Finding nothing sinister, we were emboldened to open the other doors more quickly. They were all rooms from Sister House, all from various timelines – from the inception of the home in the late 1800s to the house we knew today.

Merry squealed when she found our old playroom, filled with teddy bears and dolls and Ruth Anne's Nancy Drew books. "Raggedy Anne!" Merry exclaimed, holding up her old rag doll. "And Ruth Anne, here's your Andy."

Ruth Anne grumbled, but smiled all the same. She took the doll, tucking it into her canvas backpack.

We moved on to the next room, and then the next. Aside from providing a few moments of nostalgia, the rooms were neither helpful nor frightening. Their only purpose seemed to be to confuse us further. *Or delay us?* The doors went on endlessly, opening into rooms, and sometimes rooms within rooms.

We were ready to turn back, to find the nursery again, when Eve pushed open one final door. Frigid air billowed out, enveloping us.

Eve's eyes were as large as quarters. She took three steps back, pointing inside and whispering, "Merry, I think this one's yours."

Merry stepped inside, unafraid, and we followed. It was as cold as winter in this room, though a soft yellow moon outside cozied up to the window. Miss Sasha's sewing machine sat untouched in a corner, tucked near her ironing board, and several fur coats hung in an open wardrobe. But it was the tree that drew our attention.

A pine tree grew proud and tall from a pot in the center of the room, its top brushing the ceiling. I remembered this tree from childhood. We all did. Merry had retrieved it from the forest as a sapling and brought it home to surprise us one Christmas. But we had replanted it back in the forest, and that was twenty years ago. Now here it was, alive and thriving. The whole room smelled of fresh pine.

Merry took small steps forward, bowing before it reverently. She touched its needles and smiled. "I can't believe it."

"But wait, there's more," Ruth Anne said, pointing up. Tucked into a higher branch was a small white owl. It shivered and hooted, watching us with one round eye from behind a wing.

"Merry, is that your owl?" I asked.

"Starlight!" She gently rattled a tree limb, coaxing him down.

The baby snow owl spread his tiny wings, revealing a face that seemed to smile. He hooted his pleasure as he fluttered down and landed gracefully on Merry's shoulder.

"I missed you so much!" She nuzzled her companion, who nuzzled her back. "I never thought I'd see you again."

Paul gently petted the owl's wing. "Eve told me how you found Starlight one Christmas, after wishing on a falling star. It was a beautiful story."

"Oh? Why haven't I heard this story?" Michael asked

Merry stroked the owl, dreamy-eyed, oblivious to Michael and everyone else.

"This is fascinating," Ruth Anne said, circling the room to take pictures with her high-tech camera. "Starlight clearly remembers Merry, even though she was a child when they last saw each other. I believe he recognizes her by her aura. I should document this." She put her camera away and began scribbling in a notebook from her back pocket.

"What should I do with him?" Merry asked. She looked at Starlight, and Starlight looked back. Then they both looked at me.

"This presents a problem," Ruth Anne said clinically. "His destiny most likely changed the moment you interacted with him. In the Upper World, a star guided him home."

"Oh, no!" Merry said. "Should we leave him here, then? Or take him with us?"

Ruth Anne scratched her head with the tip of the pencil. "I'm not sure what happens once we close these doors again. And I'm not even sure if his destiny in this world will affect the Upper World."

"I'll take him with me," Merry said firmly. "Maybe there's a star in this world he needs to find as well?"

I worried that Starlight would disappear the moment we left the room, but I didn't say anything. Merry was too determined and I was in too much of a hurry.

How much time do we have anyway?

I spotted Mother's Coca-Cola clock hanging above the ironing board. The hands spun around, slowly then quickly, not settling on any one time. I felt around and found the small hourglass in my skirt pocket. Its inscription was now gone, covered by a tape label with the typed words: 'Start Netherworld Timer Now.'

How bizarre.

I didn't feel any new magick on it, so I decided to do as instructed. I peeled the tape away. Though I held the timepiece sideways, the sands began to flow from one side of the funnel into the other. I flipped it upside down, trying to restart it, but the sand was unforgiving. *Was this all the time we had?* I quickly slipped it back in my pocket before anyone else noticed.

We left the nursery and returned to the hallway - one owl richer - opening door after door as we sought our way out.

"Montana's link is growing dimmer," Shane said. "We'd better hurry before I lose him altogether. This place isn't... *situated* right."

"There's one room left we need to enter," Merry said. "I have a feeling the house won't let us leave until we do. I think we've all been avoiding it."

Mother's bedroom door appeared before us in the hallway. How had we not come across it already? *We were afraid.*

Merry knocked three times, and the door swung wide open.

The room smelled sweet at first, like cedar and lilac, but then the aroma of mildew filled our noses. "This isn't Mother's room," I said. It was far too formal and stiff for Mother's tastes.

"If I had to guess, this was your grandmother's room," Paul said. "Or maybe even your great-grandmother's room. This flocked rose wallpaper hasn't been popular in nearly a century. And I can't imagine your mother using a porcelain chamber pot." He pointed towards a 'chair' hunkering in a corner.

Eve gave him a curious look and he shrugged.

"I have a fascination with the Victorian era. Poe, Jack the Ripper, steampunk." He lifted a silver brush on a vanity and set it back down again. Next, he opened a book and smiled, commenting on its smooth leather binding. Ruth Anne joined him in marveling over the craftsmanship of the novel.

I walked over to Juliana's portrait; it was hanging in the same place it had hung my entire life. She was young but her expression was dour. I'd always feared this picture, feeling her eyes on me. But since her spirit had helped find her missing ankh, I felt bonded to her. Still, there was something different about this painting. *She's wearing her ankh!*

"Holy Mother of Mary!" Ruth Anne exclaimed, forgetting to use her inside voice. "*The Complete Works of Edgar Allen Poe*! First edition! Hardbound!"

She and Paul ogled it, neither able to speak for several breaths. "I feel like I should pray to it or something," Paul finally said.

"That's bordering on idolatry," Michael commented. "But I understand what you mean, and I'm sure The Big Guy won't take much offense."

"Think we can take the book too, Mags?" Ruth Anne asked, like a kid who had just found a stray puppy. "Nothing happened when I took the Andy doll."

"So far," I said, rapping my knuckles against a wooden chest near the foot of the bed. "Just please use your judgement. I have no idea how the rules work here. I just hope we aren't undoing anything that shouldn't be undone."

Ruth Anne nodded and slipped the book into her backpack. The moment she closed her bag, the floor tilted again. No... not tilted, lurched. We held out our arms to keep steady.

"We need get downstairs, now!" Shane said, his eyes darting nervously upwards as the hall lights began to flicker.

"There they are!" Merry said, pointing.

Sure enough, the end of the hallway appeared, and so did the staircase. Was that Shane's command that had brought them out? Or had we simply not gone far enough?

The stairwell was steeper than I remembered, and windier, too. Candle sconces lined the walls, though the light was eerily scant. Shane led the way and Michael took up the rear, with the rest of us crowded between. Halfway down we heard voices on the landing below, and we froze. It was Aunt Dora, Miss Sasha and Jillian, but not as I knew them. "They're so young," I whispered.

"And beautiful," Merry added.

Mother didn't look a day over forty. Aunt Dora was in full health, with rosy cheeks and tinted hair. Jillian's hair fell almost to her waist.

"They're not real," Merry said. "It's a memory the house has kept. I think we can get closer, so long as we don't disturb the ripples in the memory fabric."

Ruth Anne's jaw dropped. "How do you know that?" she demanded.

Merry shrugged. "I just do. Look, they're talking now."

We inched down a few more stairs, holding our breaths even as Merry assured us we could breathe.

"I t's foolproof," Sasha said, clapping her hands together once, and then once more for good measure. "Armand won't find the child or know that it's his. The Council is sworn to secrecy. And even if they break their oath, my spell is far too powerful. Armand is clever, but he needs to remember who taught him."

"He's no fool," Dora said, shaking her head. "He'll figure it out sooner or later. I been watchin' him since the day he arrived. He knows more than he's sayin'."

"I still can't believe it," Jillian said, unzipping her long coat to reveal the swelling in her belly. "Armand has never actually hurt anyone. It's hard to consider he would do what you're suggesting."

"He hasn't hurt anyone?" Sasha asked, her eyes falling to Jillian's pregnant belly.

"I'm to blame as much as him. I loved him."

"Love blinds you," Sasha said.

"Love saves us!" Jillian replied. She lifted her chin and stormed out the front door.

"It's no one's fault," Dora sigh, watching Jillian go. "It's the will of the Fates, and only the Fates can alter it." Dora put on her coat. "Yer threats and yer spell won't silence her forever. She'll want to see her child."

"She can be an auntie, just like you."

"That won't be enough."

"It will have to be. Or all is lost."

The scene dissolved, sucked back into whatever cosmic time vault it originated from. We all continued down the stair case, except Ruth Anne, who stayed behind. She fumbled with her pack, her brow knit in frustration.

"Let's go." I urged. "While the getting's good."

She cut me off with a chop of her hand. "Really, Mags? How can you be so callous? I just saw my dead mother. And not haggard and losing her marbles, but healthy. I didn't realize how much I missed her." She crumpled up on the step, her head in her hands.

I walked back up and sat with her. "I understand," I said. Unlike the rest of us, Ruth Anne was Sasha's only biological daughter. After giving birth to a child myself, and meeting my own real mother, I understood the power of blood bonds. "I miss her, too."

"You do?"

"Every day. She raised me, taught me, and gave me my sisters. We had our problems, but we had our 'come to Jesus' meeting at the end."

Ruth Anne sniffled and cracked a smile. "She'd whack you with her wand if she heard you say that."

"She'd have to catch me first," I said.

E ve called to us from the living room, and Ruth Anne and I raced down the stairs. The living room was in the correct location, but nearly three times bigger. A fire roared beneath a portrait of a young Sasha, no older than sixteen, wearing ringlets and dimples. Her eyes twinkled as she gazed over her shoulder - a twinkle that would later disappear, along with her youth. A grand candelabra lit the room, aided by candles and sconces of various sizes. An orchestra belted out waltzes on a phonograph.

An assembly of distinguished ladies and men paraded in through the front door, fog rolling at their feet. The women wore elegant dresses and elaborate eye masks. Their hair was piled high in pin curls. The men were in coats and tails, wearing masks just as fanciful as the women's. Once they stepped inside, they paired up and began dancing, whirling around the room on a downy blanket of mist. Miss Sasha stood out among them, now a full-grown woman. She wore a red-sequined dress with her hair long and loose and danced with a soldier from a long-ago war.

"I think that's Mom and Robbie!" Eve said. Robbie was Mother's only love. He died during WWI, and she never forgot him for the rest of her life, even as she entertained herself with various lovers. "I've never seen a man look at a woman like that," Eve said, shooting Paul an accusing glare.

Merry rose up on to her toes and swayed. "The music is mesmerizing," she said, waltzing her way into the crowd. She turned with open arms, and became a spinning pink cashmere blur, mixed in with all the others.

"Look who else is here," Shane said, nodding to a corner. Wearing a similar red ball gown, with dark spiraled curls and snarling red lips, was a young Larinda. She was watching Sasha and Robbie, intently. Sensing my anger, Shane said, "Remember, this is all just a memory, Mags. You can't get to her yet."

This was true. Besides, if I interfered with her younger self, I might never find her older self, the one who held my son captive. I looked away from her, and focused on the dancers instead.

The colorful celebrators whirled around the room as the hands on the grandfather clock spun erratically. I tried to seize Merry as she passed by, but she was too lost in the music. She pirouetted out of my reach, not seeing me at all.

"When in Rome," Shane said, hooking my arm. I didn't know how to waltz, but he did. We spun around the room, succumbing to the music and forced gaiety. I say forced, because there was desperation in the laughter - a need to squeeze the moment for all it was worth. The clock, however sporadic, would chime soon enough.

How had I never danced like this before? My hair and skirt fluttered around me as Shane expertly wove us through the throng. Miss Sasha's eyes were locked with Robbie's, showing more joy than I had ever seen on her face. I wished I had known her then, before life had taken its cruel toll.

Ruth Anne snapped pictures from the sidelines, though the dancers were oblivious. Her lens lingered on Sasha and Robbie the longest.

I could stay here, I realized, as the hands of the clock moved back several hours. It was safe inside this fabricated ballroom. I rested my head on Shane's shoulder and continued to dance.

"Maggie."

It was like a whisper through a forest, without direction.

"MAGGIE!"

This was no whisper. A firm hand shook my shoulder. The room became bright as day, and shrank to its original size. Except for the seven of us, it was deserted.

Shane stared at me. "What did you see?"

"The ball. Mother and Robbie were here. And Larinda. You saw it too, right?"

"I saw it for a moment," Merry said. "But then it vanished."

"But you were dancing. Don't you remember?"

"You were the only one dancing." Merry said.

"I would call it flapping around like a wounded goose," Eve said. "Ruth Anne got some great pictures of you."

"You took pictures Ruth Anne! Did they come out?" I asked.

"Sort of. The good news is that my camera works here. The bad news is, you may want me to burn these before anyone sees them."

We searched her images. Sure enough, I alone hopped and hobbled around the floor. I felt myself redden. We hadn't even made it to the Netherworld proper, and already I had succumbed to its madness.

"I caught some cool orb photos though," she said. "If we make it back, I'll analyze these on my computer." She put her camera away and knocked on her bag for luck.

If.

"I'm sorry you guys weren't there," I said. "It was a really nice place."

"After watching you, I can truly say I'm glad I wasn't there," Eve said.

"Shall we?" I asked, feeling the pull of the front door - the same door that Jillian's younger memory-self had stormed through.

"Let's go," Shane said.

I took a deep breath and turned the knob, proceeding through a blinding tunnel of warm light.

∾

I was standing on the front porch of Sister House, the others slowly phasing in behind me. Judging by the blooming flowers and the budding lilac bushes, I guessed it was early spring. The sun was so yellow it seemed painted on, but its warmth was real. The grass, too, was impossibly green. Merry's garden spade lay muddied on the porch steps. *This timeline must be recent.*

"Is this paradise?" Merry asked, sniffing the air as she spread her arms wide. Starlight flew from her shoulder, circling us. "I just feel so...light?"

"Me too," Ruth Anne agreed. She skipped down the steps, wrinkling her nose as a dandelion floated by.

I didn't share their cheerfulness. Eagle Mountain loomed in the distance, above the tree line, looking more ominous than it ever had before.

Ruth Anne sat down in the grass and removed her shoes, dumping out a spray of pebbles. "The air feels charged," she said.

"Refreshing," Michael agreed.

"Can you guys stay out of trouble for a few minutes?" I asked. "I need to talk to Shane, privately."

"Talk?" Michael asked, not hiding his disdain.

"We'll be fine, Maggie," Merry said.

"You want to check on the tree, don't you?" Shane asked, when we were out of earshot, behind the house.

He knew me too well. We headed into the forest to look for Jillian's tree. I looked back several times, making sure the others stayed in sight.

We reached the spot, but there was no tree.

"Shane! Where the hell's the tree?" I asked.

He scratched his head. "Jillian said hers was a representation of the original Tree of Life, which is probably hidden deep in this world."

I searched my pocket, drawing out the silk-wrapped acorn. I looked down at the open space where the earthly tree had stood. "Do you think I should I plant it? Jillian said *I'd know.*"

Shane knelt down and touched the dirt with his bare hand. "Does it feel right to you?"

I crouched beside him, touching the acorn to the earth, hoping it would somehow speak to me. But there was not so much as a whisper. "What if I don't plant the seed here, but I was supposed to? I could ruin everything."

"If it's fate, you can't mess it up."

I hoped he was right.

I needed to check Jillian's old studio. We quickly returned to the others, who by now were all reclining on the grass. "Sorry to interrupt your sunbathing," I said. "But we need to leave now."

We raced through the woods towards Jillian's studio. As in the Upper World, the magick was heightened in this part of the forest as well - I could even smell it. Even so, parts of the woods were shriveled and dying, parched and cracked, as in the world above.

When we arrived at the glade, I saw the studio, newer and cleaner looking than in my own timeline. The windows were mostly intact and the walls had only begun to crumble. And...

The tree is here!

I charged full-speed, greeting the tree as if it were an old friend. The burn mark had spread, but the tree was several feet taller than the one back home. I placed my ear against the trunk. Though faint, I heard a child's heartbeat and smiled. "My son is sending me a message. I just know it. We're on the right track."

I told them the story of finding this tree, purposely leaving out any mention of the Tree of Life. That would have to come later.

"Where's the baby hat?" Michael asked. "I'd like to see it."

I searched my pockets for it...but it wasn't there! "It's gone!" I frantically started backtracking, searching the ground. "Oh no, no!"

"Stay calm," Shane said. "I've got a new read on Montana. He's still okay."

"Are you sure?" I asked, turning my attention back towards the tree.

Merry examined it alongside me, placing a deliberate finger on the scorched bark. The color lightened slightly, and the surrounding leaves perked up. It was far from healed, but there was hope.

"Yow!" she said, shaking her hand. "That really took a lot out of me." But she smiled, letting me know she was okay.

I asked for a moment of privacy, and went into the studio alone. It smelled like wet paint and turpentine. An easel and canvas were set up in a corner, and on it was a portrait of a baby with auburn hair and green eyes. Montana.

What sick person did this? I wondered. Then I saw that it was signed by Jillian.

"1979," I read aloud.

Had Jillian really foreseen the birth of her grandson, over three decades ago? Or was this a portrait of me as a child? Or maybe it was all a delusion, another trick of the Netherworld.

I left the painting, my heart and mind heavier than before.

Outside, the sky overhead teemed with large crows, all speeding towards Eagle Mountain.

"Larinda's minions," I said. "Off to tell on us."

"Let them," Shane said defiantly. "We ride east, out of Dark Root."

Michael snorted. "I hope you're ready for a confrontation once we get there, cowboy, because I'm pretty sure we won't be surprising anyone if we take your route. And I'm fairly certain a few of those birds heard us."

Shane stepped forward, his chest expanding. "What's your problem, Michael?"

"I think you've got a big mouth and nothing to back it up."

My husband readied a fist. Merry and I quickly jumped between them, prying them apart.

"Maggie, you trust me, right?" Shane asked, spinning in the direction of his intuition.

"Yes. You're the only one who even partially understands this realm," I said. "Or at least the way it functions."

Michael scoffed, clicking his tongue as he fell behind. "You'll trust a cowboy over a priest to lead you through hell? Let's hope you're right about this."

I hated to admit it, but Michael had a point. Shane might be a tracker and a dreamwalker, but he admitted this world was much different. And Michael had spent his life studying the afterlife.

"Are you sure you know where you're going?" I asked Shane quietly, as we seemed to be moving away from Eagle Mountain.

"Just follow me," Shane said.

And we did.

~

S hane guided us through the woods that led towards downtown Dark Root. Gray clouds hunkered overhead, and there was the threat of rain. Merry sidled up beside me, lacing her fingers with mine.

"Heads up! Eve's freaking out. She had nightmares as a kid, and this place is dredging them up."

A moment later, Eve caught up with us, her eyes wide and cautious.

"You okay?" I asked.

"I don't like it here. It's ugly and I want to get out." She glanced up at the clouds and flapped her hand, as if to shoo them away. Eventually she gave up, hanging her head beneath her curtain of hair, blocking everything out. Paul didn't seem to notice her somber mood, as he chatted easily with Ruth Anne while we walked.

"We'll be all right," I said aloud, to reassure her and everyone else. "We've already fought demons and witches back home. Nothing here scares me ... except not finding my son."

"I understand how you feel," Merry said. "I like to think I'm a nice person, but if anyone tries to harm June Bug..." Her face turned the same rose shade as her cardigan. "Well, I'm not sure what I'd do. But it wouldn't be pleasant."

"At least you know June Bug's okay," I said. "Even if she is with Frank."

"Yeah..." She stroked my arm, soothing me with her warmth. "We'll get Montana back. I've seen it in my meditations."

I stopped, letting the others to pass by. "You did?"

"Yes. He was older, maybe sixteen. He was talking to a girl with long brown hair and gray eyes. Maybe a girlfriend."

"Girlfriend?" I asked, feeling strangely possessive.

Merry laughed. "I'm only speculating."

"Was he happy?" I asked, chewing my lip.

"He was smiling." Merry's brow furrowed and she licked her lips, as if deciding whether to tell me the rest. "Of course, that is only the most likely timeline."

"I see."

She held up her right index finger, as if checking the direction of the wind. "My abilities seem to be heightened here. If I sense anything that might be helpful, I'll speak up. But I'm still not sure of the rules, and I have a feeling they can change on a whim."

"Yes," I agreed, as the clouds parted, all drifting in separate directions.

"The energy here is making me ill," Eve said. Indeed, her skin had taken on an orchid yellow coloring. I hadn't realized she was so sensitive.

Merry placed her hand on Eve's lower back, and her ivory complexion slowly returned. Merry stumbled when she was done, drained by her recent healing work with Eve and the tree.

It was twilight over Main Street, with the blue quickly receding from the sky. Rolling fog collected around our ankles and the metallic scent of October rain clung to the air. We reached the spot where the Town Square should be. It was a vacant lot, with tall grass dotted with beer bottles. There were no streetlights at this end of town, and Ruth Anne used her flashlight to cut through the growing dark. Her beam found a banner strung between two telephone poles: *The Haunted Dark Root Festival.*

Eve put her hand on her hip. "Halloween? Are you kidding me? Like we don't have enough frights running around in this world. I guess it's too much to ask for a Christmas or an Easter setting here."

Ruth Anne smirked. "Do you really want to see the Netherworld's version of the Easter Bunny or Santa Claus? Because I imagine they're both quite horrifying."

"I'm going to scout the area before we move on," Shane said. "I can't quite make out which way to go from here yet, but we are close. I just need a few minutes to regain my bearings." Shane pulled a flashlight from his pack and turned it on."

"You couldn't have pulled that out sooner, Boy Scout?" Michael snorted.

"I'm no Boy Scout. You'd be wise to remember that."

I tried to steal a glimpse into Shane's open pack. "What else did you bring?" I asked, remembering all the noise he made in his apartment while packing.

"Not much. I like to rely on my wits, mostly. But I did bring this," he said, holding up the flashlight. "Also, some jerky, my lucky horseshoe, my..."

"Horseshoe?" I interrupted "You brought a horseshoe? Why?"

"I've taken it on every trip I've made since I was eleven, and it's brought me safely home, every single time. Like I said, it's lucky."

Michael rubbed his brow. "As much as I'd like to play *Guess What's in My Sack*, I think we have more pressing things to attend to."

Everyone looked at me, awaiting my direction. I shifted my weight from one foot to the other as I considered our options, shivering as the temperature steadily dropped.

"It's not really cold," Michael said. "Your mind is reacting to the setting."

"My mind knows that's true," Merry agreed, pushing up her cardigan sleeves defiantly. "But my body disagrees."

"Shane, I appreciate your offer to scout things out, but I think we should all explore the town, together," I said. "We just need to stay within eyeshot of one another. Or at least earshot."

Shane nodded. "You're right. I'm not used to traveling with a group. Let's stay close."

We walked down the center of Main Street. Black and orange banners flapped above us, announcing the upcoming festival. Yellow-eyed jack-o'-lanterns lined the sidewalk like luminaries, and home-made signs announced Samhain specials in shop windows. I wasn't certain why we were here, but it felt right, and I kept my eyes open for signs of my son or where to possibly plant my tree.

We began to see people. The crowds grew thicker with each step.

"What year do you think we're in?" I asked Paul and Ruth Anne, our resident historians.

"The late '70s, judging by the shopfronts," Paul said

"But look at the getups these people are wearing," Ruth Anne said, covering the side of her mouth. She pointed to a woman in a poodle skirt and penny loafers walking beside a man sporting a purple mohawk and a Ramones T-shirt. Others wore traditional witch, ghost and monster costumes, most of them made of cheap plastic. "I don't know who's dressed up for the holiday and who isn't."

"I think timelines are overlapping here," Merry said. "Everything is jumbled up but still working together, like when you throw random ingredients into a cauldron but the spell still takes. It's just kind of... distorted."

My ankh began to glow. I lifted it to show the others. "We must be on the right path," I whispered, so excited I nearly kissed it.

"Boy, this place looks different," Eve said, as we stood in front of Miss Sasha's Magick Shoppe. There were no curtains in the window, and the door was wood, not glass. A 'Closed for the Holiday' sign was tacked on the door, with a promise of a 'Secret Sale' the next day.

"I wish I could have known Mama when she was young," Merry said, peeping through the window. She gasped and tapped furiously on the glass. We all crowded around Merry as Miss Sasha appeared from the stock room, wafting smoke from a green candle around the shop - the color used for prosperity spells. Her hair was long and curly, and she wore bell-bottoms and clogs. She checked her stock, nodding to herself as she inspected each and every bin.

"Now where did I misplace my spell book?" she asked accusingly, loud enough that we could hear through the glass. She raised an eyebrow and looked around, her eyes sliding past us, focusing on a bare shelf. She blinked and shrugged, then returned to the stock room.

"Mama never misplaced anything in her shop," Merry said.

"I...uh...wonder..." Ruth Anne took off her pack and showed us Mother's Book of Shadows. "Gah! Did I screw this timeline up?"

There was a collective inhale as we considered the ramifications of altering time, and we exhaled in relief when Mother reappeared with her book open in her hands. Then, as if someone changed the channel, the image of Mother in her shop abruptly blinked off. The room was completely bare.

Shane turned and pointed to a neon sign across the street. 'Delilah's Deli,' he said with a grin. He raced across the street, dodging the phantom trick-or-treaters as if they were real. He knocked on the window and beckoned me over. "I think Uncle Joe's in there!"

When I reached him, he took my hand and pulled me into the café. The doorbell chimed as we entered and a few plaid-and-paisley wearing customers wearing looked up curiously, paused a moment, then resumed eating. I wasn't sure if they'd seen us or not. Were they spirits or memories? Or were we simply invisible time-travelers, watching from the safety of a future timeline?

"It was pretty nice back in its heyday," Shane said, inspecting the metal-rimmed tables and padded booths. The curtains were starched and there were fresh sunflowers on every table. The café smelled like pumpkins and coffee. The jack-o'-lantern on the pie counter, carved in Elvis' likeness, lent the restaurant a charm even Dip Stix hadn't achieved.

"I see him." Shane squeezed my hand and pulled me towards a booth in the far corner. Joe and his partner, Leonard, were huddled behind a plastic menu. "I just want to listen for a minute," Shane whispered. We got so close that I felt uncomfortable, but neither Joe nor Leonard noticed.

"I don't like any of this," Leonard said, after taking a hard bite of his sandwich. "Why Sasha insists on having that vile warlock stay here is beyond me." He crumpled his napkin onto his lap and dropped the sandwich back on his plate. "We're men. We can supply all the masculine energy needed for Sasha's domes and whatnots."

Joe laughed. "Whatnots? We are Sasha's whatnots, Leonard. I know this is hard on you, since you weren't raised in the craft like we were. She may be dramatic, but she's the strongest sorceress I've ever met. If she says something's coming, and we have a chance at salvaging this world before the shit hits the fan, then we need to do whatever we can to help. Even if means Armand is part of that equation."

"Hell, Joseph. Maybe this is all in our minds. Maybe we're all just smoking too much weed."

"Or not enough. Have faith, Lennie."

"I lost my faith when my priest said I wasn't allowed into confession."

"The world may be misguided, but we don't have to be."

The scene crackled, then splintered away and the booth was empty. The red vinyl bench was now worn and aged and covered in dust, though the rest of the diner remained unchanged. Shane and I turned towards one another.

"You saw that, right?" I asked, looking around. Everyone else had remained in place.

"I saw my uncle and Leonard," Shane said, nodding. "They were talking about Sasha and Armand." He looked back at the booth. "That was the most I've ever heard Leonard say. Damn, why didn't I get to know him when he was around? Or spend more time with my uncle, for that matter?"

"Because when we're young we have no perception of time, or the awareness that it will ever run out." Ruth Anne said, from behind us.

"Jesus! You scared the hell out of me, Ruth Anne!" I said, turning on her. "Don't do that again! Where's everyone else?"

She pointed to the window. Three faces were pressed to the glass, staring in at us. "I've been conducting a few experiments," Ruth Anne said, showing me an antique compass and her high-priced electro-magnetic reader.

"Watch this." She grinned, walking about the café, casting the EMF device over the oblivious diners. It flashed wildly, like she'd just won a carnival prize. "Paranormal activity!"

"Ya think?"

"But wait, there's more." She flipped open her compass. The needle spun, left then right, then backwards and forwards. Just like the clocks. "It doesn't work here," she said, stuffing it into her pocket.

"It's a reminder to not take things for granted here," Shane said, his eyes remaining on the empty booth.

"This diner is brimming with residual energy," Ruth Anne said. "It must've had a big impact on many people's lives."

Shane smiled and thanked her with a squeeze of her shoulder. Residual energy was the permanent imprint of memory or soul, absorbed into stones or structures or even objects. Strong emotions and memories were especially prone to imprinting. People may come and go, be born and die, but their shadows lived on indefinitely.

My wand vibrated beneath my sweater, and I saw the soft glow of its orb through the yarn. I had almost forgotten it was there. I tapped it, as an Old West sheriff taps his trusty pistol before heading in to a den of outlaws. It vibrated again and I drew it out. The light expanded, and soon the diner was awash in fluorescent yellow light. One customer actually noticed – a young woman whose eyes I recog-nized from a much older body. She was one of Mother's friends, who died in the late 1990's. There were ghosts as well as memories here.

As the light spread to all the corners of the room, other shapes were illuminated – a hodgepodge of patrons whose clothing and hair-styles spanned at least four decades. None noticed the others, and some even shared the same booth, their forms overlapping. I covered the tip of my wand and some faded away. The diner had begun to feel claustrophobic.

"Classic," Ruth Anne said, scribbling into her notebook.

"What?"

"When a place has real meaning to people, they leave part of themselves there."

She pointed to a booth where a young couple sat. I stared intently, as their faces and fashions flipped like a deck of cards. One moment they were young and sharing a milkshake, the next they were sharing a burger and their booth with two small children. And then, the woman sat alone, staring into an empty coffee mug with somber eyes.

I turned away as Ruth Anne gleefully continued her notes. I wasn't comfortable watching someone else's life so intimately. Shane came up beside me, his hands thrust deep inside his pockets.

"You okay?" I asked, brushing a wisp of hair from his face.

"I would just love a couple of do-overs," he said.

"Amen," Ruth Anne agreed. "Let's get out of here. It's starting to creep even me out."

The others were waiting for us outside of Dip Stix. Except for one.

"Where the hell did Michael go?" I asked.

Merry shrugged. "He said he'd be right back and not to worry." She smiled and rubbed her hands together, nodding towards the pie shop. "I can smell them, and its making my stomach rumble. Do you think it's safe to eat the food here?"

"I have no idea," I said, my own stomach reacting to the savory smells of cinnamon, apple and pumpkin.

"They say that in Heaven, you get to enjoy all the earthly delights," Merry noted.

"I don't think we're in Heaven," I pointed out.

"What's that noise?" Eve asked, looking down the road.

I heard it, too. A low rumbling sound rolled up Main Street. Shane and Ruth Anne cast their lights down the foggy road.

"It sounds like a parade," Merry said.

"It *is* a parade!" I said. "The Haunted Dark Root Parade."

A horse-drawn cart appeared through a curtain of haze. A scarecrow was mounted in the bed, with a large pumpkin for a head. Its mouth was carved into a cruel smile and its eyes blazed as its straw hands flapped in the wind. The horse slowed as it passed by, snorting and sniffing the air, but it didn't stop. Next came a family of vampires, packed into a wagon. They waved jovially to the bystanders, tossing out treats. And then came a procession of pallbearers, carrying a wooden coffin filled with candy.

The costumes were simple, not the elaborate outfits Mother made for us in later years. I scanned the crowd gathered on the sidewalk. It seemed the entire last century was represented among the spectators.

Michael reappeared next to me, his face grim as he took my wrist. "Maggie, we need to leave. Now."

"Why?" I asked.

"I see why!" Ruth Anne's flashlight fell on a group of people pushing through the crowd on the other side of the street, heading straight for us. Their hands were reaching and their eyes were feral. They were focused on Michael.

"What did you do?" I demanded, as both he and Shane pulled me away by my elbows.

Michael's free hand went to the cross dangling on his chest. "I may have uh... tried to save a few souls."

"You did what?"

"They saw the cross and... responded to it. I just let them know their sins were absolved and they could move on. I guess they misunderstood the latter part of my message."

"Beware of false prophets," Shane growled. "But we'll discuss that another time." He closed his eyes, quickly trying to get a read on which direction to go. Eagle Mountain was no longer in sight.

"I say we leave Michael here and let him sacrifice himself," Eve cried out, dodging an open-mouthed specter grabbing for her hair. "This is his fault."

The spirit horde gathered other souls on its way toward us, like a tumbleweed collecting debris as it rolled. Peeling off of Main Street, we ran for the quickest cover – the woods.

"Those aren't memories, they're ghosts," Ruth Anne confirmed, firing a heat sensor device over her shoulder. "See, the bars are red, which means they're emitting energy."

We scanned the trees, looking for a path into the forest. So much of the landscape was altered from what I knew. The woods were thicker, deeper, darker and more ominous.

"I got a lock on Montana!" Shane said, pointing. "Let's hurry before I lose it again."

I glanced over my shoulder as we ran. The ghost army was still coming, some spryer than others. I caught site of a familiar face in the crowd, one with a particular lightness to his step and a glowing aura.

"Albert? "I called out, stopping abruptly. He was the first spirit I directly communicated with, and he had inadvertently helped me find my ankh. "Albert!" I ran back to him, parting the advancing throng, my arms out. They ignored me, their focus still on Michael.

"I'm so happy to see you," I said, hugging him. He felt surprisingly solid. "But Albert, why didn't you go into the light?"

"We can't find it," he said, returning my hug. "It just closed up." He leaned in and whispered. "They say that things are changing in the worlds. We're not sure if anyone finds the light anymore, but they must, huh? Or else there'd be more of us, right?"

I nodded, wondering if this had anything to do with the ailing Tree of Life. "It will reopen. I promise you," I said.

"I hope so. Thank you."

We hugged again. "I wish I could do more." I felt the weight of the responsibility I carried in my pocket.

"Send my wife my love," he said. "That will give me peace."

"Hey! She can talk to us!" A shrill female voice cried, her bloated hand pointing at me. The others all stopped, diverting their attention from Michael.

"Uh-oh," Albert said. "You'd better go."

But they were already on me. Their fingers, in various forms of decay, raked at my hair and pawed at my clothes. "Help us!" they moaned.

I screamed, swatting them away. The more I pushed back, the

THE SHADOWS OF DARK ROOT

more appeared. I was being swallowed in the crowd. "I don't know where your light is!"

"She lies!" an old man accused, grabbing for the glowing tip of my wand. "She has the light! She stole it!"

They pressed in on me. They smelled like winter and dirt. "Mine!" They chanted in unison, and I didn't know if they meant me or the wand.

"Look! Here, ghostie ghostie!" Ruth Anne shouted. She held her EMF reader high, so that the flashing red and green lights were visible to all. "Look! I've got the light! Follow me!" She danced around, holding the reader above her head. A few shook free of me, heading for my sister, and slowly the others joined. Ruth Anne easily outran them, zigging back and forth like a dog keeping a Frisbee from its owner.

Shane reached me, wrapping his arm around my waist and pulling me towards the woods. "You're a beacon here, Maggie. Luckily, Ruth Anne seems to be right in her element at the moment."

We found a narrow game trail and raced into the woods. I looked back and caught sight of Ruth Anne, who seemed to be enjoying her game of ghost tag. When she saw us reach safety, she broke off and raced towards us, leaving her new friends in her dust.

"Thank you," I said to Ruth Anne, once she caught up to us. "That was brilliant."

"I may not be able to cast spells, but I'm pretty good at running away from things," she said, grinning in the dark.

"Maggie, that ankh of yours is glowing again," Eve said. "You may want to hide it before you attract anymore loonies."

It blinked slowly, sporadically. "Interesting," I said. I moved to the right and the frequency increased. I then moved off to the left, and it slowed.

"It's an inter-dimensional version of hot and cold," Ruth Anne said. "Badass."

"I think it wants us to head right," I said.

Shane looked at me, skeptically. "That's not the direction I'm locked into."

I was torn. Did I follow Shane's tracking abilities, or the magickal ankh? We looked both ways, the forest dense and dark in all directions.

"Let's follow the ankh," I said.

Shane's face fell, but he nodded. "It's your journey."

We crept carefully forward, picking our way through the undergrowth and the inquisitive tree limbs. How long we walked, I couldn't tell. I checked my hourglass, but there was no light to see the falling sand.

And then suddenly, there it was. A dazzling golden archway stood in the midst of utter blackness. My ankh blinked excitedly.

Was this our gate?

We gathered around it. The archway was braced between two trees, and there was nothing but a void at its center. I suspected it was similar to the closet portal, and I flinched as I poked my hand at it, dreading the cold that would follow. But it was a solid surface, and my finger bent upon impact. "What the..."

Shane and Michael tried too, pushing on it like a jammed door.

"Is there a keyhole?" Merry asked. "Your ankh kinda looks like a key."

"Not that I see," I said.

"Let me check it out with my... wait, that's me!" Ruth Anne said, her mouth falling open as she stood before the gate. "Can you see me in there?" she asked, looking at us.

We crowded in. It took a moment, but then I *did* see Ruth Anne's image staring back at her. She was wearing different clothes and her hair was much longer. But it was clearly Ruth Anne.

She poked at it, and it rippled like water.

"Neat," she said. "I think we should..."

But that was all we heard. My sister was pulled through, disappearing before our eyes.

I felt myself thin out along the edges. I was being pulled in, too. I clutched my crystal bracelet and my ankh, praying I'd end up with the others. And that it was one step closer to finding my son.

5

THE EMPEROR

*R*uth Anne's eyes darted to the cabinet above the kitchen window. *Inside, there was a jar – a jar Aunt Dora kept filled with money. Not just change either. Crisp twenties and even hundreds.*

"Ya want more tea, dear?" Aunt Dora asked from across the cozy kitchen table. She was wearing her gardening clothes, and Ruth Anne wondered how much longer until she actually gardened.

"Nah, I'm good." Ruth Anne shook her head, nearly dislodging her glasses. She smiled cheerfully, though her toes tapped spastically beneath the table. Her aunt refilled both tea cups anyway, and leaned back in her chair. Ruth Anne snuck a peek at the clock over Dora's shoulder. She'd been up all night, wondering how she'd finance her trip. And then like magick, the answer came to her - Aunt Dora's money jar.

Ruth Anne opened a book and pretended to read, hoping it would bore her aunt into the garden. Her mother, the flamboyant Sasha Shantay came in the back door and took a seat beside Dora. The two women chatted about candles and missing socks.

"Honestly, Dora," Sasha said. "I had no idea children cost so much when I decided to have them."

"Aye," Dora agreed. "They'll squeeze yer last penny out." She winked at Ruth Anne and she blushed, wondering if her aunt knew.

In the adjoining living room, the screams of her younger sisters interrupted the conversation. They were playing some sort of chasing game and fighting over a rule. Moments later, they filed into the kitchen. Ruth Anne had made up the game herself, so it fell under her jurisdiction to decide the outcome. She gave her verdict and they took it, knowing she valued fairness. Plus, she loved rules - they appealed to her logical mind. As she watched her siblings leave the kitchen, Ruth Anne realized how much she would miss them. She consoled herself with knowing she'd soon be able to read her books without constant interruption.

Sasha patted Ruth Anne's hand. "Those girls are giving me a headache the purest willow bark couldn't cure."

Ruth Anne resisted responding. If Sasha didn't like being around children, perhaps she shouldn't have had so many?

"Now Sasha," Dora said. "They'll be grown an' gone soon enough, an' ya'll miss all that carryin' on."

Sasha took a long draw from her cup, her eyes both amused and doubtful of Dora's prediction.

"Ruth Anne!" Merry burst back into the room, rosy-cheeked and flaxen-haired. Her blue eyes twinkled as she caught her breath. "Can you talk to Maggie again? She's trying to cheat!"

"I'm not cheating!" Maggie marched in, defending herself. She put her hands on her hips, ready to argue, drowning in her cherry-red curls. "I tagged Merry with the end of my broom, fair and square. Now she has to be the witch flying in the sky. That's the way it goes, right?"

Eve trailed in behind, dressed head to toe in lavender and lace. "Ruth Anne knows everything," she nodded with certainty.

Ruth Anne adjusted her glasses, frustrated by yet another distraction. "If you're playing Witch-in-a-Ditch, then Maggie is right."

"See! Told ya!" Maggie stuck out her tongue and then ran outside. Merry and Eve followed, all giggles and screams, slamming the door behind them.

"I better get out there, too," Sasha said. "Before they dig up the entire garden."

Ruth Anne raised an eyebrow, hoping this would be her lucky break.

"Can I get ya anything, luv?" Aunt Dora asked, standing to rinse her cup and saucer.

"Uh... maybe. Do we still have any of those pickles you canned last year? I've been thinking about them."

Dora grinned, rubbing her hands. "Have ya, now? Me, too! I have a few jars in the cellar."

"Need help?" Ruth Anne asked, knowing Dora would refuse. Sure enough, Dora waved her hand and plodded over to the basement stairs, the door shutting halfway behind her.

Ruth Anne waited a moment, listening to the creak of the old wood stairs, before springing to her feet. Then she scrambled onto the counter, opened the cupboard, and quietly slid the jar to the edge of the shelf. It was heavier than she imagined and she nearly dropped it. In full sunlight, she could see the wealth inside the glass: a leprechaun's pot of silver, gold, and green. She reached in and pulled out the entire roll of bills. Then she slid the jar back into place, closed the cupboard, and hopped down from the counter. Looking around to make sure she was still alone, she stepped into the adjoining laundry room to count out her haul.

Nearly $1,700!

She swallowed, trying to control her shaking hands and rapid heartbeat.

Farewell Sasha Shantay! Farewell Dark Root! Nice knowing you!

She heard her sisters return through the back door, giggling on their way to watch TV in the living room.

Ruth Anne curled her fist around the wad of money. This wasn't right. Maybe she should return it before anyone noticed. But before she could, Aunt Dora and Sasha were back in the kitchen, talking. Ruth Anne pressed her ear to the laundry room door and listened.

"Those girls are harder on the garden than the bugs," Sasha said.

"Aye, but cuter," Dora agreed.

"Oh, Dora. I'm so tired and frustrated lately. The girls are wild and won't listen. And not one of them is practicing their spell-work! I'm afraid everything we're working for will be lost."

"Don't ya worry. They're all talented. They'll come 'round."

"Even Ruth Anne's has become rebellious. She's talking back and hinting she knows things." Sasha sighed. "It would be easier to take if she showed any

sign of being gifted. Ironic, the one daughter who actually shares my DNA doesn't have a drop of magick."

"Her talents may be latent," Dora said.

Ruth Anne stopped listening. Her mind went back to her mother's comment. She'd always had her suspicions about her sisters, and had even confronted her mother about them once.

"What an imagination you have, Ruth Anne," Miss Sasha had said in response. "Perhaps you should be a writer."

And now, here she was, hearing the truth spoken out loud for the first time. It angered her, and now she was glad to have the money in her hands.

"Armand is still out there," Sasha continued. "We must expedite their training."

"I told ya he was dangerous."

"Oh Dora, I knew he was dangerous. But if I didn't train him, someone else would have. Or worse, he would have trained himself. Armand has his own fate, and we have ours. We must stay vigilant, and keep the girls away from him, no matter what. So mote it be."

"So mote it be," Dora confirmed.

Ruth Anne knew about Armand. She was old enough to have met him, to feel his contempt as he looked her over coldly. She hadn't seen him in years, but her memory of him frightened her to the core. Why were they still talking about him? That was it. No more delays. She was getting the hell out of Dark Root.

When she'd talked to her father on the phone, she'd told him she'd get the money. And now she had it. Surely, they could live on this for a long time.

When her mother and aunt finally left the kitchen, Ruth Anne slid out of hiding and went into the living room. Her sisters had collapsed on the couch in a heaping pile of sweat and laughter, their brooms piled on the floor beside them.

How can I leave them?

Then she remembered her mother's words about DNA.

She looked down at the roll of bills one final time, then tucked it into her pocket.

~

R uth Anne was the first one in… and the last one through. Her face was a pale mask of shame as the portal spit her out. She stumbled, looking up at us with wide eyes, massaging one side of her head with her knuckles. "I had the worst dream."

"Yes, we all saw your dream," Eve said, narrowing her eyes.

"In vivid detail," Merry agreed, petting Starlight on her shoulder.

"You guys saw that, too?" Ruth Anne asked us, her knuckles now digging into her temples, trying to extract the unwelcome memory.

"Afraid so," Michael confirmed.

"It wasn't that bad," Paul said.

Eve jerked her head around and shot him an outraged look. "Whose side are you on?"

"I didn't know this was a 'sides' thing," Paul said. "It was obviously a traumatic event for Ruth Anne, and I was just trying to reassure her that it was okay."

Eve's face froze like a Gorgon, and I wondered how Paul wasn't turned to stone. "I might need reassurance, too. Have you thought of that?"

I looked at Ruth Anne. Her lips trembled, and her gaze fell to the long shadows cast by her legs. I followed the line of the shadow, taking in the new landscape. It wasn't night, but it wasn't quite dawn, either. The sky was that dreamy azure that only comes when the sun and moon are about to trade paths, their lights tickling each other flirtatiously. There was a refreshing coolness to the air.

"Let's ask Maggie," Merry said, pulling back my attention.

"Ask me what?"

Merry lifted her hand and began counting on her fingers. "What do you think of the fact that Ruth Anne, one - took money from Aunt Dora, two - never told us she was leaving, or said goodbye, three - knew Sasha wasn't our real mother, and four, knew your father was a danger to us, and left us there anyway!"

Until she said it aloud, I hadn't given any of it much thought. We had all done regrettable things in our teen years. But now that Merry had laid it all out, I began to get angry. I joined Merry and Eve in crossing my arms and staring her down.

"How could you?" I asked. "How could you have left us there with crazy Mother? I always thought your dad just showed up and you left spontaneously. But you planned to leave us, didn't you? Ruth Anne, how could you?"

"Et tu, Mags?" She looked down at her feet and sighed. "In my defense, I didn't know Armand was your father. He was just one crazy warlock among a bunch of other crazy witches and warlocks. You know, a typical day in Dark Root. And Gah! I was fifteen!"

She ran her hands through her short hair, then lifted her face, palms up. "I was scared, okay? Mom was doing all this voodoo shit, putting curses on people, and talking about the end of the world. Basically, going nutso." She snorted and jammed her glasses onto her nose. "I felt horrible about it, but I had to get out of there. I had forgotten... buried, the whole thing, until now."

"Does Aunt Dora know you took her money?" I asked.

"No. I never told her. I couldn't bear the look on her face. I'm sorry."

"Are you?" I asked. Sasha had blamed me for the missing money. I very clearly remembered the look Aunt Dora gave me, the same one Ruth Anne couldn't take. She locked her cabinet thereafter. "Are you really sorry, Ruth Anne?"

"Of course, I'm sorry! Leaving was the hardest thing I ever did. But I didn't know how to save myself, let alone you girls. It was always my intention to come home and make it right."

"But you never paid Aunt Dora back," I said. In honesty, I wasn't mad about the money anymore. I was hurt. Now that I had come to know her as an adult, it was harder to believe she could have left us as kids.

"I didn't do a lot of things I should have done."

"Your sisters are here for you now, Maggie," Shane said gently. "All of them." If it had been anyone else, I would've shot them one of Eve's Gorgon looks. But he was right.

"You all could show a little compassion," Ruth Anne said. "I just had my guts splayed out to everyone I love. I took one for the team. You're welcome."

She might be right. Jillian had warned that our secrets would be used against us. Perhaps with Ruth Anne's unwitting help, we had maneuvered that obstacle.

"We'll talk about this later," I said, thinking it over as I examined our surroundings. I needed time to process the conflicting emotions: Anger. Betrayal. Abandonment. And countless others chiming in to get their say. I knew Ruth Anne never meant to hurt us. Like each of us, she needed to get away. And like each of us, that meant casualties.

"Let's figure out where we are," Shane said, as Ruth Anne tapped and shook her wonky compass.

Michael whistled quietly. "This place has a strange atmosphere. Ancient."

Ruth Anne looked up from her spinning compass. "I know what you mean. It feels so familiar. Like I've been here before."

The gate we'd come through was no longer there, nor the surrounding forest. My eyes adjusted as a radiant dawn flooded the world. We now stood in an endless wheat field. The stalks were in clumps that varied in height from up to our ankles to as high as a tree. We had left one forest for another, of sorts.

My ankh flashed. I smiled, and looked for Eagle Mountain. Though I couldn't see it, I knew we were on the right track. My mood improved as the sun warmed the earth, and the wheat swayed in the breeze.

"How long should we wait for your boyfriend to do his magic tricks before we move out?" Michael asked, his eyes scanning the horizon.

Shane shot a quick reply. "That's husband, if your ministering credentials aren't as shifty as you are."

"Ignore him," I whispered. Then, to everyone else, I added, "We'll stay as long as it takes for Shane to get a lock on Montana."

Shane relaxed and closed his eyes. His fingers twitched at his sides while we held our breaths, waiting. A wisp of a smile fell over his face and he looked at me. He had it. "That way," he pointed.

"We call that forward," Michael said. "Brilliant."

The wheat field stretched for miles, and the further we went, the taller the wheat. Soon, it was up to our waists.

The skies brightened, rivaling the crystalline blue of Merry's eyes. Geese flew overhead, arranged in a deep V, headed into the lazy marshmallow clouds. The wind tickled my cheek and the scent of summer was so rich I felt giddy. It was the smell of freedom and adventure. The fragrance of life.

I wasn't the only one whose mood had lifted. Merry spun in wide-armed circles ahead of us. "It smells like Kansas," she said, breathing deeply. "I miss this."

"It does smell like Kansas," Michael agreed, giving Merry a smile of acknowledgment.

We walked on and on, without stiffness in our legs or the slightest sense of exhaustion. The day was invigorating, and even though I still didn't see the mountain, I felt wholly inspired. Only Ruth Anne straggled behind, her face long, as if the weight of her pack had doubled.

I wasn't angry anymore. The anger had fled before the beauty of the day.

"Ruth Anne, you study things," I said, falling back to join her. "Why do you think we're in a wheat field? Is this symbolic?"

My sister wrinkled her nose. "That's been bothering me, if you want to know the truth, Mags." She picked up her pace, taking a spot in the middle of our formation. When she spoke again, she spoke to all of us. "I read about a place called the Elysian Fields. It was where souls went to rest after a hard life. Energy was restored there, and burdens were lightened.

"I always found that story creepy, souls just wandering fields endlessly. With or without their earthly burdens, all I could picture was the hopelessness of it all." She looked around and sighed deeply, and as she exhaled the skies seemed to darken to a dusky blue.

Wandering fields endlessly.

Endlessly?

It did seem to be endless and unchanging. My earlier euphoria gave way to panic. I felt my ankh, but it was now dormant. Shane forged ahead determinedly, and I tried to reaffirm my faith in him.

"Why would anyone want to go to a wheat farm when they died?" Eve asked.

"Wheat is highly symbolic," Ruth Anne volunteered. She stretched out her hand, high-fiving each stock she passed. "In many ancient cultures, bread is associated with fertility, life, and abundance. Ancient people found it comforting to enter an afterlife of such extravagance."

"That's not much of a sales pitch," Eve said.

"Wheat is also associated with the modern church." Paul, who rarely talked unless a subject interested him, was suddenly animated. "For instance, breaking bread is an expression of charity. And the grain itself represents the resurrection, that all things will be born again."

"Preach it!" Ruth Anne said, joining Paul. The two continued discussing wheat fun facts, while Eve rolled her eyes behind them. *Is she still upset with Ruth Anne for that long-ago indiscretion, or was there something else?*

Flocks of birds crossed the sky at various intervals. And while there were certainly worse places we could have ended up, every step increased the urgency of my mission. I checked the timer – the sand continued to fall.

Soon we had guests. Dozens of black ravens collected, perching on the faraway stalks, watching us.

"Are we getting closer?" I nervously asked Shane.

He lifted the rim of his cowboy hat. "I *feel* like we are, but it's frustrating. I have no control over this landscape like when I dreamwalk."

"But you can still feel Montana?"

"Yes, very strongly."

"Oh, thank god." I kissed his cheek and he smiled. "Does he feel... healthy?"

"Mags, I can only see flashes of him for a second at best." He saw my fallen expression and quickly added, "His energy is strong or I wouldn't be able to get a read. We just have to keep moving forward and not take anything at face value. These landscapes are deceiving. What looks like miles may be only a dozen steps…what the hell?"

Shane stopped abruptly. We all did. We had come to the edge of the wheat field, and the setting changing like a slide in a View-Master. We stood before another field, this one of gray-white flowers. Asphodels.

I bent to pick one, remembering how I had planted one on the Upper World, how it was said the flowers connected the living to the dead.

"I'll be," Ruth Anne said, scratching her head. "Is this really Asphodel Meadows?"

"What?" Eve asked.

"The place where apathetic souls went in the afterlife," Paul jumped in. "At least, according to the ancient Greeks."

"I don't see any souls here," Merry said. "Apathetic or otherwise. Just us and nine trillion sad-looking flowers."

I looked behind me, but the wheat field was already gone. Shane motioned for us to keep going. Our moods ebbed to a dishwater blah, as we considered how long we'd be wandering this new field.

"I used to dream about these fields," Ruth Anne said. "I read about them in Uncle Joe's library. I'm not sure why I was so frightened of these places. They seem a bit boring, really."

Michael stopped, holding his finger to his lips. "You hear that?"

"What?" we all asked.

"Maybe I should say, 'did you 'feel' that?'"

"I have no idea what you're talking about," I said.

He looked around warily, his fingers grazing his cross. Michael wasn't the easily frightened type, so this worried me. "There's a bad storm brewing, Maggie," he whispered, so that only I could hear. "Mark my words."

Shane gave him a hard glare as he moved on. Tensions were amplified here. Eve was eying Ruth Anne, while Shane and Michael argued back and forth. For a place of apathy, we weren't very apathetic.

The temperature rose and I grew uncomfortably warm. It might be a trick of the mind, but the sweat rolling down my neck was real.

"Maggie, can you ask your *husband* where he's leading us?" Michael barked. "Because as far as I can tell, the mountain is nowhere to be seen. Moses found his mountain in less time than we will."

Shane stopped. He thrust his hands in his pockets, turning to face us. "We all want to get out of here," he said. "You're not the only one with a life to return to."

"Why should we trust you?" Michael asked, stepping up to Shane's chest. "You've done nothing but take us on a hike so far."

"You're welcome to lead, if you feel you're qualified."

"I'm probably more qualified than you," Michael countered. "As the child's father, I'm able to sense where he is. And while you spent your youth being 'dream-boy,' I spent mine studying the afterlife."

"So, in your expert opinion, is this heaven or hell?"

Michael's face turned the color of the asphodel field. "I'm leading," he said, then started marching to the left, through the field.

Shane shook his head and turned right.

The others all looked at me.

"What should we do?" Merry asked.

I trusted Shane's abilities, but Michael was Montana's father. *Oh, fuck!*

Why the hell couldn't those two stop fighting long enough to see this through?

"Stop!" I bellowed. The asphodel's around us trembled from the force of my words. Michael and Shane both stopped, turning their heads back towards me.

I balled my fists and stamped my foot, and the ground rumbled. "I'm Montana's mother. I know best. You'll both stop these schoolyard antics right now." A bolt of silver lightning scorched the blue sky then disappeared.

"Chill out, Mags," Eve said. "We don't want to draw any unnecessary attention."

"What are you suggesting we do?" Merry asked me.

"We are standing right here, right now. There are no coincidences, so this is where we need to be. We wait here, and look for a sign."

"A sign?" Eve asked. "Like a 'This Way to Munchkinland' kinda sign?"

"I don't know what the sign will look like," I said, flustered. "But we've been walking forever and not much has changed."

Ruth Anne sighed and Eve looked doubtful, but Merry gave me a supportive arm squeeze. Michael and Shane still stood on opposite sides, their backs to us, as if waiting for someone to yell "Draw!"

Screw them both, I thought. I stood still, surrounded by bleak flowers, quietly waiting for... my sign. Finally, Shane turned back towards me.

I didn't realize I'd been holding my breath, but I let it out gratefully as he drew nearer. I smiled, watching him all the way into my arms. Michael never returned. He continued walking, until he was a blip on the horizon. I wondered if he was doing this to find Montana, or just for spite? I let it go. Perhaps we had a better chance if we split up anyway.

"I'm sorry," Shane said, kissing me. "Your ex brings out my stupid pride."

"He brings out a lot of stuff in me, too."

"Hoo-hoo...." Starlight hooted.

"Uh...Maggie." Merry tapped my shoulder. Straight ahead, my sign appeared. It came in the form of an orange cat's tail, cutting through the milky-gray flowers.

"It can't be!" I smiled, jogging to catch it. "Wait!"

The tail stopped. It was Maggie Cat! How had he gotten here?

The orange tabby opened his mouth, coughing up a sleek black feather. Then he turned and waded back into the flowers. He looked over his shoulder, waiting for us to follow.

I nodded. And we did.

~

"Where did Maggie Cat go?" Merry asked, when the seemingly infinite asphodels finally began to thin out. My cat had disappeared, leaving us standing before a colorful, living panorama –a photograph without a frame.

There were people, too, all going about their afterlives. Couples walked hand in hand, families rode bikes together, a teenage boy played with his dog, and toddlers splashed in fountains. In the far distance I saw a river, dotted with bobbing rowboats. And in the sky there were stars, though it was the height of a sunny day.

The mural-world was inviting, as if Michelangelo himself had painted paradise and then brought it to life. There was no color in the Upper World that matched the green of the grass, or the red in the apples hanging on the trees. A storybook world had opened up in front of us, and we were about to step into the first page.

As delightful as the scene was, I felt anxious. My ankh hadn't glowed in a long time and Shane wasn't picking anything up. Plus, we hadn't seen Michael since we parted ways. I worried that we'd be split up forever if we went on.

"Dare we?" Merry asked, bouncing from one foot to the other. "It's prettier than Disneyland," she added dreamily.

"I'm afraid I'll track in mud," Paul joked.

"It could be a trap," Shane said. "That cat could easily have been one of Larinda's minions."

Ruth Anne carefully poked at the mural, and then her face lit up. "Summerland!" she said, snapping her fingers and smiling sheepishly. "Now I remember! As you may know, I'm a bit of a geek…"

"A bit?" Eve asked.

"A *bit*," Ruth Anne reiterated. "And while you all squandered your childhoods playing games, I spent mine learning about the world. Worlds in fact. One of them was Summerland."

"What can you tell us about it?" I asked Ruth Anne.

"Yes, oh wise one," Eve said. "Please fill us in."

Ruth Anne tapped her temple. "Let me think. Sorry, it's been a while."

"Summerland is a stopover for souls," Paul added hesitantly. "Right? It's the place souls rest *in between* lives and are reunited with loved ones. They can stay as long as they want."

"That's right! I remember now!" Ruth Anne said, scratching out more notes.

"How many worlds do the dead get?" Eve asked.

"As many as they need, I guess," Merry answered.

"Well, we aren't dead," Eve countered. "I'm ready to get on with what we came here for."

Shane pointed to a section of the mural. "Isn't that the garden where you escorted Sasha and Leo?"

"Is it?" I stepped closer, bringing my face up to the invisible border, as if mesmerized by a Christmas window display. "It is!" Sure enough, I saw the garden. *They are in there! They have to be!*

I turned to my sisters. "Mother and Leo are in there. I'm going in." I stepped across the threshold, bracing myself for whatever came. But, except for a blink of my ankh, I passed through smoothly. I realized this wasn't an actual portal, and I beckoned the others to follow.

I sprinted for the garden. The park-goers ignored me as they went about their business, dressed in styles popular during their lifetimes. There was a weightlessness to my body, and I ran faster than ever before, as if there were springs beneath my feet. When I reached the lavish garden, I looked around, expecting to see Mother waiting for me. If anyone knew how to navigate the Netherworld, and could protect my son from Armand, it was Sasha Shantay.

"How's your day, Miss?" A handsome young man in a floppy hat and vest asked me. There was a deep scar on his cheek and his eyes were bright but vacant.

"Fine," I nodded courteously, and continued on.

"Maggie, wait!" Merry called. "It won't save us any time if we lose track of each other." She caught up to me as Starlight circled overhead.

Time.

I took out the hourglass, and was dismayed to see how many more grains of sand had fallen.

"What's that?" Merry asked, as the others joined us.

I lifted the timer, like a scientist examining a beaker. I flipped it over several times, showing them that the sand only ran one way. "This is how long we have," I said, frowning. "Or at least I think so."

"How long we have until what?" Eve asked, warily.

"Um…"

"Never mind," Eve said. "I think I know. Put that thing away, please." She shivered, stepping close to Paul.

Our mood sobered as we waded through the lovely garden, looking for Mother. Merry stopped to smell the flowers, but her heart wasn't in it. "Sasha," I called out, realizing how much hope I had pinned on finding her here.

"Maggie?"

I turned towards the familiar voice, grinning even before I saw him. "Leo!" I said, rushing for him. "Oh, Leo!"

I collapsed against my friend's chest and sobbed. He was younger than when I'd seen him last, no older than thirty, his brow now worry-free. His arms were muscular and there was a healthy glow to his cheeks. Even his clothes appeared new. He hugged me, comforting me in a soft voice. "It's all right," he said. "Whatever it is, it's all right."

I looked into Leo's eyes. He seemed so tall now. Had he always been this tall? "I'm so happy I found you," I said, sniffling. "I'm glad you are OK."

"You look beautiful," he said, touching my cheek. "Just like I remember."

I laughed, tugging at a leaf caught in my hair. "No Leo, I'm a mess." I told him my story and he listened thoughtfully, while my sisters added details here and there. Shane and Paul hung back, clearly uncomfortable.

"I wish I could help," Leo said. "But I don't know what lies beyond. When your mother disappeared from here, I…"

"Miss Sasha disappeared?" I asked.

"Yes. I'm told it happens when we feel ready to move on. Some stay forever, while others go quickly. I'm happy here, so I think I'll stay." He put his hands in his pockets and looked around, nodding in satisfaction. "I shudder to think where I would have ended up if I hadn't met you. You redeemed me."

"You redeemed yourself, Leo. You are no longer the person I met playing pool at the bar. You shine now."

"But Leo, where do they go?" Merry asked. She often ruminated on whether Mother might end up in a 'dark place,' working off the karma of all her curses. In my opinion, Merry needn't worry. Even if Mother ended up in the heart of hell itself, the devil was no match for Sasha Shantay.

"I don't know where they go," Leo repeated. "We don't talk about it much here. We mostly just acknowledge that it happens. But there are whisperings…"

"What kind of whisperings?" Shane asked, stepping up beside me.

"Some say we start the whole process again." Leo shrugged. "Others say you move on to the next level, and it's even better than the last, like a video game. But I have a hard time believing anything's better, so I'll stay here if I'm allowed."

My sisters and I exchanged glances. I couldn't dwell on this now. Getting help from Mother was no longer an option. I looked around, wondering at which direction to go, as Eagle Mountain still hadn't reappeared.

"I can take you to the border. It's not far," Leo said. "But I can't go beyond."

Shane bristled, but stayed silent. I'd forgotten Shane had once believed Leo and I were lovers. Even after he knew the truth, he was still uncomfortable with our relationship.

"You seem so alive, Leo," I said, as he leisurely guided us towards the edge of his world.

"I *am* alive," Leo said. "More so than I've ever been. It was my previous life that was illusion."

"I, for one, am ready to get back to my illusionary life," Eve said with a snort. "All these dead people are creeping me out." She ducked a Frisbee sailing over her head, expertly caught by a little girl in a crinoline dress.

Leo chuckled, pointing to a line of stubby trees at the base of a hill.

The boughs of one tree were intertwined with the next, as if guarding what lay beyond – a dark and unfamiliar forest.

"I wish I could go on," he said, "but I'm already starting to feel pulled apart. I think you'll find what you're looking for in that direction."

I nodded gratefully, my eyes watering as I gave him a fierce hug. "Thank you, Leo. I love you."

"I love you too, Maggie." He took my hand and saw my wedding ring, then cracked a smile at Shane. "Congratulations. You're a lucky man. Take care of her." He dropped my hand and winked at my husband. "Just a warning, you'll have competition in the afterlife."

Leo flexed his arm and I burst into a fit of bittersweet laughter.

"Roger that," Shane said, pulling me into his side.

Leo turned and ambled back, his manner more weighted on his return trip. My heart was crushed. *I couldn't say goodbye to one more person! I wouldn't!*

We moved along the stunted trees, looking for an opening. The scenery was changing once again, though the shift was slower, more gradual. Green fields turned damp, then marshy. The scent of meat cooked over an open fire seeped into the air. And then twilight came, dusting the world with purple fog dotted by fireflies the size of gold coins. I had begun to accept the constant changes of the Netherworld, and so I just sank into this new landscape.

"I think I found it," Shane said, marching purposefully towards two trees spaced farther apart than the others. My ankh blinked in confirmation and we pushed our way through, entering immediately into a hidden bayou. Long-legged cranes stood on the shore, and a large reptile slithered through the water, its bulbous eyes watching us.

"Reminds me of the Delta," Ruth Anne said, as we carefully skirted the swamp. She scratched at her neck, as if the location caused an allergic reaction. She looked around, anxiously.

"What's wrong?" I asked her.

"Oh, uhh..." she shrugged. "This is just bringing up some memories, that's all."

I nodded, letting it go. Ruth Anne had confessed to me that she had fallen in love with a voodoo priestess who lived, and then died, in a similar environment during her time away from Dark Root.

As dusk deepened, our party huddled closer together, walking at half speed. Shane led the way while the rest of us kept our eyes on the strange birds roosting in the bushes and the ripples in the black water.

Merry slowed and put a finger to her lips. "Listen," she whispered, the whites of her eyes gleaming in the dark.

I heard it. A repentant moan echoed around us. It was soon by joined by other laments, growing louder and closer by the moment. The voices were all female.

"Let's hope those aren't banshees," Ruth Anne said.

Banshees. Please, not banshees.

Banshees were thought to be the souls of wronged or wicked women who exact their revenge by inflicting pain on others – particularly children. A single banshee in the Upper World was difficult to ward off, but a clan of them in the Netherworld could prove impossible. I looked to Shane. Despite the deepening darkness, he continued forward, not breaking step.

"Ah, Geez," Ruth Anne said, shrugging off her pack. Up ahead there was a flickering torch. She raced towards the light, running full speed. I chased after, calling her name. We came to a row of straw huts. Ruth Anne twined through them, until she came upon a particular shack. A young black woman with long braids stood in the doorway. She had wide almond eyes and a secret smile. Ruth Anne wrapped her arms around the woman's shoulders, gasping for air as she sobbed against her neck. But the woman just stared vacantly ahead, not seeing Ruth Anne at all.

"Who's that?" Eve asked, catching up to us.

It was Ruth Anne's former lover, who had died in a fire while exorcising a demon. "An old friend," was all I said to Eve.

Ruth Anne was frantically trying to communicate with the woman. Not getting a response, she kicked the doorframe and punched the thatched wall in frustration. I watched, heartbroken, until I couldn't take it anymore.

"Ruth Anne, please! Can we talk?"

She wiped her eyes and gave the woman a final glance, then returned to me. "She doesn't know me, Mags," she whimpered.

"I'm sorry."

"I just wanted to tell her I loved her, and to apologize for not being with her when she died."

"She knows that already. See how peaceful she looks?"

Ruth Anne nodded and sniffed. The woman hummed to herself, then stepped back into her house, shutting the door behind her. "Yes, she does look happy, doesn't she? That's all I could ever ask for."

The light inside the hut window went out, and the entire world went silent.

My sister dried her face with her sleeve. "We need to leave this place, please. I can't handle being here, if I can't be with her." She put her hand on her hip, looking around. "But damn, I'm glad I saw her. At least I know, you know?"

"Yes, I know."

"It's strange that the truth-portal didn't show how we parted. Leaving her was my biggest regret, and my darkest secret."

"It's not a secret," I reminded her. "You told me."

We stood, listening to the only sound remaining – that of our own breaths. Ruth Anne sighed, and then spoke to the small house. "Goodbye my love. I'll see you again, one day." She kissed the palm of her hand and offered it to the air. A breeze rolled back the darkness and the huts disappeared, one after another.

"I didn't know you were so magickal," I said, impressed.

"It wasn't magick," she said. "It was just letting go."

"Everything okay?" Paul asked, as we rejoined the others beneath a weeping willow tree.

"Yep. Just pondering my existence in this vast universe," Ruth Anne said, cracking a tight smile.

"Can you ponder a little faster," Eve asked, looking at the swamp, now in daylight. "Less chit-chat, more skit-skat."

"Yes, ma'am," Ruth Anne saluted, taking her bag from Paul and slinging it over her shoulder.

We fell in behind her, marching through the swamp, looking for a way out. I did my best to ignore my wet feet, knowing it was only an illusion. Looking ahead at my sister Ruth Anne, I realized we were leaving pieces of ourselves in the Netherworld, and I wondered if we'd ever find them again.

"I hear music!" Merry said, as we neared a winding river. "It's a flute!"

A light, whimsical tune whistled through the trees and skimmed along the water. Then we heard people singing along, their stamped cadence reminiscent of an upbeat chain gang. On both sides, a row of people appeared, singing as they marched towards a single point ahead. We watched as they disappeared from view.

We followed them curiously, as we had no other particular way to go. They eventually converged on a monstrous gray boulder, covered in moss and vines, stationed at the base of a hill. On the front face of the rock was a metallic disk with a pull handle. The singing procession phased right through the disk as they marched. Their song disappeared with them, though the flute played on.

We drew in closer and the disc became a mirror. We stared back at our reflections. Shane tightened his jaw. "I think this is it."

"Think?" Eve asked. "I'm not entering a Netherworld manhole unless we're damned sure."

Shane nodded, sounding more confident this time. "Yes. This is it."

Starlight flapped his wings, hopping along Merry's shoulder. "It's owl-approved," she said.

"Sorry, Eve," I said, pulling rank as I reached for the handle. "We don't seem to have a choice."

The door wouldn't budge. The others pitched in, without effect.

"It's worse than one of Aunt Dora's preserve jars," Merry lamented, wiping her hand with a tissue from her purse. "Why is it no one thought to bring wet wipes?"

Ruth Anne's eyes widened as she leafed through her bag and withdrew Mother's spell book. "Surely there's something in here we can use.

We searched the book, and found many spells to unlock jars, car doors, vaults and even hearts. I tried a few, but nothing seemed to work.

"Here we go!" Ruth Anne said, stopping at a cracked page written in tiny calligraphy. The title read: 'Master Realm Access. Prepared by Goodwife Snow. 1694.

"What if it sends us to the wrong realm?" I asked.

"We don't even know what realm we're in, or what realm we're going to, so how could it be the wrong realm?" Eve asked.

Everyone stood back as I recited the incantation:

> *From this realm, we wish to flee.*
> *Let our bodies be the key.*
> *Guide us through the closest veil*
> *Towards the light and far from hell.*

"You forgot to say, "so mote it be," Merry whispered.

"So mote it be," I added, slamming the book shut. I didn't like some of those older spells. Even the helpful ones could sound ominous.

There was a great trembling in the earth around us. The ground tilted and lurched, and rocks higher on the hill were shaken loose. We covered our heads and stepped back. The sky darkened considerably, and the wind picked up.

From the earth before us, a crude human form rose up, shaping itself from clay. Twigs, leaves and moss were pulled into it, and the body took on a rough texture, with bark for skin and red foliage for hair. It was a giant, at least seven feet tall, broad and muscular. He stretched the budding branches emerging from his torso and they became arms and legs. His green eyes surveyed each of us, turning ember red along the way. Two enormous antlers sprouted from his head.

"None may pass through my gate without my consent!" he bellowed, appearing angry at having been awakened. The tree-deer-man lifted his 'root' legs, shaking off dirt.

Was he friend or foe? I wondered. "May we have your permission?"

He bent low, his branches rustling, and sniffed at each of us. "Only the dead may pass from Summerland," he said. "And you're not dead."

"No, but I need to go inside. Please, I need to find a witch named Larinda."

"Larinda?" he asked. "The witch who resides on Eagle Mountain? Consort of Armand?"

"Yes! That's her."

"I will let no ally of Armand through. He has polluted our world already!" He roared, and the ground shook again.

"We should go, Mags," Ruth Anne pulled at my sleeve.

"Go? Go where?" I spread my arms, looking around. I took a step towards the creature, and explained my story. I showed him my ankh and told him of my son. I hoped I wasn't making a mistake, but I sensed he tolerated liars even less than the lost. "Please," I asked again.

The creature's eyes softened. He reached into his leaves and produced a richly carved flute, polished to starlight silver. He lifted it to his lips and played three long notes. Then he lowered the instrument and his appearance shifted. The shape of an actual man emerged, with sharp pointed features, wavy autumn hair, and long delicate fingers. His antlers shrank to mere horns, and his rich brown skin became smooth. He was adorned in lavish, colorful clothing. He was quite handsome and... regal.

"You're a prince!" I said.

"Not a prince, a king. Though in the Upper World, they call me a god!" He cocked his head and smiled, seemingly amused by the notion. "I am Cernunnos, and I am the ruler of this place. You must have a gift, red-haired lady. Only a goddess can pull me from my guise unless I'm at my court."

He stepped forward with long, rickety strides. His feet were hesitant to leave the ground, as if his legs were rooted. His eyes matched the color of spring foliage, sparkling like two gems against his tan skin. He lifted a strand of my red hair, several shades darker than his own. "So lovely," he said. "Like unrefined silk." He bowed low, one long arm gracefully extending behind him. "And who are you?"

"Maggie Maddock, from Dark Root." I introduced the others. He nodded at each, though his eyes stopped at Eve. He examined her, head to toe, then kissed her hand. It seemed that even Netherworld kings were not immune to her beauty and sensuality.

"Your musical instrument is exquisite," Merry said.

At this, he dropped Eve's hand and showed us his flute. "You have good taste! It is carved from the finest wood, found only in my kingdom. Its sound is sweet enough to summon even the shyest of souls, and the most mischievous of fairies. My role in this world is to assist those who are ready to move on from Summerland. Would you like another tune? I composed one just this morning, though no one wants to my new stuff," he said, lowering his eyes. "They say 'Stick to the classics!'. Don't they understand I'm an artist?"

"I would love to hear more!" Merry said, clapping her hands.

"No!" I stamped my foot. "We need to find my son, and we need to get through your kingdom to do so. May we have your consent?" Cernunnos furrowed his bristly brows, his flute poised at his lips. "If you let us inside," I continued, softer now, "Merry will listen to your music. We all will."

He lowered his flute, as if deciding. His eyes grazed both Merry and Eve with interest. "Fine, though it is Feast Day. We are celebrating the Feast of the Crone! You will be expected to attend the festivities if I guide you into my land."

I felt my timer, wishing I could look at it without drawing attention. I wasn't sure how long a 'Feast Day' took, but I felt forced to agree. "We'd be delighted to be your guests," I said, bowing.

Shane offered me a quick smile, showing his approval of my budding diplomacy skills.

"Perhaps after the feast, you can show us the way to Eagle Mountain," I pressed, while I took one of Cernunnos' arms and Merry took the other.

He rubbed his chin thoughtfully, his eyes shifting left and then right. His arms were covered in a soft layer of fuzz that was both primal and masculine, and I found myself aroused in his presence. The way my sisters flushed, I sensed their reactions were similar - including Ruth Anne.

"I cannot show you the way to Eagle Mountain, but perhaps I can find you another guide inside." Cernunnos smiled, his grin stretching across his face. I noticed then that his teeth were pointed. "But first, we feast and partake in merriment! I will even give you a tour of my kingdom. I'm sure you will find rest and rejuvenation within. And then, you can go off and find your son."

Though he spoke to me, his eyes and attention were on Merry the entire time.

6

THE HIEROPHANT

*C*ernunnos waved his hand and the giant circular door unscrewed itself three full revolutions. He pulled it open and bade us enter. "It's safe, nothing to worry about," he said, winking at Merry.

Ruth Anne was the first to step up. "Why do I feel like I'm walking into a bad Grimm fairy tale?" she asked.

"Hopefully not Hansel and Gretel," Paul said. "Eve's been fattening me up."

We went into the dark hole, only to emerge into a vast and radiant woodland. The sun seemed so close here, yet the temperature was perfect. Once we were all through, the doorway sealed behind us, camouflaged by tulips and rose vines.

"Things keep getting more and more beautiful in the Netherworld," Merry commented, as a butterfly the size of her hand fluttered around us. Starlight hooted and flapped his wings, as if asking to join in. "I only wish Michael were here to see this."

"Michael?" Cernunnos asked, but Merry was already lost again in her surroundings.

"Are these tomatoes?" she asked, bending to inspect a soft red fruit, as large as a cantaloupe.

"My very best," Cernunnos acknowledged, a smile tugging at the corner of his mouth. He then took a step towards her, cocking his head. "You have Gaia's blood, Merry. You are an earth mother, and it is an honor to meet one so beautiful... and young."

As Merry marveled at the vegetation, Cernunnos lifted her hand, studying her fingertips, from knuckle to nail. "I have never touched a creature so soft and exquisite."

"Okay, that's enough, pal," Shane said. "That's my sister-in-law you're pawing."

Merry put out her arm and smiled. "It's okay, Shane, I'm a big girl. Although it's nice to be called your sister." She looked at me, her blue eyes shining. "He fed me some of his energy. I feel so alert now! So alive!"

"Guilty as charged." Cernunnos beamed. "I could sense that your heart was... heavy."

"Yes," she sighed. "It was. But I'm feeling better now."

"This garden is nothing," Cernunnos declared, opening his arms. "When you see the real fruits and vegetables of my labor, your smile will be seen from the moon! And if that doesn't impress you, my banquet tonight will."

"I hope we're not the main course of this meal," Eve whispered.

Cernunnos and Merry walked ahead, giving us a tour of the abundant plant life. Some I knew from the Upper World, and some could only be found in a dream. Merry fawned over each and every one, petting petals and tickling stems.

Then we came upon a patch where a few of the vegetables had withered. Cernunnos's brows knitted. "All ugly and worthless," he said, pointing at the worm-eaten food. "I shall get rid of it, so that you won't have to look upon it." He pointed, and an eggplant crumbled into dust.

"Stop!" Merry pulled his arm down as he moved to the next. "Let me try."

She touched a giant snap pea, gingerly caressing it as she hummed a sweet lullaby. And then she blew the vegetable a kiss. "Grow," she said simply.

And it did.

The plant doubled in size, no longer afflicted, but robust and healthy. Cernunnos inspected it carefully. When he returned his attention to Merry, he was entirely enamored. "You are a descendent of Gaia herself!" he said.

"He's smitten," I whispered to Shane, as we followed behind them on a cobblestone path, a shaped hedge on either side. "Perhaps he's never met a Nature Witch before."

"You Maddock girls cast quite the spell."

The path twisted and turned between the hedges, though it wasn't quite a maze and we didn't quite get lost. I fell back with Ruth Anne, who was mapping the path as we walked.

"Watch this." She looked around, then took out her pocketknife and cut a leaf from the hedge. It grew back instantly. "The flora in this world is amazing, and don't even get me started on the fauna."

"I won't."

"Penny for your fortune," a woman's cracked voice said as we rounded the next bend.

"Not a penny, fool!" said another woman's voice. "We charge a nickel now."

"Bah! I remember when a penny could buy two fortunes!"

Three woman appeared in an alcove within the hedge, all grasping the handle of a giant silver ladle. Together they stirred an enormous black cauldron, tossing in ingredients they summoned out of the air. We should've been surprised to see them but we weren't, which was more surprising. This place had already started to claim us.

I looked ahead to see the others continuing along the cobblestone path, oblivious.

"Witches?" I asked, stupidly. These were not just witches, but storybook witches with pointed hats and curly-toed shoes and missing teeth. The oldest caught me staring at a growth on the back of her hand.

"You like?" she asked, tapping on the lump. "I could arrange for you to have one."

I shook my head. "Let's keep going," I said to Ruth Anne.

"But don't you want your fortunes read?" asked the youngest witch. She was shorter than the others, but made up for it in girth.

"There are too many variables in this world," Ruth Anne countered. "So there are no fortunes."

The middle witch, her age somewhere between the other two, smiled. Her eyes were covered in milky clouds, as if she had cataracts. "That is true. But there are some things in your path that are unavoidable. Look closely."

The trio stirred the soup, and soon a picture bubbled up to the surface: Me, staring back.

"Most souls are free to roam and explore, but some paths are set at birth," said the cloudy-eyed witch. "Especially for those born with the witch's mark."

"Who are you?" Ruth Anne asked, waving away the steam with her hand to get a better look.

"You already know," said the middle one, with a hearty laugh.

"The Fates!" Ruth Anne declared, and the cauldron answered with a hiss.

Aunt Dora often had often spoken of the Fates. They were real, she insisted, said to establish the journeys of some souls at the time of birth. Though given free will to navigate the twists and turns, if you were touched by the Fates, there was no way to avoid the ultimate outcome.

"You know what happens to my son!" I said. "Please tell me!"

The young one surveyed me, still churning the ladle. "Maggie, your journey does not end in the Netherworld. You have much work to do."

"So I get out of here?" I asked. "With Montana?"

"You will get out of here, yes," said the middle witch. "Whether with or without your son has yet to be decided."

"But you decide!" I objected.

"No," said the oldest. "We decide the final destiny, not how one reaches it. Your son will reach his destiny - here, or in the Upper World."

"No more games!" I shouted. The cauldron hissed and I yanked the silver ladle from the witches' clutching hands. The heat scorched my palms, but I didn't care. "What's his destiny?" I demanded.

"If we told you, there would be no point." They all spoke in unison. With that, the steam from the pot thickened, shielding them from view. When it cleared, they were gone - cauldron, ladle, and all.

I stared at Ruth Anne. Her bangs were limp and her face was damp. "Worst. Fortune. Ever," she said.

"Those Fates were no help at all!" I said, stamping my foot. "They just showed up out of nowhere, screwed with our heads, and then disappeared."

"Actually, they were some help, Mags." We quickened our pace, trying to catch up to the others. "They said this isn't the end for you. That's comforting."

"But what about Montana fulfilling his destiny, either here or back home? That didn't sound sinister to you?"

"True, but they also said he had a destiny. And that sounds like a long life."

"Unless his destiny is to be Armand's Secret Santa gift," I said bitterly. I stood on my toes, trying to peer over the hedge. There was no sign of Eagle Mountain, and I hoped we were doing the right thing in following this strange king.

At last, we exited the hedge path, pausing to survey this newest habitat. We were inside a forest, deep, lush and majestic. The height and grandeur of the trees made Dark Root's woods look like a simple arboretum. The tallest of them stretched up into the clouds. Interspersed between these giants were other trees of every shape and size, some with graceful branches and others with trunks of fur.

Birds chirped on all sides, their songs as colorful as their feathers. They hopped from limb to limb and danced from tree to tree, watching us with curious eyes. The sun sifted through the leafy canopies as Cernunnos strode forward, telling us of his realm.

"The souls I call with my flute use this forest as a place of refuge and recovery. Most had a hard life, or bore too many losses. They convalesce here, in this land of beauty. My oasis, if you will."

"I dunno," Ruth Anne said. "Summerland didn't seem so bad."

"That place will soon be overrun with demons," Cernunnos said. "Seals are breaking everywhere, unleashing them on freer lands. But here… we do not have that problem."

"The fewer demons the better," Eve agreed.

"I dream of places like this," Merry said, cooing over each new discovery. Plump bunnies nibbled on carrots, while hummingbirds hovered over blossoming flowers.

'We are in a land of dreams,' I reminded myself, guarding against accepting this place as reality.

We arrived at a plush dell, with a dozen small vegetable gardens laid out in three neat rows. Behind the gardens, a stream gurgled. The surrounding trees dripped rich fruit from their limbs. And in the center of the clearing was a circle of mushrooms, tall enough to sit on. Children with hair of silver and gold ran circles around them. They laughed easily, no worry in their faces. But it was their aura that drew my attention –a blue field contouring their bodies, moving as they moved.

"These are the Sprightlings," Cernunnos said. "New souls."

"What darlings!" Merry exclaimed, clapping for a girl who clambered on top of a mushroom and began to dance.

"Yes, they are wonderful," Cernunnos continued, though his voice sounded weary. "When they come to me their troubles are washed clean. They are given new bodies, and must unlearn all the things that weighed them down. Unfortunately, they are without a teacher at the moment. Our beloved Thelemia has moved on, and I'm unsure how long it will take us to find another."

"So they just gotta unlearn stuff?" Ruth Anne asked. "How much does the job pay?"

The king laughed, putting his hands on his stomach, as if his belly were much larger. "They also learn new things - the nature of darkness and light, of illusion and reality. Of necessity and… waste." He sneered at this last word, and the tips of his horns seemed to twitch.

"There is much for them to learn here and I am not patient enough to teach it. This interruption may delay their development."

He crossed his hands behind his back, saying no more. Soon, we arrived at a thriving forest village of small huts built around a communal well. More houses were in the trees, with rope ladders and bridges, operated by a system of complicated pulleys. In front of a large communal house, several women danced around a bubbling pot, as a trio of musicians playing wooden instruments serenaded our arrival.

"This is the hub of my kingdom!" said Cernunnos. He looked at his flute, his fingers trembling. "You will eat with us tonight. The feast is over once we coronate our honorary crone. Then I will call for someone who can lead you to Eagle Mountain. Deal?" He smiled, and his teeth shone like the sun.

"Do we have a choice?" Shane asked.

"There is always a choice," Cernunnos said. He continued his tour, showing us where the new souls learned and played, until they were ready to *move on*.

"Where do they move on to?" Merry asked.

"Hmm... I never gave it much thought. That is not for me to decide. Now let us revel!"

Cernunnos smiled at the dancing women with a twinkle in his eye, and sampled the sumptuous foods brought out from the communal kitchen. He used words like delightful, exquisite, and delectable as he popped cherries into his mouth and sampled bites of meat roasting on spits. His mood was only soured when a young female brought out a plate of grapes. "Are these grapes grown in the gutters of Hades? Tear the vineyard down and start again." He spat a seed back on the platter, emphasizing his disgust.

Shane pulled me aside. "Can't we just go now?" he asked, taking off his hat. "Cern seems swell, but we need to get the kid so we can get home and get on with our lives."

"Get the kid so we can get on with our lives?" I asked, furious.

"I didn't mean it like that, Mags. I'm just getting frustrated."

"It sure sounded like you meant it that way."

I was already rattled by the ominous words of the Fates, and by this further delay. I knew Shane meant no real harm, but I was tired of others referring to my child as a thing and not a person.

I walked away from Shane and rejoined the others. Cernunnos was now surrounded by tall children with slender frames and delicate hands. They had pointed chins and noses, and a ruddiness to their complexion. The girls were beautiful and feminine, while the boys were slender and rowdy.

"Daddy! Daddy!" They cried out, engulfing him. "Did you bring us presents while you were away?"

Cernunnos laughed heartily. "I brought you the gift of my flute!" he said ceremoniously, lifting the instrument to his lips.

"Aww…" the kids all groaned, and most scurried away.

"Kids these days," he sighed, holstering his flute.

"Oooh, she's beautiful." The village women encircled Merry, lifting the ends of her hair, fingering the fabric of her dress, and brushing her cheek. "Perhaps she can be our new mother," they said, though many looked far older than Merry.

"Stop it!' I ordered, wading into the pack and pointing a finger. A vine sprang out of the ground, wrapping around a plump woman's ankle. She squealed, and easily broke loose. "Leave my sister alone or I'll bind you all."

"Witch!" they cried, running away. I dusted off Merry's dress and she stopped me.

"It's okay," Merry said. "I told you, I'm a big girl, remember?"

"No, it's not okay. You're my responsibility and I'm going to keep you safe."

"My sister, the benevolent dictator."

"If I knew that what meant, I'd probably be pissed," I said.

"You would," Ruth Anne agreed.

Cernunnos ushered us to a lavish banquet table. It was over-flowing with jams, pies, and soups. There was more meat than even Ruth Anne could put away, and the aroma of fresh bread filled the air. There were puddings and popcorn and something that resembled cotton candy billowing from a large bowl. And then there was the wine. Jugs were crammed into every available nook on every available table. And each place setting offered two goblets on either side of the enormous plate.

"I don't think we can stay for all this," I said, eyeing our decadent table.

"I think we can stay a little while, maybe," Merry pressed.

"Merry, we…"

Cernunnos cut me off. "Enough! There is no squabbling on Feast Night."

"That is the first rule of Feast Night," Ruth Anne said with a smirk.

A well-built man emerged from the forest. He wore fine clothes and his long white hair handsomely contrasted with his coal-black eyes. His skin was ruddy, though he lacked the more pointed features of the locals. He and Cernunnos greeted one another like two old friends, patting each other on the back. He appeared younger than the forest king, though there was an aura of wisdom about him, as if he had seen many, many things.

"This is my cousin, Hades" Cernunnos said. "He owns an impressive amount of land, and his empire grows by the day."

"Hades?!" Ruth Anne asked.

"You've heard of me?" Hades raised an eyebrow. "As for my empire, I got lucky. I bought in when it was all just marshland. Later, much of it was gentrified. We've been working on things but there are still a few areas I wouldn't even go in after dark."

"You're too modest! Look at what you've done!" Cernunnos boasted. "The music! The women! The alcohol! And those food courts!"

"There is more to my holdings than that. If you'd just visit a little longer…"

"Bah!" Cernunnos cut him off. "Why see more when I've already seen the best?"

Hades face reddened then, though he smiled. Like Cernunnos, he possessed a palpable sexiness that my body responded to. As the cousins spoke, I couldn't help but notice the way his muscular arms moved, or the smooth line of his chest partially hidden beneath his loose-fitting jacket. I ached to touch him.

He caught me staring and turned to me. "Are you as fiery as your hair?" he asked, approvingly.

"Much worse," Ruth Anne said.

"Indeed?" He lifted my hands to his lips and kissed it. If it had been any other man, I would have resisted. But with Hades, there was only need. His eyes flickered to Eve, then Merry, then Ruth Anne. One by one, we inwardly crumbled.

He turned his attention directly to Eve. "I have seen you in a movie."

Eve shook her head quickly, probably embarrassed that though she possessed the looks of an actress, she never got much work.

"Too bad you are a married man!" Cernunnos jumped in, patting Hades on the back. "Our guests are indeed very beautiful."

"Yes," Hades agreed. "But that has never stopped you. How is Thelemia, by the way?"

"Bah! She is gone. And she was to be our crone!"

"If you stopped referring to them as crones once they got their first white hair, perhaps they'd stay longer," Hades said.

"I suppose you should know. Persephone hasn't left you, and you're grayer than the Asphodel Fields these days."

Hades reached inside his jacket and produced a corked bottle. "I am on my way to a meeting and wanted to bring this by. It is from my vineyard."

"Why, thank you, cousin! But where are you off to in such a hurry that you cannot stay and enjoy the feast?"

"They say there is an enraged demon on the loose. I haven't made my quota this month. If I can catch this one..." he rubbed his hands together and his black eyes gleamed.

"I find it's best to avoid demons altogether," Cernunnos said. "Nasty unpredictable creatures without a love for the finer things. Cousin, if you finish before the moon dies, please join us for the Crowning of the Crone. Bring Persephone if you wish."

Hades buttoned his jacket up to the neck. "I'd love to, but there's another deal I'm working on, that's even more important."

"Oh, what deal is this? And why are you holding out? You know how I love to be in on the action."

"It's nothing you'd be interested in. There's a hotshot entrepreneur who will be coming into vast resources soon, if the cards play out the way I think they will. We are going to discuss him purchasing land. I'm looking to unload some real estate in Slozthozia and I think I can work a good deal."

"If you can sell him that, tell him I have a tree-bridge in the Barrenlands I'd like to talk to him about."

The two laughed. Cernunnos thanked him for his wine, and they shook hands.

"Farewell beautiful mortal women," Hades said, sighing wistfully. As he strode off, our eyes couldn't help but follow.

Paul, who had been hovering close by, hastily rejoined us. "Was that the real Hades?"

"The one and only," Ruth Anne said.

"Hades? Isn't Hades the devil?" I asked, wondering if this was who my father was bartering for my son with.

"Not traditionally," Ruth Anne said. "Only in later lore. Originally, he was just an heir to the Netherworld."

"He still governs a good portion of it," Cernunnos added, "but he sold most of it off a long time ago."

"Whoever, or whatever, Armand is trying to trade Montana for, is probably much more evil and powerful than that joker," Ruth Anne whispered in my ear.

"Some boyfriend you are," Eve said to Paul. "Merry's owl was more jealous than you were."

"You want me to be jealous?"

"I want you to be... I don't know."

"Worshipful," Cernunnos answered. "That is what all women secretly want of their men. But those same women will run when they are worshipped too much." He sighed deeply, eyeing Merry. "Why aren't women as easy to understand as gardens?"

"Uh, you may not be tilling them right," Ruth Anne offered, and I elbowed her in the ribs.

Cernunnos snapped his fingers, and was instantly dressed in a velvet hunter-green tunic with gold embroidery. His thick auburn hair was tied in a ponytail, and he now looked more like a lion than a tree. "Merry, please be my guest at the head of the table. With Thelemia gone, I am quite lonely."

With that, he lifted a cornucopia brimming with fruits and vegetables. He dumped them into an empty bowl and blew the horn. Its triumphant thunder filled the air, echoing back from somewhere far away. He seemed pleased with the sound and blew it again. "The feast commences! Soon, my children, we shall all have a new crone! You've known her for ages, and will not be disappointed."

The villagers took their seats at the table. The band began a lively tune and I couldn't help but tap my foot to the rhythm. Women in long dresses and headscarves danced joyously, throwing food, leaves and even stones into the cauldron. They all sang:

> *When the longest day of the year arrives*
> *And day replaces night.*
> *We feast and dance our cares away*
> *Our hearts and toes, both light.*
> *For a new Crone takes her place*
> *To rule by our king's side.*
> *She'll be beloved until the day*
> *He finds another bride.*

While Merry joined Cernunnos at the head of the table, the rest of us found seats along the bench of the harvest table. I looked around for Shane, hoping to sit beside him, but he was nowhere in sight. I noticed Starlight hopping along a nearby branch, making friends with some of the local birds. As I scanned the trees, I thought I saw an enormous black owl, but when I blinked it was gone

I quietly checked my ankh and my hourglass, hoping to see the ankh glowing and the hourglass unmoving. But the timepiece had lost considerably more sand and the ankh was unresponsive. *I hope Cernunnos keeps his promise to get us to Eagle Mountain.* I fingered The Star card in my pocket, as if it might help.

The food was replaced as soon as it was eaten. I poked at it, wondering where Shane was as I stared at his untouched plate.

As twilight fell upon us, the band's lively music calmed to more serious tunes. The trees came alive with blinking eyes and twinkling lights. Cernunnos excused himself from the table and stepped up onto a raised wooden platform.

"Greetings friends, old and new." He smiled at his audience, lingering on Merry. Fireflies glowed obediently around him, creating a spotlight. "Tonight is a night of feast and fortune. A night of celebration. A night to pay homage to those who came before, showing us the ways of magick. Tonight is the Feast of the Crone!"

Applause erupted all around, and we joined in.

"Before I make an *official* announcement, it has come to my attention that the beautiful and talented Demi, 'Mother to All and Betrayer of None but Those Most Wretched,' has asked to recite an original poem. Demi, my beautiful angel, please come up here."

The crowd clapped politely, though they looked at one another, as if surprised. A beautiful woman in her middle years marched confidently up to the platform. She allowed Cernunnos to kiss her cheek before shooing him off her stage.

"Thank you, my darlings." She smiled as she slid her hands along her honey-colored ponytail. "And thank you Cernunnos for the introduction. Since our beloved Thelemia has left us and cannot give the proper introduction, I took it upon myself to pen what it might be like to be a crone."

She opened her hand and a scroll appeared. Clearing her throat, she began to speak. "Though I am far too young to be a crone myself, I imagine you spend your days hoping your grown children come around often enough to let you impart wisdom to your grandchildren. In that spirit, I call this poem: A Letter to My Granddaughter on Her Eighteenth Birthday.

My Darling Dear, my Guinevere
Though I have been away now, for many years
And perhaps you no longer remember my face-
Covered with folds like the pages of a book we once read
Of kings and fairies, and things that might be
When you sat small upon my knee, before succumbing to
*   your bed.*

I wanted you to see, my queen,
that my stories are not yet through
Though I've taken my place
Among the bards of yesterday
I still reach out from time and space
To tell one final tale to you.

Your future is a living story
Empty pages to be written on
With ink that cannot be erased-
As you start on your adventure
Do not rush towards story's end
Notice lilies in the morning
Count the stars that end the day
Real heroes are not forged in glory
But in quiet journeys along the way.

The greatest deeds a champion does
Are those we do not write about
Real moments that make up our lives
Are more important in the end
Than all the dragons we have slain
Or fleeting glimpse of unicorns
These cannot match the sun at morn
Or the smile of a friend.

Dream big

Act small in kindness
And my queen, do not forget
Each life is a chapter in a far greater story
Written across the universe-
It is the small words that weave
Our stories together
Be thoughtful with pen
When contributing your verse.

"Someday, I'll have that granddaughter!" Demi promised as she bowed. "Luckily, I still have plenty of time."

The crowd clapped politely and Cernunnos rushed back onto the stage. He whispered into her ear and I caught a glimpse of a scowl as she was briskly ushered away, arguing that she had several other poems to read.

"And now for the moment you've all been waiting for," Cernunnos announced with a deep bow when Demi had finally been subdued. "The coronation of our new Head Crone. As you all know, to qualify, she must be a woman of wisdom, maturity, and grace. A woman of very advanced years. A woman who has served her husband faithfully and is done with the drudgeries of marriage and childbearing. A woman who need do nothing more now than be revered."

"I like where this is going," Ruth Anne said, propping herself up on her elbows.

"And so I offer you my beloved, and soon-to-be-ex-wife, Ingrid. My love, step on up here. Band, please play the Crone's March."

The fireflies circled the crowd, searching for the elusive Ingrid. They found her cowering at the end of a long bench. Everyone clapped as Ingrid stood nervously and walked forward. As she passed by I guessed her to be no older than 35. Tops. Not nearly old enough to be considered a crone. In fact, Aunt Dora would be insulted.

"But I—I wasn't even nominated," she said timidly as he placed a crown of dried and brittle leaves upon her head. Several crumbled in her hair. "I thought I still had a few good years left."

"Nonsense! You have been a good wife to me and this is your

reward! We will have your hut in the Faraway Woods made up as soon as possible." He kissed her hand and bowed. "You are welcome, My Crone."

"All hail the Crone! All hail the Crone!"

Ingrid meekly waved one hand as a bouquet of dead roses was placed in the other. She thanked everyone, though her face had drained of all color. Then she was escorted away, off the back of the platform.

"Look at the way Cernunnos is eyeing Merry," Ruth Anne said from above a goblet that had just been filled for the third time. "I don't trust him, Mags," she hiccupped.

"This is the Netherworld," I said. "Who can we trust? Merry's smart, and I trust her judgement."

"You know as well as I do that love makes you stupid." Ruth Anne sighed and called for another glass.

"Has anyone seen Shane?" I finally asked aloud. My anger at him had all but vanished, and was rapidly being replaced by fear.

"He said he was going off to clear his head," Paul answered, pointing towards a small grove of trees as he popped a cherry tomato into his mouth.

I stood, wiping the crumbs off my lap. Small birds immediately swooped to my feet and began pecking them up. "Clear his head?" I grumbled, my anger renewing. *He could have at least told me.*

I glanced around at the whirling dancers, the drinking men, the pipe-smoking boys, and the giggling girls. Shane was nowhere to be found. I locked eyes with a man so handsome that my heart froze. He strode forward and bowed. "May I have this dance?"

I didn't say yes but I didn't say no, and he promptly swept me into the frenzy. These creatures had such power, I thought, mesmerized by his appearance and sex appeal. He pushed closer to me, and I kept trying to remember what he was making me forget.

My baby. Shane. Shane. My baby. My baby Shane. Larinda. Armand. Madness. Three Days.

I looked down at my ring. I was a married woman. *What am I thinking?* I pushed him away, hard.

118

"Sorry!" I called over my shoulder as I ran towards the grove of trees. The further I went, the easier my steps became.

Soon, the sounds of the feast and accompanying merriment were muted, leaving me with only the sound of my footsteps. I walked along a lightly trod path, ignoring the harsh squawk of the crows that traversed the violet sky. The trees thickened into a proper forest, not unlike Dark Root's.

"Shane!" I called, my heart beating fast. My voice echoed, bouncing off the dense forest. I folded my arms across my chest as the air grew damp. It was late twilight, and I wondered how long the dwindling light would hold.

I should turn back, I thought, as the woods deepened and the path narrowed. But I wasn't sure there was a 'back' anymore. The trees were now sealing shut behind me, and not even my footprints remained. The sound of crackling leaves and snapping twigs on either side of me urged me forward. I kept calling my husband's name, wishing I had been smart enough to bring a flashlight.

"Shane!"

The woods suddenly opened into a small clearing, just as they often did in Dark Root. The glade was well-lit, and at its center was a majestic tree. A tree identical to the one Jillian tended. *The Tree of Life!*

I froze as I took it in. It was magnificent, with elegant boughs and shining leaves. It was surrounded by a golden-white halo of light, pulsing like a heartbeat. It was so beautiful I began to weep.

The Tree of Life? The Tree of Mother Frickin' Life, right here before me! I felt its power. It was the heart of the Netherworld. It was the heart of my world, too.

I crept closer, feeling unworthy of gazing too long, let alone, touch it. I felt around in my pocket for the acorn seed, massaging it in my hand as I drew nearer. Was this where I was supposed to plant it? It hardly seemed likely, given the tree was full and healthy.

"*Sssssss...*"

A gray snake slithered across the toe of my shoe and I screamed. The creature was gone as soon as I saw it, disappearing into the thick grass. I stood motionless, holding my breath. When I was fairly certain the snake was long gone, I carefully circled the tree.

It was much larger than its cousin in Dark Root, but indistinguishable in every other way, with two exceptions: This tree glowed, and the scar on the trunk was more pronounced. I wanted to touch its wound and heal it like Merry did, but my touch would most likely destroy it.

My death touch.

I fiddled with the acorn in my pocket. The tree, though sick, was clearly still alive. I wouldn't be planting the acorn here.

As I completed my circle around the trunk, I was startled to find a beautiful woman standing beneath one of the branches. Luxurious sea-green hair covered her bare breasts and torso. Her eyes were white, without any pupils.

"Maggie," she said, her voice only a breath. She extended a slender arm, beckoning me.

I found myself unafraid. I stepped closer, noticing a tiara in her hair. It was made of starlight or diamonds, and twinkled along with her slightest movement. She was young and smooth, without a line on her face or a worry in her eyes. She smiled at me, her white eyes unblinking.

"Who are you?" I asked.

A pattern emerged in the grass at our feet, a circle enclosing three misshapen spokes of a wheel, with us at its center. "Greetings," she sang. "I am Hecate, Guardian of the Tree of Life."

"Hecate! I've heard of you. You're a witch!" I said. When we were kids, Miss Sasha required us to learn *The Ode to Hecate* in order to earn one of her special 'magick badges.'

> *Hecate, flying through the sky,*
> *Taking solace in the night,*
> *Like a comet burning bright,*
> *We watched your magick flow.*

Until that day when men burned down,
Your village, and all else around,
Now only ashes there abound,
And to the Netherworld, you go.

You traded solace for revenge.
But when that moment comes again,
You'll laugh at all those heartless men,
Who'll reap all they have sown

Hecate smiled and her colorless eyes shimmered. "You have heard my poem?" She shook her head and her hair fluffed out around her, rearranging itself again to perfectly cover her exposed areas. "Technically, that is not factually correct. I never wanted revenge. The cold hearts of the wicked won't be undone by acts as trivial as revenge. Karma comes for everyone, and when it does, I will not laugh, but cry."

"You're much younger and more beautiful than I imagined."

She laughed gaily. "I am many things, at many times. Do not be deceived by appearances." She shrugged and petted the trunk of the tree. "Above, I am revered as a powerful witch. Below, I am a mere tree guardian."

"You have the most important job of all," I said. "If this tree dies, we all do."

"True. But what is death? Just another phase in an endless cycle of phases, I think."

"You're cynical," I noted.

"You might be too, if you had seen all that I have seen. I took refuge here, centuries ago. It is prophesied that someday the hearts of men will be purified, by trial or fire, and I await that time."

She sighed heavily, her hand falling upon the scar on the trunk. "The Tree of Life is but a shadow of its former glory. It weakens, rapidly. Its pulse and glow are subdued. If its light is extinguished entirely, no more souls will find their way. The Upper World, as well as my own, will descend into darkness."

Is that why Albert and the others couldn't find the light? Is it because the tree is fading?

"Is there any way to stop this darkness from coming?" I asked.

"Fate is involved, and fate is more powerful than me or even the Tree of Life itself. But there are rumors of a Seed Bringer, and my sisters and I await her with hope." She smiled again.

I didn't speak of the acorn in my pocket. Though I suspected she knew something from the way her lips pursed as she watched me.

Hecate reached high into the tree and plucked a large red apple that shone like a ruby. "For you," she said, offering it to me.

The snake slithered back out of the grass, growing longer and thicker as it coiled itself around the tree. Hecate paid it no heed.

I backed away, afraid again. "I don't want it," I said. The symbol on the ground around us sparkled like a live wire, and I was reticent to cross the fabled witch's threshold.

The snake hissed, lowering its head from a branch, watching us intently. Hecate stepped closer, her bare feet digging into the earth. "Magdalene, I am Guardian of the Tree of Life. Do you not trust me?" She stretched out her hand, proffering the apple again. "One bite, and you will see the truth."

The truth? It was the way she spoke the word 'truth' that appealed to me. A simple gift, and yet one we received so infrequently. "Why should I trust you?" I asked, backing to the very edge of the circle. "Even if you are the guardian."

She paused and put a finger to her chin. "Because I knew Jillian. I was there when she took the office of guardian, though she wasn't aware of it. I have watched her grow and I'm proud of the work she has done."

Hecate rolled the apple across her palm. It teetered magically on the edge of her hand, then rolled lazily back to the other side. *Tick Tock. Tick Tock.* The apple swayed. "I also knew Armand. I see both of them inside of you. And I see the confusion that entails."

"You knew my father?"

She laughed. "Everyone knows Armand here! He has tramped through my garden many times, with little regard to nature or our delicate ecosystem. He leaves a dark trail behind him." She motioned towards a plot of barren land at the edge of the glade. "When I sense his presence nearby, I cloak the Tree. I don't trust him, or those he conducts business with."

"I'm not my father," I said, absolutely.

"That is good. Armand has too much power as it is. His daughter... and his grandson... could give him more."

"I'm just here to find my son, and keep him away from Armand! Can you help me? I'm afraid Larinda will offer him to Armand."

Her eyebrows knit and the apple stopped rolling. "That is troubling, but it is not for me to intercede. I don't challenge fate. But I might be able to help *you* help yourself."

Once again, she extended her hand. The apple rolled from her palm into my own, fitting perfectly within my cupped hand. I let it sit there a long moment. It was larger than my fist, yet felt feather-light.

"Just one bite, for now. Eat more as necessary, but you must make sure to save one bite. Save it for just the right time."

I bit into the apple. It was the sweetest fruit I'd ever tasted, juicy and refreshing. A moment of dizziness followed, the world spinning, and I wondered if I had made a terrible mistake. Just as suddenly, my vision cleared.

"What do you see?" Hecate asked.

I focused my attention on the snake hanging from the tree. It flicked its tongue and its diamantine eyes grew larger. The serpent uncoiled its body from around the tree branch, and lowered itself towards me. I was no longer afraid.

We stared, eye to eye, our faces so close I could smell fruit on its breath. It smiled, transforming into a voluptuous naked woman. She dropped to the ground and stood before me, her ebony hair billowing around her curvaceous figure.

"Lilith!" Hecate said, clapping her hands. "That is no way to introduce yourself."

Lilith hissed, as if still in snake form, then shimmied and fluffed out her hair. Her face was so perfect it was hard to look upon without feeling the inadequacies of my own appearance. She looked me over, unimpressed.

"You smell like a man," she said, crossing her arms before her bosom. "I had hoped you would be handsome, and now I am doubly disappointed."

"But she is beautiful," Hecate defended me. "In her way."

"Hmm?" Lilith clicked her tongue and shrugged. "They are all beautiful when they are young. Wouldn't you say, Hecate?"

Hecate gave her a knowing smile. "True. But the young do not realize this, until they grow old."

"What does she do?" Lilith asked, circling me, her hips swaying as she wound around me.

"I do as I please!" I said, tired of them discussing me as if I weren't there.

"Ooh! Feisty! Not a marshmallow like some of the others. I might like her after all." Lilith lifted a handful of my hair and rubbed it between her fingers.

I yanked it out of her grasp. "I need to go," I said, looking again at the circle drawn around our feet. "Thank you for my gift, Hecate."

"Why do you need to go?" Lilith asked. "Hecate's tales may be droll but her fruits are exquisite. You should stay and join us. The Netherworld needs more strong women. We are far outnumbered here, but soon our day will come." She took note of the ring on my hand. "Of course," she said, her voice tinged with disappointment, "you are leaving your sisters for a man."

"Huh? No..." I hid my hand behind me, as if it were evidence of her accusation.

"Do you know the true nature of men's hearts?" Lilith challenged, looking me in the eyes. "They want power. Control. They want us beside them, but not as equals. As slaves and incubators. You would leave us for that?"

Hecate snorted. "You had one bad experience, Lil. Let it go."

Lilith spun towards Hecate. "One bad...one bad experience?! Excuse me!" She threw up her hands. "How can you defend the likes of men? They alone sent you here to hide and babysit this tree for all eternity. And speaking of the tree, do you remember why you are here? Because if MEN ever found it, they would chop it to bits and sell it all off, acorn by acorn, board by board."

Lilith turned back to me, and I wondered if she knew about the seed in my pocket. But she returned her attention to Hecate just as quickly. "You may not care about your place in this world, but I was the first woman, Hecate. Born at the time of the first man. And what do I have to show for it?"

Hecate said, diplomatically. "It is true what you said about my arrival, however, the choice to stay here has been mine alone. And, to your point, you are also here of your own free will."

Lilith seethed. "He should have been the one to leave. Not me."

"Who? What?" I asked, thoroughly confused.

"Do not suffer my fate," Lilith said. "Marriage is slavery, plain and simple. And any woman who goes along with it deserves what comes."

My wedding ring seemed to tighten at her words, either in agreement with them or aversion to them. "I don't have time for this," I said. "If I don't find my son, Larinda will turn him over to Armand. Please let me go."

"Son?" Lilith's expression changed. Her cheeks grew gaunt and her skin paled. "Are you Armand's daughter?"

"Weren't you listening to a thing we said when you were hanging from the tree?" Hecate asked, annoyed.

"No, I was too busy trying to discern this newcomer's gender." Lilith tapped her chin several times before speaking again. "Armand once tried to make a deal with me. I told him, plain and simple, 'Honey, there is nothing you can give me that I can't give myself.'" She shrugged with just one shoulder. "How can we trust that Armand's male descendant will not be just as corrupt as him?"

"He's my baby!" I stamped my foot and the ground trembled. Their expressions changed as they took renewed notice of me.

Hecate held up a hand. "Lilith, the rise of women will not come about through the destruction of men, but through coexistence."

Lilith snarled, but relented. "Fine. We will let you go. But only because I am curious about you, and I trust Hecate's intuition."

"And because she is the Seed Bringer," Hecate added.

"She is?" Lilith asked, surprised. "Why didn't you tell me? If this is true, we cannot delay her any longer!"

"So, can I leave now?" I asked, urgently looking around for an opening in the woods.

Hecate snapped her fingers and the symbol of the three spokes disappeared. "You are free," she said. "Safe travels, and do not forget your *primary* mission here."

With that, Hecate and Lilith began speaking of festivals and solstices, no longer concerned with me. A gap in the forest appeared and I scrambled for it before they could stop me.

The trail was clear and well-worn, though I wasn't sure where it led. I considered taking another bite of the apple, hoping for clarification. Thinking back to Hecate's warning, I decided against it. *You will need the final bite.* I clutched the ankh, desperate for it to glow.

Finally, I arrived at a fork in the trail. Shane said we shared abilities, now that we were married, and I decided to put that to the test. I thought of my husband, focusing on the grey in his eyes. The more I held his image in my mind, the closer he seemed.

"Go right," I said, with certainty. My ankh glowed. I felt the magick of the Netherworld course through me - like mercury.

As I set off, a butterfly floated out to greet me. And then another. Soon, I was engulfed in a cloud of white butterflies. They fluttered around me, giving a hopeful glow to the dusky world. My ankh hummed and I nearly skipped, feeling the pull of my conviction.

7

THE LOVERS

I looked down into a small valley, nestled between the gentle slopes of two hills. Below me, a shimmering waterfall splashed into a crystal-blue lake. Glowing rocks along the beach illuminated the water, in hues of green and blue and turquoise. The ankh flashed as I peered over the ledge. I made the long climb down, easily and without fear.

The water was inviting, and I slipped off my shoes to dip a toe into the quiet water. It sent small ripples across the water, wrinkling the harvest moon reflected on its surface. The pool was pleasantly warm, and so clear that I could see deep to the bottom.

I stripped naked and waded in, wearing only my ankh and bracelet. My hair bobbed around me like red seaweed. I ducked beneath the water and reemerged, feeling as free as a mermaid. I had never been a strong swimmer, but this water buoyed me. I laid back on and stared at the stars, wondering if this is what it was like to fly.

In the stillness of the evening, I heard a noise. I trod water and listened closely. Someone was speaking. I looked towards the waterfall, and could see the outline of a man standing behind it. I quickly slipped under the surface, just as he dove gracefully in. Before I could swim away, the man caught one of my legs, pulling me further under. I turned to face him.

Shane!

He grinned as he drew me into his arms, and we resurfaced together.

"How did you know it was me?" I asked.

"I felt it."

He slipped his hands around my waist and I planted mine on his shoulders. Together we bobbed along, gently kicking our feet beneath us. A drop of water collected on his bottom lip and I wiped it away with my finger, as if it were mine now.

"What are you doing out here?" he asked, still smiling. "Not that I'm unhappy to see you, but I thought you were having fun with the wood men."

"I missed you." I kissed him, overcome with gratitude at our reunion. "I'm sorry I got so upset. It was wrong."

He kissed me back, passionately. "No, I'm sorry. I shouldn't have spoken like your son was a burden. And trust me, you weren't that scary. I've seen you far worse."

"Hey!" I said, splashing him.

"Hey yourself!" He swam backwards, splashing me in return.

I could make out the outline of my husband's nude body, and I found myself warming. He caught me staring, and gave me a sideways grin. "I'm glad to see I haven't lost all my charms on you yet," he said.

"Nope. Your charms are both noted and appreciated." I pressed my forehead to his. We stared into each other's eyes, our chests pressed flat as we floated along.

"I need you," he said, tilting my head and kissing me. His breath was hot, and every muscle in his back tensed. I nibbled on his lower lip, working my way to his neck. We twined in the water beneath the stars, his hands on my thighs, my fingers digging into his shoulders. I wrapped my legs around his torso, desperate to be as close to him as possible.

"Come with me," he said, reluctantly breaking free. He took my hand and we dove to the bottom of the pool, lit by a bed of glowing rocks. As we swam towards the waterfall, I began to make out the entrance of a cave behind it. Swimming through the waterfall and into the cavern, I saw Shane's clothes, shoes, and cowboy hat were neatly arranged on the shore.

"Mi casa," he said, pulling me up onto the sand.

"I'm a little insulted you didn't invite me," I said, wringing water from my hair.

"I was going to, but you seemed so smitten with that guy you were dancing with."

I scrunched my brows. "You saw me?"

"Uh, not directly."

It might have been the effects of the apple, but I 'saw' Shane, sitting in the cavern, tuning in to me. I poked him in the chest. "You were spying! If you watched the whole thing, you know I was an angel in the end."

"My dear, you're always an angel in the end. It's the road you take to get there that worries me."

"Likewise."

"We are soulmates," he said, kissing my chin.

"Soul twins," I reminded him.

His hand combed through my wet hair. "Have I ever told you how much I love this mane of yours?" he asked. "It's the first thing I noticed about you when we were kids. Well, that and your fearlessness. You were like a lion."

"You have strange turn-ons," I said, reveling in the feel of his fingers on my body. We kissed, easily at first, but more urgently as it went on. He hardened almost instantly.

I needed him in every way. I knew that for certain. Perhaps it was one of the truths that came from the apple. I had tried to quiet my feelings so that I could tolerate any potential loss to come. But I couldn't. He was as much a part of me as myself.

I bit his earlobe, running my nails across his chest. "Shane," I moaned as my hands massaged his hips. "I love you."

"You say that like you'll never see me again."

"In this world, who knows. But we have right now."

I lowered myself to the ground, pulling him down on top of me. Our mouths locked together, fighting for dominance as we purposely delayed the moment that was to be our first time as a married couple. It was a memory to be savored.

When we could stand it no longer, he lifted my hips. He stared into my eyes, his beautiful body poised over mine. We had made love in dreamscapes before, but the Netherworld was no dreamscape. The ground beneath us was solid, and the air actually filled our lungs.

There aren't words to describe the scene, or my full emotions. But it was beautiful, and it was real and worthy of remembering every minute detail.

~

I laid my head on Shane's bare chest, listening to his heart beat. *Thump. Thump. Thump.* It was constant and reassuring, like the hands of a moving clock.

"Oh, no!" I sat up, my hair still damp as I scrambled for my missing clothes. They were back on the beach outside the cavern, along with my hourglass and other things. "Shane, wake up! We need to leave!"

How had we allowed ourselves to fall asleep?

"Don't worry," Shane said, tucking his clothes into his pack. "I didn't come out here just for a swim. I needed to be alone to get Montana on my radar again. There was too much noise back at the feast, and I needed silence."

"You found him?"

He smiled. "I did."

I smiled, too. "Why didn't you tell me?"

"I needed to be sure."

"Are you sure?"

"I am."

I stole a final glance at his naked body before we left our hidden cave. Snatching up his cowboy hat, I placed it on his head and stood back, framing him with my hands. "We need to get you on a calendar. The Sexy Men of Dark Root. We could make a fortune."

"You'd be so jealous. You'd fume every time we sold a copy."

"I'd be more annoyed at your growing ego each time you got a fan letter," I said, poking him hard in the chest. "Or every time a woman made googly eyes at you."

"You're making up this entire scenario, you know, and it's getting you all worked up. I see smoke coming out your ears."

"You're right. No calendars. Ever."

We ducked beneath the waterfall and swam to the beach, Shane managing to keep his pack out of the water the entire way. I dried myself as best I could without a towel, then dressed quickly. Fortunately, my belongings were still all there. I looked at the hourglass. Somehow, the sand didn't appear to have progressed at all! But maybe that was just a trick of my eyes.

Shane finished dressing, pulling on his cowboy boots. "Awe," I pouted. "Someday I want you to wear nothing but your hat and boots for me," I said, winking.

"Only if you'll do the same."

We found our way back to Cernunnos' village easily, the path leading straight to the encampment. As we approached, the sounds and smells of the festivities drew us in. There was a rumbling in the air as well, as if a storm were approaching. But the revelers didn't seem to notice - they danced and sang and ate, caught up in their merriment.

"Doesn't look like a whole lot has changed since I left," Shane noted.

I zeroed in on Cernunnos. He had his arms around Merry, her head resting on his shoulder as they swayed to the music. The Netherworld was suiting her, it seemed.

"They certainly don't look to be in any hurry to help find Eagle Mountain," I said. "It's a good thing you were able to tune in to Montana again."

Shane nodded, though the vein in his neck throbbed. "The signal is getting fuzzy again, Maggie. Maybe it's this area? All the congested magick here might be gunking up my system." He put his foot on a bench and looked around. Clouds had begun gathering now, casting a dark shadow over the east. They carried with them the sound of thunder, yet there was still no rain.

"What do you think that noise is?" I asked.

"Let's not stay to find out," Shane said. "We'll round everyone up and get gone."

By now, almost everyone was draped across the tables, full of food and wine. A few were still awake, talking in pairs around the bonfire. The trio of musicians finished their set, leaving the violinist alone, playing the saddest song I'd ever heard. Though I didn't understand the words, I felt its heartbreaking loss in every note.

I was dabbing my eyes when Eve found us. "Where have you been?" she demanded, pulling us away from the crowd and behind the communal building. "Do you even know what's going on here?"

"Looks like a party," I said.

"Do you notice anything unusual?" She crossed her arms.

I rolled my eyes, not having the energy for guessing games. "You think Paul's flirting with that serving girl?" He was talking to a petite, doe-eyed woman who was sitting beside him at a table. He laughed at something she said, and a strand of his dark-blonde hair fell across his eyes. She pushed it away. I felt Eve steaming beside me, but to her credit, she didn't storm over.

"No, I don't think Paul is flirting with that...woman creature. They're just talking about trees or something." Eve took a long breath and exhaled through her nose. "I mean, do you see what else is going on here?"

"They're all drinking different wine now," Shane said.

"How do you know that?" I asked.

"It's blue," Eve lifted her glass. "Ever since one of Tree Man's minions started pouring it, everyone's been going Looney Tunes."

I peeked out from behind the building and looked again. Ruth Anne was seated amidst a small group, her mouth opening and closing very slowly, as if having trouble articulating her thoughts. I realized Merry wasn't so much draped on Cernunnos' shoulder, as holding on to him for support. And Paul kept touching the serving girl's cheek, despite the fact that his nearby girlfriend was capable of neutering him with one of her potions.

"They're all drunk," I said. But as I concentrated, their auras changed, tinged with neon blue not visible on Eve or Shane. "You didn't drink any?" I asked my younger sister.

"I learned long ago not to take drinks from strangers," she said. She shuffled her feet, her eyes flitting angrily towards Paul.

"They'll sober up," Shane said. "I thought I smelled coffee somewhere. We'll keep an eye on them and force some caffeine down their throats."

"I also noticed they only gave the blue wine to us," Eve added. She lowered her voice and stepped closer. "I heard some locals talking about us making 'good additions.' I'm not sure what that means, but I can guess."

"To hell with that," I said. If they thought they could keep us here, they were wrong.

"There's more," Eve said, her expression uncharacteristically serious. She brushed her hair away from her face and straightened her clothes. "I went for a short walk after dinner and ran into a couple of Cernunnos' cronies. They were talking to some scary-looking shadowy creatures, and the conversation didn't seem friendly."

"What did these creatures look like?" Shane asked.

Eve was visibly nervous. "They were large and dark and... fuzzy? I don't know, but they were terrifying. They had these red eyes and their energy gave me the heebie-jeebies. There's something really bad about this place."

"The shadow's growing," I said, looking at the sky. The entire woods were nearly consumed. Darkness was coming and the moon, full as it was, was in no position to stop it.

My eyes scanned the forest's edge. Two humanoid forms were scurrying from tree to tree. One stopped to look at me. He smiled, and I could nearly taste his malevolence. Before I could point them out to Shane and Eve, they were gone. "I'm going for Ruth Anne first. Keep an eye on me in case there's trouble."

I made my way to my eldest sister and her entourage, feigning the same alcohol-induced smiles the others wore. I fell into her lap, wrapping my arm around her neck. "She's my favorite sister," I said aloud, slurring my words. "Did she tell you the story about the time she swallowed a fly? No wait, it was two flies, right Ruth Anne?"

"It was a dare," Ruth Anne explained to the others, her face comically serious.

The women wrinkled their noses and took their glasses, immediately leaving the table. Ruth Anne punched me on the shoulder. "Damn. They were cute. Thanks a lot, Mags."

"How are you feeling?" I asked.

"Great, if you don't count the fly-eating story. Cernunnos was right - this place is restorative." She reached for her goblet. "I wouldn't mind staying a while longer."

I took the glass and dumped its blue contents. "Ruth Anne. We have to go. We're here to find Montana, remember?"

She removed her glasses, cleaning them while she blinked at me. "Oh yeah. I didn't mean now. But it is nice, isn't it?" She reached quickly for the wine and took a gulp straight from the bottle.

"I hate to do this, but it's for your own good." I focused on the bottle and it shattered in her hands.

"What the hell? You could've cut me," she said, teetering on her legs as I led her back to Eve and Shane.

"She's way drunk," I announced.

"Not drunk enough," Ruth Anne said, chewing on her blue-stained tongue.

"We need a drunk tank," I said. "Or a sobriety pill."

"I think there's a spell for that...in the book...hic...but we don't have time for that," Ruth Anne stuttered, waving her hand. "It 'quires like...three...maybe four nights of naked dancing or something.... we don't have time for that."

Eve handed Ruth Anne a glass of water. "One down, two to grab."

"I'll get Paul," Shane said. "Maggie, think you can pry Merry away from Cernunnos?

"No, but I'm going to try."

As I made my way over to Merry, I noticed the impish shadow

creatures darting out from the woods periodically, blending almost seamlessly with the encroaching darkness. I shivered. What were they? And why didn't anyone else seeming to notice them? I reached into my pocket, rubbing the smooth side of the apple with my thumb. Was this worth risking a bite?

"That owl is a quite suitable companion for you." I overheard Cernunnos say, as I approached. "We have a great many birds here in our sanctuary. They are all well cared for, free to roam the forest. Starlight will make many new friends."

My sister, now wearing a crown of flowers, beamed as he kissed the tip of her nose.

"Merry, how are you doing?" I asked, smiling innocently as I joined the couple.

"Your sister has enchanted me," the king answered on her behalf. "Her life-giving work with plants and animals is unparalleled. She cannot be a mere mortal."

Merry blushed and touched a ring on her left hand, one I'd never seen before.

"What's that?" I asked.

"It is a gift," Cernunnos said proudly. "Merry has agreed to be my wife."

"You did what?" I snapped my finger several times in front of Merry's face, hoping to wake her from her daze. I looked at her place setting at the table. There were three empty wine bottles lying near her plate of half-eaten fruit.

I tried to stay calm as I reasoned this out. There were too many of them to fight through, and their magick was too strong. I had to know the 'truth' of what was happening. I turned away and inconspicuously took a bite of my apple. The world spun again. When I reoriented, the entire setting had changed.

The fruit on the tables was rotted and boiling with worms. The leaves on the trees were brown and dying, their branches thick and grotesque, knotted and twisted. The dancing women, the band, even the servants were no longer brightly clothed and luminous – they were sickly gray creatures with bloated bellies and bulbous noses.

When they spoke, the sounds coming out of their mouths were only grunts and clicks. Even Cernunnos' disguise fell away, revealing soulless eyes and glistening teeth. His antlers were sharpened to knives.

The only color came from Merry, who danced with light and beauty amidst the ugliness of this world. And then I noticed the lights in the trees remained as well, tiny beacons glowing even brighter against the stark backdrop.

Did that light in the tree just move?

I wandered over, until I was directly beneath the bough. Up close, the lights in the trees weren't twinkling, they were wriggling! They looked like Japanese lanterns, glowing from within.

There is a person inside! A person cocooned in a web of light!

The trees writhed with glowing orbs, the inhabitants thumping and rattling against their cages! A grunt from a nearby bush sent me into hiding behind the trunk. One of the imps emerged. It had long pointed ears and a heavy brow. The beast poked at a lantern with a stick, knocking it loose.

It fell to the ground, bouncing twice and rolling away, the captive still inside. The shadow-creature pounced, stabbing the lantern with the point of his stick. The cage deflated and the person inside vanished. The imp creature breathed in deeply, smiling with pleasure before skittering back into the woods.

Were these the tired souls Cernunnos spoke of?

I snuck back through the trees, to behind the communal building. Shane, Eve, Ruth Anne, and Paul were waiting impatiently for me. As quickly as I could, I explained what I'd seen.

"It sounds like those lanterns are soul incubators, and those creatures are consuming them before they reach maturity," Ruth Anne hypothesized, now sounding more sober. "I know demons feed on fear. Maybe these things feed on souls?" She rubbed her head. "I dunno. I'm still groggy."

"We still need to get Merry," Paul reminded us, rubbing his temples.

"I'll get her," Shane said.

I grabbed his arm. "She's drunk. And Cernunnos will put up a fight. Anyone got any ideas?"

"Nope, but I got a speel book...er, spell book." Ruth Anne handed over Mother's Book of Shadows, upside down.

I flipped through the pages, not sure what I was looking for. How could we get Merry away from Cernunnos? She didn't see him as he truly was. Nor did she see the people in the lights, or the shadow beasts.

My fingers stopped on an incantation titled, 'Eyes Wide Open.'

"Will this work?"

Eve surprised me by opening her designer backpack and taking out a small wooden mortar and pestle wrapped in cloth. Next, she pulled out herbs, a paper fan, and a vial of peppermint oil. Reading through the spell as she worked, she mashed the oil and herbs together. When she seemed satisfied, she passed the mortar over to me.

"Go ahead, Maggie," Eve said. "You're the strongest. We can't screw this up."

I scrawled the image of an eye into the dirt, reciting the spell.

See with the mind, not with the eyes.

Reveal the truths and expose the lies.

I flipped open the paper fan and waved away the scent drifting up from the mortar. One by one, the villagers arose from their stupor. They yawned and blinked, looking around, as if seeing their world for the first time.

Suddenly, I heard Merry scream and an alarmed snow owl flew off her shoulder. "What's happening?" she asked, hunkering against Cernunnos.

I waded through the festival, releasing the scent into the air. Reaching my sister, I dropped the bowl and lifted my wand. "Merry, get away from him. He's not who he appears to be. They want to harvest our souls, Merry."

Cernunnos was aghast. "I'm sorry, my queen, but your sister is not making sense. Perhaps she has drunk too much?"

Merry looked from me to Cernunnos, then at the misshapen creatures scurrying around us. "Who are you?" she asked the king.

"I don't harvest all the souls," he said defensively. "Just the ones I need for barter. How else do you think we keep the demons off our lands? If you want to eat omelets in paradise, you have to break a few eggs!

"Do you think this lifestyle comes cheap? Hades may be my cousin, but he doesn't cut me any deals on rent. The plants, the animals, the servants...they don't propagate themselves. And don't get me started on the cost of entertaining my people." Cernunnos tilted his head, rubbing his thumbs and forefingers together. "My world runs on life energy; without it, everything falls apart."

"But none of this is real," I said. "You eat rotten food and live in filth."

"The illusion is good enough for most," he said. He turned to Merry, clasping her hands. "Stay here with me. I'll keep you in wine and jewels."

Merry pulled away to stand beside me, drawing her wand. "Let us go!"

"I can't," he said. "Even if you don't stay willingly, you will stay. And your sister," he said, motioning to me, "will be traded. With her value, we will drink real wine and eat real food. And all my demon problems will be solved. Just think, your sacrifice will be for the greater good! No more souls will need to be harvested or traded."

The imps began closing in around us, poking at us with sticks as if checking for tenderness.

"Run!" I ordered Merry. I thrust out my hands, sending a wave of creatures skidding backward across the dirt.

Cernunnos grabbed Merry and she whacked his arm with her wand. It transformed into a thick vine, though immediately began repairing itself. Furious, he roared, his antlers lengthening, their sharp tips gleaming in the moonlight. "You will pay for this!"

"You will not harm them!" said a voice I recognized. Demi, the poet from earlier in the evening, marched regally forward, wearing a long white gown. She moved slowly, and as she passed each unlit torch, they sprang to life.

"Let them go, Cernunnos," she said. "Or else."

"Or else what, *crone?*" he asked with a sneer.

"Oh, am I the crone now? I wasn't a crone when you were rubbing those sandpaper hands all over me last night, was I? I'll bet your new *queen* doesn't know about your other queens." She turned to us. "He has three wives in this district. Who knows how many abroad? Thelemia didn't decide to leave, she was forced to. Cernunnos only likes things new and fresh." At this, she morphed into a beautiful young woman. "Even if it is only illusion."

Cernunnos looked her over with greedy eyes. "If you knew your place, I wouldn't need more wives, would I?" The two began passionately quarreling, and Merry and I broke away during the distraction.

Thunder rolled all around us. Not just overhead, but truly all around us. A sense of dread covered the land.

Where are Shane and everyone else?

My heart raced as the sound of footsteps pounded up behind me. Something grabbed my wrist and I cried out, turning to fight. But it was Shane, and the others were with him.

"Which way?" I asked him.

"Not far. Follow me."

"It's getting so dark," Ruth Anne said.

The hairs on my neck prickled, and a chill touched my spine. Even the moon seemed hidden.

This isn't just a storm.

"Gahabrien," I whispered. Though I couldn't see, hear, or even smell him, I felt his presence in my bones.

I absolutely knew it was him. He had haunted me, the proverbial monster in the closet, until we trapped him in a jar and buried him in Aunt Dora's garden. *Did Larinda set him free, setting him loose in this world?* "We need to find the next portal immediately."

"West," Shane said. "I can see the gate in my head."

We ran as fast as we were able, trying to outrace the darkening sky.

139

We passed by groves of trees filled with lantern cocoons. There were hundreds of them, all swaying in the branches.

"We can't leave these souls to be devoured," Merry said, stopping abruptly.

"Yes, we can," I replied, looking over my shoulder.

She stared at me with wide eyes. "These people were loved by someone. They deserve better."

I sighed and came to a stop. "Ah, hell! But just one tree."

We heard panting and growling in the distance, growing closer every second. And Gahabrien's dark energy was gathering. We didn't have long.

Ruth Anne and Shane scrambled up the trees and pulled the lanterns loose, dropping them down to us. We batted at them with our wands, releasing the brilliant white light within. As we watched them evaporate upwards, I felt a sense of peace, one that even Gahabrien's shadow couldn't dampen.

"Just one more tree," Merry said.

"No! They're almost on top of us!"

But Merry was already dashing to the next tree, reaching for another cocoon. She jabbed at the gauzy covering with her wand, freeing the soul quickly.

"Go on ahead," I called to the others. "I'll get Merry." I reached my sister as Shane fended off three imps barehanded. "We need to go right now!"

"Okay." She looked to the sky, her eyes frantic. "I forgot Starlight! We need to go back."

Shane backed towards us, imps nipping and clutching at his limbs. "The portal's just over the hill. I think the others are already there." He pointed up the slope and I saw a flash of gold over the crest. My ankh blinked with certainty.

The horde was almost on us now, led by Cernunnos himself. We linked hands and ran for the portal.

Halfway up the hill, Merry jerked free. "Starlight!" she cried, pointing to the sky. Her owl was flying towards us, and she ran in his direction, calling his name.

"Damn it," Shane said, veering off to chase down Merry.

"Leave her alive!" Cernunnos commanded his minions. "You can do what you please with the others."

I watched, frozen, as the horde scurried past Merry and converged on my husband. Dozens of them, rolling over him like a tidal wave.

"Get off of him!" I screamed, charging down the slope. I let loose my anger and imps flew in every direction. Others disintegrated where they stood, becoming piles of dust. But more appeared to take their place, and I was pushed further and further away.

I suddenly felt Merry's hands on me, pulling me back up the hill. "Maggie, we can't wait!"

I could feel the tears stinging my cheeks now. I couldn't see him! I couldn't see my husband.

My sister was dragging me away, and I could hear myself screaming.

I reached out, feeling my heart being yanked out of my chest, as the portal sucked me in.

8

THE CHARIOT

*P*aul stared at the man with the bushy beard and thick mustache for a long time. There was gray at his temples and crescent folds beneath his eyes. But though the man had seen a few years, Paul recognized him at first glance. It was Dave Dalton, a legend in the business. He had discovered Seattle bands like Roving Danger and Butterfly Horizon, and had even had his picture on the cover of Rolling Stone.

And here he was, sitting in the front row and nursing a beer, listening to Paul and his brother Eric play through their set. This was their big chance!

The brothers played through all the cover songs they knew, weaving in their best originals. Paul made a last-minute song change, catching Eric off guard, but his brother rolled with it. They were perfectly in sync tonight.

When the set was over, Paul stood up from his piano and Eric removed the strap of his guitar. The audience, by now mostly drunk, clapped and shouted for more. Good timing, thought Paul, as he disappeared with his brother behind the curtain.

"What the hell was that change-up for?" Eric asked, guzzling down a warm beer.

"That's Dave Dalton out there," Paul said, cracking the curtain and *pointing. "He's a bigshot music producer. Or at least he used to be, back in the '90s."*

Eric took a look himself, then turned to Paul, eyes wide. "What the fuck's he doing here?" Paul's brother was only younger than him by seven minutes, but they were very important minutes.

"He's checking us out. That's why I played 'Sylvia Sleeps.' It shows our full range."

"The hell it does. 'Reefer Gladness' runs the whole gamut! You know how the crowd reacts whenever we play it. You should have called for that one instead."

"You're just saying that because you wrote it." Paul scratched his head and wondered what the protocol was. They had dreamed of the day when an influential exec would hear them and offer a deal. Should they go introduce themselves?

"We have one more set coming up," Paul continued, looking at the clock as he sipped his water. "We'll do one of your songs, then one of mine. That way he gets the full package. Deal?"

"Deal."

They spit into their palms and shook, as they had when they were kids. Paul was the heart, but Eric had the soul. Paul could write beautiful lyrics, but it was Eric who was able to convey the emotion to the audience. With their combined talents, they were sure to impress Dalton.

They returned to the stage ten minutes later. Paul resumed his seat at the piano while Eric picked up an acoustic guitar. They began with 'Nowhere to Go', a song Paul had written about a man with no idea what he wanted to do now that he was an adult. It was a song of childhood dreams lost, one that usually received nods of acknowledgement from the men in the audience, and brought a few pretty girls to tears.

It was the best rendition of the track they had ever played. The audience was as still as stone while Eric's heart-wrenching voice called to them across the bar. A few people at a far table held up cameras and lighters, swaying them in the air. When the tune was over, everyone cheered. Paul was almost certain he saw a smile crack beneath Dave Dalton's mustache.

He winked at his brother. Eric grinned back. Paul then moved on to the drums, and they began their next song. "One, two, one-two-three..."

Eric strummed into a livelier song, a fun romp about partying too much and having to work the next day. The crowd clapped and stomped along, and a few danced beside their tables. Eric was so encouraged that he let loose an unexpected guitar solo he'd only played in his garage. The audience went crazy, raising their hands and howling as Eric's fingers glided effortlessly over the guitar strings. Dave Dalton leaned forward on his bulky forearms, squinting his eyes with interest. Even Paul was stunned by his brother's genius.

Even though Eric had broken protocol, Paul did his best to keep up. Dave Dalton at least seemed to be enjoying it. After five minutes, Eric finally returned to the actual song and the crowd hollered their appreciation. How a tune about drinking whiskey and picking up women got more attention than a poetic ode to life bewildered Paul, but he let it go. He would deal with his emotions later. Now, he needed to stay focused.

By the end of their last set, the audience would have followed them into battle.

"Dude, we killed it!" Eric said, back behind the stage.

"Yeah we did! Nice solo, by the way. I just wish you had let me know first."

"Sorry about that. I just got inspired. Loved the way you just joined in, though."

"Knock, knock. Can I speak to you boys?" Dave Dalton waddled over to them. His puffy cheeks were flushed and his brow beaded with sweat. He looked a bit like the Monopoly Man, without the top hat and monocle.

"Mr. Dalton." Paul grinned, extending his hand "I'm Paul and this is my brother, Eric. I'm a big fan. A big, big fan."

"I know who you are," Dave said, reeling his hand back in. "I received a call from a good friend about the two of you. Said you had raw talent, and she was right. I'd love for you to come up to New York on me and audition for a band I'm putting together. You'd both make awesome front men and it looks like you play multiple instruments."

"Yes, sir," they said at the same time.

"Good." Dave handed Paul a card and gave them directions. "Call my secretary, Jeanine. She'll arrange everything."

The brothers looked at the card, and then at each other, trying to keep their expressions from betraying them. "Thank you," Paul said, on their behalf.

"I better be going. Good to meet you both." Dave shook their hands, but when he shook Eric's, his eyes sparkled, and he held on a moment too long. "Loved that solo. You've got something special."

With that, Dave Dalton left.

"He said I have something special. Can you believe it?" Eric slugged Paul in the arm, then whooped out loud. "Can you fucking believe it?"

"Yeah, of course you do." Paul clapped his brother on the back.

After packing up their gear and collecting their pay, Paul dropped Eric off at his apartment. "Nice work, bro."

As he stepped out of the car, Eric swore, "By this time next year, things are going to be very different for us! Me and you bro. All the way."

Paul drove a few blocks, then pulled up to the curb. He pulled out the business card Dave Dalton had given to him, and called the number.

"Jeanine? Hi, My name is Paul and Mr. Dalton asked me to call you and..."

"Paul! Yes. David just spoke to me about you and your brother. He is very excited to have you two come up to New York. Can you leave on Friday?"

"Uh..." Paul put his foot to the gas and pulled away. "That would be great, but I don't think Eric can come this time. He has... obligations."

There was a long pause on the phone, and Paul was certain Jeanine would say that if Eric couldn't come, neither could he. He let out a sigh of relief when she said, "Just come alone then. I'll book your flight."

"Can I come sooner than Friday?" Paul asked, before he could talk himself out of it.

"Well, Dave won't be here until next week, but it might give us a chance to see your talents without having him breathing over your shoulder. He tends to make people nervous. Will Monday work?"

"How about tomorrow?" Paul asked.

"Enthusiasm! I love it. Okay then. I'll call when I have your flight information. See you soon!"

Paul pulled his dented Subaru onto the freeway, ignoring the accusing glares of passing drivers when his car couldn't push past forty miles per hour.

His eyes grew red and he began to cry. "I'm sorry, Eric," he muttered under his breath.

~

P aul knelt in the tall grass, cradling his face in his hands. "Oh, God," he whimpered. "Oh, God. Oh, God!" He rocked on his heels and his eyes were red.

I looked around frantically for Shane, hoping somehow he had been pulled in, too. Jillian had told me I'd know when someone was gone, that I would 'feel' it. But I didn't feel his absence. I only saw that he was not with me. I kept staring at where the gate should be, hoping that he would come through. With every breath, my chest constricted and my heart beat quicker. *Shane.*

"That was messed up," Ruth Anne broke the silence. "Paul, you left your brother for a dumb gig?"

"I know," Paul sobbed, on his knees, his eyes squeezed shut, as if praying for absolution.

"It's okay, Paul," Merry tried to reassure him. "You were young."

"He didn't look that young," Ruth Anne said. "Not as young as I was in mine, anyway."

Paul wiped his nose and found his feet. "Ruth Anne's right. About everything."

Eve hadn't yet spoken. She stood motionless while her boyfriend tried to stop his tears, not offering a single word of consolation. Finally, she walked up to him and pushed him forcefully in the chest. "You have a twin? I've known you three years and you've never once mentioned a brother, let alone a twin. Where was he when we were in Seattle last winter?"

"Gone. He died a few months after I left." Paul's lips trembled and he lowered his head, his hair falling over his face as if to shield him. "O-o-overdose," he managed to stutter. "I never even got to say goodbye before Mom spread his ashes on Puget Sound."

"Geez," Ruth Anne said. "I didn't know. Sorry, man."

"Not geez! Definitely not *geez*!" Eve faced Paul, unblinking. "Who

146

are you?" she asked, taking a small step back and putting out her hand. "I feel like I don't even know you."

My heart broke for him, even as Eve looked at him as if he were a monster. But at least she still had him. I stretched my neck again, looking around desperately for my husband. The portal was long gone.

"Where's Shane?" Ruth Anne finally asked, noticing we were a person short.

I pressed my lips together, unable to explain. I pointed limply to where the gate had been. "They got him."

"Shane? Not Shane," Ruth Anne said, her voice begging me to tell her I was kidding. I shook my head and told her of the swarm of shadow creatures. Then, we were all sobbing along with Paul.

The Netherworld was taking its toll.

"Starlight didn't make it through either," Merry said, drying her eyes. She sucked in a breath and straightened up. "But there are more important things right now."

I turned on her, my hands now fists. "You're right we have better things to worry about than an owl! I lost my husband because of you and that owl."

"Try to stay calm, Mags," Ruth Anne said, putting a hand on my shoulder. "We need to figure this out, calmly."

I shrugged her off. "You calm down!"

"Maggie's right," Merry admitted. "If I hadn't wanted to free those souls, and then tried to get Starlight... Oh, Maggie! What have I done?"

"Oh, no you don't." I said, feeling my anger elevate further. "You don't get to play martyr. This is your fault, end of story." I pulled leaves from my hair, trying to think what to do next. I couldn't lose Shane again, but I had no way to get back to him. And Montana was still out there, somewhere.

My ankh hadn't sparked since crossing, and without Shane I had no idea what to do or where to go. I flung my back against the nearest tree. I had hoped I could take on the Netherworld, but it was winning.

"We should go," Merry said, looking up.

147

The sky was bland and colorless, as if it too had given up. There were tall gray rocks and sickly looking trees. All traces of the beauty of Cernunnos' world had vanished, and I had to remind myself that all this was an illusion anyway.

"We're not going," I said, stubbornly. "Not until we have Shane."

"He's not coming," Merry said gently. "Maggie...he's...."

"No!" I covered my ears. "I don't believe it. I don't believe you."

"Honey..."

"Don't honey me! This is all your fault. I never want to see you again."

There was a collective gasp. Even Eve's mouth dropped open.

"You don't mean that, Mags," Ruth Anne said.

"I do!"

Thunder rippled across the sky. Everyone looked upwards but me. Had I done that? Or was it the new landscape? There was no sign of the darkening shadow that had loomed over Cernunnos' land, but there was a feeling of impending... something.

"I'm so sorry, Maggie," Merry tried again.

I twisted the ring on my finger. It didn't feel dead. Shane couldn't be either.

"Stay focused, Maggie," Ruth Anne said, looking at my ring. "Can't you see what this world is trying to do? The shameful memories the portals make us watch? Even the encounters with Cernunnos. This world is trying to pull us apart. It's one of the rules of war: divide and conquer."

The air was chilly, and two half-moons were poised opposite one another in the sky. As my eyes adjusted to the new setting, I noticed more trees than I had first assumed, flanking us on both sides. We were on a wide path that cut through the middle. Patches of heavy fog billowed in shallow dips in the landscape. I gave an involuntary shiver as dozens of small yellow eyes blinked from the darkness beyond the fog. I focused on a single pair, daring them to challenge me.

"What are we going to do, Maggie," Eve asked.

I sniffed and shook my head. "I don't know."

"But Montana..." she said, quietly.

But Montana.

But Shane.

I looked back at the missing portal. If someone had plunged a knife and twisted it into my heart, it might have hurt less. I checked the hourglass. It was half full.

What are we going to do, Maggie?

I breathed deeply, trying to find calm. If Shane was alive, he would find us, even if we went on. And if he wasn't... I refused to think of that now.

"I don't like the vibe here," Merry said.

Forward was as good a direction as any. I took one step, and then another. Slowly, I made my way, my feet iron weights. Even as I took another step, hoping it would lead me towards my son, there was unease because I was leaving Shane behind.

The others followed, keeping their distance. They didn't offer words of comfort anymore, probably fearing I'd snap at them. But even their silence invoked my anger. "It's your fault," I repeated to Merry whenever she tried to get close. The accusation made me feel stronger. More resolved.

"Maggie, I didn't mean for any of this to happen," she said.

"Those souls weren't our problem. And that owl... did you think you'd bring him back to Dark Root with you?" My strides were long and purposeful now. As long as I kept moving, I felt like we were doing something. My anger combatted the gloom of this region, which was as sticky and oppressive as quicksand.

Merry eventually grabbed me by the hand, pulling me to a halt. "Now listen, little sister. I'm sorry about Shane. I really am. I loved him too, Maggie."

"Don't say *loved!* How dare you say *loved!*" *Love was present. Loved* was finality.

I had lost my son, his father, and my husband - and I wasn't sure if I'd see any of them, ever again. There was too much bottled up inside of me. Too much loss. I needed to release. I spread both hands, arcing them out to my sides, yelling at the world as I scorched the trees around us. Flames stripped their branches, blackening the trunks. The flames disappeared, replaced by drifting cinders.

"Whoa!" Ruth Anne gawked, looking from me to the trees and back again. "Don't fuck with Maggie."

"That's right!" I challenged the Netherworld. "Don't fuck with Maggie! I'll burn this whole damned world to ashes before I let you take me down!"

"Shh..." Eve said, looking around, as if my challenge might be accepted.

"I don't care who hears. I'm done being nice. Let it come for me."

"Quiet," Paul said, holding still. "Listen." The ground shook, enough to stir the puddles of water dotting the path. Then came the sound of thundering hooves, galloping towards us. "Get off the trail!" Paul ordered, pulling us into a clump of shrubbery.

A monstrous black horse came charging into view, its hooves as white as its long teeth. It was nine-feet-tall from hoof to head, breathing out billows of smoke. It skidded to a halt on the trail before us, its nose down and its eyes coal-red. The steed whipped its neck around, snorting and stamping in the dirt.

I peered through the leaves, hoping to get a better look. Riding the horse was a tall man in a long gray cloak, holding a lantern. He lifted his light and swung it in a slow arc. I held my breath, not daring to exhale.

"What the..." Ruth Anne whispered.

The rider pulled back his cloak. He had a jack-o'-lantern head with yellow eyes and a permanent wicked smile. His gaze and the lantern peered at the scorched trees. *Was he going to find us?* I tried to will my heart to stop beating, as if it might betray our location. Finally, he snapped the reins. The horse reared up and stampeded off.

"I think I just peed my pants," Ruth Anne said.

"Still want to take on the Netherworld, Maggie?" Eve asked, as she crawled out from the vegetation and brushed off her blouse. "What was that thing, anyway?"

"The Headless Horseman, I believe," Ruth Anne said.

"What the hell is he doing here?" Eve asked. "Isn't he from a book?"

Paul examined the horse's footprints, stamped into the wet earth. "Actually, he's from a short story by Washington Irving. He wrote that the horseman lost his head from a cannonball in the Revolutionary War."

"Yep," Ruth Anne agreed, grinning now that the danger had seemingly passed. "His head splattered all over the battlefield and his friends had to carry his body off without it. It's said that he rises every Halloween to look for it, taking the heads of others to replace his own. It's a great story, if you're not living it."

Eve looked between the two of them, shook her head, then walked off. Paul eventually followed.

"What's Eve's problem?" Ruth Anne asked.

"Her boyfriend is giving you more attention than her," Merry said matter-of-factly, as if it were obvious.

We continued along the trail, following the horses hoof prints, listening carefully for the sound of his return. Owls occasionally screeched from the tree boughs, causing Merry to look pitifully over her shoulder in hope that one was Starlight. The two moons moved closer together as the night wore on, until they formed a single bright yellow disk, seeming near enough to lasso. The fog grew thicker as well, and bone-chillingly cold. We were down to one flashlight and could only see a few yards ahead. Paul and Eve led the way, neither speaking.

"This place has a gothic feel to it," Ruth Anne said, removing her Geiger counter from her pack. She handed me the flashlight as she conducted her search. After several minutes, she announced, "No radiation levels, but who knows what's normal for the Netherworld?"

"How big is this place?" Merry asked.

Endless.

As we walked, the trail transitioned into a cobblestone road. Eve's boots clicked underfoot, ringing like horseshoes hammered on an anvil. Eventually we reached a crossroads. A sign was planted beside it, in the center of a spoked circle, like the one in Hecate's garden. It pointed in three directions: Left, right, and forward. I stopped to feel around for the acorn in my pocket. Was I supposed to plant it here?

"Head's up!" Paul called out as the sky darkened two shades.

Bats. Thousands of them. So dense that they momentarily blotted out the conjoined moons. Eve scrambled for Paul, but as soon as he took her hand, she pulled away.

Ruth Anne crouched low and covered her head, her eyes truly terrified. "Make them go away, please!"

As if to fulfill her wish, the bats disappeared into the night.

"Um, I think bats are the least of our worries," Merry said, tapping me on the shoulder. To our right, a stream of raggedy people filed out of the woods. They carried flickering torches and pitchforks.

A woman with frazzled hair spotted us and pointed. "Witches!"

"Burn them!" A man thumped his staff against the ground. "Burn them all!"

They ran for us, with hobbling knees and greedy fires. *We're being chased again? Why are they even after us?* I didn't have time to ponder it. I focused, and my amber bracelet sparked, shooting a blue sphere of light around us.

"Which way Maggie?" Merry asked, looking around anxiously.

"We're not running this time."

The horde was almost upon us, screaming obscenities.

"You will leave us alone!" I raised my hands high. Lightning cracked across the sky. It struck a nearby tree, halving it as it fell. I snapped my wrist, as if wielding a whip, and another round of lightning sounded. "You really want to mess with a witch?"

The ragtag mob fumbled to a halt, stepping back and lowering their torches. A few made a hasty sign of the cross.

I opened my palm and their torches went out. And then, one by one, they all began to flee. All except a solitary woman. "You'll burn in hell," she promised.

I took a step forward, sensing a familiarity about her. *Leo's mother?* Before I could know for sure, she too, disappeared into the mist.

I fell against the signpost, nearly spent.

"How...what...how?" Ruth Anne asked.

I looked at my offending hands, and then at my sister. "There's so much inside of me that wants to get out."

"You're weakened now, Maggie," Merry said. "You need to rest."

I looked to the horizon. There was still no sign of Eagle Mountain. And I had no idea which direction to go. It was more exhausting to make hard decisions than to set fires. "We have to keep moving," I said, looking at the sign. There were no words, only arrows. My eyes lingered to the left for a long moment, before I spoke. "Let's go right."

I looked periodically back at the two roads I hadn't chosen, hoping I'd made the right decision. Occasionally, I peeked at my hourglass. The sand was moving quickly, and nearly half was now drained. *What happens when there is no more sand?*

The cobblestone road reverted to gravel and the trees continued to watch us. Large barrel-trunked oaks that in earth time would be centuries old. Many were covered in layers of pungent dark moss, the smell wrinkling my nose.

"I feel light-headed," Merry said, stumbling.

"Me too," Ruth Anne admitted. "Maybe we still have some wine in us?"

"No, I think..." Eve crumpled to the ground. Paul went to her, tapping her cheek, and her eyelids fluttered open. "What happened?" she asked, groggily.

"You fainted." Merry put her hand on Eve's forehead. "Your energy is depleted."

Eve snorted as she stood up, daring her wobbly legs to defy her. "My energy is never depleted."

"You okay, babe?" Paul asked. Eve's response was to glare.

We walked on, looking and listening for horsemen and bats and witch-burning-mobs. Our shoulders slumped as the night weighed on us. "All these things were cool in the books and movies I loved," Paul said. "I had quite the collection at one time."

"Paul's always been into the dark and creepy," Eve said.

"Must be why he likes you," Ruth Anne teased.

I looked at Paul as I chewed on my lip. "You know, your subconscious may be creating this reality," I said. "The last portal we went through affected you, and it's your imagination we are catching glimpses of."

His brows pulled down over his eyes. He pressed his lips together and rubbed his hands. "Let's just hope this is as bad as it gets," he said. "I grew up on old horror movies. Who knows what else is trapped in my head?"

"Clear your mind, Paul" I ordered.

"Uh, it might be too late." Ruth Anne pointed down the road, towards a looming gray tablet protruding out of the ground, enclosed behind a rusted black iron gate. An enormous raven sat atop the stone, watching our approach. If its head hadn't been moving to follow us, I would have sworn it was stone, as well.

Paul stopped, turning to face us. He held out his arms, barring us from going any further. "No, please! We need to turn around."

"We can't," I said, noticing that the ankh had finally awoken. Its glow was dim but present. And the path we were on led directly to the iron gate.

"Nevermore," the raven squawked loudly, focusing its amber eyes on Paul. "Nev-er-more!" With that, the bird flapped its mighty wings and flew into the night, cawing as it circled overhead, twice.

I caught my breath, nodding. "The raven's gone, Paul. We can go through now."

"That's not what I'm dreading."

Ruth Anne touched his shoulder. "It'll be okay."

He gave her a grateful nod and led us towards the gate. His legs were quivering and his teeth chattered audibly, but he continued nonetheless.

More than anything, I wished Shane were here. If whatever lay beyond that gate could scare Paul so badly, I wasn't sure I wanted to face it either. Rubbing my ankh like Aladdin's lamp, I hung close behind him.

At our approach, the gate swung open, as if expecting us.

"This isn't fun anymore," Merry said. "I don't want to go in, either."

I looked at her. "Well, you're free to go back to the Tree King if you want. I have zero choice in the matter."

Merry glanced behind her, but all that was visible was the bright yellow moon and the white rolling fog. There was no way back. This was a theatre, and we were the unwilling performers.

Paul swallowed and stepped through the gate. His sneakers made a squishing sound as they sank into the wet earth. We all huddled close, making our way to the stone tablet. I jumped as the gate snapped shut behind us.

Patches of the ground were layered in thin ice, and the air was so moist I choked. We were in a cemetery, with old cracked stones and dead flowers laid at their feet. The opposite gate lay beyond the ominous monument of stone, and we could only reach it by passing by.

"I can't," Paul whispered.

"You have to," I said.

The slab gleamed like polished rock amidst the other old grave markers. It was new. Fresh. Paul fell to his knees before it and we held our breaths as words carved themselves into the tombstone.

Eric Stolson.
1987-2008.
Cause of Death: Shameless Brother.

Paul fell backwards and crawled away, turning onto his stomach and scrambling into a run. Ruth Anne raced after, nimbly leaping over tombstones to grab him. She put her arm around his shoulder as he sobbed. I looked to Eve, whose eyes showed a mixture of pity and betrayal.

"Go to him," I whispered to her.

"I can't." Eve lowered her head and turned back to the gravestone, mouthing the inscription to herself.

Merry approached Paul, opening her pouch and producing an orange flower. "I wasn't sure why I brought this," she admitted shyly. "It's a Sunrise Flower. It provides comfort to those who have crossed over. I have blessed it, and it will give you both peace."

Paul looked at Merry with gratitude as he took the bloom. "As long as *he* finds peace," Paul said. "I deserve none." Weeping, he placed the flower on the tombstone and the rest of us stepped back to give him some privacy. He spoke to his brother quietly, his entire body shaking with grief.

"That's not even his real grave," Eve said. "And Merry, there's no such thing as a Sunrise Flower."

Merry smiled softly. "I know. But he doesn't."

We didn't rush him. When he returned to us, his eyes were dry, as if he'd cried every last tear. "I can go on now," he said.

The gate beyond the grave opened, like a maître d' showing us our table.

My ankh glowed nearly as brightly as the moon. As we walked through the gate, our next portal appeared not far off. It lit up the foggy night as gloriously as any star. We ran for it, and all the while I knew it would only take me further from Shane, but would hopefully bring me closer to my son.

9

STRENGTH

I sat, rocking on the lid of the toilet seat, looking at the double pink lines on the pregnancy stick. Surely, this had to be a mistake. I'd only had sex with Michael once in the last few months, and I hadn't been with anyone else.

Once was enough, I thought grimly.

I thought I was meant for bigger things than simply being a mother. I was the Sworn One.

The Sworn One.

I'd heard Aunt Dora and Mother refer to me by that title when I was younger, when they didn't know I was listening. "Her magick is thick," Aunt Dora said while the two drank tea in her kitchen. "No one will be able to equal her, once she's trained."

"Training will take another lifetime," Mother said with an indifferent snort. "And we don't have that kind of time, even if she is still young." Sasha swirled her tea leaves, hoping for a good fortune. She frowned and put down here cup. "She's a wilder. She'll get into trouble if she isn't watched. She may even end up like..."

"We watched that man like a hawk!" Aunt Dora retorted. "Look what good it did us. If Maggie's really the Sworn One, it'll work out."

They stared at one another and swallowed, though neither any had tea left in their cup.

And now, twenty years later, I understood what they were worried about. I was reckless and undisciplined like my father.

A baby!

I couldn't have a baby. Not when the baby's father was now out of my life. And how was I going to tell Shane I was having another man's child? I was falling for him, but that would be over now.

"Fuck!" I broke the stick in half and screamed the word into my knees, then tossed the two halves into a wastebasket, burying it deep. I inspected my panties, hoping for the telltale drop of blood.

Did I look pregnant? I stood and examined myself in the mirror, turning to the side. There was a slight swell to my belly and a puffiness to my face. Even my wrists and ankles looked bloated. I put my dress on quickly, before I screamed again.

I didn't want the baby. In fact, I abhorred the idea. How could I love a child created by the man I detested?

There were things I could do. I could go to another town and do it under a false name.

But I was a witch, one of many in my family. I didn't have to go anywhere. There were pills and potions and Mother's spell book. I'd over-heard Sasha advise women when I was younger - women with dark-circled eyes and swollen bellies and few choices. Mother prescribed them herbs and sent them on their way. "Put this in your tea for three days and three nights," she'd say. "And tell no one."

I never knew what happened during the course of those three days, but I'd sometimes seen the women wandering around town soon after, a relieved look on their faces. Mother always seemed troubled after these visits, but she wore it with a look of duty and never turned anyone away.

I could talk to Aunt Dora and find out what herb that is. Or research it myself. Or search Mother's cabinets. Perhaps she still has some, from days gone by.

"I don't want you," I said, putting my fingers on my abdomen as I stared hard into the mirror. "I hate you and I just want you to go away."

~

I had secretly hoped I was immune to the truth portals. I thought I had no more secrets to tell. But my heart still had one – and now, as the smoke cleared and I stood shivering on the other side of the gateway, I felt completely exposed.

Eve, Merry, Ruth Anne, Paul and Michael stood staring at me.

"Michael!?" I exclaimed, trying to ascertain if this were real. His chest rose and fell, yet he said nothing. "Michael! Thank god!" I eventually said, wrapping my arms around his very real body. "Where did you come from?" I looked around, hoping that Shane had come through the portal, too.

He scratched his head, confused. We were once again standing in daylight - early morning from the looks of it. We were in a wide and beautiful valley, sun rising over the hills on the horizon. The grass was a vivacious green and there were whimsical flowers of every color and description - some the size of pebbles and others growing taller than my head. I had seen a painting like this once, in a gift shop in Northern California, and I'd always wished I could go there. And now I was, but the setting was too beautiful to accept the memory I had revealed.

"I thought I heard you call for me... then I was sucked in," Michael said.

"Thank god!" I said. "But how?"

"Maybe he got pulled in because he was part of your memory?" Ruth Anne offered. "Makes as much sense as anything else, I guess."

I looked around again, hoping Shane would appear, as he was also part of the memory. There was no sign of him. But Michael's return meant that anything was possible in this world, and that was enough to give me hope.

There were no roads or paths, only the open grass, but it was a welcome relief after Paul's landscape. But I knew even the most beautiful worlds could suddenly turn dark on us in the Netherworld, and I wouldn't let my guard down again. I started walking, and the others joined me. We hadn't traveled far when Michael spoke up.

"You hated me that much?" he asked, catching up to me. The gray in his hair had nearly doubled. His pants were dirty and his face gaunt. His eyes were rimmed in red, and there was an abnormal heaviness clinging to him. I wanted to know where he'd been, and what he'd seen. He obviously hadn't found our son, but something had clearly occurred.

"I know I screwed up, Maggie, but I didn't realize it was bad enough for you to consider getting rid of our son."

"Please Michael, let it go," I said. "That was a year ago, a lifetime away."

"How can I let it go?" he asked, raising his voice. "You really wanted to get rid of our baby."

"Yes, I did," I answered honestly.

"Can you blame her?" Eve said, speaking up for me. "You cheated on her. Not to mention that no one wants to raise a baby in a dumb commune."

"Maggie lived in that 'dumb commune' for many years and was very happy there."

"Apparently not that happy," Eve said.

I couldn't look at Michael. In fact, I couldn't look at any of them. Now that my mind had cleared after the portal, the guilt was unbearable. I had forgotten how badly I had wanted the baby gone when I learned of my pregnancy.

"Do you ever think you brought Montana's disappearance on yourself?" Michael asked. "You're always saying 'words have power.'"

"Are you trying to pass the blame of losing Montana on to me, Michael? Of course I didn't curse my own son," I said, speeding up, as if outrunning him would outrun the thoughts in my head.

"I'm just saying, it's a possibility."

The color of this new world sharpened, as if coming into focus. There were a few trees along the way, whimsical and exotic, as if we had stepped into a child's storybook. They twisted and twirled, climbing towards the sky. Fanciful birds chirped at us and willows danced in the breeze. It would have been lovely – a vacationer's paradise - were the circumstances not so dire.

"You never answered my question." Michael pressed. "Did you really hate me so badly you hated our baby, too?"

"Michael, I had no job skills and I was on my own. How was I supposed to feel?"

"I don't know. Joyful about creating a new life? I mean, it was a gift from God, Magdalene."

"Go to hell," I said, seething. Knowing he only called me 'Magdalene' when he was trying to shame me. "Don't try to mess with my mind, Michael. I kept the baby. I loved...*love* Montana. It was a quick thought, nothing more. Millions of women have had that very same thought. If that's my darkest secret, I can't wait to see what yours is."

"I have no secrets," he said, spreading his palms. "My soul has been washed clean."

I marched ahead silently, contemplating Michael's accusation. Was he right? If I were truly the Sworn One, had my words really cursed my own son?

Oh, what a tangled web...

I stopped in the middle of the field, realizing my ankh hadn't blinked at all, and the grass seemed to stretch on forever. Michael offered no information on where he'd been, and no one dared ask yet. His face was that of a soldier's, returning from war.

"Any thoughts?" I asked as we came to the bank of a turquoise stream, popping with fish.

Ruth Anne got out her compass and began beating it again. "According to this piece of crap, every direction is north."

"Too bad there are no maps of the Netherworld," Merry said, stopping to pick a flower. It was cotton-candy pink, as large as a teacup, and as fragrant as Eve's exotic perfume. She tucked it behind her ear and smiled.

The air was warm and pleasant, though stiff and unmoving, as if someone had set the thermostat to precisely comfortable. We walked beside the creek, and the water sparkled in sharp contrast to my mood. I was tired and my earlier optimism was quickly fading.

"Can we stop, just for a moment?" Merry looked longingly at the water. "I just want to dip my toes."

"We don't have time."

"You said there is no time here."

I palmed the hourglass, but didn't dare look. "We need to keep moving."

Soon, we were up to our calves in wildflowers and the air was sickeningly sweet.

The sun continued to rise, and Merry removed her sweater and tied it around her waist, as if simply on one of her nature hikes. "I wish I'd brought my water bottle and dried fruit," she said, glancing at the inviting water again.

I gave her a sideways look, which she caught.

"Wanna talk," she asked?

"No."

"Okay, I understand." She kept pace beside me, humming along with the sounds of nature. I couldn't help but still feel my anger. If it wasn't for her and that owl, Shane would still be with us.

"I heard you think that," Merry said.

"Think what?"

"That it's my fault that Shane's gone."

"That's not exactly classified information."

"I was trying to help, Maggie."

Her words caused me to stop. "You mean you wanted to help everyone but us?"

"What was I supposed to do? Those souls were in danger, and so was Starlight. Tell me what I should have done differently, before you put all the blame on me."

"I don't put all the blame on you, just most of it. Now leave me alone, please"

"I'm sorry," she said, her blue eyes tearing up. "You have no idea how sorry I am."

I clenched my fists. *Sorry?* She had everything, and I had nothing. And she was *sorry?*

The patch of grass where I stood withered beneath my feet. "Merry, I need space. I feel like I've been beaten up and left for dead, and the only thing keeping me going is the very thin slice of hope that

I may – *MAY* - find my son and Shane again. So forgive me if I need time alone." I fidgeted with the hourglass, wondering how much more sand had sifted away while we spoke.

"Well, I'm not leaving you alone," my sister said, defiantly lifting her chin as she folded her arms across her chest. "And you can't make me."

"I can't make you? Is that a challenge?" My fingers tingled as the magick of the world coalesced around me, begging for me to use it.

"Yes," she said. "It is a challenge."

Game on, sister. I snapped my fingers and pointed at a nearby fallen log. It rolled towards Merry, not stopping, forcing her to leap out of the way to avoid it. The log was small enough that it wouldn't have hurt her, but I needed her to see who she was dealing with.

"Oh? So, that's how it's going to be?" Merry drew her wand out of her skirt pocket and slapped it across her open hand, like a school mistress preparing to dole out justice to an unruly student.

Whispering winds
And ancient trees
Catch the witch
Before she flees

A drooping limb from a nearby tree unfurled like a long arm, and quickly wrapped itself around my leg. I tried to yank away, unable to move. Merry smiled smugly as I fought to disentangle myself, growing angrier by the moment.

"Don't mistake my compassion for weakness," she said. "I may not be a wilder, but I'm no wilting flower either." She raised her wand in warning.

I pulled out my own wand and swatted it across the limb. It quivered and turned gray, and the entire tree turned to dust. "That's on you," I said, eyeing her over my wand.

The others stepped back, staring in disbelief as Merry and I slowly circled each other, like two wrestlers seeking an opening.

"Spells are too slow, Merry," I said. "Too bad you rely on them." I flicked my wand towards a bluebird perched on a rock. It became a snake, with piercing eyes and a darting tongue. It slithered toward Merry and she screamed.

Merry muttered under her breath and blew into her hands. She pointed at the snake before it could reach her, returning it to its bluebird form.

"That was cruel and stressful to the poor creature," Merry chided. "You have no respect for nature." She scrunched her face and pointed her wand towards a grouping of pink butterflies.

"Double. Double. Double. Double.
Let's see Maggie break this bubble."

At each repetition of the world 'double,' the butterflies grew in both size and number. Soon, there were a hundred butterflies the size of rabbits, all swarming around me. They dive-bombed my hair, tickling my face, my arms, my shoulders. I swatted them away with my hands as best I could.

"Be glad that butterflies don't bite," Merry said, enjoying her victory. "Unlike snakes."

I stumbled backwards, nearly tripping over the log while I fought to escape the swarm. Exasperated, I swung with my wand wildly. With each pass, several crumpled.

When I had cleared enough to see again, I bored my eyes into the ground near Merry's feet. The earth around her began to shake. Small sinkholes formed, pulling in everything like an imploding anthill. Merry jumped and dodged, trying to avoid falling in.

"Ladies..." Michael implored. "Perhaps you should both calm down."

My sister and I turned our wands on him, and he stepped back, palms out.

"Where were we?" I asked Merry. With our concentration momentarily broken, the remaining butterflies had flitted away and the ground had stabilized.

"You're up," Merry curtsied. "Let's see what the *Sworn One* can do."

Her mockery triggered something primitive and wild inside of me. But it wasn't just her words - it was the tempting call of the Netherworld and its limitless magick. Once tasted, it was an addictive drug, and I could take in as much as I could hold.

I fanned my hands out before me. A wind funnel rose up from one of the collapsed pockets in the earth. It spiraled around her, whipping her blonde hair across her face and lifting her feet. I flicked my wand and the twister dissipated, dropping her unceremoniously onto her bottom. Merry was left on the ground, flustered and dirty.

"You look like that piglet you used to have when we were kids," I said, laughing as she tried to regain her footing. But I wasn't done with Merry yet.

"I bind you!" I stood over her, my wand pointed at her chest. A gasp arose from Ruth Anne and Eve. *Binding* bordered on gray magick, something Miss Sasha occasionally practiced but didn't condone, mainly because of the karmic repercussions. "I bind you, Merry Maddock!"

"The hell you do." Merry quickly drew a circle in the air her with her wand. Seafoam-green light engulfed her crouching body, and my spell failed to affect her.

I tried again, this time digging deeper. Once again my spell was deflected. I cast wildly and blindly, trying everything to penetrate Merry's damned bubble, getting more worked up with each failed pass.

I threw my wand to the ground and heard myself speaking words I didn't recognize. My amber bracelet sparked as a guttural voice erupted from within me. I looked at my shaking hands. *The death touch.*

"I don't need a wand to finish this!" I said, feeling the charge trickle through me as I pointed at my sister.

"Maggie, stop!" Eve said, advancing towards me, her own wand raised and leveled at my chest. "She's your sister. I won't let you hurt her."

"Sorry, Mags," Ruth Anne said, drawing her own wand. "But you're out of control"

"Stay out of this," I ordered them.

"Maggie, it's not me you're angry with," Merry said, lowering her wand. "Honey, you're grieving. This is the denial and anger stage and..."

"Shut up! I'm not grieving. Shane isn't dead, and I'm going to find my son. How dare you assume that just because ..." I choked. "Just because ..."

I couldn't get the words out - in part because I didn't even know what I meant.

Merry gently pushed my arm down to my side. And then she embraced me in a warm hug. Ruth Anne and Eve closed in around me, wrapping me in their arms.

What did I almost do?

"I don't know about you girls, but I'm getting awfully tired of this shit," Eve said.

"Amen," said Ruth Anne.

"Where in heaven did that come from?" Michael asked, pointing. I turned to see a rainbow, arching across the sky.

A rainbow.

I fell to my knees, sobbing. "A rainbow," I said, dumbly. It was so close and solid that I could touch it if I tried. But I didn't want to touch it, and ruin it the way I ruined everything. It was perfect just the way it was.

The rainbow was all you. You can do anything, Maggie Magick. In any world, dream or otherwise.

"Shane isn't dead," I said aloud and with certainty. I rubbed my nose on Merry's shoulder. "I'm sorry. I'm so sorry."

"I know, honey."

We all watched my rainbow together. It stayed a long while before slowly dissolving.

As the last colors melted, my ankh lit up like the pot of gold at rainbow's end.

"Montana," I whispered. "Son, I'm coming."

10

THE HERMIT

There weren't enough words to express to Merry how truly sorry I was. And ashamed. By brandishing my wand at my sister, and using magick against her, I had broken the rules of sisterhood. And taken another step towards becoming my father. Had my sisters not checked me, what might I have done?

I tucked my wand into my pocket, wondering why they chose to stay with me after my childish display. But I felt very grateful, and someday I'd make it up to all of them. My entire resolve now was focused on finding my son and getting us all home, safe and intact.

Shortly, we came upon a monstrous tree. Its trunk was as wide as Harvest Home, with thick twisting branches that spiraled to unprecedented heights. It reminded me of the beanstalk in the story of Jack. It was an anomaly, even here.

We stood before it, trying to take it all in. Aside from its size, there was nothing strange about it. Scattered on the rough trunk were large knots begging to be climbed. I circled it slowly, checking my ankh along the way. When I reached the opposite side, my ankh brightened even more, yet there was no portal.

"Isn't this where the elves make their cookies?" Ruth Anne asked, rubbing her tummy.

"It's ancient," Merry said, laying both hands on the trunk. The nearby leaves fluttered happily at her touch. "And friendly!" she added. She rested her head on the bark, and her smile turned to a grin. "It's got a heartbeat!"

A heartbeat! Just like the tree Montana had sent. And yet, this was no Tree of Life. At least, not the type Jillian had shown me.

Merry felt her way around the tree with her hands, like a doctor listening to a patient through a stethoscope. I watched her, mesmerized. She was so calm and loving as she attended to it, stopping here and there to heal a minor wound the tree had endured at some point in its long life. The tree responded by fanning out its branches, as if to offer us shade.

"Um... call me crazy, but I think the tree just invited us inside." Merry pursed her lips. "But I don't see a ...."

"Door Ho!" Ruth Anne called from the opposite side.

We ran around to her. Sure enough, a faded outline was etched into the tree. It formed a curved doorway. I nodded to Merry.

"All right then," my sister said, rolling up her sleeves. "Let's hope the tree is as friendly as it appears."

The door gave way easily, opening inwards. Ruth Anne turned on her flashlight and Eve lit a candle from her pack. I smelled the tree's interior before I could even see it. It was the familiar scents of moss and lichen and bark and sap and dew. But there was more. An earthiness reminiscent of Aunt Dora's garden. I felt welcomed, even before I stepped inside.

But how was this bringing us closer to Eagle Mountain? Were we about to fall into another trap of the Netherworld? I checked my ankh once more. It hummed steadily.

Michael took the lead. "Stay tight," he said. I peered over his shoulder, hoping to see our next gate within. When the last of us were inside the massive trunk, the door swung gently closed behind us and Eve's candle blew out.

"It's all right," Merry said. "The tree assured me we are safe. It's a refuge for the lost."

Wasn't that what Cernunnos had said? I didn't ask this aloud, but I was sure it was on all our minds.

The trunk seemed even larger on the inside. We hugged the perimeter, noting the many sloping corridors branching outward. *Roots?* There was a spackling of gold dust along the smooth inner wall that helped us to see, once our eyes adjusted. Ruth Anne put away her flashlight to conserve batteries.

I moved away from the wall and began to explore the middle. The ground was spongy, forcing me to move slowly. My pace was a blessing, as it allowed me to notice the dark pit at the very center before I fell in.

"A big hole," I announced, peering over the edge. The well was vast. I kicked a pebble inside, and I never heard it hit the bottom. Ruth Anne whistled in response.

"Maybe we don't have to go down," Merry suggested. "Maybe we try one of the root hallways."

But my ankh was now growing brighter than ever. "This is the way," I said.

Merry's teeth chattered. "I'm afraid of heights," she confided, pulling back from the edge. "Maggie, I don't think I can do this."

"Yeah, who knows where this leads?" Paul said.

"Oh, I think I know," Eve answered. "To hell."

"It might," I agreed somberly. Hell could just as easily be in the belly of a tree as the belly of the earth. I sidestepped closer to the pit, my ankh vibrating. I wasn't afraid of heights, but I had a big fear of the unknown. Especially in utter blackness. Can you die in the Netherworld?

"None of you have to go," I said to the others, unsure of how I'd even get down. "Stay here and wait for me."

"I'm going first," Michael said. "And that's final."

"Because you're the man?'" I asked.

"Maybe," he answered honestly. "I'm physically stronger than you. I can probably make the climb."

Ruth Anne shook her head. "I think we all have to go, just like the portals. We can't risk being separated again."

Merry was now shaking visibly. I took one of her hands and Eve took the other.

"We got this," I said to her.

"Yes," Paul agreed. "We all go together."

"Let's figure out how to do this," I said.

Paul crouched down and patted the wall of the pit. "It's pretty slick," he said. "I was hoping there were grooves or knots to use as handholds and footholds." He took off his backpack and pulled out a rope. "We... Eric and I used to go mountain climbing together." He looked at the limp nylon rope as if it were his brother. "I have no idea why I decided to bring this, but I think Eric had a hand in it."

"How are we supposed to do this?" Eve asked, looking dubiously at the rope and the pit. "You might be half-goat, but I'm not."

Paul unfurled the line and tossed one end down the well. It obviously didn't reach anywhere near the bottom.

"Now what?" Merry asked.

"Dangle me down," Ruth Anne said, wrapping the cord of her flashlight around her wrist. "I'll go as far as I can and shine the light to see what we're dealing with."

"I should go," I said.

She grinned. "Yeah, right. Look, let me contribute to my nephew's rescue, by doing something I'm good at." She raised both brows over her glasses and I knew she wouldn't back down.

With that, Paul reeled in the rope, then tied an intricate double loop around one end. He slipped the loops around Ruth Anne, then wrapped the other end of the rope around his waist several times. "Michael, help me unfurl this as we lower her down."

"Here goes nothing," Ruth Anne said, and we held our breaths.

Paul and Michael lowered her slowly, releasing the rope gradually from around Paul's waist. She walked down the wall, bouncing slightly as she went. I was reminded of old photos I'd seen, of miners walking through pitch black caverns, their headlamp their only guide.

Down she went. Down. Down. Down. The two men huffed and

grunted, digging in their heels to support her weight. Eve and I were on our knees, peering over the ledge, keeping a close eye on our sister. Merry kept a safe distance back, and periodically put a healing hand on Paul or Michael to ease their exhaustion.

"Ah, hell!" Ruth Anne shouted.

"What?" I called, alarmed.

"Rope burn."

"See anything yet?" Eve asked.

"No, and it seems to go on forever," she said, her words becoming more distant.

"You want to be pulled up?" I called.

"Yessss... no wait! I see a ledge into an opening over to the right of me. If I can rappel over, I can check it out."

"Great," Paul said. "That may be our ticket out of here. Hold on a second, Ruth Anne. If you're going to be rappelling side to side, I want to tie off my end first." He found a convenient root nodule and double-knotted it.

Suddenly, Ruth Anne screamed, loud and hysterical.

"What's wrong now?" I shouted.

"Bats! Big bats!" she yelled, frantically kicking at an unseen enemy. "Oh, God! They're organizing!"

I heard them, then finally saw them – an inky screeching mass swirling around Ruth Anne's head. She thrashed, unable to fight them off with her hands and hold on to the rope at the same time. flail

"She's phobic," Merry quickly explained. "Ever since discovering a pickled specimen in one of Mama's oddity jars.

"Quick! Pull her up," Paul said, digging his heels into the ground.

We all grabbed hold of the rope, but Ruth Anne was bouncing around too wildly. Finally, the rope started rising, until it abruptly caught. Paul peered over the ledge, inspecting the situation. "The rope's jammed pretty tight into a crevice. There's no way we can pull her up now."

"That's not an acceptable answer," I said.

"Whatever we do, we'd better do it quick," Paul said. "She can't stay dangling and tied up the way she is for long, especially with those bats going at her."

"Now would be a good time for a miracle," Merry said.

There was a sudden breeze in the air, as if someone had just turned on a fan. Floating down from high within the tree, like a drift of cotton, was a white snow owl, bathed in light.

"Starlight!" Merry gasped, as her owl flew down into the pit. There was screeching and squawking and hissing, some of it coming from Ruth Anne.

The bats began to scatter, chased away by the snow owl's fierce talons and beak. As Starlight flew up and resumed his position on Merry's shoulder, Ruth Anne quickly rappelled over to the ledge and untied from the rope. With the line free of her weight, she was able to give it a quick snap and dislodge it from the crevice.

"Thank you, Starlight! I'm so glad to see you again," Merry said, tickling the owl's chin.

"How's it look down there, Ruth Anne?" Paul asked.

"The bats are gone, so all is well! And it looks like there's a tunnel here that leads somewhere. Come on down!"

Paul repositioned the rope, so it hung directly over the tunnel ledge. "Okay, who's first?" he asked.

Merry's eyes widened as she shook her head vigorously. "I can't' do it, we need to find another way."

"Watch us first, Merry" I said. "You'll be fine."

One by one we rappelled down into the darkness. My heart nearly stopped as I stepped backwards over the precipice, but the rope held steady and I shimmied all the way to the cavern ledge, along with the others. Only Paul and Merry remained above: Paul to watch the rope, and Merry still paralyzed with fear.

Michael paced the ledge, running his hands through his hair. "I should go back up and get her."

"Are you going to carry her down on your back?" I asked.

He looked up, his brow glistening. "Merry," he called. "You have more faith than anyone I know. Use it now."

Merry's back straightened and she exhaled as she wiped her hands along her blouse. She nodded a quiet prayer. "Thank you, Michael. I can do this." With her bird protectively still on her shoulder, Merry worked her way down the rope. Her legs shook and she stifled several cries, but she made it. Paul was close behind.

Once down, she grabbed Michael, hugging him hard. He smiled and hugged her back, and I couldn't tell if his face was flushed from embarrassment or something else.

With that, Starlight lifted his wings, hooted once, and flew back up the tree. Merry raised her hand in both thanks and goodbye, tears streaming down her cheeks.

As touching as the moment was, I was eager to get moving. I took a deep breath and faced the belly of the cave, motioning forward. "C'mon, let's go."

The tunnel was tight and round and the ground was squishy, like a Dark Root forest after a strong rain. There was a strong smell of stagnant water.

"It's getting darker," Michael noted, as we walked single file. "I'm starting to feel like Jonah in the belly of the whale."

"Not for long." Ruth Anne pointed ahead, to clusters of small luminescent mushrooms glowing on the walls. The light was eventually bright enough to allow her to shut off her flashlight, saving what little battery she had left.

The narrow tunnel continued on and on without a single fork.

"I'm hungry," Ruth Anne said, patting her stomach as she looked longingly at the glowing fungus. "I used to eat wild mushrooms on my hikes." She plucked one from the wall and put it to her lips, and just as quickly Merry slapped it away. It bounced on the spongy ground, and Merry squashed it beneath her shoe.

"You should know better than to eat strange things in strange worlds," Merry scolded.

"You ate Cernunnos' pies and drank his wine," Ruth Anne countered.

"Then you should learn from my mistake."

"We've gone a long way," Paul commented. "I've counted nearly five thousand steps, which is a little over two miles. And I'm pretty sure we're going downhill, but it's hard to tell with the footing."

My ankh had been quiet since we entered the tunnel. I began to worry. *Did we take the right path after all?* For all I knew, this old tree had hundreds of roots. But as of now, we had no other choice. We could only go forward, descending into the steady tunnel of darkness, illuminated by just a smattering of mushroom light.

"Do you feel that?" Paul asked, stopping suddenly.

"What?" Michael said.

"Wind."

We all held still. A breeze tickled my cheek. "There must be an opening somewhere close by."

"We've gone about three miles now," Paul announced. "And I'm sure we're moving downhill."

I was struck by a feeling of deep unease and claustrophobia as I thought about being three miles beneath the earth. I started walking faster, searching for the source of the breeze. The Netherworld was wearing me down, step by step. No wonder Larinda was desperate to escape it. I wiped my forehead repeatedly, as I tried not to think about how much further we had yet to go.

Ruth Anne cleared her throat. "Some say that caves represent the process of birth, death, and rebirth," she said. "In fact, shamans of ancient times used caves ritualistically, to go into the spirit realm. There's even evidence that ancient cavemen weren't painting animals on the wall to showcase their art, but to invoke the animal's spirit in a sacred space. Caves are the bellies of ancient magick."

My ankh unexpectedly flashed, as if being powered on. And then, carried by the breeze, I heard my name. *"Maggie... Maggie... Maggie."*

"Ignore it, Maggie," Michael said. "They are just trying to screw with you."

I wasn't sure who *they* were, but it was working.

"Maggie... Maggie... Maggie."

The words lifted the ends of my hair and tickled my arms. My heart pounded and my breathing deepened. The number of mushrooms was dwindling rapidly now, and the meager light was fading. I pushed ahead of the others, desperate to find the exit. I listened for my name while watching my ankh.

"Four miles," Paul said from some distance behind me.

The tunnel was becoming oppressive. It took great effort to lift each foot now, as if they were weighted down with concrete. It became almost easier to shuffle than walk.

Ruth Anne took pictures, comparing them periodically for differences, but nothing changed. There was only the cellulose and sap walls, and the occasional luminous mushroom.

"Everything in due time," a lyrical voice sang, though this time no one else seemed to hear it.

Whoosh. Whoosh.

Everyone heard that.

"Is it a bat!?" Ruth Anne covered her head.

"Stop being a coward," Eve said. "It's undignified."

The steady gust grew stronger and Merry crowded in close to me. "I'm scared," she confessed.

"Hey, you made it down the rope," I said. "You can do anything." She nodded solemnly, though her eyes were faraway. "If I've learned anything on this adventure, Merry, it's that you can take care of yourself."

"Thank you, Maggie." She moved one leg forcefully in front of the next. "But there's more. I don't think I can go through the next portal. I've been lucky so far, but what if it's my turn next?"

"So? Of all of us, I think you have the least to worry about." Merry was as pure and bright as a newly minted silver dollar. "Unless you're afraid that I'll find out you sometimes eat processed food," I teased.

"I do not! Unless its offered. Then it's rude to say no."

"If anyone has to worry about portals, it's Michael," I said, loudly. He had given me hell for mine, and I greedily awaited viewing his. My secret was bad, but his had to be ten times worse.

The wind picked up and I had to hold my skirt down to keep it from revealing more than just my secrets.

"Maggie, I've done something. I can't let anyone see it," Merry whispered, keeping her gaze forward.

"What did you do?"

She shook her head quickly, the strands of her flaxen hair whipping her face "I can't tell you. I can't tell anyone"

"If it's your darkest secret, we're going to see it anyway. If you tell me, it won't be a secret anymore," I reasoned.

"I can't. I want to, but I can't." Her face was pinched and pained, and I wondered what Merry – the very best of us – could possibly have to hide. I couldn't imagine her doing anything terrible.

"it's probably not as bad as you think," I said.

"That's what you say now." She looked down at her slogging feet, and didn't look at me again.

Was she sleeping with Michael, I wondered? That would explain her reluctance to tell me. But the way Michael looked at her sometimes, with pure love and not ardent longing, suggested something else. But what could it be?

"The wind's getting worse," Eve complained, smoothing her hair as she caught up to us. "Why didn't I bring a hat?"

"Sure wish that tracker husband of yours would show up," Ruth Anne said.

"Ruth Anne!" Merry chastised.

"What? Unlike you, I don't think he's dead. I mean, its Shane Doler. I just hope he finds us soon."

"You really think he's okay?" I asked Ruth Anne, desperate for confirmation.

"Maggie, he's disappeared out of your life many times before, and it's always been for a good reason, and he's always found his way back."

"I don't think we can die here," Eve said.

"But we can get trapped," I reminded her.

"Then maybe we'll all be trapped down here together," Eve said. "Wouldn't it be fun to spend eternity with this fun little group?" With that, we all pushed forward as quickly as we could, heads down into the wind.

The root, if that's what we were inside, suddenly widened out and the wind let up. A shard of silver light beamed from ahead. *What is that?* The anticipation hastened our speed. Soon the light expanded, not to another portal but to a brilliant world of color and sunshine – a welcome relief from the confining darkness. We had emerged from the tree, only to find ourselves in another part of the woods. *A forest within a tree?*

"I'm getting real sick of shrubbery." Eve sighed. "Is the Netherworld one giant salad?"

"At least we can see where we're walking again," Merry said, wiping the bottom of her shoes, as if she were entering a newly carpeted house. The rest of us instinctively followed suit, as Merry had always been the one to establish protocol.

The air was fragrant, filled with the scents of lavender, roses, cotton, and lilacs. At least those were the smells I could differentiate. There were other scents, some pungent but most sweet, and Merry rattled off a list of possibilities.

"I brought my herb pouch so I could collect samples!" she squealed. If she was really going to harvest plants from the Netherworld, I didn't begrudge her. Even if I had my reservations on how it might affect the Upper World.

To Merry's great delight, a wide variety of plants flourished in all directions. "Sage! Mugwort! I'm not sure what this is, but it smells good!" She shrugged as she popped it into her leather bag. I watched as she loaded her pouch, marveling that it never got full. She plucked from field and forest, like a child on Easter finding limitless eggs.

There were so many birds chirping that for a moment, that's all we heard. But then other sounds presented themselves. A rushing stream. Thumps and bumps and footsteps. And – *laughter?*

I glanced at the others, wondering if they'd also heard it, too, but they were busy investigating our surroundings. It was a colorful expanse, a secluded oasis. Tropical plants abounded around a wide pond, where enormous lily pads bobbed enticingly on the water. Ruth Anne was pulling off her combat boots, ready to jump in, when Eve stopped her.

"Who knows what kind of bacteria live in that," Eve said. "Or worse."

Ruth Anne's face paled but she quickly put on her shoes. It wasn't the germs that frightened her, it was Eve's ominous 'or worse.' This place was deceptive, and anything could be a trap.

"It would be nice to get a reprieve once in a while," Ruth Anne grumbled.

"Maggie, your ankh's going off again," Paul said.

It was. A steady rhythmic blink that neither hastened nor lessened, no matter which direction I moved. Montana wasn't here, but perhaps this was where I was supposed to plant the acorn? I moved off by myself and cradled the seed in my hands. I didn't 'feel' anything, and I remained indecisive until Merry called me back over.

"A path!" she said, pointing to a hidden trail behind a large bush.

We moved past the shrub and followed the path, which led to a wooden gate with a bronze latch, draped in welcoming vines. The gate was small, child-sized, and Merry happily opened it, skipping inside as if discovering a secret garden. The dirt path turned to sienna bricks and the rest of us followed along, warily. Finally, the path opened into a rolling patch of green grass and wild rose bushes. It was all so beautiful, but I wondered why this realm seemed more suited to Merry than me, since the last portal had been mine.

Paul stretched and yawned as we entered. "Sorry," he said, looking up. "I think the sun's getting to me."

It was not uncomfortably warm, but I understood. I could've easily found a patch of soft grass and napped for hours, were my mission not so important. I squeezed the ankh, letting it anchor me.

"Those tangerines look delicious," Eve said, pointing to a fruit tree. They were perfect in size, shape and color. And the tree seemed to offer them up willingly as we passed beneath.

Just one little bite. It won't hurt a bit.

We examined the field, our eyes wide open even though everything felt warm and welcoming here. We had been deceived before.

"Hey, do you smell chocolate?" Ruth Anne asked.

"Yes," I said, looking around for the source.

"Remember the lessons of Willy Wonka," Paul advised.

A stand of trees stood watch at the top of the field. They were tall, with leaves of turquoise and salmon and even maroon. An enchanted wood, and I felt reticent to enter because of this enchantment. It was too perfect, and that meant danger. But the closer we got, the louder my pendant hummed.

"I'll bet there's a gingerbread house waiting for us in there," Ruth Anne said.

"You have nothing to worry about," Paul said approvingly. "Trim as a fiddle."

Ruth Anne grinned.

Eve scooted close to me, flipping her hair back. "I don't like the way Ruth Anne and Paul are getting so chummy." She pursed her lips as she watched them converse. "Just because she knows a few dumb things...that doesn't make her interesting."

Ruth Anne had confessed to me that she wasn't interested in men romantically and I wasn't going to break her trust. I decided to have fun with Eve instead. "They do make a nice couple. Maybe you're just not Paul's type?"

"Maggie, I'm everyone's type." She squinted as she watched them converse, as if considering what Ruth Anne had that she didn't. She shook her head, coming up empty.

"We all get jealous," I said, offering up my wisdom. "But you need to trust Paul if you love him."

Eve's face turned to stone. "After watching the way he ditched his brother, can you blame me for questioning his character? His own twin. You don't get closer than that." Her eyes gleamed as she processed the situation. "Women get jealous over me, not the other way around. I suppose this is my kar...kar...what's the word?"

"Karma," I answered, suppressing a smile. "I don't think you have anything to worry about."

Eve sucked in her cheeks and nodded sharply. "You're right. She might have the brains, but that won't keep a man warm at night." She clapped her hands together, as if confirming 'that was that,' but a subtle look on her face told me she wasn't so sure.

"Maggie," Eve said. "Before we join the others, I need to talk to you about something else." She looked cautiously around, to make sure we were out of earshot.

"Yeah?" Her tone said there was more than just petty jealousy going on inside her.

"I'm freaking out about going through the next portal. I'm praying we find Montana before my turn comes."

Unlike Merry, I was well aware that Eve had her secrets. She was as aloof as the night, and that usually indicated someone who didn't want their layers peeled away. "There's still Merry and Michael left," I said.

Eve rolled her eyes. "The worst thing Merry probably did was to steal a piece of candy from Mom's shop when she was like, three years old. And Michael claims that he has nothing to hide. Maggie, I don't trust a man who says he has nothing to hide. It's not natural."

"So, what are you hiding?" I asked. "If you tell me, then it won't be a secret anymore."

She sighed. "I would, if I knew which secret it was going to be. And how can I stay angry at Paul, if mine is worse than his?"

"This isn't a competition," I answered, but Eve was already walking back to join the others.

Finding myself alone, I heard the laughter again. It was very distinct, a high-pitched giggle. It seemed to be coming from everywhere at once. My amber bracelet sparkled. I covered it with my hand, looking around.

"Everything in due course," a voice whispered to me.

The laughter resumed. Children's laughter. And tucked in between the sounds of laughter, I heard a baby crying.

Go to your child, said the voice, calling me from the grove of trees at the head of the field.

No one noticed as I ducked inside.

~

There was no path, and I turned sideways as I waded through the undergrowth. Rough branches scraped my arms and caught my skirt, pulling at me like hands begging for food. I forged ahead, hoping it would be a few minutes before anyone noticed my disappearance.

I kept moving inward, inward. Still, the land felt pleasantly familiar, as if I had visited it before, in a poem or a dream. The growing euphoria outweighed my apprehension, and I felt giddy with anticipation of what might await me.

And then it was night.

Just like that. As if an order had been given and then obeyed. A myriad of sparkling stars appeared between the tree branches, highlighting a perfect crescent moon. There was no setting of the sun. It all just... was.

My journey led me to the bank of a gently flowing river. She reflected the light of the moon and stars on her surface. I don't know why I say her, except the whole place felt like a HER. Warm. Nurturing. Kind. Maternal.

I walked along the bank, unafraid of the darkness overspreading the woods. I crouched down to inspect the deep water and caught my own image. I didn't recognize myself, as I looked both young and old at once, depending on how I turned my face.

I knew why this was all so familiar! I'd been to this river before! It was near Harvest Home, where we often hiked as kids. A favorite game of ours was to stare at our reflections in the water at night, and ask whom we would marry.

> *River deep and river bright*
> *Show us who we'll wed tonight!*

Eve's answer was like a roulette wheel, with innumerable faces appearing one after the other. She never got the same face twice, which suited her fleeting nature.

Merry never got an image at all, just simply the letter J, which in later years proved the game unreliable, since she ended up marrying Frank.

As for me, the moment an image began to appear, I would slap the water with my hand, dissolving any attempt at a sealed fate.

I dipped my hand into the water, stirring it with my fingers. It was cool, and part of me wanted to strip naked and swim along with the slow current. But I couldn't leave this spot, for fear of losing my way back. There was no sign of 'my child,' whom the mysterious voice had teased me with, and the laughing had not returned. It was just me.

Me and my reflection.

I stared into the water as I had when I was ten, moving my head so that the moon was positioned above me like a lunar crown. The moonlight kissed my hair and nose and eyes, setting my entire reflection aglow. I focused intently, not searching for the face I would someday marry, but for the face of the woman I would one day become. My fiery red hair faded to stubborn auburn, then finally to muted silver. My skin went from smooth to troubled, as the lines of life arranged themselves around my nose and mouth and brow. But through the metamorphosis, my eyes never changed. They were always deep and searching green. Just like Jillian's. Just like Armand's.

Did seeing myself in later years mean I would make it out of the Netherworld? Or was that only one possible timeline? I studied silver-haired Maggie's reflection again. She looked very much at peace.

"Maggie... Maggie... Maggie."

My name again, this time accompanied by the sound of children giggling.

Still crouching, I looked around, searching the woods, wondering who they were. Other stolen children? Or beings born of this world? Or perhaps, and most terribly, they were simply young souls, irretrievably lost to the Netherworld.

I tried to decipher the whispers between their laughs. I didn't hear a baby's cry, and that both frightened and consoled me.

The laughter ceased abruptly. When I looked at my reflection again, I was neither young nor old, just me as I was, with pale skin, a worried frown, and red-rimmed eyes.

"I'll never have kids," I remembered telling Eve and Merry, after our husband-summoning sessions. We would lie on our backs, staring up at the moon, listening to the crickets and the bullfrogs sing their nightly song.

"Why not?" Merry asked. "You can dress them up and teach them things and cook for them."

"That sounds like a lot of work. Besides, Mother says the world's going to hell in a handbasket. Why would I want to bring another person into this world?"

"You need to stop listening to her and Aunt Dora talk," Eve said. "It'll give you nightmares. Especially when they're drinking Mom's 'Saturday Night' tea."

I should have heeded my own advice, I briefly thought, stirring my reflection with my pinky finger. I wouldn't be scouring the Nether-world, feeling this incredible void in my heart. But then, I'd have never have gotten to hold him. And love him. And that was worth everything.

I sat up on my knees, my hands folded before me as my head tilted reverently towards the moon. How did anyone survive parenthood without a thousand scars? Or love anyone at all, for that matter?

"*The truth will set you free*," a giggling voice whispered. I turned, right then left, but saw no one.

"What truth?" I asked aloud.

"*THE TRUTH!*"

I fumbled through my pocket and found the apple. It was still mostly intact, and one more nibble couldn't hurt.

"*As above, so below*," another voice said, followed by a chorus of chortles and giggles.

I took a careful bite, and waited.

And then there were ripples upon the water.

I looked at my river image once more. It shifted, bleeding outwards like watercolor across a canvas. My coarse red hair became smooth chestnut brown. My pale skin tanned, and the spray of freckles across my cheeks faded. My nose rounded and my chin soft-ened. Yet my eyes were the same.

"Jillian," I whispered, peering closer.

The image panned back. Jillian was in full view, holding a baby in the nursery of Sister House. When I saw the red hair, I thought it was Montana. She nuzzled the child's cheek and said a few words, then drew a magick circle.

"There, there, my daughter," she said, rocking the baby.

Daughter?

"I give you half my breath," Jillian said, kissing the baby's mouth. "Now, I will always be able to watch over you, no matter where you are."

Half her breath? What did that mean?

I wanted to see more, but the image shifted. Now I saw Miss Sasha staring back at me, as she looked when I was young, with a large frame and only a few strands of gray in her hair.

She sat in the parlor of Sister House, her ankles crossed as she sipped her tea. She sat opposite another woman, whose face was blocked from me.

"She'll be the end of us all," the other woman said, slamming her tea cup onto her saucer. "You know it as well as I do."

"That's not what I see in her future," Sasha said.

"You are only focusing on one timeline, but many others still forming because of your stubbornness. I've divined some of them, and they are grim indeed. Sasha, I beg you to reconsider."

"I will not!" Sasha firmly put her cup on the table and leaned forward, leveling a pointed finger at the woman. "She needs protection. And we need protection from her. We can't let her loose in the world without training. Not with her father out there. I will raise her and that is that."

"One wrong step and she'll go down the left-hand path," the woman warned, standing to leave. "And then we'll have another Armand on our hands." She turned and mumbled. "Or worse."

The image shifted back to my face, before morphing again. The eyes remained and the hair retained an autumn hue - only shorter and wavy rather than long and curly. My face narrowed, my chin squared, and my brow thickened.

"No," I whimpered, as a cowboy hat replaced my moon crown. A hat that now sat above my father's face.

"Can you blame me for not wanting to be a father?" he asked, pushing his hat down over his forehead. "Do you see what parenting does to you? It sucks the life right out of you, and it makes you forget who you even used to be."

This was not a memory. Armand was speaking directly to me.

"Go back Maggie, and leave the Netherworld. Return to your carefree existence, before you were burdened with a child. It's not selfish. It's only natural."

"Go to hell!" He may have walked away from me, but I wouldn't walk away from my child. I scooped up a handful of rocks and scattered them across the water, breaking the image.

I will not become my father.

"Or will you?" the voice asked.

I shivered, suddenly cold. I wanted to return home, and have Jillian and Aunt Dora wrap me in their shawls and tell me it's okay. I wanted to be a daughter again, not an adult.

I lifted the ankh from its chain around my neck and squeezed it in my hands. I would never abandon my son. Never. I'd battle the devil himself to get Montana back, and if the devil happened to be my father, so be it.

"Jillian," I whispered. "I hope you're still watching over me. I need you." I massaged the ankh, repeating my prayer. Even if I couldn't see her, it comforted me to know she was out there somewhere, guiding me, as promised in the vision.

"Maggie!"

It was a clear voice this time – and one I recognized. I turned, wary of more tricks and illusions. A man ran down along the river bank, straight for me.

Shane lifted me from the ground and swept me in his arms. "It's really you! Oh, Maggie. Thank God!" he said.

"How?" I asked, seeing my sisters and Paul and Michael behind him.

"I was following the moon, and suddenly got a read on you. You must have been looking at it, too?"

"Yes. That was fast."

"Fast?" he shook his head. "It took me forever to find you. But I was so happy I didn't even mind seeing Michael again."

I wished I hadn't shattered the image of my future husband in the river. I was now certain it was Shane all along. "We were destined to be together," I said.

"I've always known that. Now let's get going. I know the way to the next gate. It's not far at all."

I took his hand. Merry and Eve exchanged worried glances, though Michael looked unconcerned. I wondered if Shane had already gone through his gate. I hoped he had. I didn't want to think of him as anything but perfect.

"How'd you get free?" I asked.

"I have no idea. One moment I was swarmed, the next, everyone was running a way and I made a break for it. Must have been my lucky horseshoe."

"See!" Ruth Anne grinned as we marched for our next portal. "He's Shane-Frickin'- Doler."

THE WHEEL

"*Well, aren't you pretty?*"

The man brushed Eve's hair away from her shoulder, tucking it behind her ear, and then brought it back to her face, as if he couldn't decide which he liked best. She held still, in the way she did when her mother fixed her hair for school pictures. He stood back, examining his work.

"Exquisite, actually," he continued, as if she were a piece of artwork. "Exotic yet familiar. I've never seen anyone who looks quite like you." He lifted her chin to get a better look. "Have you considered color contacts? They look great in photos."

Eve shrugged, and in doing so, loosened herself from the man's hold. She glanced at her friend, Babs, standing beside her - a pretty French woman ten years her senior. Babs had brought Eve to Zach, assuring her that he was a 'good guy and a reputable agent,' the kind that could get her name out to all of New York. And beyond.

But for being such a high-profile agent, he didn't dress to impress. His jeans hadn't seen a washing in weeks, and his beat-up fedora was older than she was. His office was a jumble of open cardboard boxes filled with files and foreign magazine covers featuring smiling young women with big hair and teeth.

"He's eccentric and foreign," Babs had said of Zach, on their way to his studio. *"He'll take a minute to get used to."*

Eve checked her watch. She had to open the diner in less than five hours. *"Can we hurry this up?"* she asked. *"If I don't get some beauty rest before my shift, my tips – and the customers – are going to suffer."*

Babs laughed. *"I told you she was funny, Zach."* Then she looked at Eve. *"Honey, when Zach is done with you, you'll never have to worry about rotting away in some dive diner, ever again."*

Eve's eyelashes fluttered thoughtfully. She hoped it was true. Waiting tables was not the future she had envisioned for herself when she moved to New York. If Zach could help her catch her break, it would be worth missing a night's sleep. But then again, if Zach was so amazing, why was Babs still waiting tables?

She gave Babs a discreet once over. The woman didn't have Eve's fine bone structure, or her figure or hair, for that matter. She was very pretty, but she wasn't Eve. The answer satisfied Eve's inner nagging voice, and she returned her attention to Zach.

"I'll call Gerry in Angeles. I'm betting he can get you work right away, if we get your head shots to him soon."

"You'll love Gerry," Babs assured her. *"He got me several shampoo gigs and a skin care ad. But he also casts for soap operas. Eve's pretty enough to be in a soap opera, isn't she, Zach?"*

"Oh, definitely! Especially if she can act a little."

A little? Eve harrumphed. She was born for the stage.

"Babs, can I have a word?" Zach asked. She nodded and joined him near the open window, where the sounds of traffic, sirens, and catcalls rang through. While the two spoke, Eve busied herself studying the magazine covers framed on the wall. The models were pretty, but none was as breathtaking as she was. If those women could grace a cover, imagine what she could do.

Her phone buzzed. It was her sister Merry calling, and she tossed it back into her purse without answering. She hadn't talked to Merry since leaving Dark Root, and was pissed that her sister wanted to talk now – right when her life was finally about to change for the better. No, she would talk to her older sister, later, but only after she became a star. Then she'd talk to them all in person, rolling into Dark Root with a shiny new car and a personal shopper.

"Great news!" Babs said, returning as Zach disappeared into the hallway. "He likes you. Says you're a diamond in the rough."

"In the rough?" Eve said, indignant. She wasn't rough. She was elegant and sophisticated. But then again, he did call her a 'diamond.'

Her phone buzzed again. "Who's that?" Babs asked. "I thought no one but me had your new number."

"You and my sister."

"You have a sister?"

"Three. But I haven't seen them in a few years."

The phone continued to ring. "Maybe you should turn it off while we're in our meeting." Babs suggested.

Why was Merry calling so insistently, Eve wondered? Had something happened to their mother or aunt? Her fingers twitched, but she wouldn't think of it now. She had to focus on her career. If bad news was coming, she'd need some good news to buffer it. She reached into her purse and silenced her phone.

"Where is Zach?" Eve asked, after fifteen minutes had passed. The sirens outside were so frequent in this neighborhood that Eve couldn't distinguish one from another.

"He went to get his camera so he could see how you photograph. You're thin, but curvy, and the camera will either work with that or against it."

"He thinks I might look fat in my photos," Eve said, dryly.

Babs chuckled. "I doubt you'd ever look anything less than perfect." She smiled sweetly, staring at her as usually only men did.

Zack returned with a video camera, a digital camera, and a tripod. "Almost ready," he said, pulling down the window shades and dimming the overhead lights. He set up several backdrop screens, and props to go with them.

"This looks like it's going to take a while," Eve said, trying not to look at her watch.

Babs might be confident she'd be able to quit her job, but Eve wasn't so sure. Even Elizabeth Taylor probably had to wait a few weeks before the *dollars came rolling in. And if Eve didn't have the rent again, there was little chance she could convince her slumlord to give her another month.*

"Okay, sweetheart, let's start simple," Zach said. "Sit on that stool over there in front of the summer-fun backdrop. And hold this can of orange soda. That's it! Smile, like it was the most refreshing thing in the world."

Eve despised orange soda, but she was an actress as well as a model. She put on her brightest grin, jutting out her chest and tilting her head back. As if the sun worshipped her, and she worshipped the can of soda. She smiled at the camera over her shoulder, a look that never failed to break men's hearts or make women hate her.

"Brilliant! You're a natural!" Zach said, scratching his chin through his graying beard. "Since we have the summer backdrop set up, we should try a beach scene next. Babs said you are comfortable wearing a bathing suit?"

He pointed to three bikinis hanging on a doorknob, all with the tags still attached. Eve nodded and chose a thin-stringed, yellow two-piece. She changed behind an accordion screen while Zach and Babs arranged the props. When she returned, she was instructed to sit on a towel surrounded by beach balls. Zach handed her a bottle of suntan oil to hold, then began directing. "Bigger smile. More dimples. Fewer dimples. Fluff your hair. Put the bottle against your cheek. Beautiful. Fucking beautiful!"

The lights were hotter than Eve had imagined, and the work harder. "Have some water," Babs said during a backdrop change. Eve guzzled the bottle while Babs dabbed her forehead with a hand towel. She would finish this shoot, then hit the sack, and make up for lost sleep after her morning shift. Or maybe she would just call in sick.

When they resumed the shoot, Babs rubbed oil on her back as Zach continued taking pictures. "You look so beautiful," Babs whispered in her ear.

Zach paused with the camera, contemplating the scene. "Babs, can you untie just the top string of her bikini? Eve, let the top fall but keep one hand across your... chest, and hold the oil in your other hand. Then say, 'Nothing comes between me and a great tan.'"

Eve blinked, but then remembered he was European. If she modeled overseas she'd need to bare more than just her cleavage. Babs loosened the string and Eve did as instructed, though she had trouble delivering the line.

"More water," Babs insisted, as Eve fanned herself.

Hours ticked by, and Eve knew she wouldn't make her shift. It didn't matter. She felt giddy now, under their constant assurances of her beauty.

But then Zach made a face. A disapproving face.

"Did I do something wrong?" Eve asked.

"You weren't smiling in the last few shots."

"It was hot."

"Do you think acting and modeling is about comfort?" he asked, raising his voice.

"Huh?"

"Well, do you?"

Eve looked around, unnerved by his drastic change of temperament. Everything had been going so well. Had she blown her chance?

Babs intervened. "Zach, you're just tired. It's been a long day. Have a drink. Eve, forgive him. Temperamental artists, you know. He's all bark, I promise. When you see his pictures, you'll love him like I do." With that, Babs left the room and returned with three glasses of wine.

They toasted and drank, then resumed the shoot just as dawn broke. Zach promised to not let his exhaustion get the best of him, and Eve promised to try harder. But whether because she hadn't slept in nearly 24 hours, or from the heat of the lamps or the buzz from the wine, Eve began to feel dizzy. Her mind wandered, as if she were slipping into a dream.

But it was a happy, delirious sort of dream, where things morphed and changed and she was going to be a star.

Zach replaced the backdrop with a new one. A boudoir set, he called it, and suddenly there was a bed that looked too big to have possibly fit through the door. An end table and lamp were brought in by two muscular men. They were wearing red satin shorts and nothing else.

"Huh?" Eve asked, though she didn't protest as she was escorted to the bed.

"We have lingerie," Zach said cheerfully. "Though I think for European markets, we're better off without it. All you have to do is look beautiful and have fun." He smiled reassuringly. "You can do that for me, can't you, Eve?"

"Uh-huh," she said, her eyelids drooping.

She was helped out of her bathing suit, lulled by the collective 'oohs and aahs' about her exquisite beauty. The men's hands traveled along her hips *and navel, then up her arms and around the folds of her ears. The lights dimmed further. One man kissed Eve. And then the other.*

She wasn't even surprised when Babs removed her own top and joined them on the bed, kissing Eve fervently. Zach took pictures and ran his video recorder. They all took turns kissing, touching, and fondling one another. All their attention was focused on Eve.

She was queen of the world.

Her bliss was only interrupted by the periodic vibrations of her phone in her purse.

~

"Where are those videos?" Paul demanded once we were through the portal. "Eve, where are the goddamned videos?"

His fists were in his hair, yanking as he paced. His face was the color of the unsettling dusky red sky, which looked as if there were a wildfire raging in the distance. He stopped periodically to question her, or to launch an accusation. "What did you do? How could you? What else don't I know?"

I looked at Eve's ashen face. Her long lashes swept the tops of her cheeks. She trembled, and for once I felt truly sorry for my little sister.

Paul was so distraught, which caught me off guard. He was always so cool and collected, hardly speaking unless offering up retro trivia or answering a direct question. His piercing eyes bore into Eve's, as his lower jaw slid from side to side while he stormed about.

"I don't know what Zach did with the videos," Eve admitted, finally breaking his stare.

"You told me they never existed!" Paul violently rebutted. "When my friends were all telling me they'd seen you on the internet, you lied to me and said they were mistaken. They told me to watch it, that I'd see for myself, but I believed you, Eve. I believed you because I loved you."

"It wasn't me," she said. "Or at least, it wasn't *Eve Maddock*."

"So you think a stage name absolves you? I trusted you." Paul held a finger near her chin, daring her to look away. "Do you know how that makes me feel?"

"Probably the same way I felt when I learned about the dead twin you never told me about. Betrayed."

"This is different."

"No, it's not. I didn't hurt or abandon anyone, other than myself. If you'd calm down, you'd see that."

Ruth Anne stepped forward, laying a hand on his shoulder. "Paul, she was either very exhausted or slipped something. You can't blame her. Can't you see how bad she feels?"

"She didn't look like she felt bad when those two men were... I'm just glad we never got to see that part of the highlight. Although I bet I can rent it for $2.99 with a major credit card."

Eve crossed her arms, anger replacing shame. "You're mad that I was with two men, but you're okay that I was with a woman?"

"That's different, too."

"I dunno about that," Ruth Anne said. "But that's not the point. You two weren't romantically together when either of these things happened. You can't be mad at someone for what they did before they met you."

Paul shrugged. "Logically, I know you're right. But Ruth Anne, she kept something big from me, and then continued to lie about it. I wanted her to be the mother of my future children. I wanted her to be a mother to Nova."

"And you're willing to throw all that away now?" I asked, suddenly outraged. I felt for Eve, and understood why she didn't tell him. It was the same reason none of us told our secrets - we were afraid of losing the people we love. "Paul, not telling you might be one of the most human things Eve has ever done. Can't you cut her some slack?"

"What do you guys think?" Paul turned to Shane and Michael for support.

"I think she was victimized," Shane said. "We should be encouraging her to call the police when we get out of here, not berating her."

"I actually agree," said Michael.

"Well, it looks like you've got everyone on your side," Paul said, throwing up his arms. "I guess you win."

"This isn't about winning," Eve said. "I'm sorry I didn't tell you, but how could I? I was embarrassed and ashamed. The next day, I wasn't even sure it had really happened, except for the strange robe I woke up in. I wanted... I needed to put it all behind me. I thought if I didn't think about it, it would be like it never happened at all. Yes, I heard the videos were out there. All I could do was pray you wouldn't see one, because I couldn't stand for you to look at me... the way you're looking at me now."

Paul walked away.

"He shouldn't go out there alone," I said. "We don't know the landscape here yet."

"I'll get him," Shane said.

"Can you believe him?" Eve said, putting a hand on her hip.

"I remember that day," Merry said. "I knew you were in trouble. I felt it in the pit of my stomach. I kept calling..."

"I know. I wish I'd picked up my phone."

"Did you go to the police?" Michael asked.

"God, no. I just wanted to forget about it. That's all I still want. Can we drop it now?"

There was so much I wanted to say and know, but Eve was in no mood for an interrogation. And how dare those creeps do this to my sister. My blood boiled and the ground trembled. Merry gave me a sideways look and I squeezed my nails into my palms and thought of rainbows and butterflies. But it was no use. All I could think about was what I would do to Zach-from-New-York if I ever found him.

"Save it," Merry said softly to me. "We need to be there for Eve right now."

Eve's face was somber and there was a vacant look in her eyes, as if she were putting up yet another wall. That event had impacted her deeply. But just because we knew her secret now, it didn't mean she was letting us in.

"We'll get justice for this when I get home," I vowed to Merry, who nodded.

"Poor Eve," Michael said to me.

"Eve has always paid for men's insecurities," I said.

"I guess you *were* listening in Sunday School," he answered.

The sky went crimson, but there were still stars above. Ruth Anne pointed to a constellation. "The Big Dipper!" she said. "In tomato soup."

As I followed the horizon, I saw the gray peaks of mountains, not far off. My heart nearly stopped. "Eagle Mountain!" I exclaimed, pointing and jumping up and down. "It's there, it's there!" I could feel it as well as see it, and I would have run straight for it, if Shane and Paul had still been with us.

Shane soon returned with a distraught Paul, who sat on a low rock, massaging the bridge of his nose. "He'll be fine," Shane said. "In a few years." He smiled resignedly, then noticed my expression. I simply pointed towards Eagle Mountain.

"We should go now," I said.

"We can't just yet. Paul and I scouted out the way forward. An icy river separates us from the mountain. There's a bridge across it, but it looks pretty slick and rickety. I really think we should wait until daylight, assuming day ever comes."

"Are you kidding me?" I checked the hourglass and groaned at the missing sand. "Do we really have to wait until dawn. Can't we just risk it?"

"I'll go check myself," Michael said, walking past Shane. "The cowboy might be a tracker, but he's not omnipotent."

We waited, silently lost in our own thoughts until Michael returned. "The bridge is covered in frost," he admitted. "Perhaps we should wait until morning."

"That advice sounds familiar," Shane said.

Against my strong desire to push ahead, we settled in along the riverbank, waiting for the sun. The moon was fully up now, moving much quicker than in the Upper World. I hoped this meant dawn came just as fast.

We sat on the ground and watched the stars . One by one, we yawned, succumbing to our exhaustion. Jillian had told us we wouldn't need sleep or food or warmth, that it was all a product of our minds. Too bad our bodies hadn't listened to her.

I found a patch of grass and curled up with my head on my hands. As I closed my eyes, I heard a child giggle. Then, a woman's voice sang me to sleep with a haunting lullaby.

～

"*Shh... sleep. beautiful human male.*"

I wriggled on the hard ground, squinting my eyes, looking for the woman's voice. It was not yet sunrise. The others slept soundly nearby. I rose, tiptoeing between them.

"*Don't be afraid, I will take good care of you,*" the woman promised. This time I was able to follow the voice directly to Shane, who was sleeping with his back against a tree, his head on his shoulder. His hat was in his lap.

I saw the woman, naked and straddling my husband as she stroked his cheek with the back of her hand. I stormed over. "Leave him alone, Lilith."

The beautiful woman turned to me, her eyes twinkling. "But I am giving him such good dreams. He deserves as much, doesn't he?"

I crouched before her, leveling a warning finger. "He's mine. I'm sure you already have enough playthings."

"None as beautiful as him." She giggled. Her form was not solid, but translucent, and her ebony hair caught the breeze, flowing around her, covering and uncovering parts of her body strategically. Her twinkling eyes continued to travel the length of Shane's body.

Lilith ignored my presence and pressed her lips to Shane's. I reached over to push her away, but my hand went right through. I tried again and she laughed. "You have dealt with plenty of humans, and even spirits, but never a goddess. Be warned."

"What are you doing with my husband, Lilith? I thought you hated men."

"That is not the way you should greet a sister." Lilith wriggled a finger and I was pushed backwards, several feet, unable to move forward. She wrinkled her nose and frowned. "I don't like using my magick against another female, but we must carry on with some civility. That should hold you for a moment. Now, regarding your question: I do not hate men. I love men. That's what I do."

Lilith snapped her fingers and a menagerie of images appeared between us...men of all ages, shapes and time periods floated by. She snapped her fingers again and the images vanished. "At one time or another, I loved them all."

"What exactly do you want with Shane?" I demanded, trying, unsuccessfully, to push through her magical barrier.

"I told you that I was curious about you. And my curiosity extends to your mortal lover." She tapped her chin and spun to face me, her lush hair blanketing most of her pale body. "I've been following him since we met. It was I who lured Cernunnos' minions away from him. It was I who helped reconnect him to you through the moon. And when he fell asleep, it was I who placed myself in his dreams, granting him what he desires most. Look how I aroused him," she said, lifting the cowboy hat from his lap.

"Enough!" I shouted, the word followed by a clap of thunder.

Lilith smiled, looking up, undaunted. "You are fun," she said. "I would have taken him, but he..." She frowned prettily. "He managed to lock me out."

"What do you mean, locked you out?"

"He replaced my image - my body - with yours. Yours!" She raised both hands and slapped them against her bare thighs. "Ludicrous, right?" she asked, jiggling to reveal her curves. "Why, is what I'm wondering?"

"He loves me," I said simply.

"Love? Men don't understand love. It's a convenience for them. An excuse to take a slave who will cook and clean and breed minions, only to be discarded when the man grows bored." Lilith brushed a strand of Shane's hair from his face, then languidly rose to her feet. Even I wasn't immune from her sexual power and beauty. There was something compelling and primitive about her. No straight man gazing upon her stood a chance - in any world.

She turned her finger in the air three times, and I was free to move again.

"That's not the way of all men, Lilith. There are only a handful who—"

Lilith put out a hand. "Save your lectures. Men are faithful only when someone's watching," she continued. "I've seen it played out since time immortal. But in the dream world, no one is watching. Haven't you wondered why Shane returns to his so often?"

"Shane's different," I said, looking at his sleeping body. I couldn't bear to see his arousal so I willed the breeze to push his hat back over his lap.

Lilith laughed at my efforts. "Jealousy is rooted in the fear of loss. I won't take him, Maggie, I just wanted to borrow him, for a little fun." She ran her fingers through her silken hair, her hips rolling as she slowly approached me. "Normally, even the most faithful husbands give in to me, but this one... he chooses you. And I can't leave until I know why. It's troubling, and exciting. It can't be your breasts, or your figure, or your hair. Perhaps its your fire he craves?"

"I already told you, it's-"

"Shhh!" Lilith pinched two fingers together, barring me from speech. She laughed again, as if it were the funniest thing she'd seen in a long while. "Mortals are too much fun. But back to the question of fidelity and love. Your husband's response made me wonder if there was someone else who might tempt him. Perhaps someone more familiar."

She twined her hands, as if pulling cotton candy. A dusting of blue light settled over Shane's sleeping body. He rolled his head slightly and half-opened his eyes. Lilith snapped her fingers. She was now in Eve's form, completely naked. "Men are always fond of sisters."

"Shane, I'm so scared!" Lilith-Eve whispered, crouching low and grabbing his shoulders. His lashes fluttered and he tried to sit upright. "Can I sit close to you?" she asked.

Without waiting for an answer, 'Eve' straddled his lap, looping her legs around his waist. She spoke to him in a voice indiscernible from my true sister, telling him how she admired him and how unfair I was

THE SHADOWS OF DARK ROOT

to him. Shane, still asleep, lazily wrapped his arm around Eve's back and pulled her close to his chest. She turned to me and winked.

I thrust out my hands and sent a blast of energy her way, but I couldn't dislodge her. Lilith rolled her eyes, then stood up again, revealing that Shane had fallen fully back to sleep.

"So, the bad girls do little for him," Lilith mused. "Perhaps he likes the good girls?" She morphed into Merry's shape. "Or the smart ones?" she said, now becoming Ruth Anne. "Or maybe he likes familiarity."

Lilith took her time melting into her next form. Now, standing naked before Shane, was his ex-wife, Irene.

I'd had enough.

I drew from the earth and the sky and everything around, ripping the sound from my body. "Stop!" I intoned, breaking her silence spell. "You will leave us alone, now!"

Lilith looked surprised but laughed as she returned to her natural form, this one solid. We moved towards one another, standing nose to nose. I wasn't a goddess, but I was no pushover, either.

Without warning, she kissed me, biting my bottom lip before releasing me. "You smell of lavender," she said. "An earthly delight, and my favorite."

"What is wrong with you?" I demanded, pushing her back. "Don't you understand what love is?"

She put her hand under her chin. "In theory, I do. But I have yet to see it. You say he loves you now, but will he still love you when your face is covered in lines and your breasts are barren?" A sheer gown appeared on her body and her hair was now bound up in radiant jewels. "Romantic love is temporary, but the Sisterhood is eternal. Join us, Magdalene. We will drive the evils of men from the Upper World and reclaim it as our own. If you join us, I will help you prevail against both Larinda and Armand."

I backed up. "Is that why you're here? To prove to me that all men are evil, hoping I will join your cause? My son will grow to be a man one day. I won't listen to anything more you have to say."

"I merely wanted to show you the truth of things. Men cannot be trusted. They all begin as someone's sweet son, but time corrupts them. You've been privy to your father's story. Surely, you see that what I'm saying is truth."

"What did you show me? You couldn't tempt Shane. Not in your own guise, and not in any other."

"There was one image he responded to. Yours. It puzzles me the most."

My anger quickly melted. Lilith may not believe in love, but that didn't mean it wasn't real. She had spent her immortal years trying to prove it's non-existence in order to validate her own earlier betrayal, and with Shane, at least, she had failed.

"He can still be turned," Lilith said confidently. "Given time and motivation."

"Not Shane. And not me."

The smugness lifted from Lilith's face. She looked toward the emerging sunrise, her eyes flickering as she considered my words. "I hope you are correct. That might be nice. I will keep my eye on you, Maggie Maddock. And I'm taking this in lieu of your husband." She opened her hand to reveal the sprig of lavender Jillian had given me. "It reminds me of home."

Her body became less dimensional. She was fading away. "I hope you will reconsider and join us someday. There is a great battle coming, and everyone will pick a side - in our world and in yours."

Lilith disappeared, taking the remainder of the night with her.

Birdsong soon filled the sky, waking the others. They rubbed their eyes, all claiming they had never slept so deeply. I gave Shane a quick and grateful kiss.

The frost covering the bridge was quickly thawing, and I could clearly see the other side.

"Looks safe to me," Michael said.

"I agree. And I don't think the portal is far beyond," Shane said pointing to an expanse of rocks.

"Can't we just go straight for the mountain?" I asked. "It doesn't look that far."

"No, it's deceptive. If you look close, you'll see it's moving," Shane said.

I squinted. Sure enough, the mountain seemed to have shifted to the west. "I'm guessing it was created so that it can't be accessed directly."

"Another portal, huh? Aren't you worried it's your turn beneath the interrogation lights?" Michael asked Shane.

"Aren't you?"

Michael lifted the cross he wore around his neck. "I have nothing to fear."

"You'd better hope so," Shane grumbled, closing up his pack. "Because if I find out you ever did anything to hurt Maggie..."

"Let's get going," I said, stepping in before it could escalate.

The scent of salt was on the wind, and several pelican-like birds appeared along the river, landing on boulders and squawking out their hellos. Eagle Mountain was now squarely in our sights. Our fortunes had surely turned.

We crossed the wide river easily, finding ourselves on a rocky beach. White foamy waves washed onto the shore and seagulls squawked overhead. Somehow, it now felt more like an ocean than a river.

"Where do I know this place from?" Eve said. "It looks familiar."

"A movie set from one of your films?" Paul answered.

Eve glowered at him and turned away.

"This looks like the beach Mama took us to when we were kids," Merry said. "We didn't stay long, but I remember running barefoot through the wet sand." She looked at the beach longingly.

"Maybe that's it," Eve agreed, solemnly.

It did look like the Oregon beach of our youth, with towering boulders, brewing clouds, and froth along the water's edge.

I heard a baby crying, not far away. And then another. Their cries became yowls of pain. The others heard it too, their eyes darting around, chasing shadows. "Did anyone hear Montana?" I asked desperately.

"I can't tell!" Merry said.

We held still, listening as the gut-wrenching sounds rose and fell like the waves.

"Mags!" Ruth Anne punched me in the shoulder. She pointed to a cave entrance further down the beach, carved into the shadows of a low cliff. And then I saw them - squat gray-winged creatures marching out of the cave in a steady stream. They had hooked fingers and flat feet, and carried woven baskets in their teeth.

Even from that distance I could make out their bulbous eyes, rounded ears, and great bat-like wings. We watched as they climbed a set of steep stairs to the top of the cliff. From there, they pumped their wings and set sail. The baskets dangling from their mouths wiggled and shook, emitting the sounds of crying infants.

"Gargoyles!" Eve said. "I've seen them before."

I charged towards the cave, not waiting for further explanation, directing my anger at the nearest gargoyle. "Leave those children alone!" It turned its lion face towards me, hissing so fiercely it dropped the basket from its mouth. I harnessed the energy around me, blasting one beast after another with my wand. They began falling from the sky, dropping their bundles.

The largest of the gargoyles leapt at me, knocking my wand from my hand with its massive paw. As I scrambled to pick it up, the creature grabbed me with its muscular arms, its talons digging into my skin. I was lifted into the air, kicking and cursing. I flailed at its underbelly, hoping to break free.

Shane lunged for me, but was caught by another beast. One by one, we were snatched up and carried into the clouds. I cried out, feeling the sting of the gargoyles claws, but the sound was drowned out by the steady drone of their heavy wingbeats. The height was dizzying, and I watched helplessly as The Star card flitted out of my pocket and drifted away. We bobbed briskly along, picking up speed as we were carted through the sky.

A tall stone tower appeared ahead, floating amid the clouds. *Larinda's castle?* Suddenly the talons released me, and I was cast inside a high window like a thrown dice. The others landed around me, tumbling along the stone floor.

Once inside the musty turret, we collected ourselves and checked for injuries. We all had scratches and bruises, but were otherwise okay. I looked around at the gray stone, searching for evidence of Larinda. There was no door, no way of escape from our circular prison, except for the lone window. But going through the window without wings would mean plummeting to our deaths on the ground far below.

"Where are we?" I demanded.

"I don't know, but this isn't Eagle Mountain."

"It's my fault," Eve said, standing on tiptoes to stare out the arched window. "Aunt Dora used to say that gargoyles stole children who wouldn't stop crying. She had a book of fairy tales from the Old World. One day I secretly peeked at it, to see if she was telling the truth. The gargoyles made the children slaves and they never saw their families again. The story and pictures scared the hell out of me I think that was the day I stopped crying."

"That's horrible," Merry said.

"So, this is all your creation?" I asked Eve. If she had read the book, she knew how it ended. "How were the children freed?"

"I never read that far," Eve admitted.

"If it was one of Aunt Dora's old books, they were probably never rescued. They were probably eaten," Ruth Anne said. "The old fairy tales were written to scare children into behaving. They didn't have the happy endings that kid's stories have these days."

Eve nodded, tugging on the ends of her hair. "All I remember is that every night for several months after reading the story, I waited for the gargoyles to come. And now, I've come to them. Is this what irony is?"

Merry paced the room. "What are we going to do now, Maggie?"

"Hell, Merry. How should I know? All I know is I seem to be getting further away from my son." I stamped my foot, loosening dust from high blocks. I stamped again, harder, and the walls rippled. "If we can't find a way out soon, I'll tear this entire tower down."

"Does anyone else smell... coffee?" Merry asked.

It was a strange question, but as soon as she'd asked it, the rich smell of brewing coffee filled the air. It was so bitter it burned my nostrils.

"Too much?" said a woman's voice. "I just wanted you to feel at home."

The coffee smell vanished, replaced with an even stronger scent of lavender. Before I could recognize the voice, my mind went numb and I dropped to the floor like a ragdoll.

As I drifted into unconsciousness, I heard a song:

> *The wheel of fortune spins and spins.*
> *Around the world and back again.*
> *Just when the lessons have been learned.*
> *Another spinner takes his turn.*

JUSTICE

"Well, well, aren't you all sweet little birdies?"

It was hot. The room was swaying. My head ached and my stomach turned.

I was several yards up in the air, sitting. It wasn't the room that was swinging, it was the metal cage I was imprisoned in. I dangled above a bubbling cauldron, spewing steam up through the bars beneath me. There were other cages, one for each of us, and cauldrons to match, as well.

"Here, birdie, birdie." A cloaked woman whistled from the floor below us, holding out her hand like a falcon's perch. We were in a new room, one with many arched windows, and I expected to see a bird fly to her hand. But when the woman kept chirping, and no bird appeared, I realized she was mocking us.

"You okay, Maggie?" Shane called from the cage on my left. I nodded as my fingers gripped the metal bars. The cage floor warmed and I moved as far as I could to the other edge. *Was this part of Aunt Dora's storybook, too?*

I studied our new surroundings. It was a palatial room, though I was now certain we weren't on Eagle Mountain. The shadowy chamber flickered from the many torches along the walls. Mounted in between were dozens of stone grotesques, each with its own hideous face. Long paintings of fantastical creatures hung beside the arched windows. Our cages were attached to ropes, looped through pulleys high overhead.

Something sparkled near the woman's feet. I quickly patted myself down. My wand was gone, but thankfully I still had the half-eaten apple, ankh, amber bracelet and hourglass. The woman caught my troubled expression as I inventoried my belongings. She smiled, lowering her cloak. She had drab brown hair and a plain, pinched face.

"I tried to take your bracelet," the woman said. "But I couldn't get the darned thing off your wrist. But fortunately, you all were very careless with your wands."

Leah!

My half-sister's magick must be much greater here, I thought, as she was no match for any one of us back in Dark Root. "What do you want, Leah?" I demanded, my voice booming across the room. "I always pegged you for your mother's lackey, but I'm sensing you have your own agenda."

"Isn't it obvious, *sister?*" Her words were venomous, despite her smile. She snapped her fingers and one of the many grotesques disentangled itself from the upper wall, turning from stone to flesh. The small gargoyle leapt down and nestled beside her feet, seeming to purr. "I've been waiting a long time for my revenge, and now I'll have it. This is Mother's world, and I'm much more practiced here than you. I. Want. My. Justice."

My cage creaked and shifted, tossing me back and forth. I was being lowered! I screamed, startled, and held tight to the bars. The others pleaded with her to stop, my cage so close to the cauldron that steam wafted all around me. It was hard to breathe or even see. Leah laughed as I came to a lurching stop. The gargoyle at her feet turned again to stone, and she wrapped the rope to my enclosure around it several times, securing it.

"Leah, please. Let us go so I can get my son," I begged. "You know what your mother will do if we don't stop her."

She spat into the nearest cauldron. It crackled and hissed. "You're assuming my mother hasn't already done what you fear," Leah said. "And why should I care what happens to your brat? There are enough people in the Upper World. What's one less going to matter? You shouldn't be begging for my mercy, not after all you've done to me. You should be praying that whatever happens, happens quickly."

There was a flash of lightning outside the windows, blinding us momentarily. Leah lowered my cage one rope wrap of the gargoyle. The bars grew hotter and steam licked at my bare ankles.

"You'll be first, Maggie," she said, her hand on the rope. "I want the others to watch this. I was going to save you for last, and make you watch them suffer, but I'm not giving you a chance to worm your way out. Not this time."

I reached my hands out of the cage and yelled. "You will not touch us!" Through the sheer strength of my will, she was pushed back several steps. As she moved away, I saw a stash of our belongings piled at her feet – our wands, packs, and Ruth Anne's camera.

"See? That's what I'm talking about," Leah said, recovering her balance. "You have absolutely no respect for anyone or anything." She discarded her robe, revealing her usual jeans and no-frills T-shirt. She was thinner than normal, and her skin had a green cast.

"If you reach for that rope again, I'll tear this entire place apart." I pointed to a portrait, and it crashed to the ground. "It looks like you put quite a bit of work into this little world of yours. What do you want? Let's make a deal."

She pursed her lips together, eyeing the rope. "Okay," she eventually said. "I'll make you a deal. You give me what I want, and I'll let you go. If you don't, I'll leave you here for that thing Mother unleashed to find you."

That thing? Does she mean Gahabrien?

"Don't listen to her, Maggie," Shane said.

"What do you want," I asked her.

"Your hair."

She ran a hand through her stringy brown mane, now well past her shoulders. It was well-documented that a witch's powers lay in the length of her hair. I had cut hers off nearly a year ago, effectively neutering her for a time. I should have guessed that would be her revenge, to take away the source of my magick too.

Leah snapped her fingers and another small gargoyle leapt from the wall. She reached into her dress and handed the creature a silver objected that glinted in the firelight. The beast sprang into the air on its heavy stone wings, landing against the side of my cage. It regarded me briefly through the bars, then spit out a pair of scissors. Then, it flew out through one of the windows, disappearing into the lightning storm.

Leah's eyes lingered on the window. The sound of thunder reverberated through the stone walls, vibrating our cages and rattling a few loose stone bricks. *Gahabrien is coming for me.*

My hands trembled as I reached for the scissors and opened the blades. I stretched out a strand of my hair, wondering if she would keep her end of the bargain.

"No deal, Leah!" Shane yelled. "Let us go now or you'll pay!"

"Tick-tock," Leah said to me, ignoring Shane. "You know what's coming for you."

"Okay, okay." The entire building shook under Gahabrien's approach. I watched the windows nervously as I held the scissors to my hair.

So many questions raced through my head as I snipped the first lock. Would I lose all my powers, or would they just be diminished? What if my ankh no longer worked? And how would I get Montana back from Larinda, if my magick was muted? There were so many what-ifs, but I would have to deal with them later.

I made the first cut just below my ears. A long rope of cherry-red hair fell, slipping into the cauldron below.

I looked at Leah. "All of it," she said, her ferret eyes darting to the door. The walls were all shaking now, and lightning blazed across every window. "Quickly, or I leave!"

I sawed off the rest of my hair, up to my chin. I held the tresses out, dangling the long red ribbons for her to see. I felt naked, and looked at my feet rather than the crestfallen eyes of my companions around me.

"There!" I said. "Now let us go!"

Gahabrien was almost upon us. The pictures rattled, smashing to the ground, one after the other. The cauldrons sloshed beneath our feet. There wasn't much time left.

Leah paused, appearing to weigh her options. She snapped her fingers and a large silver key appeared in her hand. As she was summoning another gargoyle to deliver it, the building lurched and several high blocks toppled out of the wall. Startled, Leah dropped the key and backed towards the door.

"You can't leave us here!" I said. "Leah!"

She looked over her shoulder as she left, pulling the hood of her cloak across her face. "I'm sorry," she said, disappearing.

I looked to Shane, feeling both ashamed and exposed, wondering if he still found me desirable without my hair. But then I wondered why it even mattered.

Because in another few moments, hair or no hair, we would all be victims of Gahabrien's wrath.

THE HANGED MAN

*T*he shadow entered through the windows. It wound its way down the walls in long fingers, then swept across the stone floor. We held still in our cages, afraid of drawing its attention. But the entire shadow was angling towards me. Gahabrien had found me.

The bars of my prison were almost untouchable now, heated by the brewing cauldron. My clothes were damp, and I alternated lifting my feet to give them a reprieve from the pain.

Gahabrien's scavenging minions appeared, crawling out of cracks and dark corners. They rubbed their hands and flicked their tongues, as if anticipating a tasty meal. They were barely more than shadows, but their malevolent energy rippled through the chamber, growing stronger as more joined in.

What can I do!? We were without our wands and my magick was gone. A limp strand of my hair still lay on the cage floor, wet with steam.

I looked to the others. Merry stood with her eyes closed, silently reciting some unheard verse, while Eve stared into the cauldron below her. Paul and Ruth Anne were scrutinizing our surroundings, searching for anything that might set us free. Michael and Shane pulled at their bars, trying to physically force their way out.

I touched my roughly cropped hair, knowing I shouldn't have trusted Leah. She was the seed of her evil mother, after all. Perhaps a part of me wanted to believe she wasn't destined for a specific life path simply because of who her parents were.

The room filled with the wheeze of labored breathing, and at first I thought it was the wind. It was peppered by raspy moans. The whole world quaked, as if we were golden geese, awaiting the giant's return.

"Maggie! Please do something!" Eve called.

Please do something. They were all looking to me.

"Screw this," I said to myself. I was a wilder. The Sworn One. To hell with hair or wands. I was never good with rules anyway, magick or otherwise.

I focused on a wall torch, the one nearest the rope holding my cage suspended. Concentration was difficult, with the demon looming and the hot metal scorching my feet, but I refused to let it break my attention. "Grow!" I willed the flame.

It did. It flared into a raging bonfire as I spread my fingers apart. Soon, my rope was ablaze.

"Maggie, be careful! You're almost in the cauldron" Shane shouted as my cage rocked down a hard notch.

I was close enough to the cauldron to smell its fetid contents. Whatever magick Leah was playing with was not natural, which probably added to her newfound abilities. She had given a bit of her own soul for power in the Netherworld, just like her father.

The only way to combat dark magick, of course, was with light magick. I clapped my hands together and my crystal bracelet sparked excitedly. I commanded the cauldron flames to douse. They hissed and steamed and sputtered out, like dying dragons.

Thrusting my hand through the bars, I snapped the silver key off the ground and through the air, straight into my palm. There was nothing I couldn't do here, I realized. I had the power - hair or no hair.

I quickly unlocked the cage door and leapt out, just as the fire burned through the rope and my cage clattered onto the top of the enormous kettle. I spread my arms wide, unlocking all the cages simultaneously. My bracelet vibrated and I felt all the active energies of the room flow through me.

"Jump!" I called.

"You sure, Mags?" Merry called nervously.

"Yes! Now!"

One by one, they did. I pressed my palms to the floor, counteracting their falls with whatever remaining upward energy I could muster. Once on the ground, we scrambled for our belongings.

"Let's get out of here!" Shane said, nodding to the door.

"But the demon's out there!" Eve objected.

The turret was crumbling all around us, and even the shadow minions were scurrying to get away. "Yes. But at least out there we aren't sitting ducks," Shane said.

The stone floor around the door split wide open, siphoning nearby debris into its growing maw. Even the shadows were pulled inside. The air smelled of sulfur, yet somehow the door itself stood, trembling, as if afraid of revealing what waited on the other side.

The only way through the door was over the crevice. And then we'd still have to get past Gahabrien.

"Everyone, look!" Shane called.

As the walls continued their collapse, the remaining stone grotesques began opening their sleepy eyes, yawning as they stretched out their taloned paws. Realizing their plight, they leapt into the air. The smaller ones flew away through the windows, but the larger ones were forced to leave through the door. They massed before it, not able to all crowd through the opening at the same time.

They're our ticket out of here.

"Let's go," I shouted, running full speed and leaping across the crevice. I landed on the back of the closest gargoyle, then reached down for Eve's hand, pulling her up behind me. I covered my head as a painting crashed down on us.

Looking around, I saw Shane and Ruth Anne following my lead. Managing to get onto gargoyles of their own, they helped the others aboard. We held tight to their thick necks, and each other, as the creatures jostled through the door and sailed away from the crumbling tower.

Our mounts descended through the sky in a wide spiral, and I caught my first sight of the Netherworld's Gahabrien - a massive dark funnel of anger and rage. A tendril whipped out to snatch me from the air, but the gargoyle instinctively evaded it and kept flying.

"Where are we heading?" Eve asked, her hair whipping behind her like a raven's wings.

"This was your creation," I said.

"Only the gargoyles."

"There's another portal," Shane said. He pointed to a hilly region below. "If these things fly low enough, jump."

The gate appeared in the distance, shimmering amidst the chaos of the demon storm.

We're still too high.

"Tuck your heads and roll when you land," Shane directed.

"Wait!" Merry drew a circle in the air with her wand, finishing it with a cross inside. "That should help."

I called to Shane before slipping from the gargoyle's back. "I love you," I said. *Just in case.*

"Remember that when you see what I've done."

I didn't have time to process his words. We all jumped together.

14

DEATH

*I*t is said that at the moment of your death, your life flashes before you.

As I spiraled towards the ground, I saw the memories of my life so far - my childhood, fighting and playing with my sisters; my teenage years rebelling against Sasha; my time with Michael in his commune, how I had both loved and hated him on a whim; my return to Dark Root and the reunion with my family; the dread of discovering I was pregnant; waking from the curse of Mother's spell book; giving birth to Montana; learning that Jillian was my mother; falling in love with Shane; and finally, losing my son.

The scenes played out instantaneously, as gravity exerted its will over me. I wished for one more chance to wander Aunt Dora's garden, have tea with Jillian, argue with my sisters, or kiss Shane. But I was nonetheless grateful for the memories I had collected, even though some were tinged with regret. I had stayed with Michael too long, out of convenience or rebellion but not love. I hadn't cherished my sisters as I should have when we were young, thinking there was plenty of time to make it up to them later. I had let petty emotions like jealousy and anger rule me far too often. All those arguments... all that bickering. Why? Time in *Real Life* was a luxury, and I had squandered too much.

As I pondered this all, I realized I wasn't going to die.

We drifted towards the hilltop, as if wearing sails. Merry was the first to land, grinning up at us in exhilaration. We dropped down beside her, hitting earth that might as well have been made of cotton.

"Yahoo!" Merry whooped, dancing about, giving everyone high-fives. There was a light in her eyes that I hadn't seen in a long time. "That was my spell!" she said. "It just came to me and I didn't even need a wand!"

"Merry! I love you!" I hugged her tight. I knew now that I had mistaken my sister's gentleness for weakness. "You're a badass," I said.

She beamed. "Thank you, Maggie. That means a lot."

"There's the portal," Shane said, wasting no time.

The gargoyles were long gone and we had cleared Gahabrien's storm, but only for the moment. It raged on the horizon, working its way towards us.

I frisked myself, making sure I still had my acorn, wand, hourglass and apple. "Let's hurry."

"I suggest you make your confessions now, if you haven't already done so," Michael said, clutching his cross as we approached the glimmering doorway.

Merry's lip trembled. "I wish I could."

"You have nothing to worry about," Michael said to her, then looked at Shane. "How about you, cowboy? Got any secrets from the range you want to share? I'm qualified to absolve your sins."

"My only secret is that I want to punch that smugness from your face," Shane answered.

"That's hardly a secret," Michael replied.

Merry linked arms with Shane and Michael, nodding to herself as she took a deep breath. "I got this," she said.

With that, the three stepped in front of the portal, like Dorothy flanked by the Tin Man and Scarecrow, wondering what they would discover behind the curtain.

15

TEMPERANCE

"*'mon soldier, it's 0500 hours."*

Shane rubbed his eyes and focused on the lean man in glasses and a starched tan T-shirt hovering over him. He had seen him land by chopper the night before, but hadn't formally met him. The captain was older than Shane by about a decade, and his face wore an expression of no-nonsense, absolute authority.

Still in his sleeping bag, Shane scratched his head and propped himself up on to his elbows, looking around for his thermos. The captain handed him one, filled with hot coffee. "Drink up fast. Dawn's coming."

Shane dressed quickly and stepped out of his tent. The sun had not yet risen. The indigo-blue sky, speckled by the few stars brave enough to stick around and see this world for what it was without the cover of night - an inhospitable shit hole that even the locals called 'hell.'

He rubbed his temples and finished the coffee, only vaguely aware of its earthy flavor, which wasn't unusual in this part of the world. Everything had a slightly different taste here - and most of it tasted like dust.

"Where is everyone?" Shane asked himself, looking around for Irene and the rest of his mates. She'd been skittish the last few nights, swearing that people were listening in on their conversations. He had joked in response,

"Why wouldn't they just hire one of us to listen in? Wouldn't that be easier?"

The captain returned and Shane was able to read the name tape over his right breast - Captain Dewayne Markson. He paced and spoke while Shane laced his boots. "The others have already been given their orders for today. You'll meet up with them at sunset, if we do this right."

Shane raised an eyebrow as he tucked his T-shirt into his camo pants. He was a light sleeper and was surprised he hadn't heard them leave. "Do what right, if you don't me asking? And why are we the only two left?"

"Your questions will be answered shortly," Markson said, handing Shane his camelback and steering them towards the lone jeep parked beside the campsite.

Shane watched for landmarks as Markson drove them down a dusty road. When the captain wasn't looking, Shane peeked at his flip phone, hoping Irene had texted. But the screen was as dead as the desert. Odd, he thought, remembering that he'd charged it off the generator the night before.

Markson turned down a side road, kicking up even more dust as he hit the gas. There was no sign of civilization. Shane tried to tune into Irene, but couldn't find her. She must have 'unplugged' for her own work.

Almost an hour later, Markson pulled up to an abandoned store. The sign had been torn down, but there were barrels and shelves and other remnants suggesting the place had been used recently. Shane followed the captain into the building and through a door behind the counter. They entered a cool dark room lit only by two lanterns. It suddenly occurred to Shane that it probably wasn't a good idea to be out here alone with this stranger, no matter how many railroad tracks he wore. But what could he do now? He was weaponless.

Markson pointed to a desk formed of wooden crates. A laptop was placed on the rough surface. The captain leaned over and started tapping keys, while Shane watched his fingers out of the corner of his eye. He was pretty sure he caught the password, and quickly committed it to memory.

Markson turned the screen towards him, revealing a photograph of a teenager, no older than fifteen. The boy had dark hair and skin, like most of the people of this region, but his eyes were bright and hopeful – a rarity here. He was almost smiling.

"Who is that?" Shane asked, continuing to study the boy's features as he tried tuning into him.

"Asha. He's the reason I brought you here."

"You want me to track him, huh?" The boy had a mop of black hair and flecks of green in his eyes, and he wore a blue Dodgers T-shirt. "Is he nearby?"

"That's what I'm hoping you'll tell me," the captain said, scrolling through a series of photos. "He's the son of a rebel leader, and they've been spotted together in numerous places, including New York City. Your teammates have been taken to those other areas, hoping to get a lock on him."

"So someone gets an all-expense paid trip to New York and I'm stuck here," Shane said, shaking his head.

"You're the best. And this is the most likely spot."

"Ah, you flatter me," Shane said, taking the mouse and examining the photos. It appeared the teenager had traveled extensively during his young life. The more Shane attuned, the more he felt the boy's wanderlust.

"So who is his father?" Shane asked as the captain took a seat on the corner of the makeshift desk. "And why do we need him? Kid doesn't seem like a bad sort, if you judge by photographs."

"It's not the kid we're after. But his father is a very bad man, and seems to have some talents of his own. Our remote viewers aren't able to get a fix on him. But they've caught a few glimpses of his son, who doesn't protect himself nearly as well."

"The innocent never do," Shane said, his eyes resting on the last picture. The boy was no older than twelve in the photo, and he was holding hands with a lovely young woman that Shane guessed to be his mother.

"She's dead now," Markson said. "Intel says the father killed her."

"What the hell's wrong with this world?" Shane asked, looking into the kid's eyes. He had lost his own mother at a young age and felt a growing connection to Asha. "So you think if we find him, we find Daddy?"

"Exactly."

"But you're not looking for this man just because he killed his wife, are you?"

"No. And that's all I'll say on the matter."

"What happens to Asha then?"

The captain spread a palm across the desk. "He has other family. The father is the only one we want."

"I was raised by extended family, too," Shane said. "It wasn't an ideal situation, but I was loved. The kid won't get hurt, right?"

"As I said, we're only after his dad. Think you can do it?"

Shane paused before answering. He knew he could do it. He had already established a link just by looking at the last photo alone. In fact, for the first time since being recruited, he felt good about his job. Justice had to be done.

"What's your technique?" Markson asked. "Sleep? Trance? Meditation?"

Shane drew his lips into his mouth, wondering how much to reveal. "Mind if I take a look at the orders first?" Shane asked, knowing his request might elicit an angry response. Markson reached into his pocket and produced the appropriate documents. All seemed in order and Shane relaxed.

"I have several methods. I can locate him through his dreams, but because of the language barrier and the fact we've never met in person, that probably won't be much help."

"And your other techniques?"

Shane gave him a cock-eyed smile. "I just ask."

Shane viewed the boy's photographs again, concentrating on the eyes. They showed so much. They were the same eyes as boys the world over - full of longing, optimism, and hope for adventure. But the longer Shane stared, the more he saw sadness. There was loss there, and not just of his mother. But then again, so many people endured sadness in this region of the world.

Shane's eyelids drooped under the weight of his stare. His mind and body relaxed, and he locked onto the boy's location. He was close by - no more than fifty miles away, maybe less.

"Get anything?"

"He's not far," Shane said, squinting to get a better look. "He's in a very large house, outside of a town. There's maybe twenty others with him, mostly men."

Shane felt the captain lean in over his shoulder. "Do you see a man with a wide scar across his left cheek? That would be his father."

Shane adjusted his inner lens, scanning the house.

Asha was playing a video game on a flat screen TV that looked out of place in the otherwise stark compound. He seemed oblivious to the others in the room, even to the pretty young girl who brought him a drink and smiled.

Shane zoomed out - a daunting task that hurt his head. He saw eight or nine men huddled over a table, papers scattered everywhere. They spoke excitedly in the local dialect, sometimes arguing, sometimes laughing. Shane wasn't able to see their faces, hunched over as they were, but he knew this was happening now - not in a past or future timeline.

"They're discussing plans. Something about Time Lock."

"Do you mean Time Lift?"

"Yes, sorry. Interpretation isn't my strong suit."

"Ah, Jesus. Time Lift. That's what I was afraid of." Markson ran his fingers through his choppy blonde hair, then scribbled a note on Post-It pad lying on the desk.

Shane had never heard of Time Lift, and wasn't fool enough to ask. The military had strange names for everything, both innocent and insidious. Sometimes, the less you knew the better.

"Can you tell when they plan on making their move?" Markson asked, now pacing.

"I'll try."

It was easier this time, like going through a locked door you'd already picked the last time through. Asha must have lost a round of his video game; he cursed and was reprimanded by one of the men – a man with a wide scar across his left cheek.

"Asha, turn that thing off and join us," his father insisted. The boy reluctantly turned and trudged to the table. "I don't know why you play games, when we are living this great adventure. Look! All this is our territory now." The man stabbed his finger into a map. "And soon, all this will be ours as well." He circled the opposite end of the map, pointing at a spot Shane couldn't see. "Why be a prince of video games when you can be a prince of the real world?"

The boy reached into his jeans pocket and pulled out a thick pair of glasses. They made him look even younger. He leaned over the map and studied it, just as two women came into the room and were quickly warned away.

"Do we really need more than we already have, Father?" Asha asked. "We have so much."

"The only way to protect what's ours is to secure our borders."

"But people will be hurt," the boy protested. Some of the older men laughed, clutching their bloated bellies.

"People will always get hurt, my son. It's the way of the world. But out of chaos comes order. You'll understand, when you are older."

"This isn't what Mama would have wanted."

The room went silent and anger filled the man's eyes. He loomed over his son, dwarfing him. His arms were large and heavily muscled. A soldier's arms. His face had seen far more battles than the lone scar attested to. Shane could feel the fear rolling off Asha.

"You were warned never to speak of your mother around me."

"I'm sorry, father."

"You're always sorry. And yet, you continue to speak of her."

"I'm her son."

"You're my son! She was weak." He looked Asha over, sneering. "You are too much like her. That's why I'm trying to make you a man."

The boy lowered his head. "Thank you, father."

"Now, stop with the video games. It's time to grow up. Tomorrow, Time Lift commences and you'll deliver the message."

"The message?"

A few nervous chuckles broke the strained silence. The man reached into a box, removing a sack. It wasn't large, but judging from the way Asha strained in receiving it, it was heavy. The boy peeked inside, then quickly closed it again.

Asha raised his face to his father. "No. I won't be your messenger."

The man opened his jacket, revealing the hilt of a knife tucked into his waistband. "Your sister would be very sad if her brother disappeared, don't you think?" He nodded towards the pretty girl who had offered Asha a drink earlier, sitting in the adjoining room. She was peeling a piece of fruit. Two of the older men stared at her, as if she were a piece of candy.

"All right," Asha said, his lip quivering as he looked away from his sister. "I'll go."

"You'll enjoy yourself," his father reassured him, patting him hard on the back. "It will be just like your video game, but much more fun. When you return, we'll have a party and celebrate your found manhood."

The men congratulated him, offering him cigars. But Asha's eyes never left his sister.

Shane turned away in disgust. Damn it. Just a kid. He thought his own childhood had been hard, but he couldn't imagine what Asha was going through. He bit his tongue to fully break contact, and noticed he was bathed in sweat.

"What did you see?" Markson demanded.

Shane thought briefly of telling him he hadn't gotten a clear read after all. Then, he could maybe steal away in the middle of the night and rescue the boy and his sister.

But that was insane. Even if he did make it out of camp unnoticed, he would almost certainly be killed in the rescue attempt. He knew how to fight, but he wouldn't last long against so many armed men. Neither would those kids.

"They are planning the raid tomorrow," Shane said reluctantly, closing the laptop, so that he wouldn't have to look at the boy anymore. Asha was already going to haunt his dreams. "They're telling the boy to deliver something first. It might be a bomb."

"Ah, fuck. Fuck!" Markson wiped his neck. "Tomorrow? Are you sure?"

"That's what I saw."

"Okay, soldier."

"Shane Doler," he corrected. He hated being called a soldier.

"Whatever. Are you sure about this?"

"As sure as I can be."

Markson shook his head. "I hope for both our sakes that you're as good as they claim, because I'm putting our asses on the line with this."

"I didn't ask for this assignment. If whatever you're about to do goes bad, it's on your heads, not mine."

It was a bold statement towards a superior officer, but Shane knew he had leverage. No one could force him to track anyone. And he had no personal ties, at least that they knew of, that could be used against him.

"What's the name of the village?" Markson asked.

"I'll tell you on one condition."

The captain looked doubtful. He was obviously an intelligent man. A stupid one would have threatened court martial. But Markson understood Shane's advantage. "What's your condition?"

"You bring the boy and his sister back. Get them out of there."

"He's got a sister? This gets better and better. Yes, of course we'll get them out. We just want the man in charge. Just give me the village name."

"Do I have your word?" *Shane asked, staring into the captain's steely gray eyes.*

The man nodded curtly. "You have my word," *he said, extending a hand.*

Shane gave him the name.

As their hands locked, Shane felt a jolt, from his fingertips all the way into his heart.

~

We stood in a world of purple mist rising up from primordial ground. There were sounds around us in this world of vapor - scuffles, whistles, grunts and stomps. None of them comforting. But I didn't care about any of this at the moment, as I stared into Shane's blank eyes. They looked past me, rather than at me.

"So, that's your secret?" Eve asked, grinding her boot heel into the earth. "You got off pretty easy. Meanwhile, I bared my soul to everyone."

"That wasn't all you bared," Paul fired back.

"You're one to talk, Guitar Hero." Eve glared.

"Convenient, isn't it?" Michael asked me. "He's a dreamwalker and we're in a dream world. It's fortuitous that the portal picked one of his more noble moments to showcase."

"You suggesting I had some control of this?" Shane asked.

Michael shrugged "I'm just suggesting it's convenient, that's all."

Shane stepped forward, handing me his cowboy hat. "I've had enough of your arrogance. And your suggestions. And you ogling my wife. Yes, she's *my* wife."

"She was my wife first."

"Only in that failed little cult of yours."

"I was ordained in that cult, and my ordination married you. Still want to squabble about technicalities?"

Shane took his hat back, pulling it low, his eyes still on Michael. "You know what's really convenient? The fact that you haven't had your turn inside the truth chamber yet."

"My heart's right with God."

"But it's not right with me." Shane looked him up and down, his lip curling. "I can't wait until it's your turn. I want to see you squirm."

"It's never good karma to wish harm on others. I believe that's true in every religion, not just in my *cult*."

"Stop it," I said to them both, before things escalated further. "Let's just be glad we passed through another portal without a problem. We need to focus now."

"Maggie's right," Merry said, pulling Michael a few steps in one direction while I herded Shane in the other.

I studied my husband - the way his eyes drifted, his palms clenched, and his shoulders fell. This had nothing to do with Michael. Shane was still reliving his portal memory.

"What happened to Asha?" I asked.

"I don't want to talk about it." Shane said.

"Please. I'm your wife. Tell me."

Shane tilted his head to the side and inhaled a long breath through his nose. "You don't want to know. Trust me."

"Oh, no," I said, stepping back.

The others heard, and walked over.

"They killed him?" Merry asked, her hand at her chest.

Shane's words lingered on his tongue, and we held our breaths. It was like watching a drop of water on the tip of a faucet, waiting for it to finally break free. "They killed them all," he said simply.

They killed them all.

"No," I protested, remembering Asha's eyes and his sister's smile. "The captain promised they'd be safe. Are you sure?"

Shane turned his hands over, studying them as if they had done something wrong. "They wanted to stop them before they could carry out the raid – now that they had the location. They took out the compound in the middle of the night. The children were... collateral damage."

He shoved his hands into his pockets and turned away.

I didn't know what to say, because I didn't know how I felt. I had vowed to love him no matter what I was shown, but at the moment, I felt sick.

Michael walked past, muttering. "They say the road to hell is paved with good intentions. I guess they're right."

~

"This must be where the Beatles came up with their song, 'Nowhere Man,'" Paul said.

"They probably didn't need portals to the Netherworld in the 1960s," Ruth Anne joked. "Just a reliable lighter."

We did our best to lighten the mood as we slogged through our new setting. The air smelled like new rain falling on a stagnant swamp. The mist hindered our vision. Birds whistled and cooed, but we couldn't see them. The area was almost prehistoric, sans the man-eating dinosaurs. At least we hoped so. I found a stick and tapped it on the ground in front of me, to feel my way forward.

"If this is Shane's world," Ruth Anne said, "the question begging to be asked is: Shane, are you afraid of marshes?"

"Yes," he answered, colorlessly.

I reached for his hand but he pulled away, pretending to pick something off his shirt.

"He okay?" Merry asked me.

My husband hadn't spoken since the portal. The muscles in his cheeks twitched as he marched forward, lost in his own head. I couldn't even guess at his thoughts. He was shielding me.

"He'll be all right," I said, wishing I had The Star card back for reassurance. Its absence made me feel somehow vulnerable.

"It would have ended badly for Asha no matter what," Merry whispered. "The boy would have been killed delivering the message."

"Can you tell him that? He trusts your intuition."

"It won't matter." She smoothed her hair from crown to shoulder. "He won't hear me on this. This is his cross and he wants to carry it. It's what keeps him going."

I knew she was right. If Shane could view it objectively, he would see it, too. It didn't take any special intuition to know that Asha had been doomed from the start, but at least the village had been saved.

But what if it were Montana? Or June Bug? How would I feel then? Could I offer up one person I cared for, to save a hundred people I had never met? I wasn't sure what was fair anymore, or what was right and what was wrong. The right- and left-hand paths edged dangerously close to one another, in some matters, at least.

We continued on, looking over our shoulders as invisible creatures clicked and chittered around us. Shane no longer seemed concerned about our direction, and I looked to the ankh, hoping for verification. We forged through these wetlands, picking our way along whatever dry ground we could find, my imagination conjuring all sorts of slithering beasts watching us from the mist.

The marsh eventually eased into a waterway of thick mud, canopied by hanging trees and heavy vines. We could see again, though there wasn't much to see. It was a world of brown sludge from earth to sky. The further we walked, the heavier I felt. The animal sounds receded, and only our labored breaths and slogging feet could be heard.

"I can't keep going," Eve said, losing a designer boot to the slurping suction of the mud. She reached down, made a face, and plucked it out. She continued on, one foot bare while she worked on cleaning the mud from her shoe.

"It won't be long," I assured her, holding out my arms to keep steady.

"There's no time here, Maggie. Every moment is long."

I wasn't sure if Eve's logic was sound, but I understood it. "We must be on the right track. We keep hitting the gates."

"Ever think this world is just screwing with us?" Eve asked. "That it delights in embarrassing us for its own amusement? Or maybe that once we all go through the portals, the whole cycle will start again?"

I had considered this, but I didn't admit to it. If we were the Netherworld's reality show, we were probably getting very high ratings. Our group was falling apart. Eve and Paul now only exchanged insults; Shane walked far ahead of us without saying a word; Michael kept to himself; and Merry grew increasingly agitated about her impending portal. Only Ruth Anne seemed in good spirits, pointing out her 'flora fun facts' as she walked. And this only added to Eve's ire.

"So this is hell?" Merry said, ducking beneath a slimy vine.

"More like purgatory," Paul said.

"Gotta hand it to you, this is some landscape," Michael called to Shane. "Is this what Montana looks like?"

"Fuck you, you arrogant asshole."

Three thin bolts of blue lightning simultaneously flashed around us. One cleaved a small tree completely in half.

Had Shane done that?

"His mood seems to be affecting this landscape," Ruth Anne noted. "Not his fears."

"Reminds me of you, Maggie," Merry said. "Good thing there aren't any light bulbs he can blow out."

"I'd kill for a light bulb right now," Eve said. "Anything but this drabness. Even the plants here are brown."

Hmm. If Shane were drawing on my abilities, perhaps I could draw on his, shaping this realm as we did in our shared dreams?

I looked at the sky, willing it to change to sunny blue, or even dull blue. Nothing.

Maybe I need to be closer to him. I increased my pace, catching up to Shane. I tried again for a sunny sky, without success.

"Don't think about it," Merry said. "Feel it."

Feel it? Feel what? *Hope,* my inner voice said.

I remembered The Star card, with a picture of a woman at a well, looking up at a morning star. She wasn't focused on the empty well, but on the rain that would eventually come. And that was what sustained her.

I stared beyond Shane, beyond the gunk and the grime. I stared into my intended future, where I was safe in Dark Root, married, raising Montana, visiting my sisters and running Mother's shop. I saw sunshine and blooming flowers and a happy childhood for my son. I was calm. Serene. At peace.

"Maggie!" Merry gasped, tugging on my arm. "There's light ahead!"

"And I hear something besides sloshing mud," Eve added.

Yes, it was the sound of a gurgling brook. We watched as daylight moved towards us, cutting through the gloom, bringing clear skies and color to the world again. It spread in all directions, washing this world clean.

Only Shane remained within the mire, inside a ten-foot column of despair. He turned on me, his eyes angry, still standing in his mud. "What the hell did you do? This was my landscape. My burden. You can't just take that away from me."

"This may be your burden, but it's not ours," I said. "I love you, Shane, but I won't let you pull us all down with you."

"Don't you get it? I was responsible for that boy's death, and his sister's, and who knows how many others?" Shane covered his ears, as if trying to block out the voices in his head. "If I hadn't given them the location, all those people would still be alive."

"You know that's not true. That boy was given a bum deal from the start. What you did may have saved a lot of other people. Shane, no one blames you. You were trying to help."

"Was I?" His hands dropped to his sides. "I've been over this a million times. Did I enlist to help others, or was I there for my own ego?"

"What do you mean?"

"I've always had this ability. That's one of the reasons I loved visiting Dark Root - I felt normal there." He stretched out his hand and wriggled his fingers. "I wanted to prove I wasn't a freak, and that maybe this ability was actually a gift. No... that's not entirely true," he continued, dropping his eyes. "Part of me really wanted to be a big shot."

"We all want to feel special. It's human."

"Uncle Joe warned me against my pride, many times. 'We use our abilities to serve the world, not for personal glory,' he told me. Asha's death is my karma. And it will haunt me till the end of my days."

"Stop it, Shane. I won't let you talk like that anymore."

He laughed, shaking his head. "I can still think it."

"Fine. But leave us out of it. I have a baby to think about. And if you'd stop being so self-absorbed for just a minute, you'd be much more help. You want to save a child? Save mine!"

"Maggie, that's just it," he said, looking me in the eye. "I let Asha down. What if I let you down, too?"

"The only way you'll let me down is if you give up," I said, getting in his face, joining him in his murky bubble. "Face your demons later. I'll help you. But don't give up on me now."

Shane sighed, looking me in the eye. Eventually he spoke. "You're right. My demons will have to wait." He slid his fingers through my short hair. "You're beautiful," he said. "This new cut really frames your face."

The gloom was scrubbed clean by the rays of bright silver sunlight, and Shane's demons fled. For now. There was an important conversation we would have one day, far in the future when we were back home. But for this moment, there was only sunshine.

～

"Maggie, can we talk?" Merry asked, gently coaxing me away from the group. Everyone's mood had improved, all except for Merry. Her energy was nervous and erratic, and I knew why – either she or Michael would be next through a portal.

We found a place to sit on the stream bank, dipping our toes. "It feels so good," I said, scooping a handful of water up onto her legs.

She splashed me with her foot in return. Soon, we were both laughing and Merry began to relax.

"June Bug and I used to do this back in Kansas," she said. "We would go to a pond when Frank was away at work, and spend the day feeding ducks and splashing around. I miss that."

"You miss the ducks? Or Frank?"

Her smile wilted. "I don't miss Frank. For a while, I thought I did, but then I realized it wasn't him I missed. It was the stability he provided me and June Bug. He made me feel safe, at least in the beginning. Then, it was just easier to stay than go."

Merry pulled up a dandelion and blew the seeds into the air. "I hope I get to see June Bug again."

"You will!" I said, standing up and wiping the dirt from the back of my legs. "Even if I don't get Montana, I'll get you home."

"Maggie..."

"Don't Maggie me," I said, helping her to her feet. "You've done more than I can ever repay you for. You'll see June Bug again. I promise that."

My sister touched a strand of my hair. "I agree with Shane. This cut suits you."

"You're coddling me," I said, inspecting my reflection in the water. I looked pale without my long locks, and my mouth was thinner than I remembered. But my eyes popped, as green as clover.

"Hey, Merry!" I said, bending over and searching the ground around us. "Make a wish."

"There are no stars out," she said.

"No, but I've got something better." I plucked up a four-leaf clover and presented it to her. She clapped her hands and laughed like a little girl. Merry had often spent her childhood days chasing rainbows and searching for leprechauns. But only once had she found a four-leaf clover – the thrill of a lifetime – and she'd willingly given it to Eve, who had just lost her favorite doll. She never found one again.

"Maggie! That was truly magical."

I blushed. "Not sure how much luck it will bring you, as I have a feeling these fields are now full of them."

Merry twisted the clover between her fingers, considering her wish as three ducklings waddled past. She crouched to pet them. "I have to admit, there is a part of me that loves this world."

"I could do without the gargoyles and the haircut," I said. "And Gahabrien, too."

Merry and I looked over our shoulders, eyes wide. Just saying the name of a demon could be enough to bring it around. She cast a protective circle around us, three times, just in case.

"Let's vow to always be close, and stay together until we are crones on our porch swing, casting curses and swigging tea," Merry said.

"I promise. But I don't ever want to be a crone," I said. "That word needs a makeover."

"I'll be a crone three years before you!" Merry said.

"Yes, but you'll be eternally young," I predicted. In my mind I watched Merry's face transform through the years. Her flaxen hair would lighten further and the ends crinkle a bit. Her plump cheeks would soften and a few lines would frame her eyes. But there wouldn't be much else to mark her journey through time. Her brightness and optimism rendered her ageless.

"How are you feeling now... about going through the portal." I asked, as we walked back.

She swallowed, tugging on her sleeves. "I'm still not sure I can do it, Maggie. I'm a coward." She wiped her eyes, forcing a smile. "Maybe I'll be spared?" she asked, hopefully. "My heart is mostly clean."

"Whatever you did, Merry, it can't be as bad as what I've done in my life. Do you remember, Eve and I killed Leo?"

"That was an accident."

"But it happened."

"And you made amends for it."

"And I'm sure you have, too, whatever it is."

"Maggie! Merry!" Shane called, interrupting us. He walked briskly, the others in tow. "The next portal is up. Are you ready?"

Merry swallowed and put her head on my shoulder. "Promise me you won't hate me, Maggie. I couldn't bear it."

"Not a chance in the world."

Shane pointed to a fork in the river I hadn't noticed before. "The gate's just beyond it."

As we reached the portal, Merry hugged Michael, harder than necessary. They were in love, I knew for sure, but did they know themselves?

Merry broke their embrace and turned, head high, walking through. She was taken right away, and the rest of us were pulled in after.

THE DEVIL

"*Goddammit, Merry! Let me in!*"

Merry slumped against the front door, feeling her heart break with every desperate slam of his fists. He couldn't stay there all night. Could he?

"Just go away, please!" She called, her voice cracking. She caught sight of herself in the mirror by the coat rack. She was green around the gills, as her Aunt Dora would say. She couldn't let him see her like this. She couldn't let him see her at all.

Her phone vibrated in her purse on the floor. She thought about ignoring it, but what if it was Frank? She reached down and looked at the screen, seeing the name 'Jazz Shoes'. She hit ignore and dropped it back in her purse. Looking through the peephole, she watched him put his phone away and punch the porch rail.

How had she let herself get into such a mess? She moved away from the doorway and flung herself onto the sofa, the first piece of furniture that she and Frank had ever bought together. She remembered that day clearly. They had wandered, arm in arm, through the department store. When they'd come upon the sofa, she had gasped at how vibrant the upholstery was. She had always wanted a turquoise couch.

"Your wish is my command," Frank had said, kissing her hand. "Whatever you want, I'll always make sure you have it. Always."

Merry squeezed her eyes against the memory. In some ways, it anchored her, reassuring her that she was doing the right thing. In other ways, it made her feel ill. She and Frank had so much history together. So why was she feeling like this now?

She and Frank had kept their love affair private, as her mother would not have approved of a man his age and profession —a shrink! —dating her daughter. They had met online and then he had come to Dark Root and wooed her in person. He had told her she was beautiful. And strong. And smart. No one had ever said things like that to her before. Eve was the prettiest, Ruth Anne the smartest, and Maggie the strongest.

But Merry felt in no way remarkable. Not until Frank.

He showered her with gifts, dresses from expensive stores she had only seen in magazines. He took her to nice restaurants, and told her stories about the world she'd only glimpsed in books and on TV. He promised to show her all that she had missed out on. And eventually he convinced her that leaving her family was the compassionate thing. "If you do everything for your sisters, they'll never learn to do for themselves."

The frantic knocking on the door resumed, and it sounded as if the whole house was caving in.

Merry stood and wiped away her tears with a tissue. "If Frank comes home and sees me like this..." she sniffed to herself. After drying her eyes, she carefully tucked the tissue into a plastic baggie she kept in her purse. Frank had a habit of searching the trash.

The phone vibrated again. This time, she picked it up. "Hello?"

"Don't hello me, Merry. I'm not just anybody. C'mon. Please, let's talk. I'm shipping out soon."

Shipping out? What did that mean? She texted him the question.

We R leaving Kansas soon. I need 2 C U before I go.

Leaving? Do U have 2 go?

I don't know. Do I?

Her chest constricted as she sifted through the possibilities. If he left she wouldn't have to deal with him or the situation. But she'd also never see him again, either.

Another text came through: *Going 2 R hill. I'll be there 4 the next few hours, with a picnic basket packed just 4 U. Hoping you'll join.*

The phone went silent. She crept to the door and looked through the peephole. She watched as the man she loved turned and walked away from her, a picnic basket dangling limply from his hand. He was so beautiful. Her heart broke.

Frank would be home soon.

"Think, Merry." It had happened so quickly, escalating so suddenly. She hadn't meant for any of this to be.

Maybe she could admit to Frank she wasn't in love with him? She could tell him that, even though he had been affectionate and called her beautiful, even though he had shown her the world outside of Dark Root, that it wasn't truly love. Love was... wanting the best for someone, even if it meant losing something yourself. Love was interactive conversations, not lectures on what you were doing wrong.

Love was calling just to say hi.

Or good night.

Love was remembering the little things that mattered to the other. And not forgetting special days. And packing a picnic lunch, 'just for you.'

Frank had become her father. No, he had become her warden. He kept her here, away from everyone, picking through her trash and monitoring her calls. She hadn't wanted to admit how trapped she felt, but she saw it clearly now.

She ran to her bedroom and opened her suitcase on the bed, throwing half her clothes inside. Then she shuffled the other half around in her closet, so it wasn't immediately noticeable. She zipped up the suitcase and dragged it down the stairs, floundering towards the front door. She reached for the doorknob with one hand and her purse with the other.

The door was flung open and Merry stumbled backwards, dropping everything. Frank stared at her, standing large in the doorway. His eyes moved from her tear-stained face to her suitcase. He seemed bigger now, taller than she remembered. Why was he home so early?

Merry winced. Though he had never actually slapped her, his hand had gone up more than once. "You going somewhere?" he asked.

"I was... going to take some things to the church rummage sale. Thought I'd donate this old suitcase, too."

"Oh?" He closed the door behind him and walked to the bar, pouring himself a scotch. He downed it in one swig.

Merry glanced through the curtains and forced a weak smile. "You'll be all right without me for a few hours?"

He poured another drink, his face reddening as the buttery liquid slid into the shot glass. He swished his drink around as he spoke. "There are rumors, Merry. Rumors about some shmuck's wife whose been sneaking off with one of those religious fanatics behind her husband's back."

"Huh?" Merry feigned confusion. "What fanatics?"

"Those lunatics who set up that church a few towns over. Some doomsday cult. Brainwashed freaks, if you ask me."

"Oh." Merry scrambled for an answer. "That's too bad. Anyway, I better take this over. Jenn is waiting for me."

"She is? That's strange. I just ran into Jenn and she didn't mention it."

"Uh... that is strange."

"She did mention the rumor I just told you about, however."

The blood drained from Merry's face. Jenn was her best friend, the one person she had confided in. Did she really tell him?

"Is it true, Merry?" Frank squeezed the shot glass in his fist, stepping forward. His face was crimson, but his expression controlled.

"I uh..." What could she say? That Jenn lied? No, Merry realized she'd committed enough sins already. "Yes, it was me. I've been seeing one of them," she said, meeting his eyes.

She glanced at the door, wondering if she could get by him. If she left the suitcase, she might be able to outrun him.

Frank looked down on her, dwarfing her. "Why did you do it?"

Love?

What else could she say? She opened her mouth, to try to explain that she'd come to love a boy who didn't have anything to offer her other than his heart. And that she was willing to leave everything behind, for nothing more than that.

Frank might slap her, but the sting would disappear. A small price to pay for freedom.

"We talked about religion," she said. It was almost honest. They had talked about religion, but so much more. They talked about everything as they nursed their picnic baskets on the hill, Merry lying on his lap, or him on hers. "We talked about the true nature of love."

Frank sneered and turned, and Merry assumed he was pouring another drink. Instead, he went to the door, locking it. The house became darker as the latch clicked. Then, he walked towards her, kicking her suitcase to the side.

"God, huh?" he grabbed her face and kissed her, his sharp gray stubble scratching her chin. "There is no God, Merry. I've told you that before. Your silly mother put too many things into your head. But I'm going to get rid of them."

He kissed her so hard he drew blood. "I won't let you leave me for some religious whack job. Do you hear me?"

"Frank..."

~

Merry's face was in her hands. She couldn't look at us. I knew the voice knocking on the door. Merry had been in love with Jason. My Jason. My dearest friend from Woodhaven.

I was stung by jealousy. Although we were never physical, Jason and I certainly cared deeply for one another. We stayed up alone together on many nights, talking about life and love and the world outside of Woodhaven. And there had been moments, during a pause in our conversation, when we looked into each other's eyes. There had almost been a kiss once, when our faces accidentally moved close together - it hung between us, like an unfulfilled wish. And Jason had been the one to help me leave Michael. Until that moment, I hadn't realized that I had been keeping Jason tucked away, as a perfect memory of untainted love.

I knew Merry had come searching for me in Kansas, asking for me at our temporary compound. She'd obviously found him instead.

It was unfair for me to be jealous. Jason had never been mine. But it was true, nonetheless.

Even through my unfounded jealousy, my heart ached for Merry. I never knew Frank was so awful. No wonder she sought refuge in the arms of a young preacher. I had taken the same path myself, when Michael showed up in Dark Root. But why hadn't she told us? We surely couldn't cast stones.

I stared at her, almost speechless. "Is June Bug Frank's daughter?"

"No." She wiped her nose with a tissue from her pack. Only Merry would bring Kleenex to hell. "I met Jason when Frank and I came looking for you. And then one afternoon I ran into him in town while I was shopping by myself. He was passing out fliers. He spoke and I was fascinated by his view of the world, so different from the one we had grown up with. I asked him a ton of questions and he answered them all with such passion and conviction. We saw each other almost every day for several weeks. And I fell in love. I didn't mean for it to happen."

"What the hell?" Eve said. "You stayed with that prick even after he raised his hand to you."

Merry covered her face. "I'm so embarrassed. I should have told you all." She turned to Michael. "Especially you."

Especially Michael?

He looked at her with compassion, but there was also a new vacancy in his eyes. She wasn't as pure as he'd supposed, and in the time it took for us to view her memory, a chasm had formed between them. Michael took a step back, distancing himself. I had known him long enough to know how judgmental he was, and wasn't surprised by his reaction.

But I was surprised by Paul's.

"You let Frank think June Bug was his kid?" he demanded. "And she's with him right now?"

"Yes. Yes." Merry sobbed. "I was a married woman living in a small judgmental town where everyone knew everyone else's business. By the time I got the courage to leave, June Bug and Frank had already bonded."

"It's not just small towns that frown on things like that," Paul said. "I grew up in a city, and we weren't too keen on it either. Were you ever planning on telling her real father? Does he even know he has a child?"

Merry shook her head, looking to us for support. "I was in love, that's all I can say. It was the only time in my life I've done anything like that, but it's not who I am." Again, her eyes drifted towards Michael.

"Are you certain she's..." I couldn't choke out Jason's name. "... not Frank's?"

She shook her head, vehemently. "I wasn't with Frank at all during that time. It would have been so much easier if June Bug was his."

"You think?" Eve said. She tapped her fingers on her thighs, and her foot on the ground. "You could have come home, you know? You didn't have to stay with Dr. Jekyll if he was mistreating you. What if he tries to hurt June Bug? Have you thought about that?"

"Eve!" I said.

"It's a fair question," Ruth Anne said, now turning to face Merry. "She's our niece and we have a right to know."

"Frank wouldn't!" Merry said. "Once June Bug was born, he softened so much! She's the light of his life. I thought about telling him a million times, but the way he looks at her, and the way he started looking at me again after I'd given him a daughter..."

"But you loved Jason," I said, feeling more sympathy than I wanted. "Do you still love him."

"I don't know. It's been so long. But Jason taught me what real love looked like, and now I'll never settle for anything less." She wiped a tear from her cheek. "Eve, I couldn't return to Dark Root. I couldn't face any of you. And I surely couldn't face Mama."

I understood. Pride had kept me from going home many times. But I was still angry, mostly because I now knew how strong my sister was, and she hadn't stood up for herself then.

"Security," she whispered, reading me. "I sold my soul for security, and I'm ashamed." She straightened her sweater and smoothed her

239

hair. "When Frank ran off with that barista, I had to swallow my pride and come home anyway."

"You were more worried about your pride than your kid," Eve said.

"Can it, Eve," Ruth Anne snapped, patting Merry's back. "We've all got our secrets. And none of us are innocent. Let's just hope the Netherworld is done chewing us up and spitting us out."

Our faces turned to Michael, who alone was left. He didn't look at all worried.

With that, silence fell upon our group. Ruth Anne was right.

I brushed Merry's arm. "It'll be all right."

"No it won't, Maggie. Nothing will ever be *all right* again. The djinn's bottle has been uncorked and there's no going back."

I looked at her curiously, wondering if I truly knew my sister, or anyone for that matter.

Contemplating this, I examined our new environment. It was a rocky and desolate location, red like Mars. Merry sat down by herself on a rock and covered her face with her hands. At that, the world around us began to crack and splinter. There was a moment of noisy static and a new backdrop emerged.

I blinked.

Merry was now sitting on the arm of a sofa, in the same position as before. We were no longer outdoors, and instead found ourselves in a tired living room, with scratched wooden floors and antique wallpaper. There was a window to a sunny world outside – but no door.

The rest of the scene gradually filled in.

Cobwebs hung in the corners and a thick layer of dust covered the floor. There were piles of unsorted mail on various tables around the room, while heaps of laundry lay unfolded on the couch. Dead flowers wilted in cracked vases. Dirty dishes sat on a shelf, gathering flies. The stink of garbage was strong and it made me woozy.

"Welcome to Merry's personal hell," I said, knowing her disdain for untidiness and disorder.

My sister's face turned towards window, her expression wavering between defiance and guilt. With the toe of her shoe, she drew a large J in the dust on the floor. I wondered if it was for June Bug or Jason.

Michael massaged his scalp, his countenance softened by her fragile mental state. "I don't think she can see us," he whispered. "Poor thing." At his words Merry startled and looked around, as if hearing a ghost.

We didn't move or speak for a moment. Merry eventually slid off the sofa and walked confidently towards an open closet. I almost expected a full skeleton to fall out, rattling and clanking as its bones hit the ground. But instead, she pulled a pink baby blanket from a high shelf, touching it to her cheek.

"We can't leave her alone in her head like this. Isn't there anything we can do?" I asked. I could deal with my own grief easier than Merry's.

"Let her wallow," Eve said.

"Merry's always been so good to you, Eve. How can you say that?"

She shrugged. "Merry and I don't know who our fathers are. I can't believe she'd do that to June Bug, too."

"We're here in the Netherworld because of my own horrible father. And don't forget, only Ruth Anne is Sasha's biological daughter. DNA doesn't mean everything."

"I've heard you talk of Jason," Eve said to me. "From what I gather, he was a decent guy. Much better than Franken-Shrink."

"...trapped," Merry mumbled, now pressing her hands to the window. She banged her fists against the impenetrable glass. "Trapped! Trapped! Trapped!"

Michael went to her. She shivered, as though he were nothing more than a chill in the air.

"I need out! I can't do this." Merry shouted. Her eyes drifted towards a clock looming over a brick mantle. The hands spun quickly. "I forgot to make dinner! Frank will be home soon."

"What do we do?" I asked the others, low enough that Merry wouldn't hear. Every new sound made her jump.

"She's in her own nightmare right now," Shane whispered. "It's dangerous to wake her. We need to let it play out."

"The cowboy's right," Michael agreed. "She created this scenario for a reason. She needs to absolve her guilt."

"She never told you about this?" I asked, my eyes trailing Merry as she wandered distraught around room.

"She hinted that she may have emotionally strayed on Frank," Michael said, "but I did sense there was more."

"You sensed?" I asked, knowing he had some telepathic abilities.

"I didn't pry, if that's what you're asking. I would never do that to her." Michael looked at Merry in a way he had never looked at me, even in our early years. It was the look of someone who loves a person so much that he'd rather burden his own life than add an ounce of sorrow to hers.

Were we in a version of Merry's old house, I wondered? Or simply a pure construct of her imagination? I inspected the room more carefully. It was cool and dim, with flickering candles as well as lamps. Boxes of unsorted papers were stacked willy-nilly in the corners, and colorless houseplants sagged, as if on respirators. And the room seemed to be growing ever larger, the disorder growing along with it. The window didn't budge, and without a door there seemed little chance of escape.

A sheet of paper floated down before me, and I plucked it from the air. It was a letter.

My beloved Merry,
Soon, we'll be together. I'll come for you shortly after Christmas.
My love,
Frank.

"She was just a kid when Frank took her," I said, wadding up the paper and throwing it across the expanding room. "She didn't know what love was."

"None of us had any exposure to real relationships," Eve said. "Mother never brought her boyfriends around and Aunt Dora had no interest in romance."

"And you can see how that worked out for us," Ruth Anne noted. "And Eve, you're the queen of love potions. You know how easy it is to confuse love and infatuation. How can you condemn her for it?"

"I just can," Eve said, drawing her line.

"What crawled up her round ass?" Ruth Anne asked, once Eve walked away. "She's not normally one to concern herself with morals."

Paul sighed. "A friend of mine hinted that Nova might not be mine. He insisted my ex had been cheating on me."

"Man, I'm sorry," Ruth Anne said. "Did you get a paternity test?"

Paul shook his head. "No, and Eve's pissed about that."

"Why didn't you?" I asked.

"Because he loves Nova too much," Shane answered. "Even if they don't share blood." Paul nodded and Michael stepped in closer. The male trio stood together, a statement of their momentary unity.

Eve flopped onto a chair, and a great plume of dust billowed out from the cushion. Merry noticed immediately and ran over and began beating the dust down with a pillow. Eve choked and scrambled away.

"That would be funnier if Merry wasn't batshit crazy right now," Ruth Anne said.

I nodded as my eyes followed Merry. She adjusted the pictures hanging on the slanted walls, while repeating the word 'trapped' to herself. Her hands frequently went to her belly.

"We need to get out of here. How much longer until I can wake her, or she wakes up on her own?" I asked Shane, since he was the closest thing we had to a dream expert on our panel. The clock spun, forward and back, and the room swayed with it.

"I don't know," Shane said, gritting his teeth. "This is a whole lot different than the dreams I'm used to." He rubbed his jawline. "Let's wait a while longer. Hopefully, she'll snap out of it on her own. Maggie, if we wake her too early, she might really be 'trapped' in her world."

"But listen to her, Shane. We can't leave her like this."

Merry's rambling grew more frantic. "I can't find her! I can't find her! Trapped. Trapped. Trapped."

I couldn't take it any longer. "You can't find who?" I shouted, stepping up beside her. "June Bug?"

She turned, her eyes feral and dark. "I can't find her!" She snapped, looking past me to the window.

"Merry," I said, trying to break through the barrier. "You're safe. You're here with us, your sisters."

"Who said that?" she asked, whipping her head right and left. "June Bug? Are you there?"

Merry ran towards a hallway, which hadn't been there before. I charged after her with the others close behind me. She ran down the hall, opening doors without bothering to look inside. A tall door with a brass knocker waited for her at the end of the long corridor. She seemed so small in its shadow.

My sister put her finger to her lips and looked back at us. *Does she see us now?*

"Listen," she whispered, cocking her ear to the door. "I think it's June Bug!"

She lifted the knocker and let it fall. The door scraped open.

"June Bug!" she called into the room. "Mommy's here! We're getting out, baby. Come to me."

Merry crept inside, as if afraid to wake someone... or something. I stepped in behind her. Dozens of antique porcelain dolls with missing eyes and cracked chins stared at us from countless shelves. The dolls watched as we moved through the room, their heads twisting to follow us across the creaky wooden floor. We passed a child's tea party, with three ragged teddy bears seated around a table with one empty chair. The tea inside the dainty china cups was sludge, riddled with mold. A child's rocking chair rocked near the window, unattended.

I kept calling for Merry to turn around. But she kept going, searching for her missing daughter.

"She's not in here," I insisted, even as Shane begged me to stop. He knew dreams, but I knew my sister. I had never seen her like this, but I'd known grief, and I understood it. I had to get through to her, or we'd never be able to leave this house.

"Merry! She's not here!" I said more firmly. Her eyes flickered and she blinked. Encouraged, I tried again. "It's your sister, Maggie. I'm here with Ruth Anne and Eve. This isn't your old house and June

Bug's not here. She's with Frank in the Upper World. We need to get out so you can return to her."

"With Frank?" she asked the empty room. "But I heard her."

"No. That is the Netherworld playing tricks on you."

"Why would it do that?" Merry asked, earnestly.

She still didn't see me, but at least my words were now getting through. I tried to be as articulate as I could. "Because the Netherworld would like nothing more than to keep us here. I don't know why; I just know that it does. We need to get out, Merry. Out is where June Bug is. Not here."

Shane took my hand, lending me his support.

Merry turned in my direction, listening more closely. I took a deep breath and continued. "My son, Montana – your nephew - is trapped in this world. My child is trapped here. Not yours. Your child is safe in the Upper World. Let's find my son and then we'll find June Bug. I promise."

Her lashes fluttered and her eyes slid side to side.

"Merry, please. Trust me."

"Are you sure, Maggie?" she asked, steering her eyes to finally meet mine, our connection strengthening.

"Yes, Merry. I'm sure."

"Look!" Merry pointed to a twin bed against the far wall. It was made up with pink bedding and pillow cases trimmed in lace. There was a painting hanging over it, of a young girl picking flowers. Merry rushed past me, lifting the painting off the wall and laying it carefully on the bed. She tapped the picture, her face draining of color. "June Bug's in here! See?"

The little girl stood up from the garden and rose to her feet, turning so that we could see her face. "Mama! Help! He's not my daddy!" the girl cried, her hands beating against the picture, just as Merry had beaten against the living room window. "I'm trapped, Mama!"

"Mae!" Merry screamed, calling her daughter by her birth name. "I'm coming for you!"

I grabbed the portrait and smashed it into the bed post, then smashed it again as Merry crumpled to her knees.

"It's not real," I repeated, clutching my ankh with renewed conviction. "And I'll be damned if I let this place break us. Shane, Michael - get her up. We're leaving."

They lifted her gently to her feet, wrapping one of her arms around each of their shoulders. As we made our way back to the living room, my ankh blinked erratically, creating a disorienting but encouraging strobe light.

"Now how do we get out of here?" I asked. "Shane, is Eagle Mountain anywhere on your radar?"

"It's too chaotic in here to get a read," Shane said, nodding his head towards Merry on his arm.

"Is it just me or does this place seem to be tipping?" Ruth Anne said.

"Don't lose focus," I reminded everyone, my frustration rising as the walls appeared to be closing in around us. "It's not real."

Shane and Michael deposited Merry on the couch, while the rest of us hammered our hands against the imploding walls, searching for a way out.

"Mommy!" A child's voice called, the sound bouncing around the room. "Help me! I'm trapped!" Merry covered her ears.

"We're never getting out of here," Paul said, looking around helplessly. "If Merry thinks she's trapped, she is. And she's keeping the rest of us here with her."

Eve snapped her fingers, then reached into her bag, removing a silver comb.

"Now Eve?" I asked.

She ignored me and went straight to Merry, kneeling in front of her. Eve whispered to her quietly while Merry sniffled. Eve then produced a silver mirror and handed it over to her, along with the comb. Merry looked in confusion at the items, then a smile touched her lips and she nodded.

"Just like when we were little. Remember, Merry?" Then Eve slid down and laid her head on Merry's lap.

Merry gently lifted a lock of Eve's shiny black hair, letting the comb slide all the way from root to tip. She worked at it for several minutes, occasionally showing Eve her reflection in the mirror. And then she began to sing a haunting, melancholy melody.

> *Far away, my lover waits for me*
> *Past ancient cities, across the windswept shores,*
> *He dreams of returning home to me*
> *To feel our hearts beat together, once more.*
>
> *Dreams and wishes and too many regrets*
> *The distance that divides us is so great.*
> *But you will come again for me my love*
> *And until that day, I will simply wait.*
>
> *Two lovers bound forever, our souls tied*
> *Hoping that our destinies are fated.*
> *Beneath the great celestial dome we cried*
> *And there we sat forevermore and waited.*

Merry finished her song and set the comb down beside her. Eve looked at her reflection one last time and smiled. "Thank you, Eve," Merry said standing.

She's back.

"You're wiser than I give you credit for," I said to Eve. Merry had needed someone to nurture and mother, and Eve had answered the call. I hadn't seen Merry's true strength before this trip, nor had I understood Eve's insight.

"A girl always has to look good, even in purgatory," Eve shrugged.

The room became bright and clean. A door appeared.

"I know where our mountain is!" Shane said.

Instead of a knob, there was a groove in the door, in the shape of my ankh. "Everyone ready?" I asked, lifting the blazing ankh over my head. With trembling fingers, I placed the key into the indentation.

It sparked as it made contact with the door.

247

"It was nice knowing everyone," Ruth Anne said, swallowing.

"Is this our final portal?" I asked.

"Michael still hasn't gone through his," Shane said.

Michael shrugged, neither admitting or denying anything.

We had gone through many doors and gates and portals here in the Netherworld, but this felt the most foreboding.

We all stepped through quickly. Once my feet crossed the threshold, I found myself in a lightly wooded area that smelled of spring rain. We were all together, and ahead of us was Eagle Mountain, close enough to see Larinda's castle perched atop it.

No Michael memory?

I didn't have time to dwell on it, for I now felt Montana's presence strongly.

"He's in there!" I said, crying and laughing. "Merry, I think you unlocked our final door." I wrapped my arms around her neck and whispered. "You're not trapped anymore. Not ever again."

I lifted the hourglass from my pocket. There was only a little sand left. But that was enough.

17

THE TOWER

*W*e hiked to the foot of Eagle Mountain, looking at the grey castle perched high on the mountain above.

"You ready for this?" Shane asked me, pulling me off to the side.

"This is why we're here," I said. My eyes drifted towards his back-pack, and I remembered the racket he'd made while packing. I still didn't know what he had brought. "Just in case this doesn't work out, don't let me die without knowing what's in there," I said, smiling.

"What are you hoping for?" he asked, unzipping the pack.

"I'm hoping you brought some of your badass special forces gear. Or maybe a silver stake? Oh wait, Larinda's a witch - that won't work. Nunchucks?"

He laughed and removed a folded piece of paper from a deep pocket. "I'll show you. I was embarrassed to tell you, but I can't let you go around thinking you married James Bond or Chuck Norris."

I unfolded the sheet. It was a child's drawing - a boy wearing glasses and a wild-haired girl staring up at the moon from opposite sides of the paper. "Ta-da! I did that when I was eight or nine, I think." He quickly snatched it back and carefully refolded it, putting it back in the pocket. "I had a dream of you. It was the first one I can remember. In it, you were looking for something in the night. When I woke up, I drew the picture so I would never forget. That's when I knew I loved you."

"Wow," I said, draping my arms on his shoulders. "Your artistic skills sucked."

"Hey now! Back home I was the best stick-figure doodler in all of second grade." He punched me playfully in the arm. "I wished I hadn't shown you."

"Why did you bring it here?"

"I, uh… well, before I had an actual picture of you, I used this to tune in to you. It got a bit of a workout in my early adolescent years."

"Gross!" I raised an eyebrow, uncertain if I should be flattered or horrified. Flattery won out. We headed back towards the others.

Rejoining the others, we took a moment to share private words with one another, not knowing what awaited us at the top of the mountain. I noticed with some sadness that Paul and Eve hadn't yet bridged their gap; and Merry and Michael only spoke stiffly, avoiding direct eye contact. I hoped this wasn't goodbye for many reasons.

We began our ascent of Eagle Mountain, letting Paul choose our zigzagging path up the steep slope. He and Shane pushed aside underbrush, clearing the way, while Michael watched behind us, his cross out before him like a sword. The rest of us huddled in the middle, searching the rocks and trees and air for signs of ambush. This was a witch's domain, created with the help of a nefarious warlock, and was probably guarded by foul magick.

The mountain responded to our intrusion with slight tremors that came and went. As if a sleeping giant had awakened from a troubling dream, only to snore himself back to sleep.

The higher we climbed, the more light-headed I became. "We're still too low for elevation sickness," Paul said. But I knew it wasn't elevation sickness. It was magick - dark and twisted magick from a dark and twisted woman.

Heavy-bottomed clouds converged from all across the sky, gathering over us, forming a floating moat of gloom around the base of the castle. Thunder sounded in the distance, booming in our ears like cannons. Fearing it might be Gahabrien, we quickened our pace.

Crows and ravens followed the clouds in, crowding onto tree limbs and boulders. They squawked their displeasure at our presence. It soon became background noise, no more noticeable than a fan in a darkened room. All I could hear were my footsteps and my breathing. Climbing. Climbing.

I knew it was only in my mind, but I was growing tired and thirsty. Finally, I stopped to take a sip of water beneath a fossilized tree stacked with ravens.

"This kid better be worth it," Ruth Anne teased as she expertly skirted a tumbling rock. "I'm starting to break a sweat."

"Why are you complaining?" Eve asked, limping along. Her boots were ripped and she'd lost one of the heels. "Those ugly shoes of yours seem to be holding up okay." She turned her irritation on Michael. "You really think that cross will save you from Larinda and Maggie's crazy father?"

"Conviction is the most powerful force of all," he said.

"Yes," Merry agreed. "Faith is a powerful thing, especially here."

"Let's hope so," said Eve. "Because aside from four wands, two flashlights, and a big heaping pile of conviction, we're pretty much defenseless."

~

We stood at the top of the mountain, bedraggled and exhausted, before yet another door. The storm was gathering at our backs and the wind was rising, whipping up the mountainside. Even the crows and ravens sought cover.

The castle door stood two stories tall. It was made of redwood, fastened with thick metal bands. The tower itself appeared to be a larger version of Leah's, and I guessed she'd copied her mother's design. There was no drawbridge or moat, not even a palisade wall. We were able to simply walk right up to the door. And we did so, cautiously.

"What gives?" Ruth Anne grunted. "Larinda got to design her own castle and she left out all the good stuff? Where's the minarets and crenellations?"

Shane pointed to a set of reliefs, etched into the stone around the door. Bats, of all shapes and sizes.

"Ick!" Ruth Anne said, jumping back. "Although after riding that gargoyle, I think some of my squeamishness is going away."

"Do we have a plan?" Eve asked. We huddled beside the door, in the shadow of a tree.

"No," I admitted, looking up at the daunting structure. "I was just planning on marching in and demanding my son back. But I'm beginning to have my doubts it will be that easy."

"Too late for doubts, Maggie," Shane said. "I say we just go in."

He headed towards the door. The rest of us looked at each other and shrugged, following. No one else had any ideas and I dared not look at the hourglass for fear I was already too late. Shane didn't bother with the brass knocker, leaning his full weight against the wood. It creaked on its hinges and opened just a crack, enough for us to slip inside. We found ourselves in a vast hall, far more palatial and lavish than Leah's meager replica. The floors were marble and the walls shimmered like pearl. Strong pillars rose high into the air, supporting a circular balcony above, and multiple corridors lined the perimeter like spider legs.

There was no sign of occupancy. Shane took my hand and we went forward carefully, the others close behind. The heavy door slammed instantly shut behind us, reverberating through the hall like a gunshot.

"Yup," Ruth Anne said, and I shushed her.

We walked like thieves across the floor, our eyes searching for danger, our ears listening for voices. We investigated the bottom floor, avoiding the corridors for the moment. Though the great room appeared empty, there was the unsettling feeling that we were being watched.

We eventually made our way to the grand staircase in the center of the room. As I placed my foot on the first step, a majestic glass chandelier blazed to life overhead. And somewhere unseen, a pipe organ began playing a ghostly hymn. I quickly removed my foot from the step, pulling my wand from my skirt pocket.

A woman's laughter bounced around the vast chamber.

"Larinda, come out!" I shouted "Or are you afraid? No wonder my father left you here. He never had any respect for cowards."

It was Leah who appeared - a simpleton mouse in an elegant ball-room gown, draped on her like a flour sack. She posed at the top of the balcony, then proceeded down the staircase, as if she were a queen. I held her stare the entire way, until she broke off and looked down at her own feet.

"I've come for Montana." I lifted my wand. "Give me my son or I'll..."

"You'll what?" She sneered.

Ready to strike her down, I summoned all my remaining patience. "Leah, there's nothing you can do to stop me, but I'm willing to reason with you first. What do you want?"

"Want?" She scrunched her brow.

"You obviously want something, or you wouldn't be here." I looked at a portrait of her mother hanging on the wall, posing in a flaming red dress. "Power?" I asked. "We can make you a formidable wand. Love? Eve can craft you the perfect charm. Health? Merry can cure or fix anything. Knowledge? Ruth Anne can teach you ancient languages and help you master the lore."

When Leah didn't immediately answer, I stamped my foot onto the stair. The chandelier quaked, blinking off and on in response. What else could she want? "Money? Leah, is that what you want?"

"Money?" Leah shook her head and spread out her hands. "Is that really what you think I want from you, Maggie Maddock. Look around? Money means nothing here." She walked to the banister and picked up a pottery vase, smashing it on the steps. "Material posses-sions mean nothing here. Don't you get it? As long as Mother is bound here, I have to keep coming back. I may not be trapped as she is, but I might as well be. Her guilt is stronger than her magick. Money won't help me, Maggie."

"I can help you escape for good," I said. "We'll put a blocking spell on her so she can't contact you once you're back in the Upper World."

She frowned, then sighed. "I wasn't asking for escape or spells. Do you know what it was like growing up, alone with only Mother? I had to animate my own imaginary friends," she said, nodding towards a gargoyle pedestal. "I wanted a sister. But you can't be that, can you?"

As much as I wanted to lie to her, knowing it would help my cause, the Netherworld had shown me the repercussions of untruths and secrets. "No, I can't be your sister. Maybe before all this, but I could never trust you. You helped steal my son, and then you locked us in cages and left us there. If I acted like I loved you, you'd know I was lying. It takes more than blood to be my sister."

My answer enraged her. "Mother!" she shouted up the stairs.

I snapped my wand and unleashed on her, thrusting all my anger her way. Leah was tossed back against the stairs, her head hitting the railing as she fell. I readied to strike her again, before she could collect herself.

"Leave my daughter alone!" a shrill voice ordered. Larinda materialized at the top of the stairs. "Touch her again," she warned, "and you'll never see this child again."

She drew open her cape, revealing a wicker basket tucked beneath her arm. It wriggled as she held it out, and I caught a glimpse of auburn hair within. *Montana!* I dashed for the stairs, and was quickly flung back to the floor by a flick of Larinda's powerful wand. Her red lips twisted into an ironic smile as I scrambled to my feet, my ankle throbbing in pain from the impact.

She flipped her wrist again and I crumpled, like a baby deer with new legs. "You should know better than to challenge me. I'm older than you, and far wiser. I'm much stronger than you here in the Netherworld, Maggie. This is my domain."

Michael and Shane lowered their shoulders and charged up the stairs, suffering the same fate, landing beside me. Larinda laughed, as if it were the funniest thing she'd seen. "This must be what bowling is like."

Her wand at the ready, she made her way halfway down the stairs

254

to her daughter. "My dear, you feel trapped? I also overhead you asking Maggie for a pledge of sisterhood. Tsk, tsk... I thought your loyalties were to your mother. We shall talk of this later."

"Yes, Mother." Leah's face greened. "I didn't mean to-"

"Enough!" Larinda peeked inside the basket and smiled. "I might decide to keep this little guy, since my only daughter is so ready to abandon me."

"You don't scare me Larinda," I said, standing up and advancing slowly up the stairs. She was right, I didn't possess her age or wisdom, but I had wilder-blood running through me. I pointed at a gargoyle statue across the room, exploding it to bits.

"My pet! Make her stop, Mother!" Leah cried out.

"I'm ready to take everything down in this fragile illusion of yours," I said, drawing in as much energy as I could contain, pulling it in from the fast-approaching storm. I swung my wand in a wide arc, shattering the dozens of stain glass windows lining the hall. My sisters drew up beside me, readying their own wands.

Larinda raised an eyebrow. "Fancy display, Maggie, but you're still no match for me. Even with your entourage, although I am surprised to see you all still together. I was sure the gates would have stopped you, or at least splintered you."

"You underestimated us," I replied. "You'd be wise not to do it again."

"You may have gotten past your inner demons, but that is not the demon you should be worrying about." Larinda's eyes moved to the broken windows. An angry wind whistled through the open holes, blowing the tattered curtains. "Gahabrien has been summoned, and he is not far away. He will devour you and your friends, and then he will go after that wretched father of yours. So many birds, with just one stone. Delicious."

Merry drew a circle in the air around us, which Larinda found amusing. "Your protection spells will not keep out a true demon. Trust me, I tried. But if it makes you feel better, go ahead."

"I'm done with this, Larinda. Give me back my son," I repeated, advancing towards her. The enormous chandelier overhead rocked and flickered as we mounted the steps, the light wavering throughout the hall. Larinda looked up at the ceiling, backing away. As we reached the top of the staircase, my fingers twitched and my body tingled, begging for release.

Larinda tilted her chin and uttered a quick spell.

North, South, West, and East
Stop the witch and feed the beast

She pointed to all four corners as she spoke, and at the word witch, she pointed her wand straight at me.

I instinctively raised my palms, putting out both hands before me. My crystal bracelet spawned a silver sphere around us. In that moment, the tracers from Larinda's wand intersected with the sphere. Her spell bounced away, angling directly for Leah.

Leah turned to stone, just like one of her gargoyle statues. Only her panicked eyes were free to move, following the sounds and lights of the storm flashing in through the windows. The castle walls shook, but not from magick. Gahabrien was here.

"Look what you did!" Larinda accused, going to her daughter.

"Want to try again?" I taunted her.

Larinda looked around uncertainly. Gahabrien's shadow, that of a great muscled beast, began to drift across the walls and floor, through the open windows. Larinda clenched her jaw as his acrid stench overtook us all. She might have freed Gahabrien, but it was clear she didn't control him. No one controls a greater demon. She should have learned that lesson from Armand, who was still paying his due to the devil.

We gathered around Larinda, still keeping a safe distance. She waved her wand threateningly as she tapped on Leah's stone prison. A deafening blow struck the walls from all directions, loosening the grout between the stones. Larinda used the distraction to run, racing past us down the stairs, abandoning Leah in her dash for the door.

"Stop!" I ordered, and the door's massive metal bar slammed into place. "You're lucky. If you weren't holding my baby, I would already be done with you. Whether you give my child to Gahabrien or Armand, it still won't be enough for them. It will never be enough. Demons are insatiable and my father consorts with the devil. They'll always need more. Remember your lineage, Larinda, and do what you know is right."

"Not *The* Devil," Larinda said, hunkering over the basket tucked beneath her cloak. "*A* devil. There are many of them here in the Netherworld, exploiting mankind's weakness for power and physical desires. Demons feed off dark emotions – fear, jealousy, and rage. And Gahabrien seeks all of that, hungering for revenge against your blood-line. Armand pulled him to the Upper World against his will, and then you trapped him there. He will not relent until destroys all of you. Your entire brood."

"That means Leah, too," Ruth Anne said. "She's Armand's daughter."

I could hear Leah's muffled screams from within the stone. Larinda glanced at her daughter, but her gaze didn't stay long.

"I believe all he really wants is my father, the root of his suffering. Send Gahabrien after Armand," I said. "Then your daughter will survive and you'll be avenged. This is your last chance, Larinda." I raised my wand to the ceiling and the chandelier exploded into a million tiny shards, raining down on us like exploding fireworks.

A dark, swirling mist trickled in through the windows and down the walls, separating out into skulking shapes along the floor. The dark creatures licked at the air, searching and hungry, their coal-red eyes forming in their sharp heads. They whispered in unison, a chorus of hell. "Waiting...Waiting...Waiting."

"Waiting for what?" Eve Anne demanded, as we backed against one another, holding our wands out in all directions.

Shane swallowed. "I don't know, but I wish I'd brought my machete instead of a pocket knife."

"Waiting! Waiting! Waiting!" The dark creatures sang, content to linger along the walls.

Thump. Thump. Thump.

It was the sound of dragon's feet, poised outside the door.

A great voice bellowed, and the staircase and balcony collapsed behind us.

The Leah statue tumbled down, buried beneath heaps of rubble.

Larinda stifled a cry then snapped her fingers. A broomstick appeared in her hand. "I'm sorry, my love," she said. She squatted low, then leapt into the air and out the nearest window. Her image disappeared into the shadow of the storm. And the baby basket vanished with her.

"Why didn't you get rid of her when you had the chance?" Eve demanded. "You could have used your death touch and finished her off."

"I couldn't risk hurting Montana," I answered, looking at my hands.

"We have to go after her!" Michael said. He looked at Shane. "Think you can track her in flight?"

"I don't know," Shane admitted, "but I'll try."

Gahabrien bellowed again, and the great redwood door blew in off its hinges, splintering into fragments. My crystal bracelet shot forth its protective barrier, saving us once again as the jagged wood pieces bounced away.

The demon bent low and stepped under the door frame, his body almost corporeal, with the outlines of muscle and sinew and flesh embedded in the dense shadow of his bulk. Stones rattled in the walls around him; several broke off and were sucked into his black maw, only to be spit out the other side.

"He's feeding on our fear," Ruth Anne reminded us, as we huddled in the center of the room, doing our best to avoid the falling debris.

"Well, he's getting plenty from me," Eve said.

"I yield nothing to this demon," Michael said calmly, holding his cross out before him.

I looked at him, flabbergasted at his composure while Gahabrien towered over us. But then I realized he was on to something. "It's our fear! We need to get control of it. We need to take away everything he can use against us. Merry, you're on protection spell duty."

She nodded, and quickly focused all her powers on cocooning us within her bubble.

"Eve, sing something calming and beautiful." She tilted her head in thought, and began singing a haunting yet powerful hymn.

"Keep praying," I instructed Michael. "And everyone else, no matter what happens keep the negative thoughts out of your head. Hold hands, and focus on each other."

Gahabrien stomped forward into the hall, but then suddenly stalled. His black face swung from side to side, up and down. Shiny dark tendrils snaked out from his mass, probing into the ruins, searching for us in the debris. *He can't see us anymore!*

The castle continued to collapse, and the storm outside continued to rage, pounding in through the exposed walls and ceiling. The demon might not be able to harness our emotions, but he had collected a massive amount of dark energy around him. His strength was still great, and we were still very vulnerable.

But harnessing energy was something I understood well. I began to pull it all in. The wind, the thunder, the lightning – I opened my being and drew it in like a magnet. I let it flow into me, packing it denser with every passing second. I soon felt the pressure on my bones, my joints, my skin.

Gahabrien drew into himself slightly, deprived of his fuel. It wasn't much but it was enough to renew my flagging efforts. I was further bolstered by Michael's calming words, Eve's ethereal voice, and Shane's protective presence at my side. Merry's spell was unflinching, and I knew the collapsing castle would not harm us. I drew the storm into me, deeper and deeper, dropping to my knees.

The demon continued to shrink. My body was sweating, and my felt like I was going to faint. The floor rippled under us, and the air itself vibrated. I stretched my arms out wide, releasing everything inside me, all at once.

White light exploded like a sun. The demon roared in pain, and the entire castle fell away.

18

THE STAR

"A star!" Merry said. She was lying on her back amid the rubble, pointing up. "Do you see it?"

I turned my head, my back braced against a fallen pillar. "That's not a star," I said. "It's a flashlight beam."

Ruth Anne rolled her head onto her own shoulder and grinned, looking at me with dopey eyes. "I was thinking it might work as an SOS signal, seeing as we have no idea where we are." She flipped it off and on several more times, into the empty sky. "What's Morse Code for 'get me off a mountain?'"

"Put it away. Who knows what you'll draw in."

"What happened?" Shane asked, opening his eyes and rubbing his jaw. "Feels like I got punched."

"Demon-punched," I said.

"More like Maggie-punched," Eve corrected, standing and looking at the ruins of Larinda's castle, her expression both impressed and horrified.

"What did I miss." Shane asked, looking about. "The last thing I remember, the walls were falling and Maggie…"

"You're asking the wrong person," I said. "I blacked out, too."

"You all missed an awesome show," Ruth Anne said, continuing to fidget with her flashlight. "I just wish I had caught it on my camera, so I could analyze it later. I'm not sure if the demon imploded or exploded." She slugged me hard in the arm. "Sorry. Just wanted to say I'm impressed. And I hope to always stay on your good side. You're a badass."

I smiled, trying to recall those last moments. I could only remember Gahabrien's powerful presence, and the inner calm I felt when harnessing the storm. The next thing I knew I was staring up at Ruth Anne's faux star.

By all appearances, we were all safe and accounted for. "Thank you guys. I'm so grateful to have you with me." I sniffled and wiped away two rebellious tears. "I just wish... we came all the way to Eagle Mountain... I thought that if we got here... What do we do now?"

I looked up. There was not a single star to wish upon. The clouds had been ripped apart and stretched like gauze, muting the sky. I wasn't a badass at all. I had vanquished Gahabrien, but it had gained me nothing.

"I can't do this anymore," I said, knowing Larinda was far away by now. I didn't bother asking Shane if he could track her. He would have already told me if he could, and I didn't want to make him disappoint me. I tugged at my lifeless ankh. "Maybe we should just go home."

Merry stood, wiping stone dust from her hair and clothes. "We aren't going home. We've come this far, and we'll keep going for as long as it takes. You said we didn't have time, but we do. I know because time doesn't exist here. Every new doorway is another opportunity. This world will bend to our will eventually, never the other way around!" She leaned onto one hip, a determined look on her face.

"Merry's right," Eve said, rising to her feet. Somehow her face was still clean, and aside from a little dust on her sleeve, she was untouched. "I didn't come all the way here to fail. I mean, I ruined a pair of expensive boots for this. Failure is not an option."

I smiled weakly and joined them. Maybe Merry was right. The hourglass in my pocket felt cold, like a dying man's breath. I drew it out. There was a mere handful of grains left, and I flung it as far away from me as I could.

We stood in the middle of an island of rubble. The castle was no more. "Do the rest of you want to keep going?" I asked. "Paul? Shane? Ruth Anne? Michael? It's got to be all of us or none."

"We've come this far," Paul said, looking at Eve. I sensed that he wasn't about to go home, but he wasn't about to leave without her.

"Little Monty is gonna want to see his favorite auntie the second he's found," Ruth Anne said. "I can't deny him that."

"I'll work on finding Larinda," Shane said. "I just need to close my eyes for a few minutes and get rid of the static."

"Take your time," I said. "I want you to be sure. We'll find our things and be ready when you are."

We searched around us, finding our packs and wands. Ruth Anne's wand had cracked in two. She wrapped it with duct tape she pulled from her bag, which she assured us got her out of more messes than we could imagine. It was slightly crooked, but she insisted it was only for show anyway.

"Maggie, look," Merry said, beckoning me over to the collapsed staircase. It was the statue of Leah, turned to stone.

"Is she dead?" I asked, trying to listen for a heartbeat.

"Yes," Ruth Anne said, joining us. "Buried with her gargoyles."

I looked down at the stone remains of the sister I had never gotten to know. Had the Fates seen this end for her, or was it all her own doing? I crouched down and whispered goodbye and kissed her cold cheek, because I knew no one else would.

I noticed one of the gargoyle statues was clenching something in its fist. The Star card! The gargoyle must have snatched it from the sky as it fluttered through the air. I kissed the card and slid it beneath Leah.

"Montana's still okay," I said, with certainty. "I know we'll find him."

"I still can't see Larinda yet," Shane said.

"She took him to Armand," I said with certainty. I could see the dark witch clearly in my mind, understanding her decision. She had lost control of Gahabrien, and so she would barter with my father instead.

Michael nodded. "So, where is Armand?"

"If we can just get away from this area, I'm sure I can find him," Shane said. "Let's get to the base of the mountain."

"Shane's right," Ruth Anne said, pulling out one of her devices. "The electromagnetic frequencies here are off the charts!"

"Wait." In the aftermath of the battle, loose magick was indeed everywhere. It was a primitive, restless kind of night. Larinda's energy and that of her demon permeated the mountaintop, seeping out of the stone blocks. There was even some residual energy of my father's in this land. It was the perfect sort of night for calling up a magick circle.

"Let's put all this wild magick to use and find Montana," I said. "Ladies, your wands." My sisters nodded and we lifted our wands. Ruth Anne's dipped under the weight of the gray tape.

Merry drew a large ring in the rubble and we took our positions at each of the four directions. I needed to see the truth of what the circle would call, not an illusion or trick of the Netherworld. I removed my apple from my pocket and took a large bite, while Ruth Anne paged through Mother's spell book. She began reading from it, but I hardly heard her words.

My sisters were still with me, but a door appeared between us, slowly spinning within the circle. I knew that door, with its crystal doorknob. It was the same door my father had beckoned me from, back in the Upper World. It creaked open, revealing the flames within, as if in confirmation.

I reached out my hand, recalling the terror I had felt the last time I stood before this door, seeing my father's face inside. It was like the entrance to hell itself. And I was even more terrified now. The heat coming off of it made my clothes stick to my skin. I looked closer. It wasn't Armand's face staring back at me. It was my own.

I gasped and my reflection disappeared. I knew this was different from the others. It was a one-way door to a part of the Netherworld mortals weren't meant to see - the underbelly. I didn't have time to think of how frightened I was. I simply turned towards the others and said, "I'm going in."

And I did.

19

THE MOON

*I*didn't land in hell, but perhaps it was a subdivision. The others were pulled in behind me onto a vast plain. We didn't speak much as we collected ourselves, following the only marker in sight, a full moon. A wild moon, Miss Sasha would have said. The kind that brought out the crazy people and the drunks and the fairies.

Shane still couldn't track Larinda, and my ankh remained stubbornly dark. My frustration grew, but the truth apple had shown me the door, and I felt certain it would lead me to Armand.

"Are you sure we're going the right way?" Eve repeatedly asked.

"No, Eve I'm not sure, but I'm open to suggestions," I said after the umpteenth time. No one had any comments on where we were, or where to go, so we stumbled blindly across the night.

"This isn't so bad, as long as there's a full moon," Paul said.

"Unless there's werewolves," Ruth Anne said.

"It's interesting that it's so barren here, when the magick is so ripe," Merry said, sniffing the air. It smelled like iron and old books.

It was unbridled magick, making me feel giddy like champagne. I felt a kinship to this realm.

At last we came to a wide river, still and deep, running endlessly in both directions. We walked along its blue-black water, mesmerized by the reflection of the moon dancing upon it. The prickling sensation of magick energized me like a shot of espresso. It tugged at me, and my body crackled all over. It was the moon and the water and the earth and the air, working together, amplified by the Netherworld. Everything felt heightened.

"Moon lilies!" Merry said, bending to pluck a tiny white flower with gold-dusted edges. "These aren't supposed to be real." She put it to her nose. "It smells like... dreams?"

Suddenly, thousands of moon lilies bloomed, setting the bank aglow.

I flung back my arms as I walked, as if being slowed by the wind. But it was magick that pushed on me; it was heady and overpowering and frightening, and I wanted more. My skin crawled, as if wanting to peel away. I understood the allure of werewolves now, being able to shed their human guise and run and howl at the moon with complete abandon.

Unlimited magick was liberating. What could we do if we were able to bottle it up and take it to the Upper World? Just a taste would conjure us anything we desired. I sped through the fields and Merry skipped along beside me. Only Eve seemed immune to the night's intoxication. She glided along the bank, her sleek hair fanning out behind her. She hummed as she walked, her voice harmonizing with the river.

"We're never getting out of here." I laughed out loud. I laughed until my sides hurt. We had passed through yet another portal, and were rewarded with nothing. "And I'm never going to see my son again, either."

"You are, too," Shane said adamantly.

I had my doubts. Who was I to march into the Netherworld and demand the return of a stolen child? I was a witch, but I was mortal. I didn't belong here. I laughed again, so hard I choked.

"Listen," Merry whispered.

At first there was nothing, but then I heard the far off cadence of women chanting:

Harken witches, hear the tale
Of Goody Kind, thrown down a well
Because she cast a magick spell -
The moon will set her free.

Awaken witches, remember those
Hung by their necks in their Sunday clothes
Because of marks upon their toes -
The moon will set them free.

Listen witches, to what's been said
Of healers who have lost her heads
To the gallows, now surely all quite dead -
The moon will set them free.

Witches dance and witches fly
Across the moon that lights the sky
We'll save our magick for the night -
The moon has set us free

"It's so sad," Merry said. "But beautiful."

"Really?" Shane asked, listening with one eye closed. "Because it sounds like broken glass to me."

Shane was wrong and Merry was right. The song was beautiful. I gathered my skirt and danced along as the song began again. Merry and Eve joined me. We curtsied and twirled, then raised our hands and joined our fingertips together, as if dancing around a maypole. The chant rose higher and higher, filling the night.

"I think only the women can hear it," Paul said, joining Michael and Shane in their confusion.

Ruth Anne tapped her foot along with the music. "It's encrypted.

Only witches can understand it." She narrowed her eyes. "It's a nice song, really, although I don't have the urge to get up and boogie like my sisters do. I'm not sure if it's a slam against my magick or my femininity." She shrugged. "Let's just hope it's not nefarious. There's a legend of a witch who used song to get other witches to do her bidding."

"I know that legend. Hecate was the witch's name," Paul said, cringing at an especially high note. "She is known as the Triple Goddess, because she embodies all three aspects of womanhood: Maiden, Mother, and Crone. Hecate predates even Greek culture. It's said she is one of the few that can cross worlds at will."

"Hecate?" I asked, ceasing my dance. "I met a woman named Hecate. She gave me the truth apple. She was nice, if a bit mysterious."

I listened more closely to the song, now certain I heard Hecate's voice among the chanters. I looked to the moon. Perhaps the door wasn't meant to lead me to Armand, but to Hecate.

"Stay here," I whispered to Shane. "I need to go to Hecate."

"What? Not without me."

"She's near, I can sense her." I reached out my hands, feeling her. It was the pull of the sisterhood. "Please. Trust me."

"We can't get separated again, Maggie. Not after all we've gone through."

"Listen, everyone. Please don't fight me on this. Hecate's somewhere nearby. She'll help us. But I need to go alone. I feel it."

The others nodded. "We'll be here," Michael said.

"And please don't go through anything resembling a door, portal, gate, elevator, escalator..." Ruth Anne added.

"Got it."

I turned, wading ankle deep in moon lilies, and continued along the riverbank There was a sense of finality as I walked, and I hoped it was an omen of completion rather than of an abrupt ending. The witch's song grew louder as I walked and I caught myself humming along.

When the song finally ended, I had come to a lonely stone bench in the field of moon lilies. Looking back, I could see the silhouettes of my friends far off near the water. I sat down on the bench, remembering similar ones from the gardens of Dark Root - Mother's, where only the heartiest flowers grew - Aunt Dora's, perpetually over-flowing with fruits and vegetables - and Uncle Joe's small plot behind his shop, that we raided in late summer for tomatoes. I might never visit any of those gardens again, I realized. Even if I got out of here, Dark Root was waning, as evidenced by the dying Tree of Life. Magick all over my world might be dying. It was happening slowly, but it was still happening. Without magick, there probably wouldn't be many gardens.

Had I been called here to plant the Tree, I wondered? Hecate had been the guardian of the original Tree of Life, and had referred to me as the Seed Bringer. I took the acorn from my pocket and rolled it between my palms. I couldn't mess this up. There was too much at stake. "Jillian, if you're watching," I said, "please give me a sign."

After a disappointed pause, I returned the acorn to my pocket and withdrew the apple. There was hardly a bite left. I set it down on the bench beside me, wondering if I should eat the last of it now, to see if this is where my Tree should be planted.

"You shouldn't put that beautiful apple on a dirty bench like that." A lovely young woman with a long chocolate braid shimmered into view. She wore a flowing white gown, edged with golden embroidery. A small tiara sat atop her head. Her eyes were quiet blue and there was a maidenly flush to her cheeks. She pursed her lips as she regarded me. "Hecate would not like to see her gift treated so poorly."

"I'm sorry," I said, hastily returning it to my pocket. I didn't know who she was, but I sensed her importance. "You know Hecate? I came looking for her."

"I do know her, yes. She graces us with her presence sometimes." The woman laughed, reminding me of fairy bells. "But you must learn respect before she'll grant you an audience. Just be glad that it was I who witnessed your rudeness and not my mother. She is quite fond of Hecate and has too much time on her hands. However, had she seen you, perhaps it would have given her new purpose. Walk with me into the garden."

I stood up, and there was a garden, with tall bushes guarding the entrance. "Can you take me to Hecate, since you know her? I'm trying to find..."

"Quiet, for now please," the woman said gently. "This is a sacred place – a crossroads of sorts. We are approaching one of the thinnest parts of the veil. Please be reverent."

We wound inwards through the garden, a dizzying labyrinth overflowing with moon-magick. "I already know your story, Magdalene. We all follow it here."

"You do?"

"Yes. We have watched your generations - your grandmother, your mother, your sisters, your father. Familial lineage is part of who you are, in the past and in the future. We concede that much here, unlike those in the Upper World who believe destiny is free will." The woman placed a gentle hand on my shoulder. "Your family connections are written into the fabric of your fate. You will see how they are linked, once you hear my story. And then we shall speak more of Hecate."

"Okay" I said, having no other choice. The woman radiated a calm but regal authority. She was magickal, and no mere witch.

"My name is Persephone. I was not born of this world, but of yours. My parents never got along," she said, slowing her walk. "They separated around the time of my birth. My father was powerful, but he wasn't satisfied with all he had. He would never be satisfied until both gods and men alike bowed before him. He was a blowhard, and I'm certain Mother would have divorced him, had she not found their arrangement *convenient*.

"I was caught between their fighting and their egos. My mother was so possessive that I felt trapped. My father was mostly kind to me, although his temper was frightening. When I was hardly more than a girl, he decided to marry me off so he wouldn't have to worry about my future. And also so he could be rid of my pestering mother. So I was sent to live here."

"In the garden?"

She laughed and tilted her head, revealing a sleek alabaster neck. "You are funny, Magdalene. I wish you were staying longer. We might be friends." Persephone waved her hand and everything sparkled around us, as if kissed in moon dust. "There, a little ambiance."

"Weren't you furious at being married off?" I asked.

She shrugged. "I was young and had different expectations for my life, it's true. But there weren't many opportunities then for women other than marriage. Father didn't tell me the man was nearly twenty years older than me! And ugly, too. But he insisted he was a good match for me, and without other prospects, I agreed.

"Once I married, I learned why my father had insisted on the union. My new husband was a king and my father wanted an alliance. It wasn't long before I despised both of them. I was just their tool! My husband would have my oath, but not my heart." Persephone sighed deeply, her lashes fluttering against her cheeks.

"So you are a queen?" I asked.

She nodded. "Yes, but my husband was irritated that he couldn't impress me with his power or standing, since my own father was also a king. After years of keeping me locked away, my husband made a deal with me. If I spent one night with him, he would let me go free in the morning.

"That evening, we met in his great hall. We ate dinner together at opposite ends of a long table. We were alone, except for a solitary musician, playing romantic melodies. After dessert, my husband stood up, walked over to me, and got down on one knee. And then he sang!"

Persephone looked away, covering her eyes. "It was a song he had composed himself. It was terrible! His voice, the lyrics, it was all so wretched. And that's when I fell in love with him. Any man willing to humble himself before me in such a way has surely earned my heart."

"So, everything worked out for you, it seems," I said, wondering why she chose to share this with me.

"True. But there were other obstacles thrown in our way. Just as I had begun to find happiness, fate threw in a wild card - my mother."

"What do you mean? Tell me."

"Magdalene, we follow your story, as I said. There is much more involved than you can see. There are many players, and the balance is precarious."

"You're scaring me," I admitted. "Are you trying to say I may not find Montana?"

"I am just saying that our connections run deep. It's not easy to unbind them. While I found happiness here with my husband, my mother became deeply agitated in the Upper World. She scoured the lands, searching for me, leaving devastation in her wake. She threatened to call forth famine if my father wouldn't tell her where I was. He relented, and she marched down here to demand that Hades release me."

"You're married to Hades!?"

"Yes. Hades refused my mother's request, and once again I was put the middle. I love my mother - she gave me life and is my dearest friend - but I wanted to be with my husband." Persephone paused, touching her long braid. "Mother is a clever woman. She found her way to me, again and again, disrupting my life, until I finally agreed to visit her. Then she used her magick to ensure that I could only spend three months out of the year in the Netherworld. During the precious time I'm with my husband, Mother paints the Upper World white as a token of her grief. She is finally coming to grips with my arrangement, but swears she cannot undo her spell."

"You mean winter? Why are you telling me all this?" I asked, confused.

"I am just showing you that family sagas aren't finished just because you finish a chapter. As long as you are connected, your fates are interwoven. If you save one branch, you save the entire tree."

Persephone wrapped her braid around her hand. "I know what Hades thinks of your father, and I worry. He claims that Armand is willful, self-serving and reckless. My husband rues the day he ever let Armand in. Now, your father's alliance with the Dark One has put both our worlds are in jeopardy. I have told you my story so you will find wisdom in it later, and so you will trust me now. I will assist you in gaining passage to Armand, but the day will come when I will need your help in return. You and I have spoken at length, and now we are connected as well. From this moment on, our fates are also intertwined."

We entered the center of the garden labyrinth. Three flaming torches were set into the earth. A stately woman with hourglass proportions was already there. She wore a filmy gown and her hair was bound on top of her head in heavy looping braids. "Demi?" I asked, recognizing her. She was the poet from Cernunnos' realm.

Demi ignored me, folding her arms as she regarded Persephone. "I heard you! You act like I ruined your life. You'd think I was making you stay with me the entire year."

"Nine months, Mother!." Persephone raised her hands in frustration. "And when I do visit, you're always complaining about not having any grandchildren, yet you don't give me enough time to make them! Conception's changed a lot since you and Daddy had me."

"It's just as well. I'd hardly see them, anyway. Persephone, why do you hate me?"

"Oh, Mother! Don't be dramatic. You know I don't hate you!" Persephone hugged her. "I just need a break, that's all. I was sharing our story to make our guest feel less terrible about her own family."

Demi turned, finally acknowledging me. She tilted her head, studying me until recognition snapped in her eyes. "I am glad to see you safely away from Cernunnos! I apologize for my consort's behavior. I would have warned you earlier, had the wine not caught up to me. Please send my apologies to your nubile sister."

I shifted from foot to foot, exasperated. "Persephone, you promised to show me the way to Armand in exchange for a future favor. I accept. I don't think I have much time."

Demi laughed. "You mean Cronos? He's been gone for years. Relax." A glass of wine appeared in her hand and she lifted it, winking. "You get all the time you want here, darling. All you have to do is ask."

"I need to go back," I said, moving past Persephone. Coming here was turning out to be as disappointing as going to Eagle Mountain. And I wanted to return to the others before they got worried.

"Wait," Demi stopped me. "We cannot allow your child to be raised by Armand in the Netherworld. He is gaining too much power already. I forbid it."

"Then help me get him! I don't think Armand intends on raising my son. He owes the Dark One. If the deal goes through, things will get worse for all of us."

Demi considered my words. "What you say may be true, but Hecate specifically told me not to intervene. She has the gift of divination. If she says to stay out of this, we should."

Persephone put up her hand. "Hecate also told you to stop looking for me, do you remember? But you kept on, anyway, because I was your daughter. Just because it's messy, doesn't mean we shouldn't try."

Demi shrugged, pulling a torch from its holder. A dog howled from somewhere beyond the garden. "Even if I could, it is not up to me. We would need Hecate herself to open that portal. Tartarus is not accessible, even to Hades."

"Tartarus?" I asked, saying it slowly.

"Hell," Persephone said. "Very few that go there ever return, with the exception of your father and a few others. It is for VIPs only, and Hecate is one of the few who can navigate the crossroads. And Mother is one of the few who has access to Hecate."

"Please," I said, turning to Demi.

"Please," Persephone echoed.

"Fine! But if she's cranky, it's on you." Demi drew a circle with her slippered foot around one of the torches. She lifted a chain from her neck, with a golden key attached, and spoke words beneath her breath. A column of mist rose up around the torch, and when it cleared, an old woman with scraggly gray hair and one glass eye stood before us.

Hecate? Except for the colorless eye, there was no resemblance to the beautiful young tree guardian I had met before.

"Persephone! Demeter! Why hast thou summoned me? I was in the middle of important work." The woman thrust a sharpened stave into the dirt, sniffing at them with her hooked nose.

"Cut the crap, Hecate. I know you were just taking a nap," Demeter said. "Maggie needs help finding her baby and you're the only one with a key."

Hecate turned my way, pretending to notice me for the first time. Her face was lined and ancient. The lines on the back of her hands bulged like worms. She had lost all semblance of her earlier beauty. But as I studied her face, I recognized her from somewhere else. "Are you one of the Fates, too?" I asked, remembering the middle witch who had advised us on destiny.

"Yes. It was supposed to be a part-time job, but it sucks up most of my life. But someone has to do it." She sighed, her thin shoulders slumping. "I have given you advice already, which you ignored, and I have given you an apple, which you have used inappropriately. Why should I give you the key?"

"She's grumpy when she's in her Crone phase," Demeter said, "but for some reason she seems to like that form the best."

"It keeps people away," Hecate grumbled.

"Maiden, Mother, and Crone," I said, understanding.

"Took you long enough." Hecate snorted, lifting her tattered clothes and shuffling forward. "Without time, you are not limited as to who you can be. You can be all ages at once. It is one of my few consolations here in the Netherworld." She coughed into her fist and looked up at the night sky. "If you were seeking your daughter, it would make my decision easier. But another man walking around... there are so many already. The world has become a dangerous place under their rule."

"You are being dramatic," Demeter said. "I think you've been hanging around Lilith too much lately."

"Am I the one being dramatic about the ways of men? Why is it then that you wrote that poem? Yes, it was long ago, but I still remember it! Shall I recite?" Without waiting for an invitation, Hecate cleared her throat and tapped her walking stick on the ground. Her appearance instantly changed, transforming into the beautiful young tree guardian I remembered, with thick hair and creamy skin and milky white eyes. Her voice drifted through the air.

> The witch is burning on her cross
> Flames mirrored within her eyes.
> Another maiden has been lost
> To the Darklings battle cry.

275

Villagers cast stones and names
As they call out her sins.
They didn't see this was the way
To let the Darklings in.

Her body is taken down,
The death stench fills the air.
A child laughs within the crowd.
He is his father's heir.

Festivities are over now.
They lie in slumber deep,
With memories of the day's events
Embroidered through their sleep.

In the Netherworld, a Darkling laughs.
His work 'above' is done.
Wrong is right and right is wrong,
The framework has begun.

Hecate bowed at the waist, then stamped her staff and returned to her Crone form.

"I was drinking the night I wrote that," Demeter said. "I just made it up on the spot."

"I heard you rehearsing it beforehand."

"Did not!"

"Did too!"

The two powerful women looked at each other, then collapsed against one another in a fit of laughter.

"The point is that men cannot be trusted," Hecate said, regaining her composure. "Maggie, you should stay with us. We need more strong women in the Netherworld. We will find your son and you can raise him here, among us. We will beat the filth of his gender out of his heart."

"I'm not sure how long you've been down here, but the world has changed. Most of the men I know are good people," I said, thinking of Shane, and Paul and Michael. And my son.

"They are until they aren't," Demeter shrugged.

"I won't let my son feel he isn't worthy because of his gender," I said. "Sasha and my Aunt Dora didn't trust men either, but even they started to come around."

Hecate pulled her cloak back on and regarded me with her glass eye. "Sasha? Dora? From Dark Root? Do you know them?"

"Don't you keep up with anything from the Upper World?" Persephone asked her.

"Who has time!" she said, with a wave of her hand.

"Sasha was my adopted mother, and Dora my adopted aunt," I answered.

"I knew them, in another lifetime…" Her eye drifted. "They are good strong women, though Sasha had some rogue notions I did not care for. But they are honorable. Because you are kin to them, I shall take your request more seriously. Give me a fortnight and you shall have my answer."

"Whatever a fortnight is, I'm sure I don't have that much time!" I said. "Every moment that my newborn son is with Larinda or Armand is one more moment that may seal his fate forever."

Hecate shambled back towards Demeter, looking up at her. "You are the protector of newborns and the lost. This clearly falls under your jurisdiction."

"Clearly," Demeter said. "But this case is special. I cannot pass through the portal to Tartarus, and also, as you must remember, Magdalene is the Seed Bringer."

Hecate scowled as she studied me, her gaze resting on my skirt pocket.

"The seed must flourish or the Netherworld fails as well," Persephone said. "And I do not believe that can happen until she finds her son. I have seen it in the scrying pool."

Until I find my son. Was that why I hadn't felt the call to plant the seed yet? Was Montana's survival linked to their survival as well? I stood taller, now sure they would help me.

Hecate waved her hand. "What do I care? I am old and tired. I just want to tend my tree alone, until the final days."

"You wouldn't say that in your younger guise," Demeter answered. "And the End of Days will come much faster if we allow Armand to continue growing in power. You have more than a hand in fate - you have seen what happens if we do not intervene. As above, so below. Do not throw us into another Burning Time just because of your stubbornness."

"Fate? The boy's fate is sealed! And it must be important, for even I have not seen it. There is no room for a change of course."

"You said his fate would come about with me or without me," I said. "Help me and I will do my best to raise my son well."

We all looked at Hecate. She sighed, and her sigh became a thick cough. "We shall ask the winds." Hecate snapped her fingers and a signpost appeared between the torches. There were three arrows, pointing in opposing directions. The old witch rubbed her hands together, then blew into her cupped palms. She then tapped on the signpost three times. The arrows spun, slowly at first, and then became a blur. When they eventually stopped, all three were pointing in the same direction.

Hecate coughed again and straightened her cloak. "The winds have spoken," she said. "We will guide you to the Crossing, but that is all. We cannot escort you beyond Hade's realm. But if you insist, we need to hurry! The veil grows thinner by the hour. When the moon sets, the portal will close."

I looked up. The moon was descending towards the horizon.

Hecate drew three spiral symbols in the earth with the point of her staff. Around the spirals, she drew a single circle.

"My Wheel," she said. "Or Will, as the case may be. It is a very powerful symbol, used only by me and my initiates. It is a key that unlocks many portals, but you must be trained to call it up. Your fool of a father got hold of my symbol and used it without educating himself first. That is part of the reason for our current mess, because it gave him access to the Dark One."

She looked at me, as if seeing searching for any traces of my father in me. She spit onto her thumb, then placed it on my forehead. "Protection. None but the heartiest men have come back from Tartarus intact. And most of those suffer madness or bear the Dark One's mark."

"What about women?" I asked.

Hecate scoffed. "Why would a woman go there? Except to help someone escape. Even Lilith finds the place inhospitable. No matter what has been said about the evils of women, Hell is a true boy's club."

"I have opened your portal but time is short. We will escort you and your friends to Nyx. She will help you complete your journey."

"What about the hellhounds," Persephone asked. "They should come with us."

"Yes, let us bring them!" Demeter agreed.

She stamped her staff and the trappings of the labyrinth fell away. We were now standing with my companions, who were startled by our sudden appearance.

"Whoa! Give us a little warning next time, will you?" Ruth Anne asked, taking a step back.

"This is the witch Hecate," I quickly explained. "And Queen Persephone and her mother, the goddess-."

"Demeter!" Ruth Anne and Paul said together. Eve's reaction was venomous, as she studied the impossible curves on both Persephone's and Demeter's bodies.

"I remember this cutie from the feast. What's your name, honey?" Demeter asked Paul, sizing him up. Her gauzy gown seemed even more transparent now. Paul blushed beneath her approving gaze.

"He's mine," Eve said, stepping forward, which surprised Paul, since the two had hardly spoken since their memory reveals. Eve didn't match Demeter in stature, but her shadow made up for it, growing in both length and proportions, until it rivaled even the shapeliest of women. Demeter smiled, as if the trick were cute.

"Mother, remember when we talked about true love?" Persephone said. "You are not supposed to interfere."

"True love? What do these two know of true love? All I see is jealousy, suspicion and pettiness. This is not the way of true love."

"They are learning."

"That is the problem with mortals – they are always learning. As soon as they learn their lessons, their time is done." She blew a tendril of hair from her face.

"The moon is low," Persephone said. She pointed to the brightest star in the sky. "That is Nyx. She will appear when the moon and the horizon meet. She only makes one trip a night, so we must hurry if you are to embark this evening."

"I don't like this," Shane whispered to me. "You don't know these women. They could be leading us to…"

"To where?" Hecate said, with a shrug, overhearing him. "Won't anyplace be better than limbo?"

"I suppose," he admitted.

"Now let us not dally or the boat will leave without us. Let us fly."

∾

We followed Hecate, who ran with surprising grace and speed along the river. Persephone and Demeter carried their torches. A silver chain appeared in Demeter's hand, attached to two snarling dogs - the hellhounds, who barked and bit and howled at the fading night. The air felt surprisingly light, lacking the usual pull of gravity, and I felt like I was swimming rather than running.

"Witch's dust," Persephone explained our swiftness. "Made of moon dust and fairy magick. Witches once used it to ride on their brooms in the Upper World, when there were more fairies than today."

Persephone noticed my frown. "Don't worry. They are returning. They have been hiding for a millennium, waiting and preparing."

"Waiting for what?" I asked, but she pulled too far ahead. The field became a forest, which gave way to rolling hills. Our feet hardly touched the ground as we raced to beat the moon.

"For there not being any time in the Netherworld, it sure feels like we're always rushing around," Ruth Anne said.

Our pace was forcefully slowed as we encountered a thick fog that even the blazing torches couldn't cut through. Rumbling growls emerged from the mist, spooking even the hellhounds, who whimpered and tucked their tails between their legs.

"Some guards you are," Demeter scolded her dogs as three sets of yellow eyes peered at us from the fog. The torches revealed accompanying sets of sharp, yellow fangs. The beasts growled and snarled as they stepped from their cover.

"No wonder the hounds are afraid. We've got Netherwolves!" Demeter said, thrusting out her flame. "Someone really wants to stop you," she said.

"Don't show fear." Persephone said, stepping forward and brandishing her own torch. The beasts were twice as large as the hellhounds, muscled and quick. One braver wolf stepped into Persephone's torch arc, singing its fur. It yelped and receded back into the mist, but two other wolves moved up to take its place. "Fear makes them hungry," Persephone continued. "One bite, or even a mark from their foul claws, will surely kill you."

"Move back!" Hecate commanded the wolves. "Or I'll send you someplace even worse than hell." Their growling deepened into what sounded like menacing laughter.

"Our magick is no match for them," Demeter said.

"But you are goddesses."

"And these are the pets of the Dark One. They are his eyes and ears. He won't let anything happen to them. They are untouchable."

"We're screwed," Eve said.

I readied my wand as the eyes and fangs advanced, circling us. Even Hecate appeared hesitant. "Something is wrong. The wolves are supposed to be hibernating now," she said, pushing one back with her stave. The wolf whimpered, and retaliated with a sharp snap of his teeth. Demeter's hellhounds crowded in protectively around the old witch, snapping their teeth defensively. They may not be able to best the larger animals, but they weren't going to let anything happen to their guardians, either.

The hulking Netherwolves licked their lips, discerning who among us was weakest. "My staff, two torches and these hellhounds won't hold them for long," Hecate said. "We need more."

Shane pulled out his pocketknife; it glinted in the flickering torchlight, giving the wolves pause.

"They think your knife is silver," said Persephone. "Silver is the only thing Netherwolves really. Let's run while they are distracted."

We raced headlong into the growing fog. Shane held them off for several moments, then sprinted to join us. It wasn't long before the wolves collected themselves, snarling behind us as they sought an opening between the flashes of Shane's darting knife.

"We're gonna need something more than one small knife," Ruth Anne said, between breaths. "We'll be overrun in 5...4..."

"Turn right!" Eve called out.

"Why?" Ruth Anne asked.

"I don't know. Just do it."

"Do it!" Hecate agreed.

We veered hard-right, as instructed. A wolf moved to flank us. Shane reached out, slashing its leg. The wolf rolled to the ground, disappearing before it hit the earth. Shane regained his feet and quickly rejoined us. "Can't believe that worked," he said.

"Go left now!" Eve called out. "I think."

"Always trust your instincts," Hecate said "That is why they are given to you."

More gold eyes closed in around us, blinking through the blanket of fog. Their breath smelled of rotted meat. Shane veered left and right, trying to guard both our flanks at once, brandishing his bloodied knife. A few bolder wolves stretched out their jaws, hoping to catch us off guard.

One of Demeter's hellhounds suddenly leapt into the midst of the wolves. "No!" Demeter screamed, as her dog disappeared into the blur of fangs and claws.

"Oh, Mother, you can always conjure more of those dogs. You can't create more of us," Persephone said.

"Keep going," Eve cried, now pulling to the fore alongside Hecate. Her eyes were half-closed, as if entranced. A Netherwolf appeared beside me, nipping at my arm, before being driven away by Shane's knife blade. I snapped my wand in its direction and it yelped.

At last, we cleared the fog and the Netherwolves fell behind.

"My poor baby," Demeter said, of her missing hound.

"Your baby saved us all," Shane said. "It stalled the wolves long enough for us to get away."

"His sacrifice shall not be forgotten," I said to Demeter.

We were back at the river. It looked different now, like slick oil instead of running water. "This is our destination," Hecate announced.

I looked around for the mysterious guide. "Where is Nyx? Did we miss her?" There was no sign of anyone, up or down the river.

"The moon still shows a sliver. She will be here," Persephone promised. "I must go now. Hades does not like me venturing too far from our borders. If he finds out, there will be souls to pay." She faced me, taking my hand. "Good luck finding your son, Maggie. We will meet again."

Persephone disappeared before I could thank her. Demeter stepped up before me, adjusting her tilted crown. "I understand the strength of a mother's love, Maggie. Stay true to your heart. You are more important than you know. You are the Seed Bringer."

"Thank you," I said. "I'll do whatever I can."

She frowned, looking at my arm. There was a troubled expression on her face. "You have been scratched by a Netherwolf! And yet, you appear fine. You truly are a remarkable witch, Maggie. We will meet again." And then she, too, disappeared.

Finally, Hecate spoke. "Do not let your seeming importance cloud your judgement in the times ahead. We are all replaceable. The Fates giveth and they can taketh away. And remember, women are the true expression of magick. We are the creators of life. Stay strong. The future of both worlds rests on what you do next."

She reached into her cloak and drew out a flat clay disk, fastened on a piece of string. She placed it around my neck, and it clanked against the ankh. "My Wheel," she said. "It will take you to the Dark One's lair, but the wheel won't get you out. That, you must do on your own."

She stepped back and looked us carefully over. "Offices are required in the Upper World, too, and elections will be held soon. Finish your mission and get out quickly. Our worlds need you." With that, she stamped her staff into the earth and a ribbon of silver lights twinkled above her. Hecate was gone.

"What the hell just happened?" Ruth Anne said, looking around.

I inspected my new medallion. It was a crude piece of work, and felt very old.

"Now what?" Merry asked.

Eve pointed and we saw a long narrow boat approaching, manned by a single standing oarsman. "We go with Nyx," Eve said.

The boat made no sound as it approached. No waves lapped at the beach. The longboat glided towards us across the inky surface, coming to a smooth stop before us. An unbearably lovely woman with indigo hair and onyx eyes stepped out of the boat, her gown shimmering and provocatively translucent. With every step, her breasts swayed hypnotically beneath the sheer cloth, and her ample hips fought the strain of the dress. The emptiness in her eyes was beautiful rather than frightening. They were the eyes of eternity, seeing both the past and the future.

"I am Nyx," she said without emotion, as she surveyed us. I couldn't get angry at Shane for staring. Even I found it hard to look away.

"Sister," Eve said, stepping forward and extending her hand. "I am Eve."

"I know who you are," Nyx said, brushing Eve's hair with the back of her hand.

"Uh, do they know each other?" Ruth Anne asked me.

If they didn't, there was at least a mutual understanding. Nyx and Eve faced one another, their palms pressed together, like two beautiful reflections in a mirror. Even their shadows aligned. Moon shadows – from which the midnight dreams of young men every-where sprang.

Eve turned to us, smiling. "It is set."

"It is?" Ruth Anne asked.

Eve extended her arm to the boat like she was inviting us into a grand hotel. I shrugged my acceptance, and we all found seats on the simple wood benches. Nyx resumed her position in the stern, then tapped the boat with her oar. It lurched out into the river, and made for the opposite bank. Eve lifted a lantern from the bed of the boat, while Nyx steered us along. The two began to sing.

> *A canal of stars, we glide upon*
> *Deep into the night,*
> *With only the moon to guide us home*
> *And a speck of candlelight.*
> *Our lovers wait for us at home,*
> *They keep the fires burning,*
> *We are the daughters of the night*
> *We rule until the morning.*

It was a beautiful harmony and the stars overhead responded with a shower of bright light.

"Spooky," Merry whispered behind me. "Or it would be, if this all wasn't so normal anymore."

Paul tapped my shoulder. "What's happening to Eve?"

"I don't know," I admitted, but I watched her closely the entire boat ride. She seemed so at home here, so in her element. I had never seen my younger sister so poised and certain.

The river undulated like Nyx's hips. We passed a kaleidoscope of images along the banks as we drifted downstream. The images blurred together; some I recognized, while others were entirely foreign.

"Look, Michael, our old van! Shane, that's your Uncle Joe's cafe. And there's Harvest Home! Miss Sasha's Magick Shoppe!" In front of her shop, I saw Mother, flashing through the many incarnations in which I had known her – from being in thick brown hair, tumbling to her slim waist, to a more severe version of her high-collared dress and done-up hair. And everything in between and after. The images slid from one to the other, passing through time, all shadows of Dark Root itself.

The pictures continued, becoming dim and tired, and finally quiet. This wasn't the home I knew. "Is this our future?" I asked. I looked for signs of familiarity. "What happened to us?"

Nyx put her finger to her lips. "Hush, Magdalene. Sleep now. Morning comes."

I was floating.

I dreamed of nothing. I was, at last, at peace.

20

THE SUN

*J**n the world between worlds there is a door.*

I had no memory of arriving at the door. I only remembered Nyx lulling me to sleep. But here I was before it, and it was taller than I ever imagined. There was nothingness above our heads and below our feet. The only light came from the door itself, and it raged like a bonfire on a lonely road. We stared at it, none of us speaking. This was our last door.

I reached for the handle, and the radiating heat singed my hand before I could touch it.

"Wait!" Shane grabbed my wrist. "Let me."

"Your time for chivalry will come later," I said. "

"Hold on, Maggie!" Merry demanded, taking my hand. "I need to heal that first."

"I should have brought oven mitts," I said, prepping myself to try again. Then, I noticed markings on the door frame – strange symbols surrounding horned figures in various stages of a dance. They were terrifying, but also fascinating.

Ruth Anne adjusted her glasses and peered closer. "I think the symbols translate as, *Only Angels and food may hinder.* Wait, that's not right, I'm reading this backwards. I forgot that in Ancient Sumerian it's 'Eye before Elysian Fields, except after Wheat.' Let me try again. It says, *Only Demons or Fools May Enter.* I guess that's us."

As I followed the drawings down the frame, my eyes rested on a circular groove carved into the wood. There was a spiral etched into its center.

"Hecate's Wheel," I said, lifting the pendant from around my neck and pushing the disk into the notch. The knob turned on its own, and the door swung inward, releasing billows of heavy steam. I jumped back to avoid being scorched.

Michael stepped in front of me, reciting the Lord's Prayer while ignoring the hot vapor. When it cleared, he appeared to be untouched. There was pure conviction in his eyes.

"It's time," I said. I gave Shane a quick kiss and the others a grateful smile.

I stepped into blinding light. Abruptly, I was surrounded by leaping orange and red flames. Magma flowed some distance beneath my feet. I appeared to be suspended within a cavern, with rock walls that flickered with torchlight. For a single moment, the blistering heat consumed me.

And then I could breathe again. Opaque walls separated me from the inferno. There was now a floor beneath my feet, though I could still make out the magma rolling beneath. I thought I was alone, until I heard Eve.

"I don't ever want to do that again," she said, reaching for my hand. The others appeared around me.

"Do what?" Michael asked.

"The burning thing," I said.

"Was there a burning thing? I didn't notice."

"It wasn't that bad," Merry shrugged. "Like getting your ears pierced."

"I don't think we had the same experience," Eve said.

"Montana's nearby," Shane said excitedly, as the rest of the room phased in.

Everything was now white - from the lush drapery, to the exquisite wardrobe, to the plush carpets on the translucent floor. Four white stone gargoyles guarded each of the corners, surrounded by pillars with tall candles. Larinda materialized at the far end of the room, wearing a wedding dress and veil that covered only her eyes. At her feet, a white baby cradle rocked all on its own.

"Welcome," Larinda said, as we advanced on her.

My hands shook as I walked. I would have unleashed already, were she not standing next to my son. I stopped a few yards before her. "Don't welcome me, Larinda! You know why I'm here. Give me back Montana or I'll destroy this house too." I pointed my wand at the lava below our feet.

"That would be foolish. You would kill yourself, and your son."

"She's right," Shane said. "Let me rush her."

"You wouldn't dare," Larinda said. She raised her hand over the cradle. "I will end this child's existence before you take one step."

I held still, considering our options. Larinda looked to the side and a white clock appeared on the wall. Its hands were both nearing XII. "At midnight, I will marry Armand and become as powerful as any other woman in the Netherworld. The boy will be my dowry. You will go back to your dull little lives, forgetting all about this."

"Go to hell!" I said. "I'm not giving you my son."

"Who said give?" She raised her wand and her eyebrows, and simply laughed. "Just one more minute and your father will be here. You can all be our witnesses, our festive little wedding party. Much more apropos than having these stone gargoyles as witnesses," she said, gesturing to the nearest pedestal.

"If you hadn't turned Leah to stone, she could have been here," I said. At this, I saw one of the gargoyles open its eyes. "But now your daughter is dead and it's your fault. You won't kill my child, too."

"Dead?" Larinda said the word as though she didn't understand what it meant. Her eyes softened, and there was an expression on her face I'd never seen before. Was it grief? Or regret?

The four gargoyles began coming to life, their joints crunching as they stretched their muscular limbs. They eyed Larinda menacingly from their posts, crouching like cats preparing to leap. Larinda raised her wand with one hand and held the cradle handle with the other, hesitating.

"Leah's dead. You killed your daughter. And it's all on your hands," I said, wiping mine clean.

The gargoyles all sprang at the same time. I was expecting Larinda to strike them down instantly with her wand, but she didn't. Her eyes were dull and her wand dropped to her side. She let go of the cradle as she covered her face. The creatures clawed at her, until one grasped her by the shoulders and lifted her into the air. It flew directly through the faltering wall, her illusion wavering. Larinda kicked and screamed as the gargoyles escorted her into the nothingness.

I sprinted for my son.

The walls were crumbling and the floor cracked, but I didn't care. I lifted Montana up, crying as I held him to my chest. He was as beautiful and perfect as I remembered. He was worth everything, and so much more. My son! My sun!

I smelled his skin, and a hundred wonderful memories flashed through me - feeding him, bathing him, taking him sledding down Shane's hill in one of my stupider moments. He cried against my shoulder, his mouth opening and shutting. *How had I forgotten his bottle!*

"You're safe, honey," I whispered. "Mommy's here."

The others crowded tightly around us. Michael kissed his son's forehead and Shane stroked his small hand. My sisters cried as they tickled his fingers and toes. "Thank you," I said, looking up at each of them. "I'll make it up to you, somehow."

I lifted Montana's face to my own. His green eyes recognized me and he smiled. "I'm never leaving you again," I said. "And that's a promise."

There was a new voice. "Let us just hope you're better at keeping your promises than your old man is."

We all turned. Standing beneath the clock was a man I knew very well through both my dreams and the memory globes. But we'd never met in person. He was wearing faded jeans, a fringed suede jacket, and a cowboy hat.

It was exactly midnight.

"Hello, my daughter," he said, grinning as he removed his hat. "And my first grandson. It is so nice to finally meet you."

21

JUDGEMENT

*T*he memory globes didn't do Armand justice. It wasn't just that he was physically striking– which he was. It was his forceful presence; his magnetism. His aura filled the entire room. As he drew closer to me, my thoughts seemed to scatter.

He was young, no older than thirty, and handsome in the way that demons were. He had been born a warlock, trained by the most powerful witch of her time, and he now consorted with the Dark One. I trembled in a way I have never trembled in Gahabrien's presence.

No one spoke. My breath refused to leave my lungs as Armand marched forward with long strides. I finally gathered my wits and clutched Montana as the others crowded in front of me. Armand laughed and parted his hands, as if stepping through a curtain. My companions paused and then unwillingly moved aside and froze in place, allowing him access. He was as strong as any god, here.

I raised my wand and was gripped with pain, paralyzing me. Armand easily lifted Montana from my arms and stepped back.

"There. That was easy." Armand pulled the blanket away from Montana's head. "So, you're who all the fuss is about. I can see why. You have my hair."

The warlock then looked around the room as the agonizing pain of his spell threatened to break me. "It seems I missed my own wedding. But we should at least have the reception." He snapped his fingers and we were free to move again. He snapped them again and we were all holding wine glasses, filled with clear liquid.

"Too bad my bride left me at the altar. She does loves champagne. Oh, well. We drink without her." He raised the glass to his lips and drew in every drop before it vanished again.

"Don't do this," I said, dropping the wine glass. It shattered on the floor before disappearing, too. Not a drop of wine or a shard of glass was left. "I know this isn't who you are, not deep down. I saw Aunt Dora's memory globes! You used to care about... some things. Someone."

I didn't mention Jillian's name but I could tell by the gleam in his eyes that my father knew whom I referred to. He put a hand in the pocket of his long coat and laughed. "That was a long time ago, daughter. Your mother betrayed me in not telling me about you. With her betrayal, went the last of my heart."

"She deceived you because she knew what you were planning."

"And what is that?" he asked, his brows meeting.

"You would have traded me to the Dark One, in exchange for even more power."

"Is that what they told you?" He shook his head. "First of all, you are not a male. And though I might have found a loophole to close the deal anyway, that was not my intention. I wanted my daughter."

"You have me now," I said, inching closer and glancing towards my son. "If you let me leave with Montana, we can start to forge a real relationship."

Armand laughed so hard he choked. "Forge a relationship? Forge a fucking relationship? Who the hell do you think I am?" He turned angrily, as if looking for something to punch. He pointed at one of the empty pedestals and it burst into flame, as if made of paper. "I do not need your pity, Magdalene. I wanted my daughter only because she was Jillian's, never because she was mine. I do not have that kind of ego, despite what you have been told. But now, seeing you only reminds me of her. You have her eyes. Do you think I need that kind of mind fuck at this stage of my life? "

"Please, then give him back and you'll never have to see me again. You said you could have figured out a loophole. Figure one out now. Please! For Jillian!"

He snarled, his eyes gleaming like those of a Netherwolf. "I said I lost all love for her! And even if I didn't, you have no right to invoke that woman's name in front of me." He took a long step froward, his grip tightening on Montana. "No right."

"You have no right to...to... "

"Rights? Oh-oh! Let us talk about rights!"

Armand snapped his fingers again and the walls shimmered, changing in color and texture. Larinda's bridal suite vanished and we were standing in a brick room, with stained wood wainscoting. My father stood behind an imposing podium, a gavel in his free hand. On a table beside him was a bronze scale. We were in a courtroom.

"Now, let us have that discussion about rights." He waved his hand and we were forcefully pushed down onto high-backed benches that suddenly appeared behind us.

"Let us go," Eve said as she struggled to stand. "This isn't funny."

My father laughed. "That is not true. I find it quite funny. Now, to keep further unnecessary comments to a minimum, I am going to insist that only one of you speak at a time. And only when I have called on you by name." He slid his pinched thumb and forefinger across the air in a zipping motion. I tried to speak but I could only gurgle. We'd been muted.

"Just like Babel, right Michael?" Armand said. "If the peasants are conspiring with one another, it is better that they not speak at all."

"You are not a god," Michael said. "What you're doing won't make you immortal. There's a battle between hell and heaven that has been raging for years, and..."

"And years. Yes, I know. And your poor world is caught in the crossfire. But the battle's end is nigh! And I plan on being on the winning team when it is all over." Armand left the podium and carried Montana down the aisle, stopping before Michael. "I give you credit man, for still having some of that faith. Fuck, I'd of lost mine when half my followers disappeared, but you took it like a man. Good for you."

Armand kissed Montana's cheek and held him to his chest. Michael's face reddened as he struggled against his invisible restraints, cursing Armand with every breath.

"You, yourself predicted these days, back when people still listened to you," Armand continued, "You wanted them. You could see and even taste the destruction coming. And then you were bummed out the end didn't come about. But man, they're almost here! You should be happy that Montana will help usher in a new age! After a bit of turmoil, I hear it's gonna be golden. A party, all the way to the end. You could ride it out too, if you knew whose bread to butter."

The cross around Michael's neck levitated up, and Armand shook his head. "Fool," he said, reaching out to touch the crucifix with the tip of his finger. It melted like wax. "Your God has been gone a long time, buddy. He did not help my 'priest father,' and He certainly didn't do anything for me. You should look into finding another savior." Armand shrugged, walking away as Michael stared at his melted chain. "And now, I mute you."

I struggled silently, trying to free myself while Armand returned to his pulpit. I tried to remember spells that might free us, but I couldn't work long as my father turned his attention to me.

"My daughter says I have no right...no right to what, Magdalene? My first male heir? I say I have every right. I made this deal long before any of you were even created, and it is time for me to pay up. My boss grows weary."

He pointed to me, granting my voice again. I choked as the constriction lifted from my chest and throat. "Do you really hate us that much?" I asked.

There was genuine confusion in his eyes. "No. I don't hate you, Maggie. You are a part of me. In fact, your son is so valuable that as part of the deal, I plan on asking my boss for an extension of time, on your behalf. He has waited this long for the war, what's another decade or so?"

"A decade? And then what?"

"And then we see." Armand put Montana into his cradle beside the podium, then banged his gavel three times. Somehow my son slept through it. "But we are here concerning other matters. Let the trial begin."

"Trial?"

"The Trial of Rights." Armand grinned out over his captive audience. "Just think, this little guy might buy all of humanity another ten years. Twelve if you are on good behavior. Isn't that worth it?" He motioned towards the scale. A feather sat on one copper plate, and a pulsating human heart sat on the other. "In the old days, they measured a man's heart against the weight of a feather, then later, against the weight of his sins. Today, we weigh one life against another."

Now floating above the scale plates were two holograms - one of Montana, the other of Earth. "One small life for ten years of peace on earth.The request seems more than fair, if you ask me."

"That's not fair at all!" I protested, slamming my hand against my bench.

"Isn't it? We make decisions like this all the time. Don't we, Shane?" He turned to my husband. The images over the scales shifted again, showing Asha on one plate and a ramshackle village on the other. "The boy is not the only child whose blood is on your hands, is he *tracker*? If you had to do it again, who would you save this time, besides yourself?"

"You're an asshole," Shane said, his face as red as the bricks in the wall.

Armand twisted his finger in the air and Shane's hat lifted from his head, floating all the way to the podium. He inspected it and frowned."I prefer my vintage one," he said. With that, Shane's hat melted , just like Michael's cross.

"If I ever get the chance..." Shane said, writhing to break free.

"You'll do what? Track me? I see how adept you are at that. How many times did you fail my daughter here? You had one job, Shane. One."

"I was going to say I'd kill you."

My father shrugged. "You've done plenty of that before, haven't you?" Before Shane could speak, Armand silenced him again with an aerial zip. "You're an arrogant fool, just like your uncle."

Armand paced the front of the room, scratching his head beneath his hat. Eventually, he circled over to Merry, gently lifting her chin.

"You're such a sweetheart, aren't you? With your big eyes and your morals and your heart?" He pointed to the scale and there was Merry's image hovering over one plate and her daughter June Bug on the other. "Yes. A real sweetheart."

Merry sobbed.

"Stop it!" he said, pushing her face away. "You are only crying out of shame. No one receives atonement from shame. You earn atonement through absolution and making amends."

"I've made amends!"

"Oh, you have? So where is that kid of yours? Oh yeah, with her cuckold father. Maybe its better you don't have a hand in raising her."

He silenced Merry's crying and moved on to Paul, sitting beside her.

"And you. How much is a life worth to you? A record deal? You sacrificed your brother for sex, drugs and rock and roll. I think we could have a beer sometime."

"Leave them alone!" I said. "This is between you and me. Keep everyone else out of it."

Armand rapped his knuckles against the back of a bench. "Is my little girl jealous she's not getting enough attention? Don't worry, Maggie. I have not forgotten you." My own image appeared on the scale opposite Montana's.

"As a trained witch, you knew how much power the spoken word carries. And yet, you selfishly denounced wanting your own child. Your own flesh and blood. Do you think that perhaps you brought this whole thing upon yourself? That maybe you set the avalanche of Montana's fate in motion? Destinies are created before birth, you know." He grinned and licked his lips. "You're not so different from me after all, if you think about it."

My entire body trembled, but I gauged my words carefully. He was baiting me, playing on my fears and my guilt. "I'm sorry I ever said that," I admitted. "But you don't get to decide the worth of my soul." I looked defiantly at the scale. One of the plates collapsed.

"You're a spitfire," he said. "I admit I find that endearing."

Armand made his way towards my bench. As he passed Ruth Anne, she grabbed for his arm. He broke away easily. "I wondered why Sasha kept you around after learning you were a failed witch. She must have found your pluck useful and entertaining. Too bad you didn't show her the same loyalty. But I understand. I had a hard time being loyal to her, too." He winked. "Did Dora ever forgive you? I wouldn't be surprised if—"

"I said leave them alone!"

My body quaked with anger. My bench rocked and jerked violently beneath me, the legs drumming on the floor, trying to beat themselves free. *How dare him*, I thought, releasing so much energy that the bench splintered into pieces, and I was free.

I stood and eyed him over my raised wand. I might be younger and less experienced, but I was also a wilder - and not one to be trifled with. Even by an warlock of his stature.

"That's my girl," he said, nodding as he backed towards the cradle. "I knew you had some of my coursing through you."

"I have some of Jillian's, too."

"I said never to mention..."

With still-trembling fingers, I pointed at the nearby pews, collapsing all of them. My sisters quickly gathered themselves and drew their wands, the men close beside them. Merry drew a protective circle around us as we advanced.

"Give him back!" I demanded, aiming my wand at Armand's chest. I pulled from the rich magick of this deeper world. It was a dark and polluted energy that made me want to retch, but it was potent. The gem at the tip of my wand sparked in anticipation. "Give back my son, Father. I'm not sure what will happen if I let everything go, but I guarantee, if we go down, you'll go down with us."

Armand's eyes shifted from side to side. He started to snap his fingers and I quickly flicked my wand. A red welt appeared across his palm. He retracted it, stung.

"Don't make me hurt you, Maggie," he said. "Or my grandson." His aura flashed silver around him, as if he'd stepped on a live wire. "You might be *The Sworn One*, whatever the hell that means, but sworn to who? And why? It is because of my bloodline that you can do all those nifty tricks. You owe everything to me."

"I owe nothing to you!" The charge building within me grew, threatening to overload my system. I aimed at what was left of his justice scales and they flew into the wall, clattering to pieces. I looked around for something else to throw as the courtroom lights flickered wildly around us.

"You have your mother's spirit," Armand said calmly.

"But I don't have her forgiving heart! I must have inherited that from you. Time's up!" I pointed at a clock, and it burst into flames.

Armand stretched his arms and cracked his knuckles, a smile pulling at his lips. "Don't make me do this, Maggie. Can't you see I'm trying to reason with you? I am not the bad guy here. You saw for yourself how Sasha treated me, using my abilities for her own gains. She used everyone – Dora, Jillian, Joe - even her daughters. She didn't take you in out of love - she took you out of necessity. And I am the bad one?" He spat spit from the side of his mouth, and the floor hissed as the saliva evaporated.

"Sasha has nothing to do with this," I said, making my way towards the cradle, never lowering my wand. "You had free will. You could have used it to do some good in the world. But no, you wanted more. You blew it."

"Free will? Free fucking will? Are you kidding me? Do you know how many souls are locked up in this part of the Netherworld? Countless. More than the stars in the sky, my dear. And it is all because of free will."

Armand flicked his tongue, as if he were a lizard searching for the sun. "No one has free will in the Upper World. Not when personal survival is on the line. Sure, they tell you you do, then they leave you out there, starving, naked, and alone. Merry didn't have free will when she lied to her husband, because she knew he'd beat the shit out of her if he found out. And Shane didn't have free will when he signed that kid's death order. Free will is all an illusion, created to make you believe you're in charge. Free will doesn't exist, Maggie."

"Yes, it does. And I'm using mine now."

I released everything that was left inside me, sending it through my arm, my hand, and my wand, and straight at my father. He was the epicenter of my storm. The room tremored and lurched, as if it were a boat in the eye of a hurricane; the air whipped around us, loosening the podium from the floor and scattering the fragmented benches; the walls began to disintegrate, along with the floor.

The whole place was crumbling down around us.

"Maggie! Stop!" Shane called out to me. "You're going to kill us all."

I kept channeling - pushing, pushing, pushing... throwing everything at my warlock father. My sisters added their own wands, lending their own strength to mine.

"Stop!" Armand commanded, holding out his arms. His face gleamed with sweat, and his breathing was labored. "I cannot stop the wheels, Maggie! Don't you understand? They were set in motion by the Fates long ago. A sacrifice must be made. I would rather destroy everything than tell the Dark One I cannot meet the terms of our agreement. You would too, if you met him."

We were no longer standing on a courtroom floor, but on a large flat rock floating in the river of magma. All illusion was gone as we drifted along a vast, yet suffocating cavern. The cradle rocked precariously near the edge of the rock, and Shane continued to beg me to stop. He needn't have worried. I was nearly spent and there was nothing left to tear apart. My sisters' arms began to waver too, and they dropped their wands to their sides.

"Ah, the follies of youth," Armand said. "They think they can charge in with only rudimentary training, and challenge the establishment. But the establishment has remained there for a reason. With age comes wisdom, Maggie. Remember that."

Armand stretched his arm towards the magma river, and raised up his hand. A shape rose up, formed of the lava itself. It towered beside the floating slab on which we stood, a faceless beast with six thick arms. Armand lowered his hand, and the shape descended back into the depths.

"You and that puny wand are no match for me," he said.

He was right. Our wands, even combined, were no match for him. I looked to each of my companions, and then to my son. There was only one option left to me.

I dropped my wand, letting it roll off into the river. And then I stepped up to meet my father.

There was only the death touch.

I held out a single finger, an arm's reach away.

He knew what I was planning before I spoke.

"Where do you think you got that talent?" Armand asked. "Certainly not from your mother." He raised up his own finger, poised a short inch from my own. I could feel the currents traveling between us, fingertip to fingertip. "You cannot destroy me, Maggie. I am too strong. Only a god wields that power now."

"Or a goddess," said a female's voice.

Two beautiful women appeared beside us, walking barefoot along the surface of the magma river. They stepped up onto the rock, stopping before Armand. Lilith and Hecate in her younger form.

Armand tightened his jaw. "Why have you come? You ladies have no jurisdiction here."

"Oh?" Lilith smiled, jutting out a hip. "That is not what your patron says. As a matter of fact, he has invited me to come over any time. Day or night. Preferably night," she winked. "No key required."

"And I have my own key," Hecate said, holding up her wheeled pendant. "We can gain an audience with him whenever we please. Now release the child, or we shall please."

For the first time, my father seemed agitated. He stood over the cradle, licking his parched lips. "You two should know that deals like this cannot be broken. *He* will not allow it."

"That is true," Lilith conceded. "The laws are binding here. But perhaps there is a loophole."

Hecate opened her palms and a scroll appeared. She unfurled it and began reading. "Henceforth... to be held accountable... by the year... here it is! You owe your benefactor your first male heir. That is the entirety of what you owe."

"Offer me instead," I said. "I'm not male, but I'm the Sworn One. That must have some value."

"No," Lilith said. "Your importance is tied to many things, including the seed and the child. Neither will grow without you. And even if they could, you return to the Upper World to fulfill your own destiny. The Fates are very clear about that."

"Yes," Hecate agreed, as the scroll vanished from her hands.

"Magdalene wouldn't count anyway," Armand grumbled. "Trust me, I've asked. It needs to be a male."

"Then take me!" Shane said. "I'm Maggie's husband. So that makes me your son. Technically."

Armand shook his head. "Valiant effort, but you are not my first male heir, nor is your heart pure enough to trade. You've got far too much baggage to be of any real value. Why do you think the Dark One prefers children? They're not all soiled, like the rest of us."

Michael opened his palms and looked lovingly at his child, still sleeping in his cradle. "Consider this: Montana is my son, and I'm his legal guardian while he's a minor. Therefore, until he's eighteen, I'm the trustee of whatever he's heir to. That makes me your first male heir, for now."

Armand rubbed his chin thoughtfully.

"No! You can't take him either. He's a grown man," I argued.

"But my heart is clean," Michael said. "Armand, you know that. You didn't show me on your scale."

"True," Hecate agreed. "He has purged his guilt and asked for forgiveness. It is a rare concession from a man - especially one who has made so many mistakes."

Michael dropped to his knees, his hands clasped. "Take me, Armand, I beg you. Please don't take my son."

My father turned to the goddesses. "Will it fulfill my contract?"

"It should," Lilith shrugged. "Technically speaking."

Without another word, Armand pressed his finger into Michael's forehead, twisting it, as if extinguishing a cigarette. It all seemed to happen in slow motion – Michael shrieking as his body turned to ashes, holding his form for the span of a breath, before falling into a loose pile on the drifting rock .

Then, everything went silent. I couldn't even hear my own scream.

This wasn't real. This couldn't be real. The father of my child, my former lover, and my friend. Murdered by my father, right before my eyes.

"No!" I roared, rushing Armand.

Shane grabbed me before I could strike, pulling me into his arms and out of Armand's reach. "Not today, Maggie. Montana needs his mother."

"Listen to the man," Armand said, raising his chin. There was resignation in his eyes as he adjusted his cowboy hat. "I'm sorry. It's business. Speak well of this man," he said, stepping over Michael's ashes. "It was an honorable death. We'll take good care of his soul."

With that, my father snapped his fingers and transformed into an eagle. He squawked and took flight, disappearing into the darkness of the cavern.

I crumpled to my knees near Michael's ashes. "I'm sorry," I said, as some floated away.

Eve reached into the cradle and handed me my son. I was afraid to look at him, for fear of seeing Michael in his face. "I love you," I said, pressing him to my chest. He smelled like rose petals and salt.

"You should go now," Hecate warned, looking around the cavern as if expecting someone. "Your father's patron won't be pleased about the new deal, even if he has to abide by it. We should all leave, in fact."

I looked at the pile of ashes, shedding my final tear in the Netherworld. "Goodbye Michael," I said, rising to my feet. "I promise, Montana will know who you are."

"We'll all make sure of that," Shane said.

"And thank you," I said to Hecate and Lilith, hugging them.

"Don't thank us," Hecate said. "Thank Jillian and that aunt of yours. If we hadn't heard they're prayers, we wouldn't have known."

"We'll meet again, I promise," Lilith said, backing away.

"I can't wait. Now, we'd better go home."

Shane, Paul and my sisters crowded around me while I gripped the ankh. I said a silent goodbye to the Netherworld and snapped the chain.

"Safe travels, Seed Bringer," Hecate said.

Seed Bringer!

I had forgotten to plant the seed! I desperately rummaged through my pocket, searching for the acorn as I felt myself thinning out. At last I found it. I scrambled to pass it to Hecate, hoping she could plant it on my behalf.

But it fell through my dissolving hand, bouncing into the magma .

22

THE WORLD

I had never really *seen* my world before the morning I emerged from the Netherworld. The rainbow of colors in our garden; the crisp green leaves that framed our home; the white fence that marked our property; the majestic blue sky that camouflaged our domes. Nor had I ever truly savored the smells of my hometown – the summer apples, the fresh grass, the wet earth, and the eternal scent of impending rain.

I was awakened now, to every birdsong, to every whisper of the winds. I breathed in the real air and tilted my head towards the real sun, relishing that the warmth was not a product of my mind.

I looked into the bundle in my arms. My son was real, too. And we were home.

"Where'd he get that?" Shane asked, standing beside me. He could have been there a moment or a millennium. He lifted the blanket from Montana's face, revealing a blue knitted baby cap. "This kid has talent. If he's a wilder like you, we're gonna have our hands full."

One by one, I noticed the others: Merry, Eve, Ruth Anne, and Paul. We were all together, standing in front of Harvest Home. Only it wasn't the desolate property we had left behind. It was brimming with life and color, overflowing with abundance. The garden was full. The paint was new. The flowers bloomed. The blight had not only been lifted, but had possibly reversed

"Home," I said to Montana, lifting him high to see.

"Someone must've brought in a cleaning crew," Ruth Anne said.

"Or cast a cleaning spell," Eve agreed.

"I just hope this isn't another dream," I said.

Jillian and Aunt Dora bounded from the back door, smiling and crying as they ran to meet us. A willow branch was cradled in Jillian's arms and Aunt Dora no longer used her cane. We all embraced, more tightly than ever before.

"Ya did it!" Aunt Dora said. "I knew ya would. And so quick, too."

"Quick?" I asked.

"Aye. Was hardly more than a breath."

Was she kidding? Her face was unreadable as she cooed over Montana.

I looked at the branch in Jillian's arms and panicked. "I...I didn't plant the seed! It fell into the magma river and now it's gone forever!" What good was bringing Montana back to a dying world? We were all doomed now. "Oh, Jillian. What have I done?"

Jillian smiled as her eyes lingered on my abdomen. "As above, so below. You are the vessel that carries the seed planted in the Netherworld. Soon, that seed will bloom in ours. And your daughter will be a part of both."

"I'm pregnant with a little girl?" I asked. "How did this happen? I can't have two children so close together! I just lost my baby weight."

"Ya know how it happened," Aunt Dora said. "An' if ya need a refresher, I'll show ya the globe."

"No, it's okay," I said, feeling myself blush. I guess they really had kept a close eye on me.

"Whoo-hoo! I'm going to have a daughter!" Shane grinned, setting his hand on my stomach. "And you've never looked more beautiful."

"Oh, hell no!" Eve said, shaking the sand out from one of her boots. "Maggie gets two husbands and two kids before I get even one? So unfair!"

"Mark my words," Aunt Dora said to me. "Any daughter o' yers is gonna be a handful. I better stick around a few more years. Yer gonna need me."

I looked down. Really, it was all such happy news, but I was grieving for Michael. "My son will never meet his father. He gave himself up for us."

"Aye," Aunt Dora said. "So don't squander his sacrifice."

"I won't."

"We brought Montana a gift," Jillian said. She opened her hand and revealed a crystal globe mounted on a pedestal, just like the memory globes I had seen my father's story play out in. She tapped the globe twice and snowflakes spun within it. When the white powder settled, a scene appeared.

"Look closely," Aunt Dora said.

It was a moving picture of Michael - painting Montana's crib in the nursery. He hummed as he carefully dipped the brush into the yellow paint. I tapped the globe again and another picture appeared, that of Michael sitting beside me on the porch swing, singing to my pregnant belly. I was laughing at the goofy faces he made.

"This breaks my heart," I said, touching the globe to Montana's hand. "Thank you."

Aunt Dora shrugged. "I ne'er trusted a warlock, but he grew on me. Now, Montana will have a few memories o' his father."

As everyone talked and caught up, I stepped quietly away. I rocked Montana in my arms as I wandered the now plentiful gardens. The magick and balance of Dark Root had returned. And somehow, reclaiming my son had been the key.

Even so, I knew that time was short. Time might not matter in the Netherworld, but there was no stopping it in the Upper World. My father and the goddesses had spoken cryptically of wars and endings. What were our roles in all of this? And what of my unborn daughter, conceived in the Netherworld and brought to life on earth?

I found the apple in my pocket. There was one bite left. I could take a nibble, and it might show me the future if I asked for it. I lifted the apple to my lips.

But did I really want to know what was coming? Could I live a normal life knowing how it would end? What were the odds that my story concluded with Shane and I sitting side by side on our porch rockers, white-haired and recounting our glory days? I threw the apple core into the woods before I succumbed to temptation.

"You're going to love growing up here," I said to Montana, as he gummed my finger. "You'll be so spoiled! We'll eat fresh tomatoes every morning and carve pumpkins grown from our garden. And we'll dress you up every Halloween and take you to Haunted Dark Root. No one will be more loved than you."

My son cooed and smiled, revealing one crowning tooth.

I looked at the others, all still chatting. Paul and Eve shared an embrace as Ruth Anne regaled Jillian and Dora with a dramatic recounting of our adventure. Merry stood off to the side, dabbing her eyes. I promised myself that I would be there for her; she was going to have a rough time ahead.

We had all had our lives splayed out before one another - our most embarrassing moments, our darkest deeds, and our innermost secrets. Nearly a year ago we had all straggled back to Dark Root, carrying those secrets like wounds. But Dark Root had healed us. And now that we had traveled to the Netherworld together - and had shared those intimate moments - there was a bond between us that wouldn't - couldn't be broken.

Shane wandered my way. "How are you doing?" He asked.

"I don't know. It's surreal, isn't it? I still can't believe we made it out alive."

"I told you, it's my lucky horseshoe. It gets me home, every time."

"Then you are never allowed to leave without it!"

"Deal." He looked at Montana, and then at me. "I still can't believe we're having a baby. A little girl! I just realized that between us, we'll have three kids. How are we going to handle that?"

"I have no idea," I admitted. "But it will be a fun adventure. And I wouldn't want to do it with anyone other than you."

"I love you, Maggie. Forever. And I'm sorry about Michael."

"I am, too. It's funny - I never really forgave him, until the moment he died. Why did I wait so long?"

"We all take time for granted."

We made our way back to the others, and Jillian noticed my new wheel pendant. "Keep that safe," she whispered. "It's priceless."

"Should I be worried?" I asked.

"Not now. That day will come, but not now. Stay present, Maggie. Stay awake."

Jillian took my hand. I took Shane's. He took Eve's, and so on. We formed a circle around Montana.

I settled into the moment, vowing to squeeze every ounce of joy and meaning from it that I could. And to do it again the next moment. And the next.

Life went by far too quickly to always be looking towards future. The only real time, was now.

I kissed my son and my husband, but promised them no happy endings. I refused to think of endings, as there were far too many livable moments in between.

So mote it be.

$\approx$

(Coming Summer 2018)
The Children of Dark Root

BONUS READING: A TOUCH OF LIGHT

Please enjoy the first chapter from Book One of my new series: Touch of Light: A Paranormal Mystery

A Typical New England Town

There are many beginnings to the same story.

Perhaps mine began two years before my return to Reed Hollow, when my husband, Ryan, went on a weekend hunting trip and never came home. His friends all testified that he was there one minute and simply gone the next.

Or maybe it began on the evening of my parents' demise. Edward and Vivi Bonds, married thirty-five years to the day, were driving home after an evening out. A flash of blinding light illuminated the gray winter sky and my father lost control of his truck, plunging into a steep ravine. My mother died on impact. My father's body was never found.

It could possibly be traced back to the morning I received a phone call from my brother. After six months of incarceration, he was finally eligible for release, but only if I took responsibility for his supervision.

But these events were only the catalysts that brought me to my current story – a montage of prologues to a much deeper and longer tale. For in the nine months since my return to Reed Hollow, there has been nothing noteworthy to report. The sleepy New England town functioned as it had for the last three hundred years. Quaint shops opened and closed like clockwork. Children went to school, parents went to work, and then everyone gathered around the dinner table to discuss their day. Church bells rang on Sunday mornings and police sirens interrupted bar fights on Friday nights. The only difference between this year and any other in Reed Hollow was the unpredictable weather.

Winter was especially harsh, coating the world in a thick layer of white, too deep to venture out into without full Eskimo attire. The frost persisted well into spring, robbing gardens of their normal color and ushering in a summer that was inhospitably warm. Even the tourists that kept Reed Hollow's economy churning reacted to the heat, grumbling over store prices and the terrible cell phone reception. We all breathed a sigh of relief as the last of the summer visitors packed up their campers and boats. Now, in early autumn, we were holding our breaths, awaiting the next round of invaders - weekenders carrying baskets and cameras, eager to capture the town's famous autumn foliage.

Though I can't pinpoint the exact moment my new story began, I think perhaps it was on a Thursday. It was early September, of that I am certain. I stood inside The Aunt-Tea-Query, at the end of the coffee line, watching maple leaves swish across the cafe's large front window. The leaves had already begun to yellow and crinkle at the edges. The heady scent of ripened apples wafted through the door whenever a customer entered or exited. And the children in the cafe toted shiny new lunchboxes as they held the hands of their caffeine-inhaling mothers.

The line inched painfully forward, as there was only one person manning the latte machine. I listened to the conversations ahead of me – most regarding the pumpkins and squash growing in their gardens.

"It's gonna be a bountiful harvest this year," someone declared.

"Yup," someone else agreed.

Dreadfully boring, I thought, stifling a yawn. But that was Reed Hollow. There was so little to talk about that even pumpkins were interesting after a while.

"It doesn't matter," I reminded myself, stepping forward. I wasn't planning on staying much longer than the new year, anyway. Let the locals be happy with their pumpkins and squash. I had my eye on the future.

That, and a large blueberry muffin in the center of the glass dessert tray, dusted with powdered sugar.

"My stars," I whispered, tapping the glass with my pinky finger. "Where have you been all my life?"

I'm normally a woman of discipline, but when I took ownership of my parents' business - complete with illegible ledgers, mountains of debt, and shoddy inventory management - I rediscovered my childhood sweet tooth with surprising ease. It was cheaper than alcohol, I reasoned, even as my skirts began to feel the strain of my addiction.

I surveyed the muffin, studying its sugar-to-bread distribution, before moving on to the strawberry shortcake beside it. The presentation was magnificent - topped with homemade cream and garden strawberries - but not exactly what I was looking for. When the line finally dispersed, I stood up straight, pulling my vintage gray hat with its raspberry rosettes down over my ears. Looking the barista in his sleepy brown eyes, I asked, "Might you have any crumpets?"

"Now what the hell's a crumpet?"

"It's like an English muffin, but from England."

"Wait, aren't all English muffins from England? Never mind." He shook his head. "Do you want an English muffin?"

"They're not the same. Are you sure you don't have any crumpets?"

"No, Baylee. I don't have any crumpets."

"How about scones?"

"Not today."

"But you said that yesterday."

"And I'll say it again tomorrow." He leaned over the counter, planting his knuckles on the glass like a gorilla. "In fact, here is my official statement on the matter: Baylee Scott, I don't have any crumpets or scones. I never have and I never will."

I touched my gloved finger to the name engraved on the man's gold-plated badge. "Alexander," I said, batting my lashes. "If you have a customer who asks for something every day, perhaps you should oblige. It's smart business sense."

"Don't call me Alexander." He yanked the badge from his chest and tossed it into the nearest waste bin. "You know I hate that name."

"And I hate that you don't have any crumpets or scones. It seems that we are at an impasse, doesn't it, Alexander?"

"Damn it, Baylee. I would take your abnormal love of crumpets and scones more seriously if you helped me make them, or even worked the counter, for God's sake. But since you're my sister--"

"I'm also part owner! I while away my life here, sorting through boxes and cataloguing people's things and...*sniff*...my hands get calloused...and.... *sniff*..."

"You're so dramatic, Baylee. I know for a fact that you don't ever cry. Still, great performance." He clapped twice, slowly. "Your eyes misted up that time. You should have been an actress, like Mom."

"But then I'd be in Hollywood and you'd have to run this place alone." I waved my arm, to demonstrate the enormity of my sacrifice.

"I'd get by." Alex crossed his arms and gave me his sternest look, though it melted almost immediately. He had a reputation in Reed

Hollow for being *gruff* but he couldn't wear that mask around me for long. "I'll think about it, but I'm pretty swamped right now with running the tea shop and my current laundry situation." He leaned across the counter. "Between you and me, I think the squirrels are stealing my socks from the clothesline. I'll have to either hunt them down or find new ones."

"You're going to hunt the squirrels?"

"I'm going to hunt down the socks! Not the squirrels. Never the squirrels!" Alex wiped his hands several times on a nearby towel, cleansing away the horrific idea. "What I'm saying is, I'm a busy man. I don't have time to learn how to make scones."

"Have you tried Pinterest?"

"Now what the hell is Pinterest?"

"A place where all your dreams come true." I took my phone out of my Italian purse and pulled up the website. After typing in a few words, I handed it over. "I just set up an account for you. You're welcome."

Alex backed away as if I were handing him a vial of poison. "No."

"Just no?"

"Hell no."

"You, sir, are no gentleman."

"Now you're mixing your movie quotes with some real emotion. Why Scarlett, you're not a robot, after all."

We exchanged smiles, softer ones without guile or agenda. We hadn't lived or worked together since childhood and we were still trying to figure it out as adults. I knew Alex would never use Pinterest or learn to make crumpets, or do anything else contrary to his stalwart nature. He was a creature of habit and ritual and was slow to change. When he took over our parent's tea shop, he swore on a stack of American-authored books there would never be any "English froufrou crap in the cafe." So far, he had stuck to his guns, but I was wearing him down.

"Would you like anything I actually have?" he asked.

"A cup of mint tea and a plate of cucumber sandwiches, please."

Alex knocked his head against the old-fashioned cash register that guarded the bagel basket. "Seriously?"

"*Pretty* please." I beamed innocently, knowing my last request would send him rooting around our sun-scorched garden, searching for the last edible cucumber. It was a fitting punishment, after his refusal of my Pinterest help.

"Fine." He brandished a butter knife inches from my nose. "But don't tell anyone cucumber sandwiches are on the menu. I can't manage the shop, find my missing socks *and* keep up the garden. I'm only one man, Baylee."

"There's always the grocery store," I reminded him.

"No. Grocery store produce is swimming in toxins. I won't have you growing a third eye or an extra limb. I'll go dig up your cucumber."

My brother exited through the large solarium to the right of the café that also served as the High Tea Room in the afternoon. He soon returned with a limp, withered vegetable dangling from his fingers. "Pathetic," he said, slapping it onto a cutting board. "It's El Nino, I tell you."

"Can you remove the seeds too, please?"

With that, Alex stormed into the kitchen, where he could finish the task in private. I remained at the counter, calling out helpful instructions, until I felt a firm tap on my shoulder. A quick jolt shook me and I grabbed onto the nearest barstool to steady myself.

When the shock subsided, I turned and leveled a finger at the man who had tapped me. He was tall and handsome with wide blue eyes set against an overly tanned complexion. "Never touch me without my consent again," I said, dusting off the space on my shoulder where he had made contact.

"Sorry about that miss, but I think you may have dropped a twenty." The stranger opened his hand to reveal a crumpled bill, presenting it with a smile as white as The Aunt-Tea-Query's finest bone china.

"It's not mine," I replied, conducting a more thorough inspection of the man. I had seen him before, but never up close. He was good-looking, in a contrived way, with moussed hair and eyebrows shaped

316

at a spa. The color on his cheeks and the scruff on his chin advertised him as rugged and outdoorsy, though his perfectly white sneakers argued otherwise. He was in his mid-thirties but could pass for younger, if he shaved.

"Are you sure it's not yours?" He stepped closer. He smelled of bar soap and expensive aftershave, the kind my husband only wore on special occasions.

"Quite sure, thank you."

The twenty-dollar bill fluttered between his fingers. "How do you know?" He lowered his gaze and took my hand, wrapping the bill in my palm. As we made contact, the letter "J" flashed in silver light above his head, then fizzled out.

"You would be wise to keep your distance, Josh or James or whatever your name is," I said, yanking my hand away. "I already warned you not to touch me without asking. You won't get another chance."

"J" blinked and retreated a step, clearly caught off guard. "I'm sorry. I didn't mean to appear creepy."

"Oh? How *did* you mean to appear?"

"Helpful?" He smiled with one side of his mouth, a look he had no doubt mastered in front of a mirror over the course of many hours. "Can we start again? My name is Jake." He nodded towards the twenty. "How do you know this isn't yours? We're the only two people here."

Despite Jake's intrusiveness, I didn't sense he was dangerous. Plus, I had time to kill while waiting for my cucumber sandwich. "Alright, Jake, I'll tell you how I know it isn't mine. It's all in the details."

"What?"

"Listen closely. I never wad up my money. I'm very careful with my things, especially money. It doesn't grow on trees, Jake."

"No..."

"And I rarely carry more than ten dollars in cash. I have a tendency to indulge myself, especially in accessory shops and bakeries, and it's too tempting to carry more money than I need. After time and good health, money is our most valuable resource."

Jake's eyes glazed over as my words rolled around in his head like the mismatched socks in Alex's washing machine. After a long pause, he grinned. "You're honest. I appreciate that in a woman."

"Do you appreciate honesty in men, too?"

"Yeah, men too," he amended, scratching his jaw. "It's just that women…well, they are…" He waved both his hand in front of him and clenched his teeth.

"I'll just surmise that you've had some bad experiences with the opposite sex."

"Boy, could I tell you stories…"

"Please don't."

My brother returned and handed me a scattering of thin sandwiches on a cracked plate. "The Queen's meal is ready," he said, bowing. "Now let me get back to my work, Baylee." Alex glanced at Jake. "You need something, too?"

"No."

"Good. I've got dishes to do." Alex returned to the kitchen and I took my sandwich to a small table near the front window, where my mother, Vivi Bonds, sat waiting.

"Who's that coming our way?" Mom asked, smacking her lips appreciatively.

Sure enough, Jake had left the counter and was sauntering over. "Ignore him," I said, as he took the chair between us.

"I heard that guy call you Baylee," Jake said, tapping his knuckles against the table. "It's a pretty name."

"It *is* a pretty name," Mom agreed, patting herself on the back. "She was named after the bay leaf, which is a plant of protection. Tell him, Baylee."

I ignored my mother and dropped my sandwich, giving my full attention to my new stalker. "Let me save you the trouble, Jake. I'm not interested in you or any other man at the moment."

"Why not?" Mom asked, her eyes taking in Jake's muscled arms.

"Because Ryan's not dead," I said.

"Who's Ryan?" Jake asked.

"My husband."

"Ex," Mom corrected. "Or maybe estranged? What do you call it when your husband goes *poof?*"

"Missing," I said to them both. "My husband, Ryan, is missing."

For once Jake's eyes showed real emotion, as well as some confusion. "I'm sorry. That's terrible. How long?"

I looked down at the table, blinking into my tea cup. "Two years, ten months, four days." Nearly three years, but I couldn't say that out loud. Two sounded more manageable.

"Are you over him?" Jake pressed. "I don't see a ring underneath those satin gloves. Classy touch, by the way."

"You're still hitting on me after I told you I lost my husband? And people accuse *me* of being insensitive." I removed my wool hat and satin gloves and arranged them neatly beside the vase on the table. Then, I turned my chair towards him and looked deep into his eyes. "Jake, you said that I was honest, but that isn't an accurate assessment of me. I'm a writer and have been known to have quite an imagination."

His dark brows knit together. "Yeah?"

"Though I may not be a pillar of honesty, I am quite blunt, which I suppose is a form of honesty." I stood and motioned for Jake to do the same. He rose uncertainly, and we faced one another. With my heels on, we were nearly the same height. "Would you like to hear my honest assessment of you, Jake?"

"Uh... I'm not gonna like this, am I?"

"Probably not." I cast a glance around the first floor of the stately farmhouse that now served as our home and business. The cafe and the solarium were both empty, save for Alex who clanked dishes around in the sink. To the left of the cafe an arch opened, revealing the antique shop I inherited. There was no one in there, either. Now certain we were alone, I crossed my arms across my chest. "I saw you pick up the money outside the men's room."

Jake grinned and nodded. "See? I'm a good guy."

"But the men's room and the ladies' room are at opposite ends of the building. One is near the solarium, and the other is near the antique shop." I pointed to the opposing doors, like a flight attendant highlighting the facilities. "Since I am obviously not a man, why did you ask if it was mine?"

Jake shifted his weight from one foot to the other, his eyes pausing at the Exit sign. To his credit, he stayed. "I thought I'd ask everyone in here. When I came out of the restroom, you were the only one still here."

"Did you notice the *man* behind the counter? He seems a far likelier choice, given the location of the found money." *Much more likely, actually.* Alex had a sharp mind but lost most everything. Our mother joked it was the reason he was so thin - he lost his appetite as a kid and never found it again.

"I hadn't thought of that." Jake glanced at Alex, who was now poking a fork into the toaster to remove a stuck bagel.

"It's not his money, either." I said. "Alex never uses public restrooms, even here."

"What are you getting at? I'm not trying to take anything from you. I'm trying to give you something."

"What I'm getting at is that I don't appreciate games. You just wanted to talk to me, didn't you Jake?" I smiled sweetly, deepening my dimples, though my arms remained crossed across my chest.

Jake raised his hands in the air. "Alright. Busted. I hope it's at least a little flattering?"

"I'd be far more flattered if I hadn't seen you chatting up every female who comes in here." I pointed through the arch, into the antique shop. "That's my office. I've watched you work your charms, many times on many women."

The bronzer momentarily faded from Jake's face. He blinked three times, slowly. "Okay, so I'm a flirt," he confessed. "Is that so wrong?"

"Not necessarily. In every society, young men and women of courtship age exchange glances, smiles, and trivial conversation meant to create intimacy and heighten sexual tension." I looked over his shoulder, wondering if I had an anthropology book handy to reference. "Flirting is often a necessary first step in securing a mate in societies where mates aren't chosen for you."

"I have no idea what you're talking about."

"That makes two of us," Mom chimed in, still sitting at the table.

"Jake, hold out your hand," I instructed.

"No."

"Hold-out-your-hand."

He pointed to a wooden sign above the solarium that read: *Palm and Tea Leaf Readings: Ten Dollars.* "I get it. You want to earn the money, huh?"

"That's my cousin Kela's business. She'll give you good news. I've got other plans for you."

I grabbed Jake's right sleeve and turned his forearm so that his palm faced up. I didn't read tea leaves or love lines, as my cousin Kela did, but I had talents of my own. I exhaled a breath into my bare hands to warm them, then wrapped both palms around Jake's right hand. Next, I braced for impact.

A flash of orange light exploded between my temples. My hands tightened around Jake's and he crumpled to his knees. "What the hell! Let go!" he begged, trying to pull loose.

But it was too late. Our bodies were fused, linked together like a stout chain, my mind probing his. I had plugged into Jake - into his past, present, and possibly even his future, if destiny were involved. Despite his calculated outward appearance, it was a jumbled mess inside Jake's head. So many random thoughts flying around. Jumping into a person's mental landscape was like freefalling into the eye of a tornado. It was dangerous, but also beautiful from a certain vantage point, if you didn't get lost. I held on as thoughts and remembrances whooshed around me, connected to Jake like a plug in a live socket, until I had absorbed all the information I could carry.

At last, I was thrown back and contact was broken. I trembled as I collected myself, shaking off the darker images before they embedded themselves in my own consciousness. Some thoughts had to be vanquished right away or they became a permanent part of you.

Jake stood slowly, shaking his palms as if they burned. "What did you do?" he demanded, looking from his hands to me and back again.

When I regarded him this time, it was with compassion. "I'm sorry. Losing Beth must have been terrible. She was too young."

"What? How did you know about Beth?"

I had learned many things in our shared moment, and most of them broke my heart. "It's a gift, I'm told," I answered, shrugging.

He clenched his jaw, his expression part anger, part embarrassment. There was pain there, too. He wanted to run. They all wanted to run, once their secrets were revealed.

"I'm sorry," I said, meaning it.

He didn't speak, but rather shuffled from one foot to the other, his hands now stuffed into his pockets. I was going to say something comforting, that Beth had loved him, and that she was in a better place, when a perverse gleam lit Jake's eyes. "Hey, I remember you! You're Baylee Bonds. The witch-girl. You were gone what...nine years? Ten?"

"Eleven years, seven months, thirteen days. More or less."

"Baylee Bonds, all grown up." He whistled appreciatively. "City living was good to you, wasn't it?"

"It's Baylee Scott now," I corrected him.

His smile widened as Alex passed by with a broom. "And that's your weird brother! The one who 'speaks' to animals? Wasn't he locked up? Wait till everyone hears he's out and sweeping floors!"

I observed Jake coolly as I returned my gloves to my hands. "Jake, let me be clear on this. My brother's incarceration is a family matter and I suggest you mind your own business."

"Only if you promise me a date. I've never gone out with a witch before."

"I will not promise you a date, but I will promise you this: If you spread any gossip about my brother, or anyone else in my family, I'll let everyone in town know what I saw in your head."

"Everyone already knows about Beth."

"That's not what I meant."

"Oh? What else did you see, *witch*?"

There was an entire cinematic reel Jake kept hidden beneath his expensive haircut: abandonment, sexual inadequacy, and debt. An extraordinary amount of debt. From gambling, most likely, as images of dice showed up repeatedly in my memory scan of him.

"You are in serious financial trouble, Jake. Is that why you gallivant about, seducing women?"

"Gallivant? Who uses words like gallivant? You're insane, lady." He checked his watch, sidestepping towards the front open door. "I'm a business consultant. I'm financially secure. You don't know anything."

I kept silent. While my visions weren't always relevant, they were uncannily accurate. Sometimes, I wished they weren't.

"I gotta run." Jake put on his sunglasses and planted one foot outside. "Don't worry. I won't be *gallivanting* around this place anymore. It's practically a cemetery anyway. No one comes here anymore except old ladies and Prozac moms. And even they're getting wise."

"So, no date then?" I called after.

Once the doors shut behind him, I slumped back into my chair, feeling the physical and emotional drain that came with reading someone so fully. I picked up a limp wedge of cucumber sandwich and nibbled at the corner, all joy in the meal now lost.

"He seemed nice," my mother said from across the table.

"He's not nice, Mom. He seduces women for money."

"I'm sure they don't mind." Vivi Bonds turned her broad shoulders towards the window, watching Jake's chiseled form disappear into the landscape of downtown. She smacked her lips together, twice. "Mmm-mmm. If I were still young…"

"And alive," I reminded her.

"Why do you keep bringing that up?"

"Because you keep forgetting you're dead."

"I don't forget. I just don't like remembering." She eyed my sandwich with the same lustful look she'd just given Jake. "You need to enjoy your life, Baylee. Play the lottery. Dance naked in the moonlight. Kiss strange men. Live it up, girl! You don't know how lucky you are to be young and beautiful and alive!"

I regarded my broad-shouldered mother over the napkin

dispenser. She was as imposing in death as she was in life. "Being dead hasn't stopped you from living," I said.

"I make the most of what I have." She sat up fully, her lips puckered as she gave me a thorough once-over. "It wouldn't kill you to cut out the muffins, though, Bay Leaf. Men like slim women. It's a subconscious thing, left over from the caveman days. Slim women are easier to hunt for. It's biology."

"Mother, you have no idea what you're talking about."

"I do, too! I read it in a book. Or maybe I saw it on *Discovery*. I don't know, but it's a fact."

"And who are you to talk about indulging in muffins?"

"What, this?" Mom patted her plush belly. "It's my winter weight."

She prattled on while I half-listened, wondering how I could gracefully leave the conversation. While she had been doting in life, she was positively smothering in the afterlife. There was no place in the farmhouse I could hide now that she didn't need sleep and could move through walls. I was constantly subjected to her pearls of wisdom, whether I wanted them, or not.

"You never know when I'll cross all the way over," Mom reminded me. "I need to spend as much time with you as I can. I don't want to leave with any regrets."

Regrets.

Now there was a subject I knew plenty about, and none of them involved not kissing strange men or dancing naked in the moonlight.

"Baylee..." Mom tapped my wrist. It felt like a cool breeze brushing against my arm. "You aren't listening to me."

"I was listening."

"What did I say?"

I lifted my hand, raising a finger with each point. "Let's see. Why haven't I remarried? Why won't I give you grandkids? Why do I wear my hair long when short would be 'much more becoming to my angular face?' Did I miss anything?"

Mom studied me with narrowed eyes. Then a wide smile crossed her face and she laughed, sending her entire body shimmying. "You had me going until you mentioned your hair. That's what we talked about yesterday. I knew you weren't listening."

I sighed. It was impossible to argue with a spirit. They had endless time to make their point and nothing better to do. I cupped my chin in my palm and cast a jealous glance at Alex, who was wiping the table beside us. He neither heard nor saw our mother. What I wouldn't give for a *Freaky Friday* moment. "I don't mean to sound insensitive, mom, but I really wish you'd find someone else to haunt."

"Now why would I want to do that? You've been gone ten years. We have lots of time to make up for."

"You talking to Mom?" Alex asked, pulling the fake rose from our faux crystal vase and replacing it with a fake sunflower.

"Do you see any other ghosts around?"

"Nope, but I don't see her, either. Send her my love."

"Mom, Alex sends his love."

"I'm dead, not deaf! But please, tell him the new yoga teacher next door is cute, and probably vegan, and very bendy, and..." Mother paused, wondering what other qualities might entice her perpetually single son into settling down. "She doesn't know about his legal problems," she whispered, as if that alone should settle it.

"Mom sends her love too."

"Ask her if she took my keys?" Alex said, patting himself down.

"I didn't take his keys! Why does he always blame me when his things go missing?" She exhaled a loud "Humph," sailing a paper napkin into the air, where it glided to the hardwood floor.

"Hey, I saw that!" Alex gave Mom's chair a thumbs-up as he plucked the napkin from the ground.

"What are you going to do this afternoon?" Mom asked me.

"Oh, I thought I'd organize the shot glass collection, or maybe restore the glass eyes on the creepy clown doll that's been taking up shelf space since the 1950's. If I'm lucky, someone will dump off a Hefty bag full of used clothes that should have gone to Goodwill."

"You need to get out and find treasures, Baylee. You can't wait for people to bring them to you." Mother reached for my teacup, frowning as her hand passed right through it. "The point is - this job is what you make of it. Reed Hollow isn't London, or New York, or even Seattle, but it's home, and if you give it a chance I know you'll come to love it again."

I offered her a wry smile, the most I could muster at the moment. Vivi Bonds loved Reed Hollow, but I didn't share her views. "I promised you I'd make this business a success before I go, Mom, but I can't stay here forever."

"You just need to get out more. Have you tried joining a group? There's a drum circle on Fridays at Lake Crystal."

I sighed, ready to launch into the myriad of reasons why I was not going to join a drum circle, when the doorbell chimed inside my office. *Odd.* Most people entered through the cafe doors. Though I wasn't particularly enthralled with interacting with anyone new at the moment, it would get me away from Mom. I excused myself and hurried into the small antique shop that took up the east side of the restored farmhouse.

The cozy room was empty by the time I stepped under the arch. But there was a strange new energy inside the room I couldn't trace. I hurried to my office window and caught sight of a woman's long, silver braid tick-tocking down the busy sidewalk. By the color of her hair, I would have guessed her to be an older woman; but her gait suggested someone much younger.

Hmm, probably just someone trying to sell us something.

Yet something felt out of place. I looked around the jam-packed room. Sure enough, perched on the corner of my mahogany desk was a black velvet case the size of a pencil box that had not been there before. The case was open and five opulent rings glittered up at me. "My stars," I said, making my way over. They were beautiful and looked quite old, though I doubted they were precious stones.

I resisted touching the rings, even as they called out to me from the case, flickering like stars against a dark night. Objects, like people, retained their memories. The older an object, the greater the likelihood it had gathered a few scars during its life.

My hand hovered an inch above the case, feeling a pull that was hard to resist.

There was more to this collection than met the immediate eye.

I caught my breath, my emotions vacillating between excitement and fear.

Magick was present – an ancient, earthy magick I hadn't sensed in a very long time.

Download Touch of Light

ABOUT THE AUTHOR

April Aasheim learned to love magic at an early age. Her mother was a fortune teller who always had books on magic and the occult in the house, which April devoured. April fell so in love with the paranormal world, in fact, that at age eight she declared herself a witch and wore a pointed hat for nearly an entire summer. It was at that time that she also discovered books (written for kids) about witches and April hunted them out in libraries and supermarkets. Her favorites were always the ones where witches and ghosts 'could be real'.

April continued her love of the supernatural into her adult life, studying the occult, spirituality, and world religion. She also loved writing but never thought of combining her two pastimes, until the day she accidentally wrote the sentence "If I were a real witch…" and The Daughters of Dark Root series was born.

April currently lives with her husband and family in Portland, Oregon. When not writing she enjoys dancing, reading, hiking, crafting, and binge netflixing.

aprilaasheimwriter.com
amaasheim@gmail.com

ALSO BY APRIL AASHEIM

Want to read more by this author?

The Daughters of Dark Root Series: (Click Link to Buy)

The Witches of Dark Root

The Magick of Dark Root

The Curse of Dark Root: Part One

The Curse of Dark Root: Part Two

The Shadows of Dark Root

Children of Dark Root (Coming Summer 2018)

Dark Root Companion Novellas and Short Stories: (Click Link to Buy)

The Council of Dark Root: Armand

A Dark Root Christmas: Merry's Gift

A Dark Root Halloween: The Witching Hour

A Dark Root Samhain: A Lesson in Magick (Coming Fall 2017)

The Reed Hollow Chronicles (Click Link to Buy)

Touch of Light: A Baylee Scott Paranormal Mystery

Touch of Shadow: A Baylee Scott Paranormal Mystery (Coming Winter 2017/2018)

Other Books by April Aasheim (Click Link to Buy)

The Universe is a Very Big Place (A humorous look at second chances)

The Good Girl's Guide to Being a Demon (A Woodland Creek Urban Fantasy)

If you enjoyed the book please consider leaving a review! A short review is fine and greatly appreciated. Word of mouth is essential for any author to succeed.

∾

Made in the USA
Las Vegas, NV
25 March 2021

20135299R10199